I0692084

Changeling Press, LLC
ChangelingPress.com

Intergalactic Brides Vol. 4

Jessica Coulter Smith

Intergalactic Brides Vol. 4
Jessica Coulter Smith

All rights reserved.
Copyright ©2022
Jessica Coulter Smith

ISBN: 978-1-60521-823-6

Publisher:
Changeling Press LLC
315 N. Centre St.
Martinsburg, WV 25404
ChangelingPress.com

Printed in the U.S.A.

Editor: Crystal Esau
Cover Artist: Karen Fox

The individual stories in this anthology have been previously released in E-Book format.

Table of Contents

Ella and the Alien Gamer (Intergalactic Brides 10)

Jessica Coulter Smith

Ella has had a hard life as a single mom who barely makes ends meet. But she's never once asked for help, and she never would. When Valero barrels into her life asking for things she's not ready to give, she holds herself back. Mostly. The thought of taking the sexy alien to bed is more than a little tempting... except he's playing hard to get.

Valero has wanted a mate ever since he was old enough to think of having a family of his own. He's never thought of claiming a female with a child in tow, but Connor's amazing gaming skills intrigue the video game designer. Asking the small family to move in with him seems reasonable enough since he plans to claim them as his, but Ella's commitment issues prove to be a problem.

What's a geeky gamer to do when the Cinderella of his dreams wants sex, but nothing else?

Chapter One

Small hands tugged on the hem of her sweater. "Mama, I'm hungry."

Ella briefly closed her eyes and said a prayer before smiling down at her young son. At the age of five, he was always hungry, and it broke her heart every time she'd had to tell him no or had to send him to bed with an empty belly. She was doing the best she could, but most days it just wasn't enough, no matter how hard she worked.

"Honey, we just had breakfast a little while ago." She smoothed his hair back from his face. "How about some peanut butter crackers? I think there's still some in the drawer by the fridge."

Connor scrunched his tiny face. "I ate the last one yesterday."

Her heart sank at his words. How had she not noticed the snack drawer needed to be refilled? She always kept crackers and a package of chocolate chip cookies in there. Even if it meant eating cheaper dinners, she tried her best to give Connor everything he needed, even if she couldn't give him everything he wanted.

"What about some peanut butter toast?" Ella asked.

He glanced across the kitchen and she followed his gaze to the empty bread container. Right. They'd finished the bread this morning. Her heart was heavy and her eyes were damp as she swallowed the knot in her throat. She'd failed her small boy in so many ways, and continued to fail him every day. There were times she wondered if he'd have been better off if she'd put him up for adoption, and then she'd mentally slap herself. Yes, he might have led a more privileged life, but no one would ever love Connor as much as she did. And love was far more important than material things.

"It's okay, Mama. I can wait until lunch."

"I'm sorry, baby. Just let Mama look through the paper a little longer and then we'll go to the store. Maybe we'll stop at the burger place you like so much and you can get a cheeseburger for lunch." Somehow. Even if she had to tear the couch apart for change. She had money in her account, but it was supposed to go toward rent, even if it wasn't enough. She was still short two hundred dollars, and that wasn't including the money she needed to spend on groceries to get them by a little longer.

The small hands tugged on her until she bent down. Connor kissed her cheek and she hugged him tight. He wiggled to be set free and ran off to his room, probably to play a game on the Xbox 360 she'd found for a steal in a pawn shop several months ago. It had just been the two of them since she'd found out she was pregnant. Ella would do anything for Connor, but even she couldn't create a miracle.

Connor peeked out of his room. "Mama, do you think I could have one of those birthday cakes from the bakery this year? Like the one I saw last week with dinosaurs on it? I promise to be extra good."

"Maybe, sweet boy. I'll see what I can do, okay?" Ella wasn't sure her bank account could handle the expense. As it was, she didn't know how she was buying the fire truck he'd asked for the last time they'd gone walking at the mall, or how she was keeping a roof over his head. It wouldn't be the first time they'd had to live in her craptastic car, but she'd vowed the last time it wouldn't happen again. Their apartment might have cracked walls, water stains on the ceiling, and a strange smell that would never go away, but it was dry and far better than living on the streets.

"I love you, Mama."

"I love you too, baby boy. You and me against the world, right?"

He smiled and nodded.

Ella kissed his brow then sent him back to his game before she went back to the kitchen. She braced her hands on the counter and bowed her head. It felt as if the weight of the world had settled on her young shoulders. She started every morning optimistic that something wonderful would happen, and went to bed every night feeling defeated.

Casting her eyes toward the stained ceiling she couldn't help but beg. "I need a little help. Just a little. I can't do this all alone. I refuse to fail that little boy any more than I already have."

Realizing that divine intervention wasn't happening anytime soon, she huffed a breath and started washing the breakfast dishes. Things always worked out, one way or another. Unfortunately, the diner where she'd worked had closed and she'd had to get a job at the local coffee shop, making minimum wage with any tips earned split between everyone on shift. It didn't help that she could only work part-time during the hours Connor was in school. She needed to catch a break, and fast.

With the dishes set on the draining rack, and her hands pruned from the water, Ella quickly cleaned the rest of the kitchen before collapsing on the couch. The newspaper was spread across her scarred coffee table and she picked up the classifieds. She'd searched the jobs a hundred times already today, and no matter how many times she scanned the pages, nothing new magically appeared that she was qualified to do. Ella flipped through the rest of the paper, searching out coupons to help stretch their grocery money a little further. A big colorful ad for Gamer Plus caught her eye. They were hosting a special Pokémon event today to celebrate their latest game. Connor loved all things Pokémon.

"Connor," she called out.

She heard his little steps run from his room.

"Yes, Mama?"

"How would you like to go to Gamer Plus today? We can't buy anything, but I thought you might like to look around, and they're having special things all day to celebrate the new Pokémon game."

His eyes lit up and he dashed off to put on his shoes. Ella slipped hers back on then went to the bathroom to run a brush through her hair and smooth on a little lip-gloss. When they had their jackets on and Connor's hand was firmly clasped in hers, they set off for the game store. Her ancient Toyota still ran well, even if it wasn't pretty to look at, and they puttered through the streets of town.

The parking lot at Gamer Plus wasn't as packed as she'd expected and they got a spot near the door. She was barely parked before Connor was out of the car and running inside. She'd have to talk to him once more about safety and stranger danger, but for now she just shook her head and tried to keep up. There were various stations around the store set up for the event and Connor was running from one to another. As she tried to chase after him, she collided with a woman close to her size.

"I'm so sorry!"

The woman turned and her eyes widened. "Ella?"

"Rory? I haven't seen you since…"

"High school," Rory finished for her. "How's your son?"

Ella motioned toward the bundle of energy that was zipping around the store. "Hyper as ever."

Rory laughed. "It's so good to see you. I feel terrible about losing touch after graduation. You still live here in town or are you visiting?"

"I live here, in the apartments over on Berkshire."

Rory frowned a little and it made Ella self-conscious. She knew the apartments weren't in the greatest part of town, but it was the best she could do with what little she had. She remembered Rory had planned to go to college, paid for by her rich politician father. Ella had been envious of Rory, of the future she would have, but not once had she ever wished Connor away.

A tall Terran at Rory's side nudged Rory. "Introduce me."

Rory grinned. "Ella, this is my husband, Zwyk. We just got married last month."

"Congratulations!"

"Are you married or seeing someone?" Rory asked.

Humiliation burned through Ella. Of course she wasn't. She was broke, single, and had been a teen mom. Could she have been more of a cliché? "No, there's no one. Just Connor and me." Ella turned toward the last place she'd seen her son. "Connor! Come here, please."

Her son scampered over. "This is so awesome. Can we stay a little longer?"

"Of course, but I want you to meet someone first. Connor, this is Rory..." She stopped and looked at Rory. "I don't know your new last name."

Rory knelt and held her hand out to Connor. "You can just call me Miss Rory. And this is my husband Mr. Zwyk. It's a pleasure to meet you, Connor. I went to high school with your mom."

Connor's eyes went wide as he looked up at Zwyk. "You're a Terran!"

Zwyk chuckled. "Yes, I am. Have you seen one of my kind before?"

"Not up close."

Zwyk laughed harder.

"I have a fabulous idea!" Rory said, clasping her hands together. "Why don't you and Connor come over tomorrow for lunch? We were going to have a few friends over and have a buffet. Wings, nachos, sliders... you know, all the unhealthy stuff guys like to consume." Rory knelt to look at Connor again. "And we happen to have an Xbox One with tons of games."

Connor jumped up and down. "Can we, Mama?

Please?"

Rory had backed her into a corner by tempting Connor with video games. How could she say no? If she did, she'd break her son's heart and seem like an ogre. She didn't know what she'd have in common with a college graduate and some aliens, but what would it hurt to stop by for an hour?

"All right. What's the address?" Ella asked.

Rory pulled some paper and a pen from her purse and wrote down the address along with her phone number. Ella waved goodbye as Connor dragged her over to one of the gaming stations to talk her ear off about things she didn't understand. She always listened when he talked about his games, but she never understood a word he said. Gaming had never been a big draw for Ella, not even in school. She'd always preferred books and movies.

She somehow let Connor talk her into a ten dollar used game and then they were on their way to Big Bart's. She didn't let Connor eat fast food very often, but he loved the cheeseburgers at Bart's and they only cost a dollar. She ordered one for each of them and a medium drink for them to share. They sat at a table outside in the play area and after Connor had inhaled his cheeseburger, he ran off to slide and climb through the tunnels. With some luck, he'd wear himself out and take a nap when they got home.

Ella let him play for a half hour then called him back to the table. "We need to stop by the grocery store if we want to eat dinner tonight. We'll come back another day, okay?"

Connor pouted, but he took Ella's hand and walked to the car with her. At the store, he was especially good and didn't ask for a lot of extra things. She did throw a box of animal crackers in the basket as a treat for another day, restocked the peanut butter crackers, and bought a package of chocolate chip cookies. She restocked their dinner options with a variety of Hamburger Helper, two types of pasta, and some fresh fish that was on sale. Connor loved seafood, but they were seldom able to get any.

She winced a little at the total when they checked out, but swiped her bank card, then gathered the sacks and carried them to the car. Once the trunk was loaded, she buckled Connor into his booster seat and drove back to the apartment. By the time she'd put the groceries away and figured out what she was making for dinner, Connor was passed out in his bed.

Ella smiled as she entered the room and gently removed his shoes. She pulled the blanket over him and kissed his brow. No matter what the future held, she would always have Connor, and that was what mattered most. Everything else was just material, and could be replaced. With a sigh, she went back to stare at the classifieds one more time, in hopes they looked a little better than they had that morning. The problem was that she couldn't work full-time without having to pay for childcare, and that would eat up any extra she'd have in her paycheck.

Being a single mother was hard as hell, even if it was worth it. Every tear she dried, every boo-boo she kissed, reminded her that even while they struggled she was far more blessed than most people. Connor was the bright spot in her world and she would do anything for him.

Well, almost anything. The one thing she wouldn't do was call her parents. They'd thrown her out after graduation and told her to never darken their door again, and she hadn't. In five years, she'd never once spoken to them or tried to see them. They didn't deserve to have Connor in their lives, and she knew that any help they provided -- if they provided any -- would come at a steep price.

No, she'd figure things out on her own, just like she always did. There would be another paper tomorrow with different ads. Just because the right job hadn't presented itself today didn't mean tomorrow was a lost cause too. As long as she believed that things would work out, as long as she held out hope for a brighter future for Connor and her, then tomorrow would always be another day, another opportunity.

Tomorrow. She chewed her bottom lip as she thought about going to Rory's. Her friend seemed to be doing well for herself. Maybe she'd know of someplace hiring, somewhere that hadn't placed an ad in the paper. It wouldn't hurt to ask. The worst that could happen was Rory would say no… and Ella wouldn't be any worse off than she was right now.

Yes. Tomorrow would be another day. A brighter day. Even if she still didn't have a better job lined up, at least they were going to enjoy a good meal for lunch and Connor would get to play some games. Maybe she would even make some new friends. Those had been in short supply these last five years. Ella would go to Rory's tomorrow open to the possibility of something more, and she'd enjoy herself even if she had to step out of her comfort zone to do it.

* * *

Valero growled as he jabbed at the buttons on the controller. Rory and her damned dragons! When she'd said she couldn't beat this level, he'd thought it would be a piece of cake. How hard could a game be that centered around an adolescent purple dragon? *Harder than fuck, that's how hard.*

"Bust the gem, turn the wheel," he muttered as he went through the steps. Little green things attacked him. "Argh. Die, you little bastards!"

"My mama will wash your mouth out with soap," said a small voice.

He glanced to his right and nearly dropped the controller when he saw a small human child. Where the hell had he come from?

"You're doing that wrong," the boy said.

No shit. That was why he'd been trying to put out the fires for the last half hour without success. What the hell did the small child know about it though? He held out the controller.

"Since you seem to know what you're doing, want to show me how it's done?" Valero asked.

The boy grinned from ear to ear, snatched the controller, and started playing with the finesse of an advanced gamer.

"How the hell did you know where the buckets were?" Valero asked.

"Soap," the boy replied in response to his bad word. Apparently *hell* wasn't allowed either. "And I have this game at home. I beat it on the second day. I probably would have done it sooner, but Mama wouldn't let me stay up playing all night."

The boy beat the level and handed the controller back.

"What other games can you play?" Valero asked. He'd never met such a young gamer before and he had to admit he was a little fascinated. He hadn't even known such a small human *could* play video games.

"I have *Minecraft, Sonic, Lego Harry Potter, Lego Star Wars,* and a few others."

"What about *Halo* or *Gears of War*?" Valero asked.

"Mama says they're too violent for me. But I wish I could play them. The kid games are too easy. I don't see why the adults are the only ones being challenged."

Valero's eyebrows went up. A challenging children's game? Was there a market for such a thing? Unless this child was a gaming prodigy, then there were probably others out there feeling his same frustration. Definitely something worth looking into.

"What types of challenges would you like to see in a game?" Valero asked.

"Well, I like the time challenges where you have to complete so many tasks in a certain amount of time. I like the fighting levels in Lego Star Wars. But collecting stuff like the rings in Sonic or the gems in Spyro can be fun. I just wish you could do more with it."

The kid was rather insightful for someone so young. And he was giving Valero an idea. His game company was still in the fledgling stages and he needed something new and edgy to put him on the map. Or so he'd thought. Maybe he was looking at the wrong demographic. He'd been thinking of a game adults would like where you blew up stuff, but if gamers were starting out as young as this kid, children who weren't allowed to play the more violent games, then maybe he needed to tap into that audience. The only problem was that his game testers were Rory and Zwyk, and neither would be able to give him the information he needed.

"He's not bothering you, is he?" a soft voice asked.

Valero stood and faced the woman, and damn near swallowed his tongue.

"I, um… No! He's not bothering me. He actually helped me figure out the level on the game I was playing."

She smiled a little. "He loves video games."

"Can I play some more, Mama?" the little boy asked.

"Connor, this man was already playing. Mind your manners."

Valero handed the controller back to Connor. "I think you're doing a better job than I was. Why don't you finish playing? Or if you prefer something else, Zwyk and Rory have a ton of games. I'm sure there's at least a few your mother would approve of."

"Can I, Mama?" he begged.

"All right. But if someone else wants a turn, you give them the controller."

The little boy gave a whoop and leapt onto the couch to settle in and play the game. Valero smiled at his enthusiasm before facing the mother once more. He moved a little closer and held out his hand. "I'm Valero."

"Ella."

His hand closed over hers and a little jolt went up his arm. Since moving to Earth, he'd never felt such an instant attraction to someone before. He'd gone on dates, but they were lacking. There was humor glinting in her eyes as she smiled a little wider and he realized he was staring at her like an idiot and hadn't released her hand. "Do you play?" he asked.

"Me? Um, no. I've never understood the draw of video games. I'm more of a reader."

He leaned against the sofa and folded his arms over his chest, feeling a bit of a thrill when her gaze was drawn to his muscles and she licked her lips. Good. The attraction wasn't one sided. The question was, what did he want to do about it? He'd never dated a mother before. He knew others of his kind had adopted human children as their own, like Reyvor and his houseful of girls.

"What do you like to read?" he asked.

"Romances." Her cheeks flushed. "I like the hope in them. No matter how dire the heroine's circumstances in the beginning, she always finds her happily-ever-after. Whether it's a knight rescuing her from a tower, a billionaire who falls for the poor waitress, or a shapeshifter who finds his mate, everyone falls in love at the end and all their dreams come true."

He smiled. "And what's your dream?"

Her expression sobered. "To provide a happy and stable home life for my son. I hate telling him he can't have things, or wondering if he'll have a good Christmas or birthday. And I'm tired of struggling to pay the rent."

She blinked at him in surprise, as if she hadn't meant to admit so much to a complete stranger. He'd been told he was a good listener and people divulged secrets to him even if they didn't want to. His family had tried to get him to become a warrior, a spy to be exact. Valero hadn't had the slightest bit of interest in it. He'd gone through the warrior training, but in the end, he'd been miserable. When others of his kind started making their homes on Earth, he'd jumped at the chance for a new start. A chance to be anything he wanted. It hadn't taken him long to discover video games, and shortly after that, he'd figured out how to create them and had discovered his true passion.

"I'm sorry," Ella said. "I don't know why I said all that."

"Not to pry, but are things hard at home? Since you're here alone, I'm assuming Connor's father isn't in the picture?" At least, he was hoping the bastard was long gone.

"No, we split up in high school and I haven't seen him since. Not in person anyway."

His brow furrowed. "How do you see him if not in person?"

"He's a football star now. I would sometimes see his college games on TV and now he plays for an NFL team. He's done well for himself, but he's not part of our lives. He didn't even want to know if I was having a boy or girl, so I had him sign away his rights to Connor."

"Your job doesn't provide everything you need?" he asked.

"I can only work part time while Connor is in school, and all I know how to do is waitress. I took some computer classes in high school, but all of the office jobs around here are full time. Whatever extra money would be in my check would just go straight to daycare, and I don't like the idea of strangers raising my son."

What the woman needed was a husband, but he wasn't about to say any such thing to her. No, he wasn't about to offer his services no matter how tempting. With that fiery red hair of hers, she'd probably slap the hell out of him for even suggesting it. He'd discovered early on, and the hard way, that redheads were feisty and quick to temper. That didn't mean he couldn't help her though.

"What if you could work full time and the daycare was on site and completely free?" he asked.

"What do you mean?"

"The Terran Station is looking for a new receptionist. Our last one flirted with one too many warriors, even the married ones, and was asked to leave. Most likely because she especially flirted with the married ones. It would be during the day and there's a daycare at the station. You could see Connor during your break and even have lunch with him."

"He goes to kindergarten until two o'clock. I'd have to pick him up."

"How about this: you apply for the job tomorrow, I'll even put in a good word for you, and if you get hired we'll figure something out for picking up Connor. Avelyn and Thrace aren't here today, but their daughter Lily goes to the elementary school. I'm sure she'd be delighted to pick up Connor and bring him to you."

Her lips tipped up on one corner. "You're volunteering someone without even asking them?"

"It's Avelyn. She loves kids."

Her eyes narrowed a bit. "Why are you helping me? I'm a complete stranger."

He rubbed his jaw. "My reasons aren't completely altruistic. There's something I want. Two somethings actually."

She tipped her chin up. "And what's that?"

"I'd like Connor to help me sometime in the near future with a game I'm developing. I need a game tester who is around his age, and he seems to love playing. He'd get to try something new no one else has played, and in return he could tell me what he liked or hated about the game."

"I don't know…"

"I'll pay him. Whatever amount you think would be fair."

Her eyebrows went up and he could tell she was thinking about it.

"What was the other condition?" she asked.

He grinned widely. "You go on a date with me."

Her lips parted and her eyes widened a little bit. She looked so stunned he had to wonder when the last time was that she'd gone out and had fun. *Stupid human males.* Although, he should probably be thanking them for their idiocy. They may have left her unattached, but Valero had no intention of letting this little beauty slip through his fingers.

"You want to go on a date… with me?"

She made it sound like it was the most absurd question she'd ever heard. Since she had a child and an ex, he had to assume she'd been on dates before. She opened and closed her mouth several times, staring at him as if he'd grown three heads.

"You make it sound like a ridiculous idea. I'm trying to decide if I should be insulted."

"No! It's not that. It's just… no one has asked me out since…" She glanced in Connor's direction.

Valero had no idea how old the boy was, but he found it hard to believe that no one had asked her out in years. She was stunning, and seemed sweet. Of course, she did have that red hair. It was possible she had a wicked temper and that tiny body contained a tempest waiting to break free at a moment's notice. He smiled a little at the thought.

"It's amusing I haven't had a date in five years?" she

snapped.

"No. I was just thinking that luck was on my side. If you haven't had a date in five years, then you don't have a boyfriend right now."

"Oh." Her anger deflated. "You want to date a broke single mom? You're a Terran. Don't tell me that the women aren't lining up for a chance to go out with you."

"I've been on dates. They bored me, but something tells me that you're quite entertaining to be around."

She looked at Connor again. "We're a package deal, you know? Dating me isn't as simple as last minute plans or going out for all hours of the night. I'd have to arrange a sitter for Connor on the times he didn't go with us, and there would have to be times he went too. Are you sure you know what you're getting into? I mean, no offense, but you don't exactly seem like the type to hang out with kids all the time."

His smile faded. She'd seen one interaction with her son and already she knew he wasn't well versed on small humans. Maybe he really did need to borrow Reyvor's kids for a day or two. How hard could it be to wrangle a few kids?

"Just give me a chance," he said. "I may surprise you."

"Very well. I'll give you one chance. You'll either pass with flying colors, or you'll run screaming in the other direction."

Valero wasn't sure if he should be scared or not.

"Puck's Pizza Palace." She smirked. "You. Me. Connor. Tomorrow is Sunday so it shouldn't be too busy. We can meet there at eleven."

"What is a Puck's Pizza Palace?"

Ella's grin widened. "A children's paradise."

Something told him this wasn't going to be an ordinary date. The evil glint in her eyes told him he might not survive the day.

Chapter Two

Ella knew it was mean to make Valero meet them at Puck's, but if the man couldn't handle being surrounded by screaming children it was better to know up front. Besides, it might be amusing to see the look of stark terror on his face when he stepped inside. She should have picked somewhere cheaper, but selfishly, she'd wanted her son to have a good time. The last time they'd come to Puck's was for a party Connor had been invited to. It wasn't a luxury she could usually afford.

"Mama, can I please go play?" Connor asked for the hundredth time.

"In a minute, baby. We're waiting on Valero, then you can get a wristband and ride some of the rides or play in the tunnels if you want. Just stay out of the bigger kid areas."

"But he's taking forever," Connor whined.

Ella looked at her watch. 11:15. He was late, but not horribly so. Of course, that fifteen minutes might as well have been an hour to Connor, who danced around her feet like a hyper Pomeranian. She was about to give up and break Connor's heart by telling him they had to leave when Valero strolled through the door. And froze.

Yep. There was the look of fear she'd waited for. It was downright comical and she wondered if he stood there long enough if his face would freeze that way. She didn't want to give up their prime table so she waved like a lunatic, even jumping up and down, until she caught Valero's attention. He still looked shell-shocked when he reached her side.

"Is it always this loud?" he asked, leaning close to be heard.

"Nope. This is a quiet day."

The horror-stricken look made her laugh.

"Kids can't be like this all the time," he said. "They'd

all be homeless and their parents would be committed."

She snickered a little. "It's not so bad once you get used to it. I'm going to let you go with Connor over to the counter to get everything we need to get the fun started. I'll make sure no one takes our table."

Connor lifted his hand and when Valero gave him a puzzled look, Connor gripped the alien's fingers and began leading him away. Ella smiled as she watched them make their way to the counter across the room. Connor was waving his hand wildly and she knew he was explaining how things worked, and probably trying to wrangle the most expensive wristband out of the alien. Maybe she should have warned Valero ahead of time.

When they returned, Valero and Connor were in an animated discussion.

"What about a dinosaur hunting game?" Valero asked. "That wouldn't be as violent as, say, *Gears of War*. Surely that would be mom approved."

Connor shrugged. "I think it's been done already."

"Well, what kind of game would you like to play? If you could play anything at all…"

"Maybe something kind of like World of Warcraft but not so adult?" Connor asked. "I'd love to play a troll and smash things with a giant club."

Valero rubbed his chin. "You know, I can't exactly copy World of Warcraft, but what if we had a mountain troll, with a giant club, who had to smash fairies that would be depicted as yellow glowing lights in order to gain health points?"

Connor's forehead scrunched. "Can he use the club to bash other things?"

"Sure. He can use it to break down doors, or maybe he can use it to attack the bad guys. What sort of bad guy do you think a troll would fight?"

"An evil wizard?"

Valero was nodding. "With a beard and a walking

stick that he uses to cast his spells."

Connor grinned. "I think I like this game. Are you really going to make it?"

"I think I just might. But I'm going to need your help, and if your mom approves, you'll not only get to be the first little boy to play the game, but I'll pay you too."

Connor's eyes lit up. "Then I could come to Puck's whenever I wanted."

Valero smiled a little. "You want to be paid in Puck's gift cards?"

Connor nodded eagerly.

"If you two are finished discussing video games..." Ella held out her hand. "Hand me the wristband, Connor."

He pouted a little at having his grownup conversation cut short, but handed over the band. Just as she'd thought, it was the blue one, which gave him unlimited everything and moved him ahead in line of everyone wearing a green wristband. After she fastened the band on Connor's wrist, she shooed him away. Then she held out her hand to Valero.

"What?" he asked.

"Receipt. I think you got hustled by a five year old." He handed it over and she shook her head. "One cheese pizza would have been sufficient with three drinks and a green wristband. He talked you into both a cheese and a sausage pizza, breadsticks, an unlimited pitcher with three keepsake cups, and an upgraded wristband."

Valero shoved his hands in his pockets. "Does he get to come here often?"

"No. Maybe once or twice a year."

"Then what's the harm if he gets a little spoiled today? If you're worried about the money, don't. I have it covered. Today's activities aren't going to deplete my accounts."

She blinked. "Accounts plural?"

"I have a checking account here, a savings account, then there's my stock portfolio, and the funds I still have back on my world in case I return at some point."

"What is it exactly that you do?"

"I design video games. Now. I was a warrior on my world. It paid handsomely, but I hated it. Going into battle didn't fulfill my dreams like it did for so many others. I wanted a different life, so I came here about two years ago. At first, I worked as a guard at the Terran Station. Again, excellent pay, but not what I wanted to do. Then one of my friends introduced me to video games and I fell in love right away."

She smiled. "Now you sound like Connor. All he talks about are video games."

"He's rather good at them, from what I've seen. He could be a professional gamer one day."

"That's a thing?" she asked.

"It's not something people generally do for a long time, but he could easily go pro for several years. If he's a top gamer, during that time he could earn two hundred thousand or more. Maybe even closer to five hundred thousand."

Ella's jaw dropped. "Are you serious? He could make that in a few years? It would take me a decade or more to earn that much."

Valero motioned to the table. "Should we sit, or do you need to follow Connor?"

She plopped onto the bench seat. Valero gracefully slid into the seat across from her. If a gamer could make that kind of money, she could only imagine how much the creators made. No, actually, she couldn't. As someone who had worked for minimum wage her entire life, having that kind of money was just beyond her reasoning. She'd thought there would be a huge gap between them because she was human and a single mom. Now, she had to add that he was apparently rather wealthy. If she dated him, would he think she was after his money? The thought sickened her a little.

"You're not smiling anymore," he said.

"We're just so different."

"Don't humans claim that opposites attract? Which by the way is true. Maybe I'm a positively charged proton and you're a negatively charged neutron."

"Why do I have to be the negative one?"

"Because you're frowning."

She had the sudden urge to stick out her tongue and blow a raspberry at him.

"I'm not a negative person." She tipped her chin up. "You've just caught me at a bad time."

The merriment left his eyes. "Did you apply for the job at the Terran Station?"

"I thought I'd go tomorrow while Connor is in school."

"You don't work tomorrow?"

"Right now I'm only on the schedule Tuesday through Friday from nine in the morning until one in the afternoon."

"That's not enough hours at minimum wage for you to pay rent, much less feed a growing boy like Connor. How have you managed to this point?"

She shrugged. "I had a better job at a diner where I made decent tips, but the diner closed."

"Tell me something interesting about you. Besides the fact you're a single mom."

A teen in a Puck's polo came over with a pitcher of soda and three cups. "Your order will be up in a minute."

Valero thanked him and then focused on Ella again. That intense gaze made her want to squirm. It had been a long time since anyone had wanted to get to know her. Something interesting? She didn't do much besides work and take care of Connor. She didn't think that counted as interesting. And he probably didn't want to hear about her cleaning methods, or lack of culinary skills.

"There has to be something, Ella."

"I like to draw. Not professionally or anything, but as a hobby. I took an art class in high school and fell in love with sketching."

He smiled. "I'd love to see some of your work."

"Maybe." She bit her lip as her cheeks flushed. "I'm not very good at it."

"All that matters is that you enjoy doing it. Beauty is in the eye of the beholder. Margaret Wolfe Hungerford said that, or rather she wrote it in her book. The point is that while you think you may not have much talent, I may think your drawings are fantastic."

She smiled a little. "You like to read?"

He scoffed. "You're surprised? What, because I like to play video games I can't be well read?"

"I didn't mean..."

"I'm teasing you, Ella. But to answer your question, yes, I like to read. I tend to read a book a day, or close to it. And I don't have a particular genre I love more than another. They all fascinate me."

"Quote something to me."

"The brightness of her cheek would shame those stars as daylight doth a lamp; her eyes in heaven would through the airy region stream so bright that birds would sing, and think it were not night."

"What's that from?" she asked.

"Shakespeare's *Romeo and Juliet*."

"It's beautiful," she said.

"You're beautiful." She cast her eyes down and he reached out to touch her hand. "Why do you do that?"

"Do what?"

"Whenever you receive a compliment you deflect in some way. You look away, bite your lip, come back with a smart remark."

Did she do that? She didn't used to, back before

getting pregnant with Connor. She'd thrived on attention back in those days, and look where it had gotten her. Ella had gone from being well liked with lots of friends to being alone the last five years. She'd learned the hard way not to let anyone get close, but for some reason, she wanted to get closer to Valero. He seemed sweet and a little geeky. Heaven knew Connor could use a positive male influence in his life. Even if they never went on another date again, maybe she could convince him to spend some time with Connor.

"I was a different person before I had Connor, but the last five years have been hard. I never let him see just how bad things are, but I think he understands anyway. His birthday is coming up and he's asked for a store bought cake and there are some toys he'd really like to have. I can't even make rent right now, much less give him a birthday. So, I have a lot on my mind. To me, compliments are empty words. If you want to make me smile, you'll have to find another way to do it."

He studied her and didn't say anything. She half expected him to get up and walk out, and she couldn't blame him. There was a hard shell protecting her heart, but the only thing that stood between Connor and a broken heart was her. And she would do anything for her son.

"We'll discuss Connor's birthday later, when he won't possibly overhear us. For now, we're going to eat and get to know one another, and Connor is going to run until he can't run anymore."

"All right."

"I've never met anyone like you before, Ella. You're strong, far stronger than any human female I've met, and I admire that trait. And you are capable of great love. Anyone can see that. It's in the gentle touch you have with your son, the way you put his needs before your own."

"He's my entire world."

Valero leaned forward. "Do you think there might be space in that world for one more? Because I'm genuinely interested in you, Ella. And I tend to pursue the things I want."

She smiled. "You're a bit of a contradiction, aren't you? Funny, geeky, gamer one minute and intense warrior on the prowl the next."

"Perhaps I am a contradiction, but my past has made me who I am today. I can't separate the warrior in me any more than I could set down my controller and walk away from the latest *Call of Duty*. Going into battle might not be my passion, but that training is ingrained in me. So, do you think you want to take on a domineering… how did you put it? Funny, geeky, gamer?"

"Maybe. And that's all you're going to get today."

He winked and leaned back in his seat as their food was delivered. She had a feeling he wasn't going to let the matter go, and she wondered just what methods he would use to persuade her to give him a chance. If he ever found out the way to her heart was through her son, she was a goner.

* * *

Valero had a headache to rival all headaches, but he'd enjoyed his time with Ella and Connor. Although, if he never went to Puck's Pizza Palace again, he wouldn't exactly cry over the loss. The important thing was that Connor had had a good time. The little boy had been all smiles until he'd finally worn himself out and started yawning. Ella had gathered their things and herded Connor out to their car, which led him to his current predicament.

Ella tried to crank the engine again, but it made a horrible grinding noise and nothing happened. He tapped on the window and motioned for her to open the door. Ella gave him a disgruntled look, as if it were somehow his fault the car wouldn't start. He leaned down to talk to her.

"I don't think your car is going anywhere, Ella. Why don't you get into my truck and I'll take you home? You can make arrangements for your car in the morning."

"I can't afford arrangements for the car, as you put it. It's going to crank. It just needs a little more time," Ella said.

She twisted the key again and this time the grinding sound came to a halt and nothing happened. Ella slammed her hands against the steering wheel and let out an unladylike curse that had him smiling a little. She was definitely an intriguing woman, one he hoped to get to know better.

"Come on, Ella." He held out his hand. "If you need help getting the car towed, I know someone who can help."

"You're friends with a tow truck driver?" she asked skeptically.

"No, I'm friends with a mechanic who owns a shop nearby and he has a driver who can come get your car."

She nibbled her bottom lip. "Then can we call him now? I don't want to leave my car here overnight. What if it gets impounded for being in the lot after hours?"

Valero pulled out his phone and made the call. Dryden answered almost immediately. Valero could hear the clank of machinery in the background and wondered if he was at his local shop or working on one of the shuttles at the Terran Station.

"Dryden, I need a car towed to your shop," Valero said. "It's for a friend."

"A friend, hmm?" Dryden asked with humor lacing his voice. "I'm guessing this friend is curvy and delicious, because you've never asked me for a favor before."

"Maybe." He glanced at Ella. "Could you send someone now? She doesn't want to leave her car in the parking lot of Puck's Pizza Palace overnight."

"Ouch! You got suckered into going to that place? It's a complete zoo in there! I dated a woman with a kid for about two seconds. One tour of that place and I was out of there. I can do without all the screaming."

"It wasn't so bad." Minus the headache.

"I'll have my driver over there in a few minutes. He was about to head home for the night, but one more haul won't hurt. Am I sending the bill to you or the driver of the car?"

"Me."

"I figured. All right. I'll take a look at the car tomorrow and see what I can do."

"Thanks, Dryden."

Valero disconnected the call. "He said he's sending someone."

"I'll pay you back," Ella said.

He waved a hand dismissively. "It's no trouble." Truthfully, he could buy her a new car and it wouldn't deplete his accounts. Ella motioned for him to have a seat in her car while they waited. He slid into the passenger's seat and glanced back at a sleeping Connor. He hated that they would have to wake the boy in order to transfer him to Valero's truck, but he wasn't sorry he got to spend more time with the little family. Despite the chaos of Puck's, it hadn't scared him off.

Ella was quiet as she stared at him. He could tell there was a lot on her mind and hoped she'd talk to him. He didn't want to press her though. Slowly, he reached over and grasped her hand, lacing their fingers together. Her breath hitched and her eyes widened. How long had it been since someone held her hand? From what he'd learned so far, she'd been alone the past five years. No boyfriends, no family, no friends.

"I know things are bad for the two of you," he said. "Just how bad is it?"

"We get by."

"Your car is falling apart. You've admitted that your son doesn't get to come to places like this very often, and you mentioned yesterday that you're tired of stressing over the rent. So, I'm going to ask again, how bad is it?"

She sighed and looked away. "I have a week to come up with the rent money or we'll be living out of the car again."

"Again?"

Ella shrugged.

"Will you let me help?" Valero asked. "I know you're proud and you want to do it all on your own, but it's okay to admit you can't do everything by yourself."

"You may have survived a date with us, but it doesn't mean you're responsible for what happens in our lives. Connor and I have gotten along just fine on our own so far."

"Ella, living out of your car is not getting along 'just fine.' You need help, even if you don't want to ask for it. Even if you get the job at the Terran Station, there's no way you'd be paid in time to make your rent. Either let me pay your rent for a month, or…"

Her brow furrowed. "Or what?"

"Move in with me."

Her mouth dropped open. "Are you insane? I just met you. I can't move my son into your house. Besides, I'm not going to be your kept woman."

"My…" He burst out laughing and immediately tried to stifle his amusement so he wouldn't wake Connor. "Ella, I have enough space in my home that you could have your own room. When I bought a place on Earth, I decided to get one large enough for the family I hoped to one day have."

"I still can't just move in with you."

Before Valero could argue the point further, the tow truck arrived. He got out to greet the driver while Ella woke up Connor. The sleepy boy stumbled out of the car and Valero lifted him into his arms. Ella put his booster seat into the back of the truck and Valero carried him over, buckling him into the backseat. He motioned for Ella to climb in. He started the engine so the heat would run while he spoke to the driver.

After Ella's car was off to the shop, Valero climbed behind the steering wheel of his truck and looked at her expectantly. She just blinked at him and he fought a smile.

"I need your address, Ella, unless you want me to take you to my place."

"Oh." Her cheeks flushed. She gave him the address and he couldn't stop the frown that tipped down the corners of his mouth.

He was familiar with the area and knew the apartments she mentioned weren't safe, but arguing with her didn't seem to be getting anywhere. He drove in silence and pulled up in front of her building. Ella fidgeted with her seatbelt and seemed to be at a loss for words.

"Why don't you let me carry Connor inside?" he offered.

She nodded and slipped out of the truck. Valero got out and picked up Connor, following behind Ella as she led the way to her apartment. When they got to her door, he was far from impressed. The hallway reeked and there were water stains on all the walls. At least, he hoped they were water stains. There was a faint smell of urine and he could have easily believed the inhabitants of the building had been peeing on the walls. She opened the door and he followed her inside.

"Connor's room is through there," she said pointing to a door across the room.

He carried the small boy into the bedroom and laid him on the bed, stopping to remove his shoes and covering him up. Valero backed out of the small room and pulled the door mostly closed before facing Ella. She was standing uncertainly in the living room. The pillow and blanket on the couch told him that was where she slept. The same funky smell from the hall permeated the apartment, even though he could tell that she'd cleaned it well.

Ella moved the pillow and blanket before sinking down onto the cushions. The couch groaned from her slight weight and he wondered if he'd break the damn thing if he sat on it. Valero looked around the tiny apartment and wondered what he could say to convince her to move in with him. He'd give her anything she wanted if she'd only listen to reason.

"I know it's not much," she said softly. "But it's ours."

"Ella, I can't let you stay here. You said you only have a week left before you're evicted. Why prolong the inevitable? I have empty rooms in my house and plenty of space for the two of you and your belongings."

"We just met."

"So you've said. What does that have to do with anything? Do you think I'm going to hurt you? Demand sex as payment for a roof over your head?"

She shook her head slowly.

"Then why won't you move in with me? It can be temporary. Just until you find a new job and save a little money. Give it a month or two, and if during that time you decide there's no future between us other than friendship, I won't stand in your way when you move out. I'll even help you pack."

"But you want there to be something between us?" she asked.

"I find you intriguing, and I love the fact Connor is so into video games. I'd be lying if I said I didn't look at the two of you and see a future I'd very much like to grab and hold tight. I wouldn't be the first Terran to claim a human child as my own. You said the boy doesn't have a father. I could fill that role."

Ella looked around her apartment, her shoulders slumping. "I've done everything I can to give Connor a good life and I seem to fail at every turn. Why do you want someone who's such a mess? I barely graduated high school. I never went to college. I'm not smart like Rory."

Valero sank onto the couch and winced when it sounded like it was going to open up and swallow him. He reached over and took her hand.

"Rory is a wonderful woman, and I'm very happy that Zwyk has her in his life. But her college degree isn't what makes her wonderful. Do you think it matters to me that you never went to college? I don't care that you wait tables for a living or fix coffee for people. You have the biggest heart of anyone I've met since moving here, and the way you take care of your son tells me that you're a wonderful mother."

"Being a good mother isn't enough," she muttered.

"It's more than enough. I can only hope that the same love you show Connor would also be shown to your future mate. And if that male were me, then I would count myself very fortunate. I'm not asking you for a commitment right now, Ella. Just let me help you, and while we're roommates we can get to know one another better."

"What happens if Connor gets used to living in your big house and isn't satisfied with the life I can give him?"

"We'll cross that bridge later."

She nibbled her bottom lip. "All right. We'll move in with you."

"How much do you need to pack?" Valero asked.

"Just our clothes and shoes, and Connor's toys and his game system."

"I'm going to go get some boxes and return so we can pack tonight. I'll leave it to you whether we move you in tonight or in the morning. Connor can nap while we get everything together."

She nodded, seeming resigned. He wished she were happier about the move.

Valero hated to leave her, but he got into his truck and went to the nearest storage facility. He remembered from his friends' previous moves that places like that carried boxes and packing tape. He hadn't thought to ask Ella how many they would need, so he started with ten boxes and two rolls of tape. When he got back to Ella's, she'd already started making stacks of clothes on the couch.

They worked together, getting all their stuff packed in a little over an hour. The hardest part had been packing Connor's room without waking him. When Valero had seen just how few games the boy had, he made a promise to himself that he would take Connor shopping at Gamer Plus at his first opportunity. He'd just have to figure out how to keep Ella from getting upset over it. She seemed like the type who wouldn't appreciate someone buying her son a bunch of games, or much of anything else.

They woke Connor, who nearly bounced out of the bed when they explained why there were boxes around the apartment. Ella packed the used bedding last and then Valero began loading everything into the bed of his truck. After he was finished, he waited for Ella to turn in her keys to the apartment manager, then he drove to his house, stopping along the way to treat everyone to a milkshake.

"This is the best day ever," Connor said as he slurped his strawberry milkshake.

"It's just temporary," Ella stressed. "Once I get a new job, we'll move into our own place again."

Valero watched Connor's expression in the rearview

mirror and saw him frown, but the little boy didn't say anything. It was hard for Valero not to tell Connor that he could stay as long as he wanted. Forever, even. Something told him it would only piss off Ella if he did that, and that was the last thing he wanted to do. He tried to watch Connor and Ella as he pulled into his subdivision. His house wasn't as grand as Reyvor's, but it was in the same community.

Connor pressed his face to the glass as he watched the homes pass by. When Valero pulled into his driveway, he heard a very quiet "Wow," from the backseat. Ella seemed nervous, her hands twisting in her lap, and he wondered what he could do to put her at ease. He opened the garage and pulled inside then turned off the engine.

"Are the two of you ready to see your new home?" he asked.

"We're really going to live here?" Connor asked.

"Just for a little while," Ella said as she got out of the truck.

Valero ushered them inside and gave them a tour. When he told Connor to pick one of the four empty bedrooms, his face lit up and he examined each of them carefully. He finally chose the blue room, with a full bed, matching dresser, and small entertainment center with a TV and Blu-ray player. Valero put all of Connor's boxes into his room and Ella's into the yellow room next to it. It wasn't surprising that she'd choose a room beside Connor. It just happened to be next to his as well.

"Do the two of you like Chinese?" Valero asked.

Connor's eyes went wide. "We never get to eat Chinese."

"Do you have a favorite dish?" Valero asked.

"I had orange chicken once," the little boy said. "It was really good. The rice had bits of chicken in it too."

"And for you, Ella?"

"I can share with Connor."

Valero shook his head. "You each get your own meal. Now, what would you like me to order? I figured we could eat here tonight while the two of you get settled and then tomorrow night we can go out to celebrate."

"Sweet and sour chicken," Ella said. "And, Connor, after we eat, it's time for bed."

"Egg rolls?" Valero asked.

Connor jumped up and down so he took that as a yes. While his new houseguests got settled in, he placed their order then tried to stay out of their way.

When Connor came to him a short while later, asking about hooking up his game system, Valero was happy to help.

"Do you have any favorite movies?" Valero asked.

"I like mostly Disney movies. Mama doesn't let me watch much else. I also like Pokémon and Scooby Doo, but the original Scooby, not the new one."

Valero had no idea what the difference was, but he'd make sure he got the correct one when he shopped online tonight. After Ella and Connor went to sleep, he'd go to Amazon and order a bunch of children's movies for Connor to keep in his room. He wanted the boy to be comfortable and think of this as his home.

With some luck, in the next month, he'd convince both Ella and Connor to make this their home permanently.

Chapter Three

Ella lounged in what had to be the most luxurious tub she'd ever seen. Valero had insisted she use the one in his master suite, and she was glad she hadn't put up much of a fight. The tub in the guest bathroom was nice, but it was just a regular tub. The garden tub she was soaking in had jets and let her soak up to the neck without scrunching down and her knees sticking up out of the water. She'd never been able to take a bath before where all of her was covered in the hot bubbly water.

She did have to wonder why he kept bubble bath in his bathroom, since he'd mentioned he rarely used the tub. Surely, he didn't have someone special in his life if he'd asked her out on a date and then moved her into his house. It was innocent enough, since she had her own bedroom, but she'd be lying if she didn't admit to being more than a little attracted to him.

She'd watched his muscles bunch and flex while he'd moved her boxes out of her apartment and into the house. More than once she'd had to squeeze her thighs together to ease the ache building there. It had been so long since she'd been attracted to someone, and even longer since she'd felt the touch of a man. Really, she'd never had a man's hands on her, because she hardly counted her high school boyfriend as a man.

Her hands cupped her breasts and she lightly pinched her nipples, sending a zing straight to her clit. Ella moaned a little as she spread her legs. She'd give anything to have a toy right now, but she'd never bought one since she didn't have privacy in her apartment. Her fingers brushed over her clit and she bit her lip to stifle any noises she might make. Other than some quick showers after Connor went to sleep, she hadn't been able to indulge in any adult time in the last five years.

Her clit was slick and swollen as her fingers rubbed

harder and faster. Her pussy clenched, aching to be filled. Eyes closed, she pictured Valero kneeling beside the tub, his hands under the water teasing and tormenting her. Would his touch be light or would he be forceful? Her fingers eased inside of her tight channel and she imagined it was his cock filling her. She came, crying out his name, and hoped like hell he hadn't heard her. Her cheeks flushed with embarrassment as her heart thumped wildly in her chest.

She heard something in the other room and tensed. "Hello?"

Footsteps came close to the bathroom door. "I didn't mean to interrupt, Ella. I just needed to get something."

His voice sounded strangled and she was certain he'd heard her. How would she ever look him in the eye again?

"Ella, I..." He grew silent. "I think we should talk when you get Connor into bed tonight."

Of course he wanted to talk. She'd just come harder than ever before while screaming his name like a banshee. She nibbled her bottom lip and stared at the disappearing bubbles. What would she say to him?

"Ella?"

"All right. Connor should have already been in bed, but I'll take care of it in just a minute."

"Take your time," he said softly. "You don't have to rush out of the tub. Connor is busy playing a video game."

How could she possibly enjoy her bath now? She quickly washed and drained the tub before drying off and slipping on her pajamas. Looking in the mirror, she questioned whether or not she should wear the skimpy tank and super short sleep shorts. Her nipples poked at the thin top and she wished she had a robe that covered her from neck to ankles.

Blowing out a breath to steady her nerves, she

opened the bathroom door and carried her dirty clothes to her room. She could hear Connor chatting animatedly and she smiled a little. He'd never had someone to talk to who shared his passion before, and she was thankful that Valero seemed to enjoy spending time with her son. She peered around the corner and into Connor's room. Valero and Connor were sitting on the end of the bed playing something on the Xbox.

"Do you always play Yoda?" Valero asked.

"He's my favorite. And his lightsaber is green!"

Valero chuckled. "So I see."

Ella cleared her throat. "I'm sorry to interrupt, but it's a certain little boy's bedtime."

Connor groaned. "But, Mama…"

"You have school tomorrow."

"Can I stay home just this one time? We just moved and I don't wanna go to school tomorrow."

Ella shook her head. "Mama needs to look for a new job tomorrow, and Mr. Valero probably has work to do as well. I doubt he would get much done with you running around the house all day."

"But he said there's an indoor pool. I wanna swim."

Ella smiled a little. "I'm sure you do, Connor, but it will have to wait until after school lets out. If you don't have homework tomorrow, then you can swim when you come home."

He pouted but shut off the game and put the controller away. Valero unhooked his own controller and eased out of the room, but paused in the doorway.

"Goodnight, Connor," Valero said. "I'll make sure my work is done tomorrow by the time you come home and we'll all check out the pool together. Then maybe we can play another game."

Connor smiled widely as he scrambled under the covers. Ella tucked him in, kissed his brow, then shut off the light. She stepped out of the room and pulled the door mostly closed before she realized Valero was leaning against the wall, waiting for her no doubt. Her heart thumped like crazy as she looked at him uncertainly.

He held out a hand and she grasped it, letting him guide her down the hall to the living room. He put up his controller and then tugged her onto the couch next to him. Ella felt the heat of him pressing against her naked thigh and part of her wanted to crawl into his lap, while the more rationale side of her wanted to move further away. Her gaze jerked up to his as he laced their fingers together, placing their clasped hands on his thigh.

"Ella, I want you to know how happy I am that you decided to come stay with me," he said. "I didn't have altruistic reasons for asking you though."

She tensed. "I won't be a whore for a roof over my head."

His grip tightened on her hand. "I would never ask that of you. I won't lie and say I don't want you, because I do, but I would never make you sleep with me just for a place for Connor and you to live. If I wanted sex for the sake of sex, then I would find some random woman in a bar."

"Have you done that?" she asked.

"When I first came here, the thought of being with a human female was intriguing. When one offered herself for just one night, I didn't say no. Looking back, she wanted the novelty of saying she'd been with one of my kind, and while the sex had been good, it left me feeling empty afterward." He winced. "And while I'm being honest, I've also used the services at the floating brothel that hovers near my world. But I seldom went there."

She licked her lips. "So, you want sex to mean something?"

"Ella, I wanted you to come stay with me so you could see that I'm more than capable of providing for Connor and you. I had hoped that when you got here, you'd see that I had a large enough bank account that you'd never have to worry about another thing the rest of your life. I had thought it might make me an acceptable mate."

"Mate... like in married?"

He nodded. "I won't rush you, but I do want you to think about it."

"What if something happens between us, but I'm not sure I'm ready for that step?"

He smiled a little. "I think it's safe to say you're sexually attracted to me, and I've admitted I'm attracted to you. Are you suggesting that we have something a little more casual for right now? More of a... How do you humans phrase it? Friends with benefits?"

Her cheeks flushed because she was very tempted by the idea, even if she didn't want to sleep with him just to have a place to stay. But sleeping with him because they were mutually attracted to one another was a different matter altogether.

"Ella, while I would love to take you to my bed, I don't want to do anything that could end with you getting hurt."

Her heart warmed at his words. She couldn't remember a man ever being worried about her getting hurt. Then again, she hadn't been serious with anyone since Connor was born. The last time she'd had sex was with Connor's dad back in high school. She wasn't sure if that made her picky or pathetic.

"Valero, you should probably know there hasn't been a man in my life since Connor's dad. I never really dated, and since I didn't have a bedroom I couldn't exactly bring home a one-night stand. Not that I would have let someone like that around Connor anyway. He's always been my priority."

Valero reached over, gripping her waist, and lifted her. She settled across his lap, her legs splayed on either side of him. She could feel the hard ridge of his cock pressed against her, and it was hard not to squirm. His hands cupped her hips and he bucked against her. A gasp escaped her lips and her eyes widened.

"I thought you didn't do casual sex," she said, her panties getting wetter by the minute.

"Something tells me that being with you would be amazing, but right now this is about you. I think after everything you've done for your son the last five years, maybe it's time for you to get something you want."

"Something I want?" she asked.

"I was thinking maybe an orgasm that didn't come from your fingers? We don't have to go all the way, as you humans say, but it doesn't mean I can't make you feel good."

"Are you suggesting we fool around?" she asked with some amusement.

"That's exactly it." He smiled. "What do you say? Will you let me make you come? Maybe more than once?"

"You really want to do that, without getting anything in return?"

"Ella, bringing you pleasure is all that I need. I'm not asking for you to return the favor, I'm not asking for us to go all the way… I'm only asking you to let me make you feel good. You've sacrificed so much since having your son. Isn't it time that you get something that's just for you?"

He bucked against her again, his cock pressing against her soaked panties and damp shorts. Ella had never wanted anyone as much as she wanted Valero. Was it wrong that she wanted him to lose control and do more than just please her? She wanted to feel him inside of her, wanted him to claim her.

No. She gave herself a mental shake. Not claim her. But she wanted… something. It had been so long since someone had held her, had kissed her, had made her ache to be with them. She wanted more of those feelings, and she knew Valero could give them to her. Did it make her selfish to hold so much of herself back from him?

"I need a yes or no, Ella. I won't do anything without your permission."

Her heart beat wildly as she contemplated what she wanted.

"Yes," she said softly. "But only if I can make you feel good too."

Valero groaned and pulled her closer for a kiss. His lips were soft against hers and she opened, welcoming him in. His tongue stroked hers and she wondered what it would feel like to have his tongue stroke other parts of her body. She rocked against his erection, her clit throbbing with need. When his hands slid around her back, and slipped under her tank, his touch left a fiery trail. She pulled away long enough to remove her shirt, then grasped his hands and placed them over her breasts. Her nipples hardened against his palms and she claimed his lips again.

Valero tweaked the pebbled tips as she continued to rock against him. Their kiss was fierce and earth-shattering, leaving her gasping for breath and wanting more. His mouth trailed a path down her throat before his tongue slipped between her lips again. Ella could feel herself getting close. He pinched her nipples and it was just what she needed to send her over the edge. She cried out against his mouth as she rocked out her orgasm against his cock. Valero stiffened and groaned beneath her and she felt dampness on his pants.

He pulled away, panting heavily, as he stared at her with an intensity that took her breath away.

"That wasn't what I had in mind," he said. "And I have to admit I've never come in my pants before. Let's keep that between us."

She giggled a little and rubbed against him again. "I like that you were so turned on you couldn't hold back."

"I think I need to go get cleaned up."

Ella bit her lip and wondered if she was brave enough to ask for what she wanted. His hands gripped her and he lifted her off his lap, setting her on her feet. She wobbled a moment, trying to get her balance as he stood in front of her. Before he could walk off, she reached out and fisted his shirt to hold him still.

"Can I join you?" she asked.

"Ella, I…"

"Not for sex. I know you want it to mean something when that happens, but maybe we could play some more?"

He tipped his head back and groaned before giving her a nod. "You're going to be the death of me. But yes, you may join me."

She picked up her shirt and followed him to the master suite and into the bathroom. Valero started the shower and stripped out of his clothes, hesitating a moment on the fastening of his pants. After what they'd just shared, she found it amusing that he seemed a little shy now. She moved closer and reached for him, her hands gently moving his out of the way. She unbuttoned and unzipped them before shoving them and his boxer briefs down over his hips.

Valero kicked them out of the way and let her look her fill, and look she definitely did. Ella licked her lips as she watched his cock grow impossibly large. If they ever did get to actual sex, would that even fit? She had to admit, it would be fun to try. After her sex life had been lacking for so long, she felt like something inside of her had been unlocked and set free.

Valero held out his hand and helped her into the shower. He followed behind her and closed the shower door. The water was so hot the glass walls were foggy with steam. The surround shower meant no one had to freeze while the other stayed warm under the spray. There was even a bench seat along the back wall. Ella had never seen anything so fantastic as Valero's home and its many features. She was going to get spoiled, living here.

They took turns washing each other, letting their hands explore. After they were clean, Valero eased her onto the bench and spread her thighs wide. Ella braced herself on her hands, arching her back as his tongue swiped along the seam of her pussy. She moaned and fought the urge to get closer to him. No one had ever put their mouth on her there, but if she'd known how incredible it would feel, she might have asked Connor's dad to give it a try. Ella decided no woman should ever have to spend her life not knowing the amazing sensation of having her pussy licked.

Valero sucked on her clit as his fingers slipped inside of her, her channel clamping tight on the digits. Her hips bucked as her nipples hardened. Ella gripped the edge of the bench and fought not to slide onto the floor. His fingers thrust faster, harder, and Ella cried out as her body bowed off the bench. She came so hard she saw stars. As the aftershocks faded, Valero pulled away from her. Her legs shook and her body trembled from the force of her release.

Tackling the sexy alien, she pinned him to the shower floor before sliding down his body and admiring his hard cock. The tip was a little darker shade of purple than rest of his body and she tentatively leaned down and lapped up the pre-cum. The salty-sweet taste of him exploded on her tongue and her mouth watered, wanting more. She worked his cock with her lips and tongue, her hand twisting around the base. Valero said a string of words she didn't understand as his body tensed beneath her.

Ella sucked him long and hard, wanting him to come

in her mouth. He seemed to be fighting his body though. His cock popped free of her mouth and she ran her tongue along the underside.

"Give it to me," she said as she licked him again. "You know you want to come."

"Fuck, Ella. Your mouth is incredible, but I don't want to choke you when I come."

"You won't. Just do it. Let go."

She sucked him into her mouth again, doubling her efforts, until he erupted. His cum shot down her throat and she swallowed every drop. When he lay panting beneath her, she crawled up his body and cuddled against his side as the water beat down on them. If every night was as great as this one, maybe moving in with Valero wasn't such a bad thing after all. Her son had a stable home and she had had multiple orgasms.

She heard the comforting *thump* of Valero's heartbeat and she smiled a little. He might not want to have sex with her without more of a commitment, but she was certainly going to have fun trying to get him into bed.

Chapter Four

Valero stared at his computer screen and tried to focus, but his mind kept drifting to the previous night. When he'd moved Ella and Connor into his home, he hadn't expected things to move quite so fast. He'd thought he'd give her time to get adjusted, take her out on some dates, and then work his way to asking her to become his mate. And then he'd walked into his bedroom and heard her pleasuring herself and crying out his name. It had nearly snapped his control.

She'd been so soft and sweet in his arms, and he'd ached to take her, to possess her, claim her as his. But that didn't seem to be what she wanted. Oh, she wanted sex, she hadn't been too shy about going after what she wanted, but she didn't want a commitment to go along with it. Sex for the sake of sex had its place, and he'd enjoyed those moments in his past, but that wasn't what he wanted with Ella. He wanted forever with her, but it didn't seem the stubborn woman was going to submit so easily.

It wouldn't be easy to deny her, but he was going to try. It was too soon to say he had feelings for Ella, but he genuinely liked her, and while he'd never thought he'd mate with a single mom, he had to admit that Connor was pretty great. How could he not love a little boy who liked gaming as much as he did? He smiled a little as he thought about how they would make an excellent father-son team when it came to creating new games. Connor had already given him some great ideas.

Unfortunately, the lines of coding in front of him didn't make much sense today. He'd already worked on some of the 3-D renderings of the characters, so Valero saved his file and shut down his computer for the day. Ella had been gone most of the morning, attempting to find a new job. He hoped the fact she'd been gone so long meant she'd found something at the Terran station. Even if they were to marry, he wouldn't stop her from working if that's what she wanted to do. He laughed a little when he recalled her words that morning, as he'd tried to keep her home for the day.

"Valero, I don't need a sugar daddy. I want a job, and I'm going to go get one. The coffee shop is fine, but it doesn't pay nearly enough."

"I have money, Ella. Let me take care of the two of you."

She'd growled and stomped her foot. "I'm not going to be your kept woman."

He'd refrained, barely, from asking if she'd consider being his wife. For whatever reason, Ella really seemed determined to *not* get married. When he'd first come to Earth, he'd thought all human females wanted to find a mate and settle down. He'd learned the hard way that most were quite happy being single and flitting from male to male. He'd have requested someone through the bride program, but those females were reserved for the males still on his world, those who didn't have access to unlimited human females on a day to day basis. And he couldn't begrudge them happiness. He just wished he could find some for himself.

The front door slammed and Valero left his office to see how Ella's day had been so far. There was a fierce expression on her face and he almost felt sorry for whatever poor bastard had put it there. She didn't seem like the type to anger easily, despite her red hair, so he wondered what had happened.

"If Tyril had said one more word, just one, about how single females only wanted access to Terran males so they could snag a rich mate, I was going to cram his words down his throat until he choked on them." She slammed her purse down on the coffee table. "Just because the last receptionist hit on anything male doesn't mean I will too."

"So, the application process didn't go well then."

She growled.

"Would you like me to make a call? Did you mention you were living with me right now?"

"Of course, I didn't say where I was living. What business was it of his?"

Valero hid a smile. "Maybe if he thought you were considering me as a mate, he might have hired you."

She placed her hands on her hips. "Oh, so the only reason I'm allowed to work there is if I want to marry one of you? I can't get the job just because I'm able and willing to do the work?"

Apparently, marriage had been the wrong subject to bring up.

"Did you apply anywhere else?" he asked.

"I tried applying at Nate's and I heard there's going to be a Mama Rosa's opening here soon. Waiting tables is all I really know how to do, so maybe I should stick with it. I know I'll get crap hours because of needing to be home with Connor, but what else am I supposed to do?" She flopped onto the couch. "Maybe I should rethink college and see if there are any grants and loans out there for single moms. Except I'd need to take classes online and I don't even own a computer."

Valero took a seat next to her. "I want to help, but I'm not sure how. You don't want me to call Tyril and speak to him about the job at the station. I doubt you'd accept a computer if I bought one for you. What do you need from me, Ella?"

She cuddled against his side and he wrapped an arm around her.

"I don't know. I'll figure this mess out. I always do." She sighed and curled into him more. "Just hold me."

Now that was something he'd gladly do.

"How much time do we have before Connor gets out

of school?"

"I need to get in the parent pick-up line in about an hour. Thanks for letting me use your truck, by the way. Any news on my car?" she asked.

"I haven't checked yet, but if you'd like I can call Dryden and see if there's any news."

"Would you mind? It sucks being without my own transportation, not that I'm not grateful for you loaning me your truck. I just wish I had my own car."

Valero nodded and extracted himself from her. He went to his office and picked up his cell phone and called Dryden's shop. He didn't know if his friend was working at the garage or the Terran Station today, or if he was even on this world. Quite often he was requested back on their home world for a job.

It rang several times before someone who definitely wasn't Dryden answered the phone.

"Dryden's, this is Rosie. How may I help you?"

He'd gotten a secretary? Interesting.

"This is Valero. Is Dryden in today?"

"No, sir. He's not expected back for a few days. Can I take a message?"

"I'm actually calling to check on the status of a car he picked up yesterday. An older sedan that wouldn't start."

"I think I know the one you mean. If you can hold a moment, I'll check on it."

"Of course."

He heard the phone clatter against a hard surface and then a door open and close. It took a few minutes, but then a male came on the line.

"This is Kevin. Are you calling about the old Honda?"

"I'm not sure what make the vehicle is. It was picked up by your tow truck at Puck's Pizza Palace."

The mechanic chuckled. "Yeah, that's the one. Listen, I don't know how to tell you this, but you're going to spend way more than this thing is worth to get it running again, and there's no guarantee it will stay running. I'd honestly recommend buying a different car."

"I see. Well, thank you, Kevin. Tell Dryden to do whatever he wants with the vehicle. If there are personal items in it, just box them up and I'll swing by another day to pick it up."

"Will do."

There was a click and Valero hung up the phone. How the hell was he supposed to tell Ella that she needed a new car? He knew the news wouldn't go over well. The woman seemed to have truly rotten luck. First she nearly lost her apartment, then she was rejected for the job she wanted, and now her car was a total loss. Maybe he could stall her and just surprise her with a new car? The females he'd previously dated would have been thrilled with such an extravagant purchase, but he had a feeling Ella wouldn't be happy about it. The woman was too damn independent.

Ella popped her head into his office. "What did they say?"

He sighed and motioned for her to have a seat across from his desk. She sank onto the chair and looked at him expectantly. Should he ease her into it, or just blurt it out, like ripping off a Band-Aid?

"It's bad news, isn't it?" she asked.

"I'm afraid so. The mechanic said it would cost so much to fix it, without any guarantee it would keep running, that you would be better off getting another car."

Her shoulders slumped and her head dropped. It was like watching an invisible weight settle on her small frame, pressing her down into the chair. There had to be something he could do for her, but he didn't know what she would accept.

"What do you say we pick up Connor and stop by a

car lot just to see what they have?" Valero asked.

"I don't have enough for a car, and only working part-time, there's no way I'd get one financed. Not that I can even afford a car payment right now. I'll just have to..." She sighed. "There's not a bus stop nearby, is there?"

"Um, no. I don't think the buses even run out this way."

"Right, because this is a rich neighborhood and everyone has several cars. Maybe if I pick up some extra shifts, if you don't mind helping with Connor, then maybe I can save up enough to get something cheap. There are cars out there for five hundred dollars, aren't there?"

"Ella... I know you're fiercely independent, and I admire your tenacity, but just this once I'm going to ask that you let me help you."

Her chin jutted out. "I'm not accepting money from you."

"If I promise not to buy an expensive car, will you let me buy one for you? I don't mind you driving my truck when you need it, but didn't you say things were easier when you had your own transportation?"

"Valero..."

He held up a hand. "I won't spend a lot of money. I'm not going to buy you a brand new high end car. If you want, I'll even promise to get a used one. Let me help you. You can't do everything on your own. There are dark circles under your eyes from the stress you've been under. If you run yourself into the ground, who will take care of Connor?"

He watched her face carefully as she struggled with his offer, and knew the moment she was going to give in. She nodded and slowly rose from the chair.

"If you'll take me to pick up Connor, then I'll agree to go look at cars. And if there's something inexpensive,

I'll let you get one for me."

"I have a feeling your version of inexpensive is different from mine. What's the max you'll let me spend on a car for you?"

She shrugged. "Three thousand?"

Valero's eyebrow went up. "I think you need to at least double that. I'm taking you to a reputable car lot, not some questionable place that will probably sell you a lemon for that price."

She smiled a little. "You know what a lemon car is?"

"I was warned about them when I decided to purchase a vehicle." He rose from his chair. "Put on something comfortable, and shoes you can stand or walk in while we browse the car lot. If you don't see something you like at the first place, we'll try another one. And if you don't find something today, then we'll try again in a week and see if they've gotten any new inventory."

She nodded before walking out of the room. One small victory. Sort of. He'd have preferred to buy her a brand new car with a warranty like he had on his truck. Maybe she'd see something she liked so much that he could talk her into it when they got to the car lot. He was going to see if the same salesman who'd sold him his truck was available.

It took Ella longer than he'd thought to change, and they barely made it to Connor's school in time. The little boy climbed into the backseat, grinning from ear to ear.

"What put you in such a good mood?" Ella asked as she smiled at him.

"Today I was like everyone else."

"Everyone else?" Ella looked puzzled.

"All of my friends at school live with their mom and dad, but it's always just been us. Now that we live with Mr. Valero, I'm just like everyone else. I told them all about my new room and the big, pretty house we live in now."

The smile slipped from Ella's face and he reached over to take her hand, giving it a squeeze.

"We're going to take your Mama shopping for a new car. Does that sound like fun?" Valero asked Connor. "She may even let you help pick it out."

Connor bounced on the seat. "Can I, Mama? Can I help pick it out?"

The smile returned to Ella's face. "I'll let you help."

"Can we get something big like this truck? I like all the room." Connor grinned. "Or maybe you can get one of those big van things so you could be a chaperone on school trips."

"We'll see, Connor. I'm sure a van is rather expensive," Ella said.

"But you'd like one, wouldn't you?" Connor persisted. "Most of the moms have one."

Ella sighed and looked out the window. Valero wondered if she really would like one, or if she was humoring Connor. He'd buy her whatever she wanted, regardless of the cost, but getting her to spend his money was more difficult than he'd ever imagined. Weren't human females supposed to enjoy shopping and spending money? For that matter, most alien females he knew were much the same. It figures he'd want the one woman who refused to let him coddle her.

Although… she probably wouldn't refuse a girl's day out with Rory. Even though he couldn't finance the spa or whatever they went to without Ella putting up a fight, he could make a trade of sorts with Zwyk. A free advance copy of whatever game he released next in exchange for him footing the bill. He knew Zwyk was more than capable of paying for such a day for their women, but he'd gladly slide him some cash when Ella wasn't looking. He'd have to make that call later.

They pulled into the car lot and Valero went in search of the salesman while Ella and Connor looked around. The guy who had sold him his truck no longer worked there, but he found someone else to assist them. The guy was a little too... something. Valero couldn't figure out why the man was so off-putting, but there was something about him that just set Valero's teeth on edge.

"So what is your wife looking for today?" the man, who had introduced himself as Patrick, said.

"I'm not sure. She can have whatever she wants."

He could practically see the dollar signs in the man's eyes.

Connor ran up to them and gripped Valero's hand, pulling him over to a dark blue van. It looked nice and the price on the windshield said it was only fifteen thousand. Ella looked a little pale as she walked around the vehicle and he noticed her gazing across the lot at a small car that was only six thousand.

"Do you like it?" Valero asked her.

"It looks really nice." She glanced across the lot again.

"Ella." She looked up at him. "Don't worry about the cost. If you like this vehicle and it's something you'd like to drive, then you should get it. Just because Connor is an only child right now, doesn't mean it will always be that way. You should get something with lots of room."

Her eyes widened. "Are you trying to tell me you want to fill every bedroom in the house?"

He shrugged. "I did buy a big house for a reason."

Her cheeks flushed and she looked at the van again. He noticed she hadn't immediately dismissed the thought of having children with him. Maybe she was warming up to the idea of being mated to him. He could hope, at any rate. He didn't know how to wear her down, but he'd eventually figure it out. Then he'd claim the two of them and make them a family.

"I can get the keys if you'd like to test drive it," Patrick said. "I just need a copy of your license."

Ella fished through her purse and handed over her license. Valero considered it a small victory and tried not to smile. If she thought for one moment he was gleeful over getting her to purchase the van, she'd probably insist on the small car just to piss him off. Stubborn, that's what she was.

By the time Ella test drove the van, they filled out the paperwork, and were ready to leave a few hours had passed. Connor looked tired and he'd been asking for food for over an hour. Valero got the booster seat out of his truck and put it into the van for Ella, then buckled Connor in. Ella didn't pull away when he kissed her softly and told her to drive carefully.

"If you'll follow me, we'll stop and get something to eat. Connor is starving and I'm sure you are too."

"It's a little early for dinner."

"Then we'll eat now and we'll snack on something like wings and fries later. I can have B-Street Wings deliver something later tonight if we get hungry." Valero smiled. "Now stop arguing and get into your new van."

She smiled widely and did as he said. Valero shook his head, but he was happy that she'd selected the van. Not only because it meant she had something she really liked, but because it meant she was thinking about expanding their family. And yes, it was *their* family. She might not have agreed yet to be his mate, but he hoped it was only a matter of time. Maybe Rory would put in a good word for him. *Crap*. He needed to set that up still.

While he drove to Ponderosa, the best Mexican place in town, he pulled out his cell phone and called Zwyk.

"Shouldn't you be spending time with Ella?" Zwyk asked by way of greeting.

"Did I interrupt something?"

"If I said yes, would you hang up?"

Valero smiled. "Not until I get what I want."

Zwyk sighed. "And what's that?"

"I need Rory to invite Ella out for a girls' day. Spa, shopping, whatever. I'll give the two of you an advance copy of my next game and some cash to cover Ella's expenses."

"Sounds like we're getting more out of the deal," Zwyk said.

"I was hoping Rory might nudge Ella along a bit, tell her I'm not such a horrible guy and to give me a chance. She seems to be fine with sex between us, but she doesn't want something more."

"And you want a family," Zwyk said. "I'll see what I can do. I'll talk to Rory and maybe she'll call to set up something tonight. She likes Ella."

"Thanks. Back to whatever you were doing, and no, I don't want to know what it was."

Zwyk chuckled and hung up the phone.

Valero pulled into the parking lot at Ponderosa and waited for Ella to park next to him. Then he went to retrieve Connor and they walked inside as a family. He wanted to call Connor his son, wanted to hear the word "daddy", and he was wondering if it would ever happen. Ella reached over and took his other hand, surprising him. She smiled warmly as they stepped inside and waited to be seated.

Connor slid into the booth and Ella started to follow, but the little boy stopped her.

"Not you, Mama."

Ella appeared taken aback, but she scooted into the booth on the other side.

"You want me to sit beside you?" Valero asked Connor. The little boy nodded.

Valero claimed his seat and felt warmth spread through his chest. Even if the mama wasn't warming up to him as much as he'd like, it seemed Connor didn't have a problem with him. They ordered their food and drinks, then nibbled on the offered chips and salsa.

"Did you work on my game?" Connor asked. "The troll game."

"I did," Valero said with a smile. "I didn't get very far but it's started."

"Does it take a long time to make one?" Connor asked.

"Well, that's a difficult question to answer. It depends on the type of game. Some games take about six months while others take a few years. It will depend on how many programmers and artists I hire. Right now, I'm trying to get a base started for everything, then I'll turn it over to a team."

"And I get to test it when it's done?" Connor asked.

"You bet. You're going to be my number one game tester for this one."

Connor beamed.

"If it's okay with your mama, when we get home we can play a game. We can play something on one of my game systems if you'd like."

Connor's eyes went wide. "You have an Xbox One and a Playstation, don't you?"

Valero nodded.

"No gory games," Ella said. "And nothing too violent."

"I'm a big boy," Connor said. "Why can't I play *Gears of War*?"

"Because you're not a big enough boy for something like that. Not until you're twelve."

Connor pouted. "That's too long. They probably won't even have *Gears of War* by then."

Valero nudged him. "They'll have something even better. When you turn ten, you can help me come up with a new game idea and maybe it will be ready for your twelfth birthday."

"I can help again?" Connor asked.

"You can help me as much as you'd like," Valero

said. "It's nice to have another gamer in the house. Maybe we can get your mom to play."

Connor shook his head. "She'll never play."

"I'm not coordinated enough," Ella said. "All the buttons confuse me."

"I actually have something you might like," Valero said. "Are you familiar with the original Nintendo systems? With the Mario games and such?"

Ella nodded.

"I have one and a box of games. Why don't we hook it up and see if you like anything? If you don't want to play after giving it a try, I won't ask again."

She smiled faintly. "Determined to make a gamer of me, are you?"

He shrugged. "The family that games together stays together."

"I don't think that's how that quote goes."

Valero smiled.

Their food arrived and Connor dug in with such enthusiasm Valero had to stifle a laugh.

"Is it good?" he asked Connor.

The little boy nodded and didn't even take a break from shoveling food into his mouth.

"Connor, stop and take a breath," Ella said. "The food isn't going anywhere."

"But we never get to eat like this. What if we can't come back?" he asked.

Valero watched Ella carefully and wished he could hold her close. She looked devastated. It wasn't her fault they'd not been able to eat out much during Connor's short life, and if Valero had anything to say about it, there would be plenty of outings in their future.

"Connor, if you like eating here, we can come again whenever you'd like," Valero said. "I know you haven't had many treats like this before, and there's nothing wrong with that. Your mom has worked hard to provide for you and I think she's done a good job. But I can assure you, the money isn't going to run out anytime soon. We can eat out several times a week if you'd like."

Ella shook her head.

"Or not. Although, I'm a horrible cook."

Ella's cheeks flushed. "I can cook. I just never had the money for ingredients to make anything nice. If you'll go shopping with me, I can make some decent dinners for us."

"We can go shopping in the morning right after we take Connor to school. Make a list of whatever you need. Don't worry about the cost. If you want to cook, I'll be happy to let you. Just don't feel like you have to."

Ella nodded and went back to eating her food.

They finished their dinner and Valero paid the bill, then they went home. Valero didn't mind spoiling Ella and Connor, and he hoped he had more opportunities for it. It was hard not to whisk them off to the mall for a day of shopping, or take Connor to a game store and let him run wild. Baby steps. Ella had let him purchase a van for her, so maybe he could talk her into some other things as well.

He'd just have to bide his time. Something he wasn't very good at.

For now, he had a game system to hook up so he could coax Ella over to the dark side.

Chapter Five

Ella had to admit she loved her new van. Well, new to her anyway. It was four years old, but it handled beautifully and was far nicer than anything she'd ever owned before. It would probably take her forever to figure out all the little buttons. She adored the leather interior and it even smelled like a new car. It still battled her that Valero had enough money to pay cash for something as big as a van, and just proved they were completely different. They'd dropped Connor off at school and stopped for coffee.

"Do you not like it?" Valero asked as she stared out the window. "Your coffee?"

Her gaze flew to his. She'd been daydreaming again and was letting her coffee get cold. Valero puzzled her. He was a great catch. Perhaps a little obsessed with video games, and she supposed that could be a turnoff for some people, but he was well-off and a tender lover -- based on what little she'd experienced with him -- and he was such a sweet guy. Why hadn't someone snapped him up by now? She kept waiting to find out something horrible about him.

"It's good. I was just thinking."

"Good thoughts?" he asked.

"Why aren't you married already?" she asked. "You seem too good to be true."

"I work a lot, or I did. Now that I have Connor and you in the house, I'm going to let a team of programmers and artists do the bulk of the work. It means not making as much of a profit quite as fast, but I have enough money for us to live comfortably."

Ella laughed a bit.

"Why is that funny?" Valero asked, his brow furrowed in confusion.

"Comfortably? Valero, you're rich. You have more

money than Connor and I have ever dreamed of. Even if you had to sell the house and get something much smaller, you would still be well-off compared to us."

Valero reached out and took her hand. "I'm not married because I never found the right woman. I dated, but I didn't feel a connection to any of those women. And most were only after me for my money."

"Like me." She shook her head.

"No, not like you. The others would have jumped at the chance for a new car, and probably would have insisted on a flashy, expensive one. Then they would have demanded a shopping trip to the jeweler's, where they would have bought the biggest diamonds. They wanted someone to buy them whatever they wanted whenever they wanted, and they couldn't have cared less who did it."

"I know there are women out there like that, but surely you dated some good ones too."

He shrugged. "I couldn't see myself starting a family with any of them. We went on one or two dates, and then I moved on. Don't ask me to explain why you're different, because I'm not sure I can. I just know you *are* different. I like having Connor and you in my home, and when I think of having more children with you, it just feels right. You're a wonderful mother, Ella. I know you don't feel like it, but you truly are. You've made Connor your number one priority in life, no matter what it cost you. One day he'll realize how lucky he is to have a mom like you."

Her eyes misted with tears. "Thank you."

"I know you aren't ready to get married. You're still adjusting to not being completely on your own, and I respect that. Just keep in mind that at any point if you decide you want more, I will happily get down on one knee and ask you to be mine."

It made her wonder if she was being a bitch by

holding out. Truthfully, she liked Valero, and she liked the way he made her feel. She'd heard enough about his kind to know they mated for life, so if she agreed, it wasn't like it would end in divorce. But she wanted to bring something to the marriage, to be able to contribute in some way. She'd called and quit her job this morning, knowing it wasn't going to get her anywhere. Valero had insisted she could stay with him as long as she wanted, with a hint of forever in his eyes. It was tempting to say yes, that she would be his.

"Just how many more children do you want?" she asked.

"I'd love a house full, but if my mate wanted fewer children than I have rooms, I would understand. Do you not want more children? You're so good with Connor."

"I want more. I think." Her brow furrowed. "I've never really pictured our lives with an adult male figure present. I guess I just figured that it wasn't likely I would ever date seriously, much less get married. I was prepared to be a single mom until Connor went off to college."

"I understand you've been on your own a long time. And I wasn't joking. You've done a fantastic job with Connor. I'd just like to help, if you'll let me. I'd like you to consider that maybe having someone by your side wouldn't be such a bad thing."

"What do I have to offer you, Valero? As of this morning, I don't even have a part-time job. You bought me a car. I'm living in your house."

He tucked a wayward strand of hair behind her ear. "Ella, do you think the only reason I want you in my life is because I think you can offer me something? I guess in some respects that isn't far off, but it isn't monetary assistance I want from you. I want someone to walk next to me in life, to have a family with, to share the good times and the bad. And maybe one day it will grow into love. All of my mated friends are wildly in love with their mates. To be honest, I already feel something for you, but I'm not sure it's strong enough yet to call it love. But I know I would be heartbroken if you were to leave."

"I don't want to leave." She bit her lip. "But I don't want to feel like I'm getting a free ride either."

"Do you know how hard stay-at-home moms work? My friend Reyvor hires a babysitter once a week to watch their kids just so Hazel can have a break and get a little adult time. He hires someone to help with the housekeeping, but she insists on cooking and taking care of the kids herself. I'd do the same for you, and even hire a cook if you didn't want to make our meals."

"I don't want to be spoiled, Valero. I want to pull my own weight and contribute to our family just as much as you do."

"What if you helped me in my office for an hour a day and then used the rest of the time for whatever you wanted? At least, until Connor came home. You could volunteer at the library, volunteer at Connor's school… anything you want to do."

"How does that contribute to the family?" she asked.

"I'm sure Connor would love it if you read to his class sometimes. And if you worked at the library, you could maybe read during children's time there. Reyvor's youngest go to that during the week. It's twice a week on Tuesdays and Thursdays. Maybe some free time would allow you to draw more, or find a hobby you really like. You can contribute to the family by not being so stressed all the time and learning to enjoy life a bit more. Do you think Connor cares if you have a job? If you're home, maybe you could use that new minivan for field trips with the class."

It was tempting, more tempting than he'd ever know. She knew that stay-at-home moms worked hard, but most of them didn't have maids and cooks at their disposal. Not that she would want a cook. She liked creating things in the kitchen. They were supposed to go grocery shopping after coffee, and she'd already planned out their meals for the next few days. She wouldn't plan more than that until she figured out what Valero liked and didn't like.

She sipped at her coffee and watched a young mother across the room with her infant. She remembered those days well, except hers had been filled with fear. Ella had Connor by herself in a hospital room she wouldn't have been able to afford without being on government assistance. It had nearly broken her to ask for help, but she'd known even then she couldn't do it all on her own. But she'd tried. What would it be like to have a baby and not have to worry all the time?

"What do human/Terran babies look like?" she asked.

"They usually take after the father's coloring, but sometimes the mother's eye color comes through." He tipped his head. "Are you thinking about what it would be like to have one?"

"Maybe." She tore her gaze away from the mother and looked at Valero. "I missed a lot with Connor as a baby because I was so scared every day. I didn't know the first thing about being a mom and I was completely on my own. I guess I just wondered what it would be like to have a baby without all that extra stress. The sleepless nights are hard enough without piling on more crap."

He smiled a little. "Well, no extra crap piled on if you decide to marry me. I'll help in any way I can, even with midnight diaper changes."

Ella toyed with her coffee cup. "What if we got married and things didn't work out? What if we ended up hating each other?"

"Ella, I'm not going to rush you into anything. If you want more time to make a decision, you can have all the time in the world. But know this... if you marry me, it will be forever. Terrans do not divorce their mates." He tipped his head to the side. "Besides, I don't see us ever coming to hate one another."

She finished her coffee and stood. "We'd better get the shopping done. I'd like to get everything put away and maybe check the classifieds before Connor gets out of school."

Valero sighed and stood, collecting their cups and throwing them away.

It wasn't that she'd meant to cut their conversation short, but... well, yes. Yes, she had meant to cut it short because it wasn't anything that hadn't already been said. She knew he wanted her as his mate, hadn't made it a secret, but she wasn't ready. Despite his words of not pushing her, that was exactly what it'd felt like.

Ella drove them to the grocery store and grabbed a cart, wheeling it toward the produce section first. Valero followed along and didn't say much, except to answer a question here or there. He seemed a little tense, and she felt bad for pushing him away again. An attractive, wealthy man actually wanted to marry her, and she was being a bitch about it. It was one thing to be cautious, but maybe she'd been a little too abrupt with him.

When Valero grabbed a bottle of wine and stuck it in the cart, her eyebrows went up. They might not have lived together very long, but she'd noticed there wasn't alcohol in the house. Had she driven the man to drink? It wouldn't be the first time she'd had that effect on someone. Her parents came to mind. Ella finished the shopping and stood back as Valero paid for everything. She tried to help load things into the van, but he shooed her away.

Ella chewed on her lip as they drove back home. Valero seemed pensive and stared out the side window. For someone who was always in a good mood and had a ready smile, he seemed rather sullen at the moment. Had she done that to him? Had her inability to commit upset him? It wasn't that she wasn't attracted to him, and it wasn't that she felt like he wouldn't be a good father for Connor. She'd thought it was because she couldn't contribute to the relationship, but Valero had made good points.

So why wasn't she jumping at the chance to marry him?

At the house, they unloaded and put the groceries away, then Valero closed himself in his office with the bottle of wine and didn't even emerge when it was time for dinner that night. Ella knew she'd fucked up, but she wasn't sure how to fix it. Unless…

After Connor was tucked into bed and soundly sleeping, Ella pinned up her hair and took a quick shower, then she dressed in the skimpiest pajama set she owned. With a determination she'd never felt before, she entered Valero's office and waited to get his attention. The wine bottle lay on its side, empty. She didn't see a glass and wondered if he'd drunk it straight from the bottle.

She edged around the desk and realized he was dozing in his chair, his hair rumpled and his shirt wrinkled. Ella eased onto his lap and ran a hand across his chest. He might be something of a geek, but he still had the body of a warrior. She could look at his naked body all day and never tire of the sight. Ella tugged his shirt free from his pants and traced the ridges of his abdomen.

Valero stirred and slowly opened his eyes. His hand reached up and cupped her cheek.

"My sweet Ella," he murmured.

"You should go to bed."

His hand hooked the back of her neck and brought her closer until his lips crashed against hers. The taste of wine hit her tongue and she briefly wondered just how drunk he was. Would she be taking advantage of him to let things play out? She felt the hard ridge of his cock pressing against her and already her panties were growing damp. Just one touch and he lit her on fire. Things were definitely passionate between them.

Valero pulled away and lifted her onto the edge of the desk. Stark hunger was blazing in his eyes as he quickly removed her clothes, leaving her bare and aching for him. The papers on his desk crinkled under her, but Valero didn't seem to care. All of his attention was focused on her. His hands slid up and down her thighs, pushing her legs apart. Valero leaned forward, his breath a hot puff against her tender skin. His mouth feasted on her, sucking at her tender folds. Ella leaned back on her hands and tried to stifle her moans of pleasure. He sucked, licked, and teased her clit, making every nerve in her body come alive.

Ella tried not to cry out as he brought her to orgasm. Her hands clutched at his desk, crinkling papers some more. As aftershocks left her trembling, he kissed his way up her body, stopping to suck and tweak her nipples. Ella tunneled her fingers through his hair and held him close. No one had ever made her feel as cherished as Valero did. As he rose from the chair, kicking it back, her heart beat a little faster. Was he going to…

Valero unfastened his pants and shoved them down his hips, his cock popping free of his confining boxer briefs. Her eyes widened as she realized he wasn't stopping this time. He gripped her hips and jerked her ass to the edge of the desk, then plunged inside her in one, deep stroke. She bit her lip and whimpered as he filled her. Valero was huge and made her ache, but in the best of ways.

He pulled back then thrust forward again. Her body sang with every stroke, her pussy clinging to him.

"So tight." He looked almost in pain. "Am I hurting you?"

"Keep going."

His hands shifted and he took her harder, faster. Ella felt her body tightening again as she strained for another release. She came screaming his name as he found his own release, warmth filling her. A little late, she realized they hadn't used a condom. She only hoped it didn't come back to bite her in the ass later.

Valero pulled free with a groan and stumbled back a step. He stripped out of his clothes and then lifted her into his arms and carried her down the hall to his bedroom, easing her down onto the cool sheets. When he slid in beside her, she curled into his side. Valero pulled the covers over them and held her close, letting loose a contented sigh. Ella wondered how much he would remember in the morning, and she hoped he wouldn't be angry with her. Just because they'd had sex didn't mean she was marrying him. Yet.

* * *

Valero woke the next day with the worst hangover. For some reason, he'd been naked in bed and his clothes were in his office. It wasn't like him to go streaking through the house, but then he wasn't a drinker either. He only hoped he hadn't done anything embarrassing. Everything was a bit of a blur after he'd closed himself in his office. Although, he thought he remembered Ella coming to him at some point. Or had kissing her been part of his dreams?

The coffee wasn't brewing fast enough. On the upside, Connor had already left for school. As much as he loved spending time with the boy, he didn't think his head could handle all the noise this morning. He grabbed the largest mug out of the cabinet and filled it to the brim. Not bothering with creamer, he took a big gulp and winced as it burned on its way down. He finished off the mug and poured himself another, but his stomach was starting to gurgle a bit. Valero wasn't certain if it was an "I'm hungry" kind of a gurgle or a "please God don't give me anything else" kind of rumble.

The front door opened and shut and he heard Ella quietly walking toward him. He leaned against the counter and crossed his ankles as he waited for her, the mug clutched in his hand. She turned the corner and froze when she saw him, the expression in her eyes leery, as if she didn't know what to expect from him. He supposed that was fair. He'd been a bit of an ass last night, and all because he hadn't gotten his way. Valero had never acted like a spoiled child in his life, but yesterday had come close.

"How do you feel this morning?" she asked softly.

"I have what I believe is known as a hangover. Perhaps drinking the entire bottle of wine wasn't my best idea, especially for someone who never drinks."

She nodded. "I can fix you some eggs and toast. That might help settle your stomach."

"You don't have to wait on me like a servant."

Ella moved a little closer and reached out a hand, placing her fingers on his forearm. "I'm not waiting on you like a servant. You don't feel well and I want to take care of you, but only if you want me to. I won't force myself on you."

Her cheeks flushed and he wondered if she'd caught the double meaning behind her words. Not that she would ever have to force herself on him. It wasn't a secret that he wanted her. He frowned as images flashed in his mind of the two of them together, or more accurately of him pounding into her. It was just a dream, right? He didn't think he'd completely lost control last night. But if he had… His gaze followed her as she worked around the kitchen. Would she say anything if they'd done more than fool around?

The smell of eggs cooking had him taking a seat at the table. When she served his plate, he slathered butter on his toast before taking a bite. The eggs were better than any
he'd ever cooked. Ella took a seat next to him after fixing herself a cup of coffee. The scent of her vanilla creamer was almost enough to turn his stomach. Too sweet.

"If I said or did anything last night..." He cleared his throat. "I'm sorry for drinking the way I did. I generally don't keep alcohol around, and very seldom drink. It won't happen again."

"You're allowed to have feelings," Ella said. "I'm sorry for making you feel like you needed that bottle of wine. I know I haven't been very open about a relationship between us. And I'm sorry."

"It's not your fault, Ella. I'm a grown male and I'm responsible for my actions. You have every right to feel the way you do."

"That's just it, Valero. I'm not sure what I'm feeling. Being with you is incredible, and I love how patient you are with Connor. I guess with us moving in, it just feels like things are moving so fast." She took a breath. "But maybe fast isn't such a bad thing. I don't think I'm ready to get married, but I promise to be more open-minded."

He nodded. "So... want to play some video games? I think my brain is too sloshed to work today."

She smiled a little. "You mean that Nintendo thing you have? Because the Xbox controller is still beyond my capabilities."

"I'll get it set up. Any particular game you like?"

"I liked the one with the raccoon outfit."

He tried not to laugh. "That would be Super Mario 3 and it's called a tanooki suit."

Her nose wrinkled. "What's a tanooki?"

"I believe it's taken from the Japanese raccoon dog called a tanuki." He spelled the difference between them.

"But I'm just guessing."

"Whatever it is, it's cute. Besides, I get to fly in that game."

"Bring your coffee and I'll get the game set up. I'll even let you be Mario."

He couldn't help but chuckle to himself. She might not be a hardcore gamer like Rory, but at least she'd try something new and seemed to like it. Or rather, something old. He'd be willing to bet they would eventually get her to play either the Xbox or Playstation. And if she never did, he'd just have to make sure he kept a working Nintendo on hand at all times. He even had an Atari he could hook up if she really wanted to go old school. When he'd first discovered video games, he'd bought every system he could get his hands on, and played tons of games.

It wasn't long after that he'd decided to make some of his own. While humans took years to make them, he'd found that he could make one a lot faster, depending on the type. He'd outsourced some of it, but liked to stay as hands on as possible. His company was still in the fledgling stages, but he had hopes it would be big one day. And if it never was, that would be okay too. It wasn't like he didn't have enough money to live off of. Earth didn't cost nearly as much as his world, probably because they had so many more resources. It was an intriguing planet.

The game was just loading as Ella came in, a fresh cup of coffee in her hand. She yawned as she settled on the sofa and reached for the controller. Valero sat next to her and waited on her to select two-player and start the game. Ella selected the first part of World One and he settled back to watch her in action. She snagged the mushroom at the beginning to grow big, then knocked the Koopa Troopa against the box, making a leaf pop up. It was fun watching her play and smile as she enjoyed herself. She cleared the level without any trouble and did a little victory dance.

Valero tried not to laugh as he started level two. Even though he had the entire game memorized, he tried to take his time. There were cheats hidden throughout the game and he knew them all, but he was waiting to see if Ella discovered them on her own. They played for several hours, not stopping until their stomachs were growling and it was definitely time for lunch.

"I can cook something," Ella offered.

"Why don't we go out for lunch, just the two of us?" he asked. "It isn't often we get to enjoy a meal without Connor. And don't think I mean that in a bad way. He's a great kid, but I want some one-on-one time with you too."

She twirled her hair. "What about one-on-one time with Connor?"

"I'm all for that."

"Maybe today after school?" she asked.

"If you want some alone time, all you have to do is ask. I have no problem picking up Connor from school and spending time with him."

"Rory called on my way to take Connor to school. She wants to do some girl stuff this afternoon, but she had a doctor's appointment this morning and said she wouldn't be free until after lunch."

Valero smiled. "I would be honored to get Connor and spend some quality time with him while you have a nice time with Rory. And if you decide you want to have dinner with her, Connor and I will be just fine here. We can either order in or I can take him out somewhere."

"You really don't mind?" she asked.

"Not at all. Now, go put on whatever you're going to wear when you see Rory and we can take two cars, that way you can go meet her straight from the restaurant."

"Could I just ride with you and she can pick me up

there? Makes more sense than us having to deal with two cars. She offered to pick me up and drop me off today."

Valero nodded. "Go get ready and I'll turn off the game."

It didn't take Valero long to turn off the game and get things put away. It took Ella quite a bit longer, however, to get ready. When she came back to the living room, her hair was curled, her lips were shiny, and she looked absolutely breathtaking. The long-sleeve shirt she had on hugged her curves, as did the jeans molded to her hips. He motioned for her to come a little closer and when she was near enough, he hooked a hand around her waist and pulled up tight against him.

"You're going to mess up my lip gloss, aren't you?" she asked, humor in her eyes.

"Maybe."

She smiled a little and then looped her arm around his neck, pulling him down. Her lips pressed against his and he couldn't help but deepen the kiss. Her gloss tasted like candy. When he pulled away, she had a dazed look, but he prided himself on the fact he hadn't mussed her hair. He wiped the gloss from his lips and led her out to his truck. While she looked fantastic, he was still wearing a wrinkled tee and one of his well-worn pairs of jeans. Not that anyone would refuse him service.

He pulled into a space near the door at Ponderosa. Even though they'd just come here the other day, he was in the mood for Mexican again. With his hand at her waist, he ushered Ella inside. The hostess sat them at a table near the window and left them with menus. They'd barely looked at the menu before a waiter arrived with chips and salsa.

"What can I get for you today?" he asked.

"I'll have sweet tea," Ella said. "And I think I want the lunch special number three."

"I'll have the same, but add two extra tacos please,"

Valero said.

They handed the man their menus and waited for their order to arrive.

"So, what do Rory and you have planned for this afternoon?" he asked.

"I'm not sure. She mentioned something about an appointment at a salon and then said we had a massage scheduled at the local spa. I've not been to a salon in a really long time, and I've never had a massage before. I'm looking forward to it."

Valero frowned. "I'm not sure I like the idea of some guy running his hands all over you."

Ella laughed. "You're cute when you're jealous."

He grumbled under his breath and took a huge swallow of the sweet tea the waiter set in front of him. It wasn't like she was his wife and he had any say over what she did. Then again, even if she was his wife, he still wouldn't try to dictate her every move. If she wanted to go off and have fun with her friends, he wasn't going to stop her. But it wouldn't hurt to have a word with Rory about only scheduling female masseurs in the future. With some luck, she'd scheduled one for today.

Their food arrived and they dug in. Lunch was passing all too fast and he wanted more time with Ella. It was selfish of him, but he hadn't had much alone time with her. They talked a little more, but he could tell that she was counting down the minutes until she could meet with Rory. When she pulled out her phone to text her, Valero knew their time was at an end for now. He paid the check and escorted Ella outside, where they sat on a bench to wait for Rory.

"I hope you have a nice time," Valero said. "Any particular rules for Connor and me?"

"Don't take him out of town. If I'm late coming home, don't let him stay up past his bedtime. And make sure he takes a bath before he puts on his pajamas. Oh!

And make sure he brushes his teeth. You'll need the sign clipped to the visor of my car that will allow you to pick him up from school."

Valero nodded, as these were all things he already knew.

"You're sure this is okay?" she asked.

"I'm positive."

Rory pulled up and Ella gave him a quick hug before running off to get into Rory's car. They waved as they pulled out of the parking lot. Valero got up and went to his truck. A glance at the clock in the dash showed that it was about time to get in the parent pick-up line at Connor's school. He drove there with thoughts of Ella weighing heavy on his mind. He only hoped that Rory would only have good things to say about him, and maybe Ella would like him even more by the time she came home.

It was stupid, but he would hold onto anything at this point that would mean Ella would be his.

Valero drove to the school and waited patiently for the bell to ring. As Connor climbed into the truck, all smiles, he couldn't help but think he wanted every day to be like this.

"Hey, Connor. It's just you and me today, all right? Your mom went off with a friend for the afternoon."

Connor gave a whoop as Valero buckled him into his booster seat.

"I take it that means you're okay with that?" Valero asked.

"Can we play Xbox?"

"Sure. Do you have homework?"

Connor shook his head. "It's fall break next week so we haven't done much this week at school. Mostly watched movies and played games." He bounced a little. "And it's my birthday tomorrow!"

His birthday? Already? He didn't get a chance to

discuss it with Ella and now he wondered if she had anything special planned. One thing was for certain, Valero needed to do some shopping so Connor would have a present from him.

"Then why don't we play for a little while and then we can either order in or if you want to go out for dinner, we can go anywhere you want." He mentally winced. "Except Puck's Pizza Palace."

Connor pouted.

"Come on, buddy. We can play whatever game you want, as long as it's mom approved. I thought maybe we could go to The Pasta Bowl for dinner. You like spaghetti and they have some with huge meatballs."

"Really?"

"I promise. Biggest meatballs I've ever seen," Valero said.

"I guess that could be cool."

Valero hid a smile as they pulled into the garage at home. Connor unbuckled himself and scrambled out of the truck and ran inside. Valero had barely gotten inside before he heard the TV turn on and the Xbox start up with Connor's favorite game. It was a good thing Valero liked gaming so much, considering he'd already played for several hours.

They settled in with drinks and snacks. And Valero let Connor take the lead, showing him tricks that even he didn't know about yet. Every time they played a game, it just astounded Valero that someone so small could be so awesome. They played for a few hours, until Connor's stomach started growling.

"Come on, buddy," Valero said as he stood. "Let's save the game and turn it off for now. Time to eat."

Connor pouted.

"It's dinnertime. Besides, your stomach is growling and mine is too. When we're done with dinner, we'll come home and you can take your bath and get ready for bed."

"Can I stay up late?"

"I promised your mom I would have you tucked in at your regular time. But we can play some more before it's time for you to lie down. Or we could find something to watch on Netflix."

"I guess that would be okay."

Connor saved the game and they turned everything off. Valero took Connor's hand as they walked out to the truck, then he buckled him in. The Pasta Bowl was on the other side of town, but it wasn't a far drive. Nothing in their small town was a far drive. Their town only had a population of fifteen thousand, not including the Terrans who had made their home there.

The Pasta Bowl was packed, but they managed to get a decent parking space. Connor reached for Valero's hand on the way in. The hostess smiled, her gaze raking over Valero like he was a prime piece of steak. He'd seen that look before, but now that he was determined to make Ella his, it made him uncomfortable. Being mated wasn't enough. He wanted wedding rings like Zwyk and Rory had, something to show he was taken. Too bad he couldn't wear one now.

"Just follow me," the hostess said. She seated them at a small table in the middle of the restaurant. "My name is Mandy, and please let me know if there's *anything* I can do for you."

He nearly snorted. "Thank you, Mandy. I'm sure we'll be fine."

Her smile slipped a little as she handed them their menus and excused herself. Connor, thankfully, didn't seem to understand what was happening. The last thing Valero needed was for Connor to tell his mom that the hostess had been a flirt.

Chapter Six

Ella looked around the empty salon and frowned at Rory. "Are you sure this is the place?"

"Zwyk booked the entire place for us. The chemicals aren't good for me right now."

"Are you sick? You said you were going to the doctor this morning."

Rory grinned. "I was going to the OBGYN. I didn't tell you before, but I'm pregnant!"

Ella hugged her tight. "That's awesome! I'm so happy for you."

"Maybe one day you and Valero will decide to have a baby. Or are you practicing already?" she asked with a sly smile.

"We've only... I mean, it was just the one time. Last night."

Rory's smile slipped from her face. "Are you on the pill?"

Ella shook her head.

"Then you used a condom?" Rory asked.

"No. I know we should have, but... I just didn't think about it and Valero had been drinking. I'm sure it's fine."

"Only one way to find out."

"Rory, it's been *one* day. I'm sure I'll have to wait several weeks before I find out if I'm pregnant."

"The clinic at the Terran Station has a test that will tell you within hours of conception. They used it on me and they've used it on all the mates I've met since hooking up with Zwyk. If you want to rest easy, then after this appointment we'll go to the clinic and find out for sure. Then we'll decide if we're keeping that massage appointment or doing something else."

Ella placed a hand over her belly. "You really think I could be pregnant?"

Rory shrugged. "I have no idea, but if it were me, I'd want to know."

Ella had to admit that she did want to know. At least, she thought she did. What if she was pregnant? If Valero found out, would he insist that they get married? She didn't want a baby to be the deciding factor. She wanted to get married because it was what they both wanted, not because it was needed. Not that she thought a baby meant you had to get married, but she really didn't want to raise another child on her own. Connor had turned out great, and she was certain this baby would too, but it had been such a hard life for them. She wanted more for her children than struggling to get by.

"Come on. We'll blow off the salon appointment," Rory offered.

"No. I can wait until we're finished here. Will there still be someone at the clinic though?"

She nodded. "It stays open twenty-four hours now that they have two doctors."

They got manicures and pedicures, then Rory talked Ella into getting her hair trimmed and styled. It took two hours before they were finished, but Ella had to admit she felt better than she had in a long time. The last time she'd gotten her nails and hair done professionally had been in high school, before she'd found out about Connor.

Rory paid for the visit, refusing any money from Ella, and then they drove straight to the Terran Station. Rory's phone rang partway there. She pushed a button and answered through the car.

"Hello."

"Why does my phone say you're driving away from the spa and toward the Terran Station?" Zwyk asked.

Rory growled. "Did you seriously just track me like a wayward pet?"

"I told you I was syncing our phones. Now that you're pregnant I need to know where you are in case I need to reach you quickly."

"Zwyk, I'm seriously going to shove my foot up your ass. I'm taking Ella to the station because she needs to make a stop there for something. Nosy, much?"

"Sorry." He did sound contrite, at least to Ella. "I'm just worried about you."

"The baby is fine. I'm fine. Now back the hell off and let me enjoy my night with Ella. I'll call you when I'm heading home."

Zwyk sighed. "Fair enough. Enjoy your time together." He paused. "Just don't enjoy it too much."

Rory smirked, blew him a kiss, and ended the call.

"Sorry about that," Rory said. "He's been a bit overprotective since we found out about the baby. I'd like to say that he's unique in that way, but all the Terrans I've seen are super protective of their mates and it seems to be amplified by pregnancy. So be warned, Valero could become a possessive freak."

Ella laughed a little, having a hard time picturing Valero that way.

Butterflies rioted in her stomach as they entered the station and made their way back toward the clinic. A male in a white lab coat was escorting a human woman out as they neared the place.

"Rory, I hope everything is all right," he said.

"Vyrex, this is Ella. She's been staying with Valero and she needs to take a pregnancy test. That one that shows almost immediate results."

He tipped his head. "And does he know you're here?"

"No," Ella said. "Until Rory mentioned it a few hours ago, I didn't even know it was possible to find out so soon. It just happened last night, so…"

He nodded. "Very well. Come back and I'll need a little blood from you."

They walked back into the rear part of the clinic and

he ushered them into a room. Ella was glad that Rory was with her. The doctor pushed up her sleeve and placed a weird looking metal cylinder against her skin. She felt a pinch and almost as fast, he was finished and backing away. He watched the vial and then looked up at her with a conflicted expression.

"I'm not sure what news you were hoping to hear, but I'm going to assume so you and Valero aren't mated you are hoping for a negative result."

Ella bit her lip. "Negative would make things easier, but if I'm pregnant I would never wish away my child. It will just mean having a serious conversation with Valero to see where we go from here."

"You're pregnant," the doctor said. "I'm going to give you a cocktail of vitamins, but I'll need to see you back in the next few weeks."

She winced as he gave her the injection and then they were on their way.

"Still want that massage?" Rory asked.

"Do you think we could just have dinner somewhere and talk?" Ella asked. "I don't think I could relax right now if I tried."

"The Pasta Bowl?" Rory asked.

"I could eat Italian." Ella smiled.

The drive was short, but not so short that Ella didn't worry the entire time. She had no idea what to say to Valero, or how he would react. Would he demand that they get married now? And should she seriously consider it? She didn't want to keep the baby from his or her father, not even if things didn't work out between them, but...

She blew out a breath as they pulled into a parking space. Rory looped their arms together as they walked inside, and Ella felt a sense of belonging. It had been a long time since she'd had a friend to do things with. She'd missed it, and hoped she would get to see Rory

more often. It had been nice doing some girly things
today.

Inside, they were seated at the front of the restaurant
in a booth that looked out over the entire place. She was
just perusing her menu when she heard a waitress
commenting about a Terran and his human son, and how
hot the guy was. Her brow furrowed. It couldn't possibly
be Valero, right? She put her menu down and looked
around, almost immediately spotting her baby-daddy
and her son. She nearly snorted. Figured they'd end up at
the same restaurant.

"Should I make my presence known?" Ella asked.

Rory looked around then smiled. "I say sit back and
enjoy the show. They get tons of attention everywhere
they go, usually of the female variety. Unless you're the
jealous type."

"I don't think I am. They were calling Connor his
son."

Rory put her menu down. "Will he be?"

"What do you mean?"

"The two of you are having a baby together. Are you
going to let him mate-claim you? Or go through with a
human wedding maybe?"

"I don't know. He wants to claim me as his mate,
but..." Ella sighed. "I didn't think I was ready for that
step."

"Are you sure that's it?"

Ella turned her startled gaze toward Rory. "Why do
you ask that?"

"Ella, it's obvious the two of you had instant sparks
when you met. Everyone in the room felt it. And you're
living with him, letting him take care of your son while
you take a night off. You're already acting like a family.
All that's missing is the official agreement between the
two of you. So what's holding you back?"

"I thought it was because I didn't have anything to

contribute to the relationship, but Valero insisted that I did more than enough, even if I don't have a job right now."

"You know what I think?" Rory asked.

"What?"

"I think you're running scared. I think you love him and it scares the shit out of you. So, you're coming up with excuses to not commit. I know you loved Connor's dad in high school and he stomped all over you heart, but not all men are like that."

Ella shrugged. "I thought I loved him, but I didn't really. I wasn't brokenhearted for myself so much as Connor. But this is different. I think if things didn't work out with Valero, I wouldn't be able to walk away without some pain."

"I tell you what. I'm going to call Zwyk to come meet me for dinner, and you're going to march your ass over to your lover and son and have dinner as a family. And then when Connor goes to bed tonight, you're going to tell Valero about the baby and the two of you are going to have a very adult conversation. And you're not going to doubt yourself or his feelings for you."

"Yes, ma'am." Ella smiled a little. "Thanks for tonight, Rory."

"You call me anytime you want and we'll hang out. Now that we're starting a family, Zwyk talked me into staying home, so I'm going to have some time on my hands until the baby arrives. And maybe after that, we can have play dates and stuff with the kids."

Ella stood up and hugged her friend before hurrying across the restaurant to Valero's table. It only took a minute for her guys to look up. Connor didn't look nearly as excited to see her as Valero was.

Valero stood and offered her his seat. There wasn't enough room for both of them to fit though, so he ended up standing until he could get someone's attention.

"I thought you were eating with Rory," he said.

"I was. Then we saw the two of you here and she offered to have Zwyk meet her for dinner so the three of us could have a meal together." Ella smiled as she looked from Valero to Connor.

Connor glared at her from across the table.

"But I can eat elsewhere," Ella said. Obviously, her son didn't want her to interrupt his time with Valero, and she couldn't blame him. It wasn't like he'd ever had one on one time with a man before.

"We're thrilled to have you with us, aren't we, Connor?" Valero asked with a pointed look at her son.

Connor huffed but nodded. "Do I still get spaghetti with the huge meatballs?"

"You can have whatever you want," Valero said.

"May I help you?" a waitress said with a bit of a simper.

"We need a larger table. And Ella needs to order."

Her gaze went to Ella and the warmth in her eyes cooled a bit. "I see."

"Or we can eat elsewhere," Valero said.

That seemed to snap the waitress back to reality. She took Ella's order and then hurried off to find them another table. When they were seated once more, it was near Rory. Her friend gave a little wave and then her smile broadened when Zwyk claimed the seat across from her. If the restaurant was excited over one Terran, Ella could only imagine the chatter now that there were two.

"Did you have a nice time with Rory?" Valero asked. "Your hair looks nice."

She fingered the slightly shorter strands. "Thank you, and yes I did. She said we could get together again sometime."

"Mama, will you be at school tomorrow?" Connor asked. "Everyone else has brought cupcakes or cookies for their birthdays."

Ella opened her mouth then let it snap shut. In all the chaos of everything going on, she'd completely forgotten Connor's birthday. Her cheeks warmed with embarrassment, but Valero came to her rescue.

"What kind of cupcakes and cookies?" he asked.

"The kind you get at the store bakery."

Valero nodded. "Any particular time we should bring these treats to your school?"

Connor's eyes lit up. "You're coming too?"

"Why not?" Valero winked at him. "I've always wondered what a kindergarten room looked like."

"You'll really bring something?" Connor asked.

"We'll be there, honey," Ella said. "Valero and I will go out tomorrow and pick up some treats for your class."

"And goodie bags?" Connor asked.

Valero frowned a bit. "I'd think something like goodie bags would take a bit of planning. Why don't we see if the party store is still open after we eat? We can let you pick out what goes into the bags and then your mom and I can stay up tonight and put them together."

Connor let out a whoop, which ended with a gleeful squeal as a huge platter of spaghetti was placed in front of him. Ella's eggplant lasagna was placed in front of her. When a massive platter of huge sausage links and spaghetti was placed in front of Valero her eyes nearly bugged out of her head.

"You're going to eat all that?"

He looked at his plate, a puzzled expression on his face. "Is there something wrong with it?"

"It's just... huge. There's no way I've been feeding you enough if that's how much you like to eat."

He laughed. "Ella, whatever you fix for me is fine. If I want more, I can always go back for seconds. I'm just especially hungry today for some reason."

"What did you do with your friend, Mama?" Connor

asked.

"We went to a salon where we had the entire place to ourselves. We had manicures and pedicures, then had our hair cut and styled. It was fun. And after that we decided to get a bite to eat."

Valero's brow furrowed. "No spa day?"

"It was getting late. Maybe next time."

He didn't look convinced, but he let it go. They finished their food, paid the check, and then went to the party store, where Connor was allowed to pick six things and a bag of candy for his goodie bags. By the time they got home, Connor was yawning. Ella got him into his bath then dressed and into bed.

She collapsed on the couch and stared at the sacks from the party store knowing her night was just beginning. Making twenty goodie bags was going to be tiring work for someone who was already exhausted. Valero took a seat next to her and reached for her hand, lacing their fingers together. She had to admit, it had been nice being together and going to the party store. Being a family felt really incredible, and she only had herself to blame for not grabbing on to Valero and holding on tight. He'd made it no secret what he wanted, and now that she knew she had feelings for him, feelings that had her running scared, then she could face things head on.

"I know we need to make these treat bags, but can we talk first?" she asked, dreading his reaction to her pregnancy.

"We can talk anytime you want to, Ella. You never have to ask."

"I lied earlier."

"About what?" He watched her intently, his grip on her hand still tight and sure.

"Rory and I didn't just go to the salon then the restaurant. We went to the Terran Station too."

His eyebrows lifted. "Did you go back to talk to Tyril

about the job?"

"No." She licked her lips and took a shaky breath. "I went to the clinic."

Valero let go of her hand only to lift her onto his lap, his hands reaching up to cup her face. "Are you all right? You're not sick?"

"I'm fine. I'm just…"

"Just what? Whatever is, we'll face it together."

Tears misted her eyes. "I'm pregnant."

His brow furrowed. "But you said you hadn't been with anyone since Connor's dad."

"Only one man."

His grip tightened on her. "I see. And will you tell him about the baby?"

"I just did."

He gave her a blank look.

"Valero, what do you remember about last night?"

"I drank too much and went to bed. Although, for some reason I got undressed in my office."

Her cheeks burned. "You didn't undress for bed in your office. Your office was in disarray because we had sex in there last night. On your desk."

He stared at her, then his gaze dropped to her belly. "So, you're saying that…"

"You're going to be a daddy. Vyrex did some test that will show a pregnancy within hours of conception."

His grip tightened on her to the point of pain and then he pulled her into his arms, hugging her. "You have no idea how happy you've just made me."

She pushed away from him, surprised to see tears in his eyes. "You're happy? You're not mad?"

He caressed her cheek. "I could never be mad that we're having a baby together. I'm only sorry I don't remember last night. But if you say it happened, then I believe you. I kept having flashes of us together, but I thought I'd dreamt the entire thing."

"I wasn't sure how you would react."

He rubbed a hand across her belly. "Vyrex said everything was all right?"

"He gave me a vitamin cocktail and said to come back in a few weeks."

"Maybe it was too soon for him to tell you anything else. How do you feel?"

Ella laughed. "I'm fine, Valero. It's a little too soon for morning sickness or anything. Maybe this pregnancy won't be as rough as my last one. With Connor, I was throwing up night and day for months. And I was always so tired."

"Whatever you need, you only have to ask for it." He kissed her softly. "Thank you for this wonderful gift, Ella."

"You're not going to push for a fast mating?" she asked.

"I've learned that badgering you about it isn't the way to go. So, why don't we do things a little differently? Instead of me asking you to be my wife, you let me know when you're ready for that next step. Until then, we'll just take things one day at a time."

"What about Connor? I don't know how to tell him. It's just been the two of us and now I'm asking him to welcome two more people into our family. And he just got you... he isn't going to want to share."

"He may surprise you."

Ella nodded. "We should put the goodie bags together. He was so excited about getting to take them to school tomorrow. We'll have to find something awesome at the bakery in the morning."

"Did you have anything planned for his birthday tomorrow?"

She shook her head.

"Then why don't we throw a small party for him? My friend, Reyvor, has a house full of kids, and Avelyn and Thrace have Lily. I think Lily is just a little older than Connor. Same with Syl's adopted son, Dexter."

"I'm sure Connor would love to meet your friends and their children."

"If you'll give me a minute, I'll go send out some messages and then come help with the goodie bags."

Ella kissed him. "Take your time."

While Valero went off to make her son's dreams come true, because he'd never had a party before, she got to work on the little bags. It was going to be Connor's best birthday ever, as long as the news of the baby didn't wreck the entire day for him. Maybe she should tell him the day after?

She remembered being stressed during her pregnancy with Connor, but for different reasons. This time she didn't have to worry about a place to live or food to eat. But now she had to worry that her precious boy would feel like he was being replaced. Maybe if he saw the kids tomorrow and how much fun siblings could be then maybe he would take the news better.

Ella sighed. Sometimes being a parent was the hardest job in the world.

Chapter Seven

Valero made some calls, starting with the owner of Puck's Pizza Palace. The man grumbled about receiving calls after hours but after Valero explained the situation, the man was only too happy to help.

"The boy is turning six and he's never had a birthday party before. I want to make sure it's a special event for him," Valero said.

"So, what exactly do you need from me?" the man asked.

"I need your largest party room and a few workers to assist with the children. I'll provide the balloons and cake, and of course we'll order drinks and pizza there. If possible, I'll need a table set up for presents. There will possibly be nine children, maybe some infants, and of course all the parents. I plan to have food and drinks for both the children and adults."

"I'll see that it's taken care of. Do you know when you'd like to start the party?"

"Three o'clock? School lets out at two so that would give everyone time to go home and change before the party, if they wanted to. And I'd say we need the room for at least two, maybe three hours."

"I can take care of that. I'll call some of my part-time workers and see if they'd like to help with the party. If you need anything else, please let me know," the man said.

"I'll pay when we get there. I'll be ordering wristbands for all of the children old enough to play."

"Thank you, Mr. Valero, for thinking of Puck's Pizza Palace for your son's birthday."

He hung up and then he called all his friends and made sure they were available tomorrow afternoon. When they asked what to get Connor for his birthday, he told them what little he knew of the boy, and hoped that

Connor would get an awesome haul. He still hadn't done any shopping and hoped there would be time between taking treats to the school and picking Connor up.

He went back to the living room and found Ella cross-legged in the floor with all the party favors around her and a stack of sacks in front of her. He smiled a little as he joined her, taking a spot next to her. She had everything organized into piles so he took one thing from each pile and a small handful of candy before tying off the bag and starting another one. With the two of them working on it, it didn't take long to fill all twenty bags. They put them in a small box to carry to school in the morning.

He'd never realized how much work it was to have a small person living with you. Not that he didn't love having Connor around, but he had to wonder how hectic things would be once there were two children in the house. He was beyond excited to find out they were having a baby, but he hoped it wouldn't be too hard on Ella. She'd done a remarkable job raising Connor and he knew she'd be just as wonderful with their baby. Would she have a boy or girl?

"You're probably worn out after all that." Valero took her hand and pulled her into his lap. "Why don't I make you a nice hot bath and you can relax?"

"If I'm pregnant, I need to take warm baths, not hot. And that sounds really nice. I was so worried about how you would react that I talked Rory out of the massage tonight. We didn't skip it because it was so late. I just didn't think I'd be able to relax."

"I'm sorry you were so stressed. I really am thrilled about the baby though. Is it too soon to set up a nursery?"

She leaned into him. "Maybe just a little. But if you're so excited that you want to get started on it, I won't stop you. It's probably going to be a while before we can find out what we're having. It's been a while so I don't remember exactly when we can find out. Maybe four months?"

"We could do neutral colors," Valero suggested.

"Like mint green?"

"I like mint green. It's a cheerful color for a baby's room. And then when we find out what we're having, we can add accents in blue or pink."

"You're painting that room this weekend, aren't you?"

"Probably."

She snuggled into him a little more. "If I take a bath, will you get in with me? The tub is pretty big. I think we'd both fit."

"If we don't, I'll sit beside the tub and keep you company."

Valero helped her stand then took her hand and led her back to the master suite. "Would it be presumptuous of me to ask you to move your things in here?"

"You want to share a room with me?" she asked.

"We're having a baby together, and we're living together. Even if you don't want to marry me right now, I'd like to hold you at night and wake up with you in my arms every morning."

"I can do that," she said softly.

While she gathered her things, he started the water in the tub, making sure it wasn't too hot. Then he added some bubbles to the water, thinking she'd like them. When she returned, she'd stripped out of her clothes and he admired the view for a moment. Her curves were perfect, but he couldn't wait to see her grow with their child. There were faint lines on her abdomen that he'd learned were called stretch marks, and she would doubtless get more with the second pregnancy, but they didn't detract from her beauty.

Valero helped her into the tub before stripping out of his clothes. He eased into the water behind her, drawing her back against his chest. When the water had filled close to the top, he used his foot to turn off the knobs. Ella gave a contented sigh and he wondered if she noticed his hard cock trapped between them. Not that he had any intention of acting on it. She'd had a stressful day, and while he'd heard sex was a good stress reliever, he wasn't going to push for it.

Ella rubbed her foot up and down his leg, making his need for her grow. When she turned, placing a knee on either side of his thighs, his eyebrows went up. The gentlemanly thing to do would have been to stop her. He wasn't feeling very much like a gentleman though. Valero leaned back in the tub and gave her full access to his body, letting her do whatever she pleased.

Her soft hand curled around his cock and stroked him several times, drawing a groan from him. She licked her bottom lip before tugging it between her teeth as her hand added a little twist.

"Fuck! You're going to make me come in your hand." His fingers gripped the sides of the tub.

"You said you don't remember much of last night. I thought maybe I could give you something to remember." She smiled a little. "Unless you'd prefer I finish this way?"

He growled a little. "Get that sexy ass up here. Or do you want me to carry you to the bed?"

"We'd get the bed wet."

She reached behind her to drain a little of the water out, then placed her hands on his shoulders as she inched her way up his body. When his cock brushed against her pussy, he thought he'd die from both pleasure and pain at the same time. He'd never wanted anything so much in his life. It sucked that he'd already been inside of her and only remembered bits and pieces of it. Hopefully, their child never asked how they were conceived, because that was a conversation he'd just as soon avoid.

Ella sank slowly, taking him inside of her. He ground his teeth together as he fought for control, fighting the urge to thrust upward and fill her completely. Once he was all the way inside of her, he let Ella set the pace. As much as he wanted to grab her hips and thrust into her until both of them were mindless with pleasure, he was going to let her run the show this time. The last thing he wanted to do was accidentally hurt her.

As she rode him, slowly at first then faster, he couldn't hold back any longer. He reached for her, gripping her hips as he met her stroke for stroke. Her nails bit into his skin as she orgasmed, her pussy clenching around him as if she were trying to milk every drop from his balls. He thrust a few more times until he found his release, coming with a shout. Ella squeezed him with her knees, as if she were afraid he'd make her move. If he could figure out how to get them out of the tub and into bed with separating their bodies, he'd just stay buried inside of her until morning.

"Think you'll remember this time?" she asked with a cheeky smile.

"Oh, I'll remember." He kissed her hungrily. "And if you aren't too tired, I'll make sure we both have something else to remember before morning."

"Only if we make it to the bed next time. So far we've christened the living room, your desk, and the bathroom. A bed would be awesome."

"As you wish." He winked at her. "Now, let's get cleaned up, dried off, and then we'll see what I can do about round two."

He liked this playful side of Ella and he hoped he got to see more of it. Maybe finding out she was pregnant wasn't such a bad thing, despite her fears. He'd just have to show her how great a family they made, and hope that she decided he was worth taking a chance on.

* * *

Ella parked the van at the front of the school and she and Valero walked in with Connor, carrying the box of goodie bags and several containers of dinosaur cupcakes. Valero had insisted they leave a little early to stop by the bakery first thing. They'd found one open not far from the house and now they were armed with thirty cupcakes and a box of chocolate chip cookies in case someone didn't want a cupcake.

"Good morning," the school secretary said with a smile. "It looks like we have a birthday boy today."

Connor nodded with a wide grin. "I'm six today."

"Well, let's get Mom and Dad signed in and then you can show them the way to your classroom."

Connor looked so happy, Ella thought he might burst. She wasn't sure if it was the comment about Valero being his dad or because she was treating him like a big boy. Once they were signed in and had visitor passes stuck to their shirts, they followed Connor to his class. His teacher welcomed them warmly.

"Connor's talked about his birthday all week, but I wasn't sure if you were bringing anything," Mrs. Coleman said.

"I should have sent a note, shouldn't I? I'm sorry, we didn't mean to just spring this on you." Ella worried at her bottom lip. "We can come back if it's not convenient."

The teacher waved away her concern. "I do ask that you leave the treats here until our snack time. I'll have an aide during that hour so we can handle everything, unless you'd just really like to be here."

Valero leaned in and whispered. "We need to do some birthday shopping today. But if you could take some pictures?"

The teacher nodded. "Of course. I have a digital camera and a printer here in the room so I'll take a few and print them off for you. I'll send them home in his daily folder. It was nice meeting both of you."

They hugged Connor and went back to the front office to check out, then Valero took them out for coffee and a bit of strategic planning. More likely he was killing time until the stores opened. Not much was open at eight o'clock in the morning. She'd let him drive the van and he parked it across from the door to the coffee shop. Inside, as they stood in line, his hand stayed at her waist, giving her a sense of comfort. They placed their order and claimed a table by the window.

"Are you allowed to drink coffee with the baby?" he asked.

"I won't have more than one cup, and I got a small. I didn't think to ask Vyrex what I was and wasn't allowed to have."

"I'll try to call him tomorrow and see if there are any foods or drinks you should avoid. I think today we'll be a little too busy for that." Valero smiled. "I think Connor is going to be pleasantly surprised with his party later. I only hope he likes it."

"He's going to love it." She reached out and took his hand. "Thank you for setting up something for him. He's always wanted a party, but we've never been able to afford it."

"Maybe next year we can invite his class."

She nodded. "He'd love that. For now, I think the cupcakes and treat bags are enough. I've never seen him that excited before."

"When the toy store opens, we'll go pick out some presents for him."

"Presents, plural?" she asked, an eyebrow raised. "Valero, he's only ever had one present at birthdays or Christmases."

His jaw firmed. "We may not be married, but as far I'm concerned he's my son and he's getting more than one present."

Her throat tightened at his words. "You really see

him that way?"

"Of course I do, Ella. I know you don't want to be more than a girlfriend right now. That is the human term, yes?"

She nodded.

"But the two of you, soon to be three, are my family. Connor is just as much my son as that baby will be my son or daughter. And while we may not have an official mating or marriage, as far as I'm concerned, I'm off the market. You're it for me."

She'd known that Valero wanted her as his mate, but she'd never understood... it had just seemed like empty words, a status and nothing more. It had felt more like he'd gone window shopping and picked her out. She'd never realized that in his heart he'd already claimed them. Ella stood and sank onto his lap, curling her arm around his shoulders. He looked surprised, but held her close.

"I never knew... I mean, you said you wanted us to be yours, but until now I didn't really get it. If you still want me as your mate, then I'm ready."

"You're not just saying that because you think it's what I want to hear?" he asked.

"I'm ready, Valero. I don't know what we have to do, but I'm ready."

"We have to finish our coffee and go to the Terran Station, and we're not leaving until the council approves our mating." He smiled. "And then I'm buying you a ring so all of the males will know to back off, that you belong to me."

"Will you wear one too?"

"Gladly."

She kissed him softly. "Then forget the coffee. Let's go."

They stood and hurried to the van. She couldn't help but notice that Valero couldn't stop smiling. She'd never seen him so happy before. At the Terran Station, he took her hand and led her to one of the conference rooms. The first two were in use, but the third had the doors wide open. They went inside and shut the doors, and then Valero used the Vid-comm to contact his council.

Ella stood beside him, feeling a little nervous. She'd never met a councilman before, nor had she ever seen one. What if they didn't approve of her? Could they deny the mating? And if they did, what would Valero do?

A room showed up on the screen with three Terrans seated at a long table.

"Councilman Larimar, this my chosen mate, Ella. We've come before the council to get your approval on our mating," Valero said.

"Welcome, Ella." The councilman smiled. "You agree to the mating?"

"Yes, sir."

"Valero, I didn't realize you were seeing anyone," Larimar said. "Why don't you tell us a little about your chosen mate, since this is the first we've heard of her."

"Ella is a single mom who has worked hard to raise her son on her own. Connor is turning six today. They've already moved into my home, and I'd very much like to make our relationship official."

Larimar nodded. "And what is it you do, Ella?"

"I, um... I was a waitress, but right now I'm out of work." Her hand pressed to her belly. "I thought I might be a stay-at-home mom."

Larimar didn't miss her hand's position. "And is there another reason the two of you should be mated?"

Valero cleared his throat. "Ella is expecting my child. Vyrex confirmed the pregnancy here at the station."

Larimar and the other two councilmen talked amongst themselves, too quietly for her to hear what they were saying. Minutes passed and she began to worry they would be denied. She reached for Valero's hand, squeezing it tight. Her stomach rolled and she wondered if maybe she shouldn't have come on an empty stomach after all. When Larimar looked at the screen again, she just knew he was going to tell her to leave Valero, that she wasn't good enough.

"Valero, most males wait until they are mated to get their mates pregnant."

"It wasn't planned, Larimar, but I'm not sorry. Even if you don't approve our mating, I'll continue to have Ella and Connor live with me, and we'll still be a family. Just an unofficial one."

Larimar nodded. "I figured you would say as much. We're going to approve your mating. I'll push the paperwork through today. Congratulations to you both, on the mating and the baby."

Ella let out a breath she hadn't realized she was holding and sagged against Valero. The screen went black and he wrapped his arms around her, kissing her softly. She looked up at him, marveling that it had only taken one conversation for them to be mated. Did that make her Mrs... Mrs what?

"Do you have a last name?" she asked.

"No, just Valero. Why do you ask?"

"Married women on Earth take their husband's last name."

"We could call the council back and ask them to assign us a last name. Would you like that?"

She shook her head. No, she didn't want to call the council again anytime soon. Valero smiled, as if he could read her thoughts. He kissed her again and led her out of the conference room, leaving the doors open for someone else to use the room.

"Maybe before the toy store we should see if there's a jeweler open." He grasped her hand and led her out to the van. "I remember seeing one not too far from here. We'll try there first."

Ella had never been to a jewelry store before and was excited and nervous. The only jewelry she'd had before Connor had come from the jewelry counter in a big-box store. The place Valero stopped at didn't look like much, but the display window was filled with diamonds, rubies, and sapphires. She'd never seen so many glittering stones at one time before.

Valero escorted her inside, the bell over the door jingling.

"Good morning," said the man behind the counter. "Are you looking for something special today?"

"Wedding rings," Valero said.

The man nodded. "And do you want plain bands or something a little flashier?"

"Plain is fine," Ella said.

Valero frowned at her before addressing the man. "Plain for me, but maybe something a little flashier for my wife."

The man nodded and began pulling out black velvet displays with glittering rings. He motioned for them to come a little closer and Valero guided her over. Ella's eyes went wide when she saw some of the larger stones, knowing she'd never feel safe wearing something like that. She'd be worried about someone stealing it or her losing it.

"That one," Valero said, pointing to an emerald and diamond set.

"It's too big," Ella said.

"No, it's perfect. It matches your eyes."

How could she argue with him when he said sweet things like that?

The jeweler held it up for her inspection and she slid it on her finger. It fit perfectly. The diamond heart on top winked under the lights, and she admired the alternating emerald and diamond pattern down the two bands. She had to admit it looked beautiful on her hand, and she liked the way it felt.

"We'll take it," Valero said. "And I'd like a band that same color."

"It's platinum," the man said as he reached for the men's bands.

"This is going to cost a fortune," Ella said.

Valero smiled. "I'm good for it. Besides, how often are we going to buy wedding rings? Can you think of a better time to spend some money?"

"I guess not."

It took a few tries to find a band that fit Valero, but once the ring was on his finger, he paid the man and ushered Ella out of the store. She couldn't believe he'd paid over five thousand dollars as easily as most people bought groceries. Just how rich was her new husband? No, she didn't want to know. As long as there was a roof over their heads and food in their bellies, that was all that mattered. Anything else was just extra.

They went to the toy store next, where she had to rein in Valero. He was like a kid in a candy story, wanting to buy one of everything for Connor. She could only imagine how he would be when it came time to buy stuff for the baby's room. She might have to confiscate his credit cards just so he didn't bankrupt them in the toy shop. Although, she had to admit he was pretty cute with his enthusiasm.

"What about this?" he asked, holding up a T-Rex that roared and moved.

"I'm sure he would love it, but it's kind of expensive."

"Stop looking at the price tags and just tell me if he'd like it or not. They have an entire set of them. We could get this one and two others so he'd have several to play with. It's not like he can do much with just one of them."

"Valero?" a male voice interrupted.

Ella looked over and saw a Terran with a blonde

woman walk up.

"Thrace. Avelyn." Valero smiled and shook the man's hand. "It's good to see you both. What brings you to the toy store so early?"

"Getting a present for your son," Thrace said with a smile. "Judging by the ring on your finger I'm going to assume congratulations are in order?"

Valero nodded. "Connor doesn't know yet."

"And you must be Ella," the woman said. "I'm Avelyn. Our daughter, Lily, will be at Connor's party this afternoon. Is there anything in particular he likes?"

"He'd love anything you picked out. It seems we're buying a few dinosaurs, but he likes trains and cars, puzzles, art supplies. He's really easy to please. You don't even have to get him anything. Just showing up at his party would thrill him," Ella said.

"Oh, we're definitely bringing something. I told Lily she could help wrap it when she gets home from school. She was really excited about making a new friend. How old is Connor?" Avelyn asked.

"He turned six today," Ella said. "How old is Lily?"

"She's seven. So, they're close in age. There are a lot of kids in our little group. I'm sure Connor will make lots of friends this afternoon." Avelyn smiled. "If you ever need a babysitter, just give me a call. We weren't able to have more children, and the last two adoptions we applied for were denied. It seems the Intergalactic Adoption Agency isn't too thrilled that Thrace is married to a human."

"I'm so sorry." Her heart ached for the couple. "What about adopting children here on Earth? Or would your council not approve?"

"We haven't asked them, but maybe we should. I really do want more children."

Ella hugged Avelyn. "I'm sure it will work out. There are lots of kids out there who need a good home."

"Thanks. I guess we'd better get to shopping or we'll still be here when school lets out. It's hard to drag Thrace out of here sometimes. If it were up to him, Lily would own the entire store."

"I think Valero is going to be the same way. It was nice meeting you."

Valero was watching her with some amusement and ushered her toward another section of the store, three dinosaurs taking up room in the shopping cart. When she saw they were heading toward the video games, she nearly rolled her eyes. Did everything with her new husband have to circle back to gaming?

She let him talk her into two video games for Connor and then she put her foot down. No more presents. As it was, her son was going to be spoiled rotten. She only hoped he didn't expect treats like this all the time.

Chapter Eight

Valero couldn't believe he was willingly going into Puck's Pizza Palace again. The back of the van was loaded with five presents, a box of more goodie bags, about two dozen balloons, and a large dinosaur cake. Connor hadn't seen everything yet, but he'd been bouncing in his booster seat ever since Ella had told him he was going to have a party. From the looks of the parking lot, they were the first of the group to arrive.

"Go inside and make sure the party room is ready. I'll start bringing things inside," Valero told Ella.

"They have a cart you can borrow to bring in everything at one time." She smiled. "No sense making several trips to the car if you don't have to."

He kissed her on the cheek. "Then let's go inside and get it. I'll let Connor and you go to the party room while I bring everything in."

Connor practically ran for the door, dragging Ella with him. Valero couldn't help but smile at his enthusiasm. He was glad they'd made an extra stop to purchase a digital camera today. Between him and Ella, they were going to fill the SD card he'd installed in it.

While his wife and son got settled in the party room, he pushed a two-tiered cart out to the van and loaded it, tying the balloons to the corners. Then he locked the van and went back inside, hoping he didn't lose anything off the cart along the bumpy parking lot. Inside, kids were running and screaming, the noise level already through the roof. He made his way back to the party room, happy to see there were two workers ready to help out. They took the cart from him and started setting things up, even tying a balloon to each chair and the remainder on the birthday boy's chair.

"Can I go play?" Connor asked.

"First, there's something we need to tell you," Ella

said. "You know how you wanted Valero to be your daddy?"

Connor nodded.

"Well, Valero and I are officially mated now. Which means, in human terms, that we're married."

Connor's eyes went wide as he looked at Valero. "You're really my daddy now?"

"I'm really your daddy."

Connor ran toward him and Valero knelt to catch him, lifting him into his arms as the little boy squeezed him tight. It was the best hug he'd ever had, and one he would remember forever. He set Connor down and took his hand.

"Let's go purchase a wristband and you can play until your guests arrive. Then you'll need to come meet everyone and have some pizza."

Connor nodded and held his hand tight as they went to the front counter. Valero made sure he had the best wristband and picked up the things he'd ordered the night before. Connor scampered off after he had his wristband on and Valero went back to the party room to wait with Ella. He knew she was nervous about telling Connor he was going to be a big brother, but maybe she was right to wait. This was Connor's day and there would be plenty of time to tell him about the baby.

Avelyn and Thrace were the first to arrive with Lily. In hindsight, he probably should have warned Ella that Lily was not of Terran descent, but if she was surprised by the red-skinned little girl, she took it in stride. Connor had seen Lily arrive and was curious about the little girl who was so different from him. He didn't stare -- much.

"Connor," Valero said. "This is Lily. She's here for your birthday party."

"Hi," Connor said. "Want to play?"

Lily smiled and nodded.

"Let me get a wristband for Lily and then you can

show her your favorite things here."

"Better get a handful," Thrace said. "I think everyone is coming."

"So… nine for the five and over crowd?" Valero asked.

Thrace nodded. "And four for the younger ones. Unless one year olds can't play here, then you'll only need three."

Valero looked at Ella, having no idea if a one year old could do anything at Puck's.

"There's a toddler area," Ella said. "Just make sure to tell them you need a wristband for someone under three. Are the others over three?"

"They're four," Thrace said. "I think."

"I'll go procure enough for everyone. I already ordered our food, I just need to get some pitchers of drinks and cups. I'll take care of that and the wristbands."

Valero took off with Connor and Lily in tow. He ordered the correct number of wristbands -- he hoped -- and enough cups for everyone, with four pitchers of soda. It was going to be a hectic few hours, but the smile on Connor's face made it all worthwhile. The kids ran off to play and he went back to the party room to wait for the next wave of children to arrive.

By the time all his friends were present, and their children off running like a bunch of wild monkeys, he was exhausted and hoped there was a nap in their future. Something told him Connor wouldn't cooperate with that idea. Everyone got along great with Ella and welcomed her with open arms. Rory and Zwyk came, even though they didn't have any children yet, and he knew Ella was grateful for a familiar face. Even though she'd met Avelyn and Thrace earlier, she'd known Rory since they were kids.

The pizzas arrived and everyone ate, decimating all the food in sight and making Valero question if he'd ordered enough. By the time the kids were finished, they were begging for cake and Connor was eyeing the mountain of presents on the table. For a little boy who had only ever received one present for his birthday, it must have seemed like he'd won some grand prize. He got a father and probably twenty presents all in the same day. Maybe he should have told his friends to go easy on the birthday spending. Ella cast a few looks his way as he handed Connor the gifts, but if she was mad about how many there were, she kept it to herself. He had a feeling he'd hear plenty about it later though.

Connor loved everything, especially the dinosaurs and video games. Thrace and Avelyn had given him a train set with a small table to put it on. Syl and Brielle had brought a gift from each of their three children, as had Xonos and Victoria. Reyvor and Hazel had probably given him the best present of all, though: a new Playstation 4 and a gift card to Gamer Plus to pick out some games for his new system. It was extravagant, but they argued the gift was from four children and not just one.

"Thank you," Connor said. "I love all of my presents. This is the best birthday ever! I get my first party and I get a daddy too!"

The adults laughed a little and the kids dragged him back out into the chaos outside of the party room. Valero knew they wouldn't have the room for much longer, so he gathered everything up. He needed two carts to get everything back out to the van, but one of the workers helped him. By the time he was finished, everyone was starting to head home. Connor looked like he was going to be wide awake for the next century, but they loaded him into the van and drove home.

At the house, Ella looked nervous and he wondered if now was the time she was going to tell Connor about the baby, or if there was something else on her mind. She asked Connor to sit on the couch while Valero carried all the new toys into his son's room. But he tried to hurry because if Ella was going to tell Connor about the baby, he wanted to be there too.

It seemed mother and son were having a staring contest when he got back to the living room. Ella's gaze broke away to look at him, as if she was seeking answers that he couldn't give. He gave her a nod of encouragement and went around to hold her hand for moral support.

"Connor, you know that Valero and I were married today and that he's your daddy."

Connor nodded, a huge grin on his face.

"I know it's a big change," Ella said. "It's just been the two of us for so long."

"But now we have a family like everyone else in my class," Connor said.

"Yes. Do some of the people in your class have larger families? Maybe they have a brother or a sister?" Ella asked.

He frowned and seemed to be thinking about it. "You mean like Dexter has Emily and Mrono?"

Well, Valero hadn't expected the boy to use Syl's children as an example, but it worked. He watched Ella to see what she would say or do next. She seemed to be thinking, but she was nodding in agreement to what Connor had said.

"Yes, like that."

"And I'm like Lily and don't have any," Connor said.

Ella licked her lips. "How would you feel about having a brother or sister to play with?"

Connor seemed confused. "But I don't have one. Are we going to adopt one like Lily and Dexter were adopted?"

"Um, not exactly." Ella swallowed so hard Valero could hear it. He decided to give her a break and take over, hoping the conversation would go a little smoother.

"Do you remember how Emily looks like her daddy but her eyes are the same color as her mother's?" Valero asked.

"I guess so." Connor scrunched his nose.

"It's because Emily's mommy and daddy made her together. So, if your mommy and I were to make a baby together, then it would be colored like me but probably have her green eyes. Would you be okay with that?" Valero asked.

"You're going to make a baby together?" Connor asked.

"We already did," Valero said. "In about ten months, your mom is going to give birth to a baby girl or boy. They will be your brother or sister, which means you'll be the big brother and have to help take care of them and teach them things. Do you think you can handle that?"

Connor's eyes went wide but he nodded. He looked at Ella's stomach. "There's a baby in there? Just like my friend Tyler's mom at school?"

"Just like that," Ella said. "Are you okay with that? I know a lot of changes are happening really fast."

"I think I'll like being a big brother. Evie seemed to like being an older sister," he said, mentioning Xonos's eldest daughter.

"Yes, she did." Ella smiled. "I'm so glad you're okay with this, Connor. I've been so worried you would be upset, or feel like you were going to lose me. Because you aren't losing anyone. You've gained a daddy and you're going to gain a brother or sister in..." Ella's eyes went wide and her gaze flew to Valero. "Did you say ten months?"

"Terran pregnancies are longer than human ones and run forty-three weeks."

Her mouth opened and shut several times before her knees gave out. Valero helped her onto the couch and then knelt at her feet. She looked a little pale, but otherwise seemed fine, if shocked.

"I'd ask if you were still certain about being married to me, but it's a little late now."

"Forty-three weeks?" she squeaked. "I'll be pregnant forever!"

He laughed and kissed her. "It won't be forever."

"Can I go play with my toys now?" Connor asked.

Valero smiled at him. "Yes, son. You may go play with your new toys. Just don't touch the Playstation 4 box. I'll hook it up for you tomorrow."

Connor gave a whoop and took off to his room.

"So, my Cinderella, any regrets?"

"Cinderella?" Her nose wrinkled.

"Well, I know I'm not as dashing as Prince Charming, and there were no missing shoes on this adventure, but I'd like to think you're my very own princess. You're as beautiful as one."

Her cheeks flushed.

"So, any regrets?" he asked again.

"No. Well, maybe one."

He braced himself for bad news.

"I should have told you before I agreed to marry you… Somewhere along the way, I fell in love with you, Valero."

He blinked, thinking he'd heard her wrong. "You love me?"

She nodded slowly, unease in her gaze.

"Oh, Ella. My beautiful Ella. I love you too. So very much."

With a cry, she threw her arms around his neck and kissed him hard.

Valero hadn't had any intention of falling for the independent single mom, but he was so very glad he'd gone to Zwyk's that day. Meeting Ella and Connor was the best thing that had ever happened to him, and he hoped he got to spend many years celebrating life every day with them. And maybe, with a little luck, he could turn Ella into a gamer too... even if it meant buying every Nintendo game ever created.

Summer and the Alien Guard

(Intergalactic Brides 11)

Jessica Coulter Smith

When her family is evicted from their home, Summer knows things can't get much worse. She blames herself. She should have done something sooner, but now it's time for drastic measures. There's only one thing left to do, even if it means tying her life to that of an alien. She drives straight to the Terran Station.

From the moment he first sees the young human step out of her car, Vordro is mesmerized. He's never seen anyone so vibrant, so beautiful... or so troubled. He wants to be the answer to her prayers, even if he knows he's too old for her. The thought of her mating with anyone other than him leaves a sour taste in his mouth. But moving Summer into his home proves to be far more temptation than he's able to withstand.

When things get off the charts hot between them and Summer ends up pregnant, Vordro knows he'll do anything to protect her and their unborn child -- even if it means defending her from her own family.

Chapter One

Summer watched as the last of her family's possessions were carted out of their home and loaded onto a truck. If she'd known things were this bad, she might have been able to act sooner, but her parents had never said a word about the bank foreclosing on their property or that they would literally lose everything but their clothes. She didn't know where they were going, or how they would survive. They'd even lost all but her beat-up Toyota, an ancient car even the bank didn't want. At twenty, she should be worrying about college. Not whether or not she'd be eating tonight.

There was only one thing she knew to do, and her parents weren't going to be happy about it. She'd mentioned the bride program once before, and her father had shot down her idea. She'd known that money was tight, but she hadn't realized how tight until now. If she'd known, she wouldn't have listened to her dad and would have joined the program anyway. She'd heard they paid well if you signed up.

"We'll stay with Aunt Martha tonight," her dad said. "And then we'll figure something out tomorrow."

"I need to run some errands after we go to Aunt Martha's," Summer said. "I probably won't return until dinner or later."

Her father nodded absently as he loaded their meager belongings into the trunk. The drive to her aunt's house was quiet and gave Summer time to think. She dropped off her parents, then drove straight to the Terran Station. When she pulled into the parking lot, she smoothed her hair and wished she'd stopped to put on makeup and maybe change her clothes. She smoothed on a little gloss, then took a breath before stepping out of her car.

As she approached the station, a tall Terran opened

the door for her. She smiled her thanks and stopped at the reception desk. The woman there was on the phone, so Summer waited patiently. There was warmth at her back, and she looked over her shoulder, and up. The same Terran who had opened the door for her was now standing extremely close. She wondered if maybe she looked like someone who was about to go postal on the place.

"I promise I'm not here to cause trouble," she said.

"I'd be happy to escort you to your destination. Are you here to meet with someone?" he asked.

"I need to sign up for the bride program."

He studied her. "Interesting choice of words."

"Excuse me?" She didn't think she'd said anything wrong. Maybe he hadn't understood her?

"You said need. Not want."

She licked her lips. "I meant want."

"We only take serious inquiries for the bride program. If you aren't entering it for the right reasons, you might as well turn around and go home."

Tears misted her eyes. "I can't."

His gaze softened, and he placed a hand on her waist, guiding her away from the desk. He motioned for her to take a seat and he hunkered down in front of her, the leather of his pants creaking from the movement.

"Why don't you start by telling me what's wrong," he said. "And then we'll go from there."

"I said I need to sign up for the bride program because it's my only hope. My family was evicted from our home today, and all our possessions were taken as well to pay off creditors. All we have are some clothes and a few pairs of shoes. My father works hard, but it's not enough. I don't know how else to help them." A tear slipped down her cheek as she looked down at her lap. "Please don't send me away."

He reached out and gently took her hand. "I'm not

going to make you leave, but I don't think the bride program is the right choice for you."

"I don't know what else to do. I can't keep a job no matter how hard I try. No one will hire me. I even saw one manager tear up my application as I exited the store."

"Are you hungry? Or maybe you'd like some coffee?" he asked.

"I don't think I could eat if I tried. I'm not a big coffee drinker, but I like hot chocolate."

The Terran rose to his full height and pulled her up. "Come on. We'll see if the café has hot chocolate."

She let him lead her through the station to a food court area. He settled her at a table before walking off. Summer looked around and noticed several of the Terrans were watching her with interest. Would it be like that on their world, if she were to sign up for the program?

When the Terran returned, he had two cups in his hands. He gave her one with a smile and then claimed the chair next to her. She was amazed he could fit his long legs under the table, but he managed somehow.

"I'm Summer," she said as she took a sip of her drink.

"It's nice to meet you, Summer. My name is Vordro. Now, why don't we talk a little about your problem and see if we can come up with a solution other than the bride program."

She nodded.

"Since I'm assuming the only reason you were signing up for the program is to help your family, I get the feeling marriage isn't something you're really ready for right now. You seem young."

"I'm twenty." Her chin shot up. "I'm not a child."

His lips twitched as if he fought a smile. "I'm thirty-five, which almost makes me old enough to be your father. On my world, males can start a family as early as sixteen years old. I believe the legal age here is eighteen."

"Yes."

"So, you're an adult by Earth's standards, which is good if you decide to proceed with your plan. What are you going to do when you're on another world and never see your family again?"

She felt herself pale a little. She'd known she'd have to leave Earth, but she hadn't really thought about never seeing her parents again. They'd always been close, or so she'd thought. With her parents hiding their financial difficulties from her, she had to wonder if maybe they still saw her as a burden and not someone who could help. She'd have taken a job to help with the expenses, even if she couldn't seem to hold onto one more than a week or two. Being punctual was not her strong suit.

"Never?" she asked.

"It's possible your mate would bring you here for a visit, but it wouldn't be often. You'd have to assimilate to our ways. There's only one restaurant on my world that serves Earth cuisine. You'd have to learn to like Terran food. Do you think you could do that?"

"I don't know," she answered truthfully. "I guess I didn't think of anything other than helping my family."

"Your parents both work?" he asked.

"No, just my dad."

"So, knowing you were having problems, your mother didn't offer to get a job in order to help, and yet you feel the need to bail them out?"

She shrugged. "Mom hasn't worked since I was born. It's always been her job to take care of us and the house. As long as she's been without a job, I'm not sure she'd have gotten hired anywhere."

"If you're determined to go through with this, to apply to the bride program, I won't stop you. But there is an application process, and you would have to be selected in order to go to my world. And even then, the financial reward wouldn't be enough to bail your family out for long."

"I don't know what to do." Summer sighed and looked around. "Why is there a bride program? Do you not like your own women?"

The Terran tilted his head to study her. "You know nothing of my world or why my people are here?"

"No. I'm sure it was on the news or something, but I was still in high school when you came to our world. I'm afraid I didn't pay much attention at the time."

"There are very few women on my world. And the last generation who mated with Terran females produced only male offspring. We had to look outside our world for mates, and Earth women seem to appeal to us the most. There are other alien species out there who are compatible, but very few of my kind have selected them as brides." He took a sip of his drink. "Could you see yourself mated to one of us?"

"I guess I don't understand the question. If you say we're compatible, you must be like human men except your coloring." Her cheeks flushed.

"Have you ever seen a naked male?" he asked, his lips twitching in amusement.

"Of course, I have." She tipped her chin up. "Plenty of them."

He chuckled, and she knew he didn't believe a word she was saying. She nibbled her lower lip and took a swallow of her hot chocolate. Who was she kidding? She'd not only never seen a naked guy before, but she'd barely even been kissed. Why would one of the handsome aliens want her? She tried not to stare and looked everywhere but at Vordro. She'd never seen a man who looked like him before and not because of his coloring. He reminded her a little of her long-time celebrity crush, Adrien Brody, just with more muscles.

"So, what was your backup plan?" he asked.

"I didn't have one."

"What type of jobs have you had in the past?"

"Fast-food places, a laundromat, answering phones at a hotel. I have this problem with getting places on time, so my jobs never last very long. My car isn't very dependable, and it takes me a little while to get it cranked sometimes." She shrugged. "I do my best, but employers want more."

"Do you know how to cook and clean?" he asked.

"I'm not a gourmet chef, but I know my way around a kitchen. I can make simple things, and I'm good at following a recipe."

"I have a house on the other side of town. It's not overly large, I don't think, but I could use some help. I work a lot of hours here, and when I get home, I don't feel much like cleaning. And I haven't quite grasped cooking human food just yet."

She sat up a little straighter. "You want to hire me to take care of your house and cook for you?"

"It's a little more than that. I would like to have a live-in housekeeper. I would expect you also to eat whatever you cooked, and I would provide a room for you. Whatever salary we agree upon you could use however you wished."

"You mean I could help my family." She bit her lip. It was a tempting offer. "When would I start?"

"Tonight."

Her eyes widened. It wasn't much time to think it over, but she wasn't certain when she'd get a better offer. She'd never lived away from home before, but she didn't think the alien would hurt her. He seemed kind, even if his bulging biceps did look like he could snap her in two if he wished to do so.

"What do you say, Summer? Will you come work for me?" he asked.

"What about when you start dating or get married?

Your new wife won't want me underfoot anymore."

Amusement flared in his eyes. "I've been on your world for years without finding a mate. I don't believe I will find one anytime soon. I honestly don't have time to search for one. I spend most of my time here."

For some reason, it pleased her that there wouldn't be a future Mrs. Vordro anytime soon. Not that a guy like him would ever look at her romantically. She was thankful for the opportunity he was giving her. Only an idiot would turn him down, but she wondered what her parents would say about it. Maybe if they knew she was doing it for them… Her dad tended to be overprotective, and she knew he would worry about her safety.

"I'm off duty today," Vordro said. "I was merely helping out on my off day, but if you would like to come work for me, I will follow you so your parents can meet me."

"You'd do that?"

He nodded. "If I had a young daughter moving in with a strange male, I would want to meet him. Besides, you might need help getting your things loaded into your car."

"I don't have much," she admitted. "Just one small bag."

He frowned but didn't say anything. Instead, he stood and held out a hand to her. Summer slid her fingers against his and let him haul her to her feet. A thrill ran through her at his touch, but she tried to tamp down the feelings. No sense getting a crush on her new boss, but it was going to be hard not to have any fantasies about him.

Summer followed him out to the parking lot, and he held open her car door for her. Once she was buckled, she pulled out of the parking space and then waited near the entrance for Vordro. A large, black SUV pulled up behind her, and a lavender hand waved to her out of the driver's-side window. She pulled forward and drove to her aunt's house.

She had no idea how her family would react to Vordro, or her new job, but she hoped like hell they didn't embarrass her. Her aunt had a small home on a barely respectable street in the older part of town. The surrounding streets looked more like a war zone, but her aunt swore it was safe to stay with her. Summer had her doubts.

She pulled up to the curb in front of the one-story home and waved to her family, gathered on the front porch. If she'd wanted time to come up with a compelling argument about her new job, she was out of luck. Summer got out of her car, wincing as the door creaked when she shut it. Vordro had pulled up behind her and was now walking her way, his long legs eating up the ground. He paused beside her, his presence somehow comforting.

"Is that your family?" he asked with a nod toward the house.

"Yes. And let me just apologize up front for anything they may say or do. I promise they weren't raised in a zoo, but sometimes they act like poo-slinging monkeys."

His lips quirked up on one side. "Noted."

He placed a hand on her lower back as they made their way up the cracked walkway. Her father stood as they drew nearer. His eyes narrowed in distrust at Vordro, and Summer had a feeling she was about to have a fight on her hands. Her father didn't do well with change and didn't particularly like anyone who wasn't just like him. It had embarrassed her on more than one occasion over the years.

"What's he doing here?" her dad barked. "We don't want his kind here."

Her cheeks flamed, and she looked up at Vordro with an apology on her lips, but it died the moment she saw the look in his eyes. He looked fierce, every bit the warrior he was, and for a moment she worried he might go after her father. Attacking a Terran was not the smartest move, but she'd never claimed her father had much of a brain. He could be really sweet to his family, but he lacked common sense.

"Dad, this is Vordro. We met at the Terran Station, and I'm going to be living with him."

Her father's face turned purple, and he barreled off the porch. "Like hell! No daughter of mine is moving in with one of them."

"He's offered me a job, Dad."

Her father puffed up. "I know just what kind of work he has in mind. I forbid you to go."

Summer pushed her shoulders back and faced off against her father. Her mother sat on the porch, wringing her hands, while her aunt looked on with some amusement on her face. Nice to know this rather public family spat was entertaining someone.

"Dad, he's offered me a job, and I've accepted. Whether you like it or not, I'm going to get my things and go with him."

"We paid for that car of yours. You can't take it with you. For that matter, we paid for everything you own. You leave, you're leaving with the clothes on your back."

Shock held her still as her breath froze in her lungs.

"You're disowning your daughter?" Vordro asked. "Because she shows tolerance for those who aren't like her?"

"If she walks out of here with you, she can never come back," her father said.

Her mother gave a little cry as she watched but said nothing. Summer knew that if she left, if her father refused to see her ever again, that he would make sure her mother did the same. If she left with Vordro, she agreed never to see her family again. It would be the same as if she'd moved to another world like she'd originally planned. The entire reason she'd not signed up for the bride program was so she could be near her family, and now they were telling her they didn't want her?

"I took this job for you, Dad. For you and Mom. I'll make enough that I can help you save for another place or another car." Summer held out her hand and let it fall when her father gave her a stony glare.

"I won't accept money from him."

Vordro rubbed her back. "If you wish to reconsider, I will understand. I don't want to separate you from your family."

Her aunt came down the porch steps and stopped a few feet away. "You can't live your life for your family, Summer. You can either sleep on the lumpy couch in my living room until your family can get back on their feet, or you can accept the offer of this Terran and start a life of your own. You can't always please everyone, but if you're going to try, start by pleasing yourself."

"But if I leave, I'll never see them again." Tears slipped down her cheeks. "What if I can't make it on my own?"

"Dear girl, you have your shit together better than either of your parents. You're going to do just fine." Her gaze strayed to Vordro. "Besides, I have a feeling someone will be watching out for you."

"I love them," Summer said.

"They know it. And your father can't be a stubborn ass forever." Her aunt smiled. "Give him a little time, and he'll come around."

She looked at her parents one last time, then turned her back on the only life she'd ever known. Vordro reached down and took her hand, leading her to his SUV. He opened the passenger door and helped her in before walking around the front. He paused before getting in, giving her family a long look. When he slid behind the steering wheel, she gazed at him tearfully.

"What am I supposed to do now?" she asked.

"Now, we're going to go buy you the essentials you need. Then I'm going to show you around your new home. I think, for tonight, we'll eat out. You can start your duties tomorrow." He turned on the engine. "You're sure this is what you want?"

She nodded and fought not to look out the window at her parents, assuming they were even still there. As the SUV pulled away, her resolved cracked, and she looked. The yard and porch were empty. They hadn't even stayed outside to watch her leave. She was truly alone. Despite everything she'd been willing to do for her family, they'd abandoned her, tossed her out like trash just because she refused to be a racist. She hoped one day her father would change his ways, but she didn't hold out hope it would be any time soon.

Wiping away her tears, she blew out a breath and determined that her life was going to be awesome, even if she was alone. Vordro reached over and gave her hand a squeeze. She held onto his hand and tried to muster a smile for him.

Maybe she wasn't completely alone.

Chapter Two

Vordro had held his temper in check when Summer's father had been spouting off. He'd done it for her. If he'd faced the man alone, his fist would have met the stupid human's chin and knocked him out. He'd dealt with his share of prejudice since coming to Earth, but he'd thought people were more accepting now. It had been over five years since the first Terran had settled on Earth in this area. They were no threat to the humans; if anything, they were an asset. While their presence did make Earth more noticeable to other alien races, no one would dare harm the little planet while his people were living here.

Summer looked so small in his SUV. The way her body curled in on itself told him she was sad about losing her family, and yet she'd still chosen to come with him. He'd been prepared for her to stay with them, but she'd surprised him. The protective feelings rising inside of him were ridiculous. The human was far too young for him, but it didn't stop him from admiring her sweetly curved body. She was petite, barely reaching his shoulder. Maybe it was her size that made him want to care for her. The moment she'd entered the Terran Station, he'd felt an urge to pull her into his arms and shelter her from the world.

And then she'd fallen apart, and his heart had broken for her.

When he pulled into the parking lot of one of the big-box stores in town, she took note of her surroundings and looked at him in confusion. Did the silly woman think he was going to make her do without just because her father hadn't allowed her to have any of her possessions? She might technically be his employee, but he would treat her with the same care he would a mate. After everything she'd been through, it was the least he could do.

"Why are we here?" she asked.

"You need clothing and other items. This place should have everything you could want or need."

"I know you said we'd get essentials, but I don't expect you to buy things for me. And I certainly didn't expect anything more than something from the dollar store."

Vordro reached out and gently touched her jaw, her skin feeling silky against his callused fingertips. "Let me take care of you. I'm still going to pay you a fair wage for the work you'll do for me, but I don't expect you to do without the necessities until your first payment."

She blinked back tears and nodded, almost as if no one had ever taken care of her before. He wondered how much her family had done for her, and just how much she had done for them. It was a parent's job to care for their children, especially daughters. Had hers failed her? It angered him that she'd had to face such hardship so early in her life. She was still young and should be looking forward to life, not worrying whether or not her parents had a place to live.

As they approached the doors of the store, he placed a hand on her hip, guiding her along. Perhaps it might have been the warrior in him wanting to stake a claim for all the stupid human males looking at Summer in a way that made him want to bare his teeth at them. It was apparent that human males didn't know how to care for a woman. When she was ready for a mate, he'd introduce her to some of his younger single friends. Maybe by then he'd have his urges under control and wouldn't picture her in his bed.

When they walked inside, he urged Summer to get a shopping cart, and he started in the beauty section. It was more difficult than he'd thought to get her to pick simple things like shower gel and shampoo. After a bit of cajoling, he convinced her that she wasn't going to empty his account if she purchased the items she needed. He'd noticed she wore makeup, even though he thought she didn't need it. She picked up a few items in that section before the real battle began.

"I don't need more than two or three outfits," she argued. "I can wash what I buy and wear it again."

"You should at least have a week's worth of clothes, maybe more. You'll need things for when you're working around the house, and other outfits for going out."

"I don't date," she said with a flush on her cheeks.

"What if I want you to go somewhere with me? Would you wear any of these outfits to a nice dinner or out to a movie?" he asked.

She looked at the items in her cart and slowly shook her head. "But I don't expect you to take me places. I work for you; it's not like we're dating."

She was right, but he didn't like it.

"Summer, if you don't pick out things you like, I'm going to memorize your sizes and buy things for you when you aren't with me. Do you want to see the kinds of things I'd purchase, or do you want to pick out your own clothes?"

She finally relented and added more items to the shopping cart, including three dresses. The shoe department was another fight, but he prevailed, and they left with two pairs and some of those ridiculous flip-flop things. He'd tried to convince her to get something better, something she could run in if trouble came her way, but she'd refused. In the end, he'd given in and secretly planned to buy her more shoes when she wasn't with him. If she wouldn't see reason, he'd just have to work on her.

At the register, the clerk gave him the total, and Summer blanched. Before she could say one word about it being too much, he swiped his bank card and paid for the purchases. He piled the sacks into the cart and began pushing it toward the parking lot. Summer took two steps for every one of his, and he slowed his pace. He loaded the bags into the back of his SUV, then put the cart away. Summer sat in the passenger seat watching him, and he wondered how ridiculous it looked for a leather-wearing alien to do something so mundane as shop at a store like this one.

When he got into the SUV, she gave him a hesitant smile.

"Thank you, for getting all that stuff for me. I'd have been fine without it, but I appreciate it."

"You're not going to do without while you're living with me. I get the feeling you aren't used to someone taking care of you."

"My parents did their best, but my dad is hard to work with, so he doesn't get the better-paying projects at work. No one wants to deal with him, and I can understand. You saw what he's like, and Mom doesn't work. Not in the getting paid sense. She does plenty around the house and for the family, but it doesn't help pay the bills."

"So you take up the slack," he observed.

"Yes. I have since I turned fifteen and was able to get my first job. I've just had a lot of them since then. I'm not exactly known for being reliable around town. I'm surprised anyone is still willing to give me a chance."

"I'm not going to fire you," he said. "There's not a particular time you need to start your day. I usually get breakfast at the Terran Station when I get to work, so the only meal you need to worry about is dinner."

"I should have looked at cookbooks while we were at the store. I only know how to make a few things, and you'll get tired of them before too long."

He smiled. "We can get one tomorrow. For now, let's drop your things off at the house and get you situated, then we'll discuss dinner. To celebrate your new job and new home, we can eat anywhere you'd like."

"I don't need much. You can just go through a drive-thru."

"No, we aren't going through a drive-thru. You're going to have good food to eat. After the stressful day you've had, I'd imagine your body could use a good nutritious meal."

She sighed but didn't argue. He began to wonder if everything would be a battle with her. Oddly enough, it wasn't off-putting. He actually looked forward to what she might say or do next. Eventually, she'd get used to him buying her things.

When he pulled into his driveway at home, he looked over to gauge her reaction. His home was small compared to the places some of his friends owned. Being a warrior had paid well on his world, and being a guard on Earth paid almost as well. He could retire and easily have enough money to live his life comfortably on Earth. The government on Earth wanted warriors like him on their world and offered a very generous conversion rate for his Terran credits into the American dollars he used while he lived here. It nearly doubled his money.

"This is where you live?" she asked, her eyes wide. "I thought you said your home was small."

He tried to see it through her eyes. To him, it seemed small enough. It was two stories with four bedrooms and three and a half bathrooms. When he'd purchased the place he'd hoped to fill it with children, but as the years passed he'd wondered if it would ever happen. When he'd agreed to move to Earth to work at the station, he'd thought his chances of finding a mate would increase. There were countless single females in the area, but he had yet to find one to bond with. Maybe he was too picky, but it seemed like most just wanted to have bragging rights about being with one of his kind, and he wanted more than that out of a relationship.

"It's small compared to the homes of most I claim as

friends."

She shook her head and slipped out of the vehicle. Vordro gathered the bags from the back and walked up the steps to let her in. He should have parked in the garage, but he'd wanted her to have a good look at the house. He was proud of his home, and he hoped she'd be happy here.

He opened the door and turned off the alarm, ushering her inside. She moved slowly, walking room to room, taking everything in. When she'd finished exploring the downstairs, he led her to the upstairs rooms and let her pick which bedroom she wanted. The fact she chose the one next to his would torture him as she slept so close and yet so far away.

He put her things in a sunny, yellow bedroom and left her to organize her new belongings. There was only one bathroom in that hall, but it was all hers while she stayed with him. He had his own attached to his bedroom. The other full bath was downstairs, but he'd turned the second master suite into a lounge for when his friends came over.

Vordro kept himself busy downstairs while Summer settled into her home. When she came downstairs, wearing one of her new dresses, he smiled. She looked beautiful, but he wasn't sure if he should say anything. Technically, he was her employer, and he damn well needed to remember that. Going to dinner tonight wasn't a date, even if it did feel a little like one.

"How do you feel about steak?" he asked.

"It was always a treat at our house, mostly when Mom found it on sale at the store. She'd marinate it all day, and then Dad would grill it when he got home."

"I was thinking more along the lines of Stan's Steakhouse. If you don't want steak, they have really good burgers too."

"You don't have to spend a lot of money on me,

Vordro. You've already done so much for me."

He curled his fingers into fists to keep from reaching for her. "Then let me do one more. Have dinner with me at Stan's. If you don't see anything on the menu you like, we'll go somewhere else. But I think you'll really like it if you give it a chance."

"We can go wherever you'd like."

It bothered him that she wasn't brave enough to ask for what she wanted. No, to demand it. Living with her bastard of a father had done a number on her. It was his hope that living away from that horrible man would help her come out of her shell some more. She reminded him of a turtle, afraid to poke her head out. She'd been willing to sacrifice her happiness for her family, but when it came to asking for things for herself she clammed up. He wondered if she didn't feel worthy, and vowed to make sure that changed. He might not be able to claim her as his mate, but he could treat her like the treasure she was, and maybe she'd start to see herself that way too.

The fact he was insanely attracted to her baffled him. He'd always gone after strong women, and he supposed she was strong in her own way. She'd have done anything for her family, but being disowned by them had damaged her in some way. She had a lost look to her as she climbed into his SUV, and he wondered what it would take to make her smile again. A real smile that reached her eyes and made her cheeks hurt.

The restaurant was crowded when they arrived, and they had to wait for a table. Vordro sat next to her on the bench seat. A noisy group of college guys came in, whooping and hollering. Summer moved closer to him, pressing against his side. He reached for her hand, giving it a squeeze. He didn't know why the males made her nervous. Yes, they were obnoxious, but he didn't see anything wrong with them. He would suppose that to human females they were even attractive.

One of them broke away from the group and approached them. Vordro wasn't certain he liked the look in the male's eyes or the cold smile that spread across his lips. Was he about to be faced with another racist asshole? Two in one day seemed like a bit much. Surely, even his luck wasn't that rotten.

"If it isn't sweet Summer," the male drawled. "I'm surprised to see you in a place like this. Isn't Burger Barn more your style?"

Now he knew he didn't like the male.

Summer gripped his hand tighter. "Hi, Matt."

"Shouldn't you be scrubbing a toilet somewhere?"

Vordro stood, towering over the male. "You will not insult her again."

"Let me guess," the male called Matt said. "The only guy you can get to touch you is an alien. That's pathetic. Everyone knows these guys will take any willing woman. Have you become a willing woman, Summer?"

Vordro didn't even stop to think, he just hauled back his fist and let it fly, knocking the bastard on his ass. The hostess rushed over with a manager on her heels. Both look flustered, but Vordro knew they wouldn't ask him to leave. He'd been coming to this restaurant weekly since he'd arrived on Earth, and he always tipped well. If anyone was escorted out, it would be the trash at his feet.

"Mr. Vordro, I'm so sorry," the manager said. "I knew this group would be trouble when they walked in."

"He insulted Summer. The others didn't take part."

The manager nodded. "I'll see that he leaves and doesn't come back. I'm sorry your date was insulted. Your meals will be on the house tonight, both of them, and I won't take no for an answer. You're a dedicated customer, and you shouldn't have had to deal with something like this."

Summer stood and took Vordro's hand. "We don't have to leave?"

Vordro looked down at her. "He insulted you. He's lucky all I did was hit him once."

The male's friends came over and hauled him to his feet. After they were gone, Vordro and Summer sat back down to wait for a table. They didn't have to wait for long as the manager went to great lengths to keep them happy. Despite the fact their meal was being paid for, he still intended to tip well. They ordered their food and drinks, and he settled back to watch Summer, something he'd discovered he enjoyed.

She took in her surroundings before her gaze clashed with his. "This is a nice place."

"I come here about once a week. We can return anytime you'd like."

"Vordro, I work for you. I don't expect you to take me out to dinner every week, or ever again. Even if you don't eat at home some nights, that doesn't mean I can't. I'd imagine you'll want to go on dates on your nights off."

Oddly, the thought of dating someone other than the woman in front of him held little appeal. He didn't understand his mad attraction to her, but he was starting to wonder whether or not he wanted to fight it. Yet he thought she deserved someone closer to her age, someone who would want to take her dancing or whatever else young human females enjoyed.

"You do go on dates, don't you?" she asked when he didn't respond.

"I have in the past, but not lately. I've found that the human females interested in me either want the novelty of being with my kind or they are looking for someone to take care of them financially, and they couldn't care less about me. Anyone with a wallet or purple skin would suffice."

"That must be hard," she said softly. "I think they're idiots. You've been so kind to me. I can only imagine how well you would treat your wife or girlfriend."

He smiled a little. "We don't use those terms. I know humans have a marriage, but on my world, we have a mating approved by the council, and once we become a pair, nothing but death will separate us."

She smiled wistfully. "That sounds so nice. My parents have been together for twenty-one years, but I don't think they should be. They argue a lot, and I don't think either of them is happy."

"The human-Terran pairings I've witnessed have done well," he said. "But if that young male up front was any indication of your species, it's no wonder so many women want to be with my kind."

She winced. "Not everyone is like Matt. He's spoiled and thinks he should have whatever he wants."

"And he wants you."

She shrugged. "At one point he did, and I said no. He tried to force the issue until someone intervened."

A rage-filled haze settled over him. "You mean he was going to force you?"

She nodded as if it were a typical discussion, as if things like that happened to her all the time. It was enough to make him want to bash heads. How could anyone want to harm the sweet woman across from him? From what he'd seen, she didn't have a mean bone in her body. If anything, she needed to learn to be more assertive. He'd be willing to bet that people took advantage of her all the time.

"Summer, if anyone tries to hurt you again, I want you to tell me. You shouldn't have to put up with males like that, or with verbal abuse from your family. You deserve better than that."

She looked at him in surprise, as if no one had ever told her such a thing. It made him question the intelligence of the human race, that she'd been so ill-treated her entire life without anyone stepping in to help.

If she'd gone to his world like she'd planned, he had no doubt she'd have had her choice of mates. Once they realized how sweet she was, they'd have fought over her.

He didn't know how long he could convince her to stay with him, but he would enjoy her company while it lasted. And when she moved on or settled down with someone, he would wish her well, even if it left him feeling empty. She'd only been in his life a few hours, and already his world was brighter for having met her.

Their food arrived, and he smiled as he saw the joy on Summer's face with her first bite. He had to admit the food was always excellent here. They enjoyed their meal, and he enjoyed the conversation even more. He found her to be witty, and quite sweet. They ordered dessert, which he insisted on paying for, and then they headed home.

When they got to the house, he wasn't sure how to act around Summer. She was his employee, and yet she felt more like a guest. One he wanted to keep. When she turned in for the night, she stood on tiptoe and lightly brushed her lips against his cheek.

"Thank you, for everything," she said softly. "I promise you won't be sorry for giving me a chance."

The only thing he was sorry about was suggesting she work for him. He should have just asked her to move in to see if they would suit as a mated pair. Despite his brain telling him that he was way too old for her, he couldn't deny the way his body reacted to her. But even more, he worried that with time, he would lose his heart to her. Summer was everything he'd been looking for in a mate, and she was out of reach.

Or was she?

Chapter Three

When Summer woke the next morning, Vordro was already gone. He'd left her a note with the number for the Terran Station and one for his cell phone. She doubted she would have much reason to call him, but it was nice to know she could reach him if she needed to. She found the cleaning supplies scattered around the house and hesitated only a moment before she reorganized so that everything was grouped together. The bathroom cleaners were stored under the sink in the downstairs half-bath, kitchen cleaners under the kitchen sink, and anything extra she stored upstairs in the hall bath.

His house wasn't messy, not like a lot of single men's homes she'd seen in the past during the handful of times she'd been invited somewhere. And unlike them, Vordro seemed to have good aim because his bathroom floors and toilet seats weren't sticky, for which she was eternally grateful. There was nothing nastier than cleaning a careless man's toilet.

Summer spent her morning scrubbing the bathrooms and kitchen before taking a break for lunch. She hadn't thought to ask about groceries, and discovered his refrigerator was almost empty. Without a car, she was well and truly stuck. Her bank account only had about thirty dollars left from her last sad attempt at working so ordering out wasn't going to work.

Her stomach rumbled, forcing her to take action. She picked up the phone and called Vordro's cell phone, hoping he would answer. Was he allowed to talk on the phone at work? She didn't want to get him into trouble.

"Summer? Is everything all right?" he asked when he answered.

"Um, I need to go to the grocery store, but I don't have a car or enough cash to cover it. There's not much here to eat. There's no way I can make dinner with what you have in the fridge."

He cursed. "And you have nothing to eat for lunch. I'll have something delivered for you, and we'll go to the store when I get off work tonight. Are you allergic to anything or do you have a special request?"

"Anything is fine, and no, I'm not allergic to anything."

"I'll place an order now, so listen for the doorbell in about twenty minutes or so. Tell them a tip is included."

"Thank you, Vordro."

"I'll have to come up with a way for you to handle monthly expenses like groceries without having to ask for money every time. We'll discuss it more tonight. If you need anything else, let me know."

She thanked him again and disconnected the call.

While she waited for her food to arrive, she vacuumed the area rugs on the lower floor and gave the stairs a baleful glare. She wasn't looking forward to vacuuming those or hauling the machine up to the second floor. She hadn't seen a second vacuum cleaner up there, though, when she'd been snooping in closets and cabinets. Vordro was such a big guy the machine probably felt like it weighed half a pound to him.

The doorbell rang, and she rushed to answer it. A man stood on the other side holding a sack from Mr. Wong's. The smell nearly took her to her knees. The last time she'd eaten Chinese, it had come from the freezer section of the grocery store, but whatever was in the bag smelled incredible. She accepted the sack and let the man know the tip had been included with payment, thanked him, and practically ran to the kitchen with her prize.

When she unrolled the sack, the smell was even stronger, and her mouth started to water. Summer pulled out a tray of orange chicken, a container of chicken fried rice, and two egg rolls. There was no way she'd eat everything by herself, but she was going to do her best to put a decent-sized dent in it. For the last few weeks, her family had been surviving off PB&J sandwiches, ramen noodles, and the occasional can of Spam. Between the extravagant meal last night and now the Chinese, she was getting spoiled. Would every day be like this with Vordro? She found it hard to believe no one had wanted him for more than his money or looks. Any woman would be lucky to have a guy like him. She could tell he was the type to take care of those around him, and just knew he would make a wonderful husband.

Her lunch settled in her stomach, making her feel drowsy and content. She put the leftovers in the fridge and settled on the couch to watch TV for a little while. The house was pretty clean, and if she did everything in one day she'd have nothing to do the rest of the week. Tomorrow she'd tackle the laundry and bedrooms. As daytime TV -- which completely sucked -- droned on, Summer closed her eyes. She told herself it would just be for a moment, but the stress she'd been under the past week or so finally caught up to her, and she ended up sleeping far longer than she'd planned. The next time her eyes opened, Vordro was smoothing her hair back from her face.

"I hated to wake you," he said.

"I'm glad you did. I only meant to take a short nap, but I guess I was more tired than I thought."

"Did you not sleep well last night? I know being in a strange place sometimes has that effect on people."

She shook her head. "I slept fine, but I guess I've just been so worried since I found out we were losing the house that the stress caught up to me. I'll be fine, though."

"Are you ready to go the grocery store or would you prefer to put it off another day? We could order in tonight, and I could have lunch delivered again tomorrow," he offered.

As tempting as that sounded, she didn't want to take advantage of him. She shook her head and stood up, swaying a little until the room stopped spinning. He frowned at her and felt her forehead.

"I'm fine," she assured him. "I probably just stood up too fast."

"When's the last time you saw a doctor?" he asked.

"A while ago," she admitted.

"Tomorrow, you should ride to work with me so the doctor at the station can check you out. Typically, they only treat brides or potential brides, but I think they will make an exception this time."

"I'm fine," she insisted again. "Really. Humans sometimes get dizzy if we stand up too fast. I'm sure that's all it is."

He looked like he was going to argue, but she placed a hand on his arm. His gaze dropped to where her fingers curled around his biceps, and she could have sworn she saw heat flare in his eyes. She scoffed at herself. There was no way a guy like Vordro would be interested in someone like her. He could have his pick of any woman in the world, so why select someone penniless like her?

"I would still prefer a doctor see you," he said.

"If I feel the slightest bit sick, you'll be the first to know."

He nodded and grasped her hand, leading her out of the house. The grocery store they went to wasn't far from his house and carried a lot of organic foods. She couldn't believe the prices, but Vordro didn't seem to mind. If she'd thought he was going to stock the house with canned goods, she would have been mistaken. He filled the cart with fresh veggies and fruits and selected the best cuts of meat. If she ate every meal with him, she was going to eat better than she ever had before.

Her eyes widened at the checkout when the cashier gave him the total. It didn't seem to bother Vordro, though, as he swiped his card and paid for everything. They loaded the bags into the back of the SUV and then went home. She had no idea what she would make for dinner out of the bags of goodies, but it was bound to be good. She'd told him she could only make simple things, though, and some of the items he'd purchased she'd never bought before. Like eggplant. How was she supposed to cook eggplant? Or asparagus?

Vordro brought the bags into the house, and she helped him put everything away. The clock on the microwave said it was nearly seven o'clock, which meant they were going to eat late. She hoped he didn't plan to go to bed early tonight. As she was perusing the contents of the fridge, she felt his hands clasp her hips and draw her away.

"What are you doing?" he asked.

"Figuring out what to make for dinner."

He shook his head. "It's too late for you to cook tonight. Besides, I have a surprise that should arrive for you shortly. Why don't we step out onto the porch and enjoy the fresh air while we wait for it?"

He wanted to go outside at night? It was chilly out there once the sun started to set. October in Virginia could either be freezing or warm, but seldom in between. The days had been in the lower seventies and the nights in the fifties, but she knew a change was coming. The closer November got, the more likely the temps would drop, and they would see snow. Summer had always loved snow in the winter, but sometimes they just got way too much of it. And she'd never been a good driver when it came to icy roads. Those were the days she stayed home.

Vordro ushered her outside and motioned for her to have a seat on the small swing at the end of the porch. She'd scarcely noticed it last night. It swayed a little in the breeze as she lowered herself onto the wooden seat.

Vordro stood nearby, watching the road. She didn't have the faintest idea what this surprise was, but he seemed eager for to her to see it.

Two cars approached. One pulled into the driveway, and the other stopped at the curb. Summer couldn't imagine what they'd brought that would require two cars. Vordro was smiling as he held out a hand to help her off the swing. They walked down the porch steps as two men dressed in polos and khakis approached. One held a large manila envelope in his hands, which he gave to Vordro.

"Mr. Vordro, it's been a pleasure doing business with you. If there's anything you ever need or if you have any questions about your purchase, my card is in the envelope."

Vordro accepted the package and shook the man's hand. The other offered a wave, and they left together in the car parked on the curb. Were they leaving the first one behind? Summer wondered if she looked as confused as she felt. Vordro smiled as he opened the envelope and pulled out a set of keys, and then handed them to her.

"I don't understand," she said. "Why are you giving me keys?"

"You'll need reliable transportation for running household errands. It was only logical that I purchase a car for you to use."

Her jaw dropped. "You're giving me a car? I can't accept it!"

"Of course, you can. Think of it as a signing bonus for coming to work for me. It's unreasonable for you only to do the shopping on my off days, or having to wait for me to get off work before you can go somewhere."

"But..." She looked longingly at the cute little hatchback. It was far nicer than her old car. She didn't need to see the window sticker to know it was nice. She had a feeling he never did anything in half measures.

"Take the car, Summer," he said softly. "I'll worry about you if you don't have something sturdy to drive around. The crash test rating on this particular car is excellent, and it's last year's model so I got it for a lot less than sticker price. It even comes with a warranty that covers your oil changes and routine maintenance for the first three years."

She wanted to accept, badly.

He pulled out his wallet and handed her a gold Visa card.

"You're giving me a credit card too?" she asked.

"It's a prepaid card. I put enough on there to cover a month's expenses for the house, but if you run out, I can always add more. I thought it would be easier than carrying around large sums of cash."

She clutched the card and her new keys. Tears gathered at the corners of her eyes as she sniffled.

"I thought these things would make you happy," Vordro said.

"I am happy. No one has ever done anything like this for me before."

"I thought we'd grab something to eat while we're out tonight."

She looked up at him. "We're going out?"

"You want to test drive your car, don't you?" He smiled. "You get your purse, and I'll lock up the house when you're done. We can just get fast food tonight if you don't feel up to sitting in a restaurant."

"Burger Barn is pretty good," she said.

"Then take us to Burger Barn," Vordro said, as he followed her up the front door. She disappeared inside long enough to grab her jacket and her purse, then they walked back to her car and Vordro got in.

She wasn't entirely certain how he fit in there. She tried not to laugh when she got in. Even though his seat was pressed all the way back, his knees were practically in his chest. A snort escaped her, then another, and then she was full-out belly laughing.

He gave her an amused smile. "Maybe we could take the SUV, and you can test drive your car tomorrow."

"I think that might be a good idea."

She leaned across the console and brushed her lips against his cheek. "Thank you, for everything."

He nodded, his cheeks a slightly darker shade of purple than before, as he exited the car. They got into his SUV and went for burgers, opting to eat there instead of taking them home. Summer enjoyed her time with Vordro, wishing she could learn everything about him. He wasn't only the first Terran she'd ever spoken to, but he was the first guy ever to get her attention. She'd been on some dates, but no one had ever made her feel the way he did. Just one touch of his hand and she wanted to curl against him and beg him to kiss her until she couldn't breathe.

She couldn't help but wonder what it would be like to kiss a man like him. He was older, more mature, and knew what he wanted in life. She didn't know if aliens were as promiscuous as human teenage boys were, but something told her that he knew his way around a woman's body. The few guys she'd allowed to kiss her had always groped her, squeezing her too hard and sometimes leaving bruises. Vordro seemed like the type to have a gentle touch when it came to women.

Not that she'd ever get to find out.

After dinner, Vordro drove them home. She knew he had to be exhausted after working such a long shift. She knew little about his job and wondered if it would be prying if she asked.

"Whatever is on your mind, you may ask," he said as if reading her thoughts.

"I don't know much about your job. Do you always work twelve-hour shifts?"

"In the past, it hasn't been uncommon for me to work long hours. Now that I have someone at home waiting for me, I will ask for shorter shifts. I know those with families have asked for the standard human eight-hour shifts, but I think I would feel guilty if I worked so little."

"You don't have to shorten your hours for me," she said. "I'm just your employee, Vordro. I don't expect you to entertain me."

"You're in my care," he said. "Whether I'm paying you or not doesn't matter. It's my job to look after you. I never understood how your males could let single females wander around without protection. And before you get upset, I don't feel that females are inferior to males, but we are much bigger and stronger."

No one had really taken care of her since she'd become an adult. Her parents might have provided a roof over her head and food in the fridge, but that was as far as their support went. She'd never had a kind word from them, no encouragement, and she'd taken care of a lot of the household chores. She wasn't sure how she felt about it.

At the house, he pulled into the garage and let her into the house. He set the alarm on his SUV before locking up the house for the night. Summer went to her room to kick off her shoes and dressed her in pajamas, a cute tank, and Capri set with kittens on it that Vordro had purchased for her. It was the furthest thing from sexy, but she loved the way they felt. The cotton was super-soft.

As she came out of her room, she noticed Vordro's door was partially open. Through the crack, she watched as he pulled his T-shirt over his head, tossing it onto a chair across the room. She'd never get tired of seeing his broad chest and large biceps on display. When he reached for the button on his leather pants, she felt her cheeks flush and willed her feet to walk away. The creak of the leather drew her gaze, and she gasped as she realized he didn't wear underwear under those pants. Her gaze flew to his face, but he was still looking away from her.

Summer tried to tame her racing heart and hurried to the kitchen for a cup of tea. Anything to try to take her mind off what she'd seen. Her cheeks were still flushed when he entered the kitchen a little while later, his hair soaked from a shower and a pair of lounge pants slung low on his waist. It should have been illegal for a man to look that damn sexy when he was dressed for bed. If he knew she'd been spying on him, he didn't say anything. He pulled a bottle of water from the fridge and a bag of popcorn from the pantry.

"Want to watch a movie with me?" he asked, shaking the bag. "It's kettle corn."

Summer smiled. "I'd love to."

And with some luck, she'd managed to look at the screen and not his naked chest and impressive abs. She hadn't realized men could get as ripped as Vordro was. Maybe it was his alien heritage because she'd certainly never seen his equal in human men. While the kettle corn popped, Summer finished off her cup of tea and got a bottle of water from the fridge. Vordro had purchased a few flavors for her to add to the bottles and she picked up the grape one, adding a few drops before screwing the top back on the water and shaking it.

"Ready when you are," she said, gripping the bottle tight in an effort not to reach out and trace the contours of his chest. How the hell was she supposed to live every day with a guy as hot as Vordro and not want to touch?

Chapter Four

Vordro was very aware of the small female sitting on the other side of the couch, a bowl of kettle corn between them. Their fingers would brush every once in a while, and he'd catch her blushing. While the pajamas she wore would be considered more cute than sexy, he couldn't help but admire the way her top clung to her breasts and the pants molded to her hips. She was a stunning woman and moving her into his home probably hadn't been the best idea. She made him want things he couldn't have.

He didn't have a clue what was happening with the movie. There was some action and a bit of romance, but other than that he couldn't say much about it. While it had been his pick, he found himself more interested in the woman watching the TV than what was actually *on* the TV. She finished her drink, a little dribbling from the corner of her mouth, and he fought the urge to lean over and lap the hint of grape-colored water from her soft skin.

After the first time she'd licked a drop of water off the lip of the bottle, he'd had to place a pillow over his lap to hide the fact he was more than a little aroused by her. What would she think if she knew the effect she had on him? Would it send her running to her room, to pack as fast as she could, or was there a chance that she was just as interested in him? He'd caught her peeking a few times, her cheeks flushing as she quickly looked back the screen.

The credits rolled at the end of the movie and he changed the channel, freezing when he realized he'd accidentally entered the number for one of those porn stations humans seemed to like. He'd asked for them to be included when he'd signed up for cable on the off-chance he could learn what human females liked. Summer's audible gasp had him fumbling with the remote, but in his haste, he only managed to turn it up louder.

Fuck! Why wouldn't his fingers hit the right buttons?

He managed to change it to an appropriate station and glanced at her. Summer's jaw was dropped, her eyes wide as she slowly turned to look at him.

"That was a complete accident," he assured her.

"Is that even possible?" she asked.

He frowned. "I assure you I didn't do it on purpose."

She waved a hand. "Not that. I meant what was on the screen. Is that even possible?"

Everything in him grew still as he pondered her question. The position the couple had been in wasn't a difficult one, and as something he'd frequently seen on the shows it seemed to him like something that would be common among humans, but she didn't know if it would work? Was she... His heart kicked in his chest.

"Summer, have you ever been with a male before?"

She slowly shook her head, her entire face red.

If he'd thought he had trouble keeping his hands off her before, now he wanted her even more. He'd never been with a female no one else had touched. What would it be like to know he was the only male who would have her? The urge to possess her welled inside of him until he clenched his hands into fists to keep from hauling her onto his lap.

"What you saw is rather common among humans, from what I've learned. Have you never seen a movie like that one?" he asked.

"No," she said softly. "I've always lived with my parents, so there really wasn't an opportunity. I've read some romances, though, and they do all sorts of things in those, but I figured it was just fiction."

He groaned and closed his eyes. His cock was pressing even harder against the pillow now. She had no idea what she was doing to him. Her innocence just made him want her more. Vordro thought of all the things he could teach her, the pleasure he could show her. When he opened his eyes, she was standing in front of him, her nipples poking through the thin material of her top. If she was trying to kill him, she was doing an excellent job.

"I've only had a few kisses," she said. "And I didn't like them."

"Why didn't you like them?" he asked, his voice hoarse from his need for her.

"They were sloppy, and the guys gripped me so tight they left bruises." She moved even closer, her knees brushing his. "I always thought kisses would be like the ones in the movies. I just wanted to experience it once, but I haven't yet."

He wondered if he looked as tortured as he felt.

"Would you…" She bit her lip. "Would you show me what a kiss is supposed to be like? I know you won't hurt me."

"You don't know what you're asking, Summer."

"I'm sorry." She took a step back. "I should have known… you aren't attracted to me. It's okay, I understand."

She thought he wasn't attracted to her? It was hell trying to keep his hands to himself, and here she was practically begging him to kiss her. He just wasn't sure he could stop at a kiss. Once he tasted her, Vordro was certain he would want more. She looked so sad as she moved farther away that before he could rethink things, he reached and grasped her wrist, tugging her closer.

Her eyes went wide as he pulled her down onto his lap, the pillow falling to the floor. Maybe if she felt how much he desired her, she wouldn't question his need for her again. His hands sifted through the strands of her hair as he brought her face closer. Her lips parted a moment before his brushed over hers. She tasted sweet, and her hesitant kiss was the best thing he'd ever experienced. He coaxed her into a deeper kiss, his tongue gliding along hers.

The way she squirmed on his lap made him question whether or not he'd manage to keep control of his wayward cock. Summer leaned into him farther, her hands curling over his shoulders. That slight touch was enough to inflame him. Vordro pulled away before he took things too far. Summer panted for breath, her eyes still closed, her lips moist and plump.

"If kisses feel like that," she said softly as she opened her eyes. "What does everything else feel like?"

"With you? It would be incredible."

She smiled, a dreamy look in her eyes, as she leaned against him, her arms winding around his neck. Vordro held her close, inhaling her sweet scent, and couldn't decide if he was in heaven or hell. No one had ever felt so right in his arms before, but Summer deserved more than what he could offer. Fifteen years was too big an age difference. Wasn't it? If her response to his kiss was any indication, the age difference didn't seem to matter to her. Could he forget about it too and just enjoy his time with her?

He set Summer away from him and abruptly stood, needing to put a little distance between them. She looked confused and a little hurt, but hurting her was the last thing he wanted to do. He reached out and ran his fingers through her hair, watching as she closed her eyes with a smile on her lips. If just that slight touch was enough to bring her happiness, what would happen if he ever took her to his bed?

"I'm going to get more drinks, and then we can watch something else," he said.

"You don't want me?" she asked.

"More than you'll ever know, but if tonight was your first real kiss, I think we need to take things slower than me hauling you off to the bedroom."

She pouted a little. "I might like getting hauled off to

the bedroom."

He couldn't help but smile as he went to retrieve some sodas for them. When he got back to the living room, Summer had already selected another movie. He sat down and handed her a drink, and she scooted closer. With her side pressed against his, Vordro had little choice but to put his arm around her. If anything, she snuggled even closer. It seemed their kiss had changed everything between them. He'd found with most human females that kissing was just an everyday type experience that didn't carry much weight in the scheme of things. The fact Summer was acting more like what he'd observed of human girlfriends showed her innocence.

With a bit of amusement, he wondered if sleeping together for her would mean they were married or getting married. Assuming they went with human tradition instead of just asking his council to give their blessing for a mating. What the hell was he thinking? Mating? Wedding? They'd shared one kiss. Yes, it had been a spectacular kiss, but still, they were a long way from being a mated couple. At least, in his mind they were. He had no idea what Summer was thinking and was almost afraid to ask. Vordro tried to pay attention to the movie, but with Summer's sweet curves pressed against him, he was having a hard time not kissing her again.

Slow, he reminded himself. What was that human term? She was a virgin. He didn't really know much about human females, except what he'd learned through working at the Terran Station and by watching TV. He'd been on dates since coming to Earth, but he'd never felt a connection to anyone before. With Summer, he wanted to shelter her, protect her, take care of her in any way possible. And she seemed like the type who would let him. The fact she'd shown up at the Terran Station to protect her family told him she had an independent streak, that she wanted to take care of others. But he had to wonder who took care of her. Her parents certainly didn't. If anything, she took care of them. He wondered how long that had been going on. How long had she taken on the role of the parent in their lives, with no one to watch out for her? How long had she shouldered the stress and responsibility for her family?

He hugged her tighter against him, determined to do right by her. He would take things as slowly as she'd allow, would help her in any way he could, and then he'd see where things led. For the first time since coming to Earth, he had hope that maybe the future he'd wanted might be within his grasp. And it all came down to the pint-sized woman by his side.

The movie went off, and he knew he should head to bed so he'd be rested for work the next day, but Summer lingered, and he didn't want to leave her alone. He felt compelled to stay by her side, if only for a little while longer. She stretched out along the couch and put her head on his lap, which conjured images of her plump lips wrapped around his cock.

"How long will you be at work tomorrow?" she asked.

"I'm scheduled for another twelve hours. I could ask to come home sooner if you'd prefer?"

"No, I don't want to mess up the schedule at the Terran Station. If they have you down for twelve hours, you should work it. I'll manage to keep myself occupied. There's more cleaning to do, and I can always watch TV if I need a break."

"What other things do you like to do when you're home?" he asked. "What about school? Don't women your age attend college?"

"I couldn't afford it, not even with scholarships. I could have taken out some loans, but I didn't want to pay them back for what would feel like forever. With the amount I would have had to borrow, I'd probably have been paying them back for twenty years or more."

"So, money is the only reason you didn't go to school?" he asked. It had puzzled him that humans spent so much time on education, and yet none of them were as advanced as his people. College seemed like a rite of passage for the human race, even though he knew not everyone went. But if Summer wanted to go, then he would make sure it happened.

She shrugged.

"If you had access to a computer and enough money to cover some classes, would you want to attend?"

"Vordro, you hired me to be your housekeeper. I'm not letting you pay for me to attend college. I appreciate the gesture. I really do. It's very sweet of you."

Vordro frowned. "I don't understand. Is it wrong that I wish to pay for you to continue your education? Isn't college something that humans are supposed to do?"

Summer patted her hand on his chest as she stared up at him. "College is something all teen humans are encouraged to attend when they finish high school, but it's just not feasible for everyone to attend, and some people just don't want to go. In my case, I wanted to go and couldn't afford it. For some, they're tired of school and are ready to get started on their lives, or maybe they excel at sports and join a professional team right out of high school. Some people don't have good enough grades to go, while others are like me and can't afford it. I think it's becoming more common for people to have a college education than it was thirty or forty years ago, but it's still not something everyone does."

"But if you want to go, why can't I pay for you?" Was this a stubborn human thing? It wasn't like he would miss the money. He didn't know how much something like that would cost, but it couldn't be too expensive, or no one would go.

"We aren't married, and you're not family. It wouldn't be right for me to accept that much money from you."

"What does it cost?"

"Over twenty thousand dollars per year and you generally go for four years. That's almost one hundred thousand dollars! I'm not letting you pay that much."

Vordro drummed his fingers on his thigh. It was more expensive than he'd thought. If this college education was expected of the young humans, why did it cost so much? On his world, education was free. Granted, instead of going to college they learned a trade, but his world didn't suffer for lack of schooling. In Vordro's opinion, people learned more by doing things than by reading books. The humans should figure out what they excelled in and then learn that after the required years of school. Maybe their world would have less poverty if everyone had a job, a purpose that would benefit all of mankind.

"So, how will you spend your time when you aren't cleaning?" he asked. "There isn't enough to do around here for you to stay busy all day every day."

"Well, I can watch TV."

"That's all you're going to do? It seems like a waste of time. There has to be something you enjoy."

She seemed to think about it for a minute. "I like to read. And I used to write poetry. I wasn't very good at it, though. It was just a hobby."

"What kind of books do you like to read?"

"Romances, mysteries, thrillers. Just about anything as long as it's fiction. I get enough of the real world already without reading non-fiction. I'm not really big on reading horror, though. I've tried a few, and they were okay, but I prefer scary movies to scary books."

"I admit, I haven't read much since coming to Earth. Perhaps you can show me your favorite books, and I can try them."

She smiled up at him. "I'd like that."

"I don't know about you, but I'm going to head to bed. Morning comes early. I don't expect you to get up when I do, so sleep as long as you'd like. If you need anything, don't hesitate to call me. If I'm unable to answer, I will call back as soon as I can."

"You'll be careful? I'm sure you get some interesting people who come through the station." She sat up and placed her hand on his thigh.

He brushed a kiss on the top of her head. "I'm always careful."

Vordro rose from the couch, missing the warmth of her body. He bade her goodnight and went to his room, knowing he wasn't going right to sleep. Even though he'd already showered for the night, he ran the water again. If he didn't release some of his sexual tension, he'd be awake all hours, thinking of the delectable woman sleeping one room away. He stripped out of his lounge pants and stepped under the spray. As the water beat down on him, his cock bobbed in front of him, the head a darker purple than the rest of his skin. Vordro gripped his shaft and stroked it. Slow, firm pulls of his hand. He added a little twist and pictured Summer on her knees at his feet, her lips parted and eager for his cock. He'd paint her lips with his cum if she were really here with him.

Vordro braced a hand on the wall as he fucked his fist, his hips thrusting faster and harder. His eyes slammed shut as he imagined Summer's delicate hands caressing his body. With a stifled cry, he came, jets of thick cum coating the shower wall and floor. When every drop had been wrung from his body, he released his cock and panted. It had been a long time since a woman had inspired him to pleasure himself. Something told him he had many more nights like this in his future until Summer was finally in his bed where she belonged.

Chapter Five

Summer blinked at the alien on the doorstep, laden with packages. He waited patiently for her to welcome him into the house and she did, stepping back to let him enter. He moved past her and set the packages just inside the door along the wall. She didn't understand where they'd come from, but the logo on one was from the local bookstore.

"What is all this, and who are you?" she asked.

"My name is Nyril, and I'm friends with Vordro. He asked me to purchase these things for you and drop them off."

She looked down at the packages. "He bought all of this for me?"

"He thought you might be bored. Since I'm intimately familiar with human novels, he asked me to stop by the bookstore. It just made sense for me to pick up the rest of the items."

Her brow furrowed. "I don't understand. How can you be intimately familiar with human novels?"

"I'm a writer. I studied the human language, both verbal and written, before coming to your world. On my world, we procure our books from other races, but I've always wanted to try writing my own book. When I came here, I was given the opportunity."

"You write?" she asked.

"Not typical of my kind. A few of us have decided to explore our creative sides. Have you heard of Liric?"

"The rock star?" she asked. "He didn't sing on your world?"

"Maybe as a hobby inside of his home, but we don't have that kind of entertainment where I come from. We work most of the day and when we relax in the evening, we usually read books we've purchased from other worlds, or we spend time with family and friends."

"It sounds… boring."

He laughed. "I supposed it could be for someone who has been offered so much like those on your world. I'm rather partial to movies and the music here. Another of my kind has taken up acting and has a big part in a new movie. I would imagine there will be others of my kind spreading their creative wings before long."

"What kind of books did you pick up for me?" she asked.

"Vordro said you liked romances, mysteries, and thrillers, so I picked up three new releases in each genre. If you've already read something, the receipt is in the bag, and it can be returned."

Summer nudged the bags with her foot. "And the rest of these?"

"One has cookbooks, in case you wanted to try new recipes. But Vordro said not to feel obligated, that he will happily eat whatever you fix. Another has some notebooks and packages of pens. He said you like to write poems and thought you might be able to make use of them."

"And the other two bags?" she asked.

"I picked up a few crafting-type things I thought you might want to try. If you don't, you can return the items. I've dated a few human females, and I tried to pay attention to their likes and dislikes. Both liked to knit, so I picked up everything you'd need to get started, including a how-to book. The other bag was Vordro's idea. There's a digital camera in there and the materials you would need to start a scrapbook."

"Vordro thought I might want to take up scrapbooking?"

Nyril scratched his chin. "Actually, he just asked me to get the camera, but I thought if you were going to take pictures you might want to do something with them. He said you were getting a fresh start on life, and I thought you might want to preserve the memories."

"Thank you." It was possibly the nicest thing anyone had ever done for her. Summer hugged him and then stepped back.

"Is there anything else you need before I leave? You have something for lunch?"

"Vordro made sure the kitchen was well-stocked, but thank you for asking. I'll just put this stuff away and then make something to eat. Did Vordro mention what time he was coming home?"

"I believe he gets off work at seven tonight. I'm sure he'll come straight home. He didn't mention anything about needing dinner held."

"Thank you again, for all of this," Summer said. "I know it was Vordro's money, but I appreciate you putting some thought into the items. I've never tried scrapbooking or knitting, but maybe I'll like them both."

Nyril pulled a business card out of his wallet and handed it to her. "That has my cell number on it. If you ever need something and can't reach Vordro, I hope you'll give me a call."

"I appreciate it."

He tipped his head to the side. "I don't suppose you have any single friends who are like you?"

Summer laughed. "No, I'm afraid not."

"Pity. Well, I'm off. Take care, Summer."

She locked up behind him and started hauling the sacks to her bedroom, except the cookbooks. She stored those in the kitchen. Summer had never thought to try a craft before, and she was a little excited about the prospect. No one in her family that she knew of had ever taken up knitting. The librarian in her home town would often knit behind her desk when all was quiet, or she had before she retired. She'd been ancient, and every time she'd climbed the ladder to reach the books on the top shelf, Summer had always worried she'd tumble off and break a hip or something.

Summer didn't want anything heavy for lunch, but she wanted something she could eat for more than one day. She decided on a pasta salad with Campanella, peas, diced carrots, mild cheddar cubes and diced ham, and tossed it all together with some Italian dressing. After fixing herself a plate, she put the leftovers in a Tupperware container and placed it in the fridge. She'd made enough to have it for lunch at least one or two more days. Or maybe she'd use the leftovers as a side dish for dinner later.

Sitting down with a glass of peach tea and her lunch, she marveled at how quiet the house was. Having grown up in a house where someone was always home, it was a little exciting to have the place to herself. Perhaps a little boring, but now that she had plenty to keep her occupied, she looked forward to her afternoon. She'd finished the cleaning and had done most of the laundry before Nyril had shown up.

Summer put her dishes in the dishwasher and then went to see which books Nyril had purchased for her. She'd been known to read two or three books in a day, so she'd have to be careful to space them out or she'd run out of reading material quickly. Maybe she could drive over to the library while Vordro was at work tomorrow and stock up. Now that she had a car, there was no stopping her. Well, unless it cost money. He'd given her the Visa card for home expenses, but she didn't think that included trips to the bookstore. Their library was small and she'd long ago read almost everything of interest. They only ordered a handful of new books a month.

All of the books Nyril had purchased were new to her. She couldn't wait to dive into them but took her time checking out the other bags as well. The scrapbooking sounded fun, and she pulled out the camera to read the instructions and get it set up. If it were spring, she'd take pictures of the garden in the backyard. She didn't know a lot about plants, but she thought a few looked like butterfly bushes.

By the time Summer settled in to read a book, the sun was already setting. She allowed herself an hour of reading time, and then she began preparations for dinner. The cookbooks actually proved helpful. She'd not had a clue what to do with all the fresh items Vordro had purchased, but after flipping through the books, she'd decided to make chicken marsala with the pasta salad and some honey-glazed carrots. She had everything she needed, and dinner finished just in time for Vordro to come home.

Summer set the table and fixed their plates. She'd just filled their glasses with peach tea when the front door opened and shut. Wiping her hands on her hips, she hurried out of the kitchen to greet Vordro. He smiled when he saw her, even though he looked weary. She wondered if he'd had a rough day, but wasn't certain it was her place to ask.

"Did you have a good day?" he asked. "Something smells incredible."

"I was just fixing our plates when you came home. Dinner is ready if you want to eat now. Or I can put your plate aside for later if you want to relax a little first."

"I'm starving, so dinner sounds amazing. Just let me wash up, and I'll join you in the kitchen."

Summer nodded and hurried back to their food, taking a seat and waiting for him. When he appeared in the doorway about fifteen minutes later, his hair was wet, and he was wearing a pair of athletic pants and a T-shirt. The casual look was a good one on him; she liked the way his shirt hugged his broad chest. He inhaled as he sat down and smiled at her.

"Everything looks and smells great, Summer."

"I hope you like it. I got the recipe out of one of the

cookbooks Nyril brought by earlier. There are a lot of recipes in there that look interesting. I saw one for an eggplant parmesan that I thought I might try tomorrow or the day after. I'm just undecided as to what would go best with it."

Vordro pointed to the bowl of pasta next to his plate. "What's this?"

"Pasta salad. If you don't like it, I won't make it again. It just sounded tempting today."

He took a bite, and his eyebrows went up. "It's really good."

"How was your day?" she asked, hoping it was a safe question. Often, her dad hadn't wanted to discuss his day at work, and some of those times he'd flown into a rage over the question.

"Hectic. We have a council member visiting for a few days, and he needs protection the entire time he's here. Especially when he leaves the Terran Station. I was scheduled to guard him for the last half the day, and he wanted to go out and explore."

"Is it common for your council to come here?"

"The council members are free to come and go as they please. It's the Chief Councilor who has to stay on our world. Although he did leave once, to retrieve his mate when she returned to Earth."

"He's married to a human?" she asked.

"Yes, a rather spectacular woman. She's mostly deaf, but it doesn't stop her from getting what she wants. And she wanted Borgoz badly. When she came back here, she was pregnant and scared."

"Poor woman," Summer murmured. "I'm glad things worked out for her."

"What did you do today?" Vordro asked.

"I set up the camera you bought for me, and I read. I also finished the cleaning and laundry." She smiled. "Thank you, by the way. I love everything Nyril brought over. And he has excellent taste in books."

"I sense a but in there."

"I read fast, and I read a lot. I'll devour those in about three or four days. But I thought, now that I have transportation, I could drive over to the library tomorrow and get a stack of books. While I prefer owning my books so I can read them over and over again, I don't mind borrowing them. If you tried to keep up with my reading appetite, you'd probably spend hundreds of dollars a month."

"I've been to the library here. It's rather nice. Will they have everything you need?"

She nodded.

"I hope you have a nice time, but please be careful on the roads. While we were out today, there was a particularly nasty accident. I'd hate for something to happen to you."

"I'm always a careful driver."

Vordro pushed his empty plate and bowl aside. "Dinner was excellent. Thank you for cooking."

"It's what you hired me to do."

He smiled a little. "Yes, but I didn't intend for you to do it every night. Whenever you want a break, just say the word, and we'll grab a bite out somewhere. I have no problem eating at restaurants; I was just tired of trying to eat my own cooking. I haven't mastered human cuisine very well, or that stupid stove. I tend to burn everything I cook."

"I enjoyed cooking today. Having so much stuff to cook, and all those great recipes, I don't think I'll run out of ideas or enthusiasm anytime soon."

"Good." Vordro stood. "Why don't I help you clear the table, and then we can settle in to watch a movie, or if you'd prefer to read that's fine too."

Summer felt warm from the inside out that he wanted to spend more time with her. Technically, she was the hired help. Even though she lived here with him, it didn't mean he had to keep her entertained. He was treating her more as a guest than an employee. It made her wonder if he'd offered her the job not because he really needed someone, but maybe because he'd liked her. She could hope anyway. The kiss they'd shared last night had certainly left an impression on her.

In the living room, Vordro set up a movie for them and then leaned back into the corner of the couch. Summer had a choice to make. She could sit a respectable distance away from him like she'd done last night until the kiss. Or she could curl up against his side the way she wanted to do. Was it wrong that she felt so completely crazy over him in such a short amount of time? A psychologist would probably have a theory about her quick attachment based off her home life. And maybe they would have been right. All she knew was that no one had ever treated her as well as Vordro did, and she'd never been kissed the way he kissed her. She wanted more.

Summer eased onto the couch and curled into his side. If he was surprised by her move, it didn't show. He lifted his arm and curled it around her body, bringing her closer. His clean, fresh scent teased her nose, and his abdomen clenched as her hand rested above his waistband. She didn't pay much attention to the movie, instead tuning into every shift of Vordro, and the growing tent in his pants. She smiled a little, loving the fact that she had such an effect on him. The question was, how did she get him to act on it?

Her fingers traced his abs through his shirt before sliding beneath to caress his warm skin. His breathing changed and she peeked up at him. His gaze was trained on the TV, but she'd be willing to bet he hadn't a clue as to what was on the screen. Summer sat up and swung a leg across his thighs, straddling him. Those purple eyes focused on her, and she licked her lips as she remembered the way he'd tasted last night. She'd never instigated a kiss before, but she was about to, and if the look in his eyes was any indication he wasn't going to stop her.

Summer leaned forward, her breasts brushing against him, as her mouth pressed against his. Vordro's hands came up to rest on her hips. She licked the seam of his lips until he opened, and then she slipped her tongue inside for a taste. The hard bulge beneath her made her want to squirm. Her clit throbbed, and she ached for him. Just because she'd never been with a man didn't mean she didn't have desires like anyone else. Granted, she'd never wanted someone the way she wanted Vordro. She had no doubt that he would leave her satisfied if she could get him into the bedroom.

She pulled away, panting heavily. "Please don't make me wait any longer."

Vordro squeezed her hips. "You don't know what you're asking. You've never been with a male before, Summer. What if I'm not the right one for you?"

"There's no one more perfect for me," she said. "I want to feel alive, Vordro. I want to feel… everything. I'm twenty years old, and I've never had an orgasm. I'm not asking you to marry me. Just show me what I've been missing."

He groaned and closed his eyes a moment. When he opened them again, he looked both turned on and tortured. Didn't all men want permission to have sex without the woman trying to tie them down? Wasn't she offering him every man's fantasy?

"I want you," she said softly. "I'm not going to change my mind, and the chances are good that I won't have the guts to ask you again. Please don't turn me away."

"What if I give you an orgasm? Will that suffice for

now?"

Her lips parted, and she nodded eagerly, happy that he'd at least partially agreed to her demands. She still wanted him, all of him, but maybe that would come soon enough. Maybe if he saw how great they could be together, then he'd want more from her. It didn't seem fair that he was going to give her an orgasm and wasn't asking for one in return. Did he worry she wouldn't be able to make him come? While she'd never given a blowjob before, she'd read enough about them that she thought she could pull it off. Or maybe his kind didn't like them.

His hands slipped from her hips and eased under her shirt. His fingers skimmed along her ribs until he was cupping her breasts. Her nipples pebbled and her panties grew damp just from that slight contact. She rocked against him, his hard cock rubbing against her in the most delicious way. Summer leaned into his touch, feeling an almost frantic need to remove her clothes. She wanted his touch skin to skin and not through layers.

Vordro popped the front clasp on her bra as if reading her thoughts. His thumbs flicked over the hardened peaks, drawing a gasp from her lips. No one had touched her breasts intimately. Summer had always worried her parents would walk in on her if she tried to pleasure herself, so she'd never bothered. Now she wondered what she'd been missing out on.

His touch was light as he teased and tormented, making her need grow. Summer's hands explored what she could reach of his body, wanting to give him as much pleasure as he was giving her. She continued to rock against him, her panties getting wetter by the minute. Her heart felt like it was going to pound out of her chest. Vordro's eyes were darker and intense as she gazed into them.

One of his hands slipped down her body and

teasingly traced the waistband of her pants. A moment later, he had them unbuttoned and unzipped, leaving Summer breathless as she thought about what was going to happen next. Her clothes felt too tight, and she wanted them off. Drawing away from him, she stripped out of her clothing, leaving it in a pile on the floor. Vordro's lips parted as his gaze caressed her from head to toe.

"You're trying to kill me," he said, his voice a soft growl.

Summer licked her lips. "I told you that I wanted you. You're the one who's holding back."

Vordro stood and lifted her into his arms. He carried her down the hall to his bedroom and pushed the door open with his foot. His bed was perfectly made until he eased her onto the mattress and mussed the comforter. She watched with a building hunger as he removed his clothes. Her cheeks burned, having never seen a naked man up close before, but she licked her lips as his cock bobbed in the most enticing way. He looked far too large to fit inside her, but she trusted him. If Vordro thought they would fit together, then she knew they would.

He knelt beside the bed, pulling her closer, her legs splayed on either side of him. No one had ever looked at her there before, except her doctor, and she was a little embarrassed. How did she compare to the other women he'd been with? His finger reached out and stroked her softly, making her want to spread her legs wider. When she felt a puff of his breath against her, she gasped and leaned up on her elbows.

"So soft and pretty," he said. "And no hair? I like it."

"I shave it off. It bothers me."

He leaned closer, and she froze.

"Wh-what are you doing?" she asked.

"I'm going to taste you, and I'm going to make you scream my name."

She was already close to doing that.

"Do you want me to stop?" he asked.

"No."

Summer flopped back onto the bed and tried to relax. Vordro's tongue traced the seam of her pussy before delving inside. Summer whimpered and gripped the comforter as he licked and sucked, driving her need higher and higher. When he drew her clit into his mouth, she nearly cried out from the sheer pleasure. It washed over her in waves until she was practically riding his face, chasing after… something. She'd never felt anything so incredible in her life.

Vordro spread her pussy open wider, and his sucking grew more intense until she was crying out his name and bucking beneath him. She saw stars and nearly forgot to breathe as her first orgasm ripped through her, leaving her boneless. Vordro placed a kiss on her pussy, then her hip, and her belly. He stood and stared down at her, a drop of cum leaking from the head of his cock.

"Do you still want me or are you satisfied for now?" he asked.

She couldn't tell what answer he was hoping for. If she said she wanted more, would he give it to her out of a sense of duty? Or did he truly want her? For all she knew, he would get hard with any naked woman lying in his bed.

"I want you," she said, knowing that if Vordro was her first, she would remember it forever. She only wished she could make him her only.

Vordro covered her body with his, the head of his cock rubbing against her pussy. Summer hooked her legs around his hips, giving him complete access to her body. She wanted him. From what she'd read, it was going to hurt, but being with Vordro would be worth a little pain.

He kissed her, and she tasted herself on his lips. Then his hips shifted, and she felt his cock ease inside of her. It burned as she stretched to accommodate him, and then he stilled. As he gazed down at her, there was an apology in his eyes as he thrust forward and claimed her innocence, making her cry out more in surprise than pain. It hurt, but nothing like what she'd expected.

As the ache dulled, she tried to urge him to move. His thrusts were shallow and slow, and then deeper. Nothing could have ever prepared her for the incredible feeling of having him inside of her. Vordro took his time, drawing out her pleasure until she thought she couldn't take another moment of it. He reached between their bodies and brushed his thumb over her clit.

Summer made a keening sound as she came a second time. As her release washed over her, Vordro pounded into her, taking her hard and fast until he found his own release. He didn't pull out of her right away, instead rolling them so she lay on top. She could feel his heart beating almost in time with hers, and she pressed kisses to his chest, jaw, and then his lips.

"I wanted to make it special for you," he said. "I didn't hurt you too much?"

"It was perfect," she said. "Thank you, Vordro. I'm so glad you were my first."

He muttered something she didn't catch, and she sighed with a happiness she'd never felt before. If only it could last... if only this was the beginning.

Chapter Six

The next morning, Vordro stared up at the ceiling as Summer slept on his chest. He'd taken her bare, not even asking if she was on birth control, not that it always worked when it came to Zelthranite sperm. Even condoms weren't foolproof. If she were pregnant... but would she tell him if she were? Or would she try to hide it and run from him? He hadn't exactly given her a reason to stay. He'd offered her pleasure, but nothing permanent. Had that been a mistake?

He was due at the Terran Station in an hour, but for once, he didn't want to go. He picked up the cell phone on his bedside table and sent a message to one of the guards at the station, asking them to cover his shift. In all the years he'd been on Earth, he'd never taken a day off unless he was scheduled for one. But today of all days seemed like a good time to stay home. He didn't know what to expect from Summer when she woke. Would she be clingy? Would she act like nothing had happened?

Not knowing what she wanted was hell. Did she want him to claim her? The last thing Vordro wanted to do was scare her off. He'd tried to take things slow, to give her time, but she hadn't wanted that. She'd wanted him. He smiled a little as he thought about her forwardness last night. It had taken him by surprise but in the best of ways. Now that she was in his bed, he'd like to keep her there. He could always ask if she'd stay in his room with him. Or should he go with his warrior's instincts and demand what he wanted?

Human females had been a puzzle since the first time he'd met one. They were all different, and not just in coloring but in temperament and desires. His people weren't all identical either, but the female Zelthranites tended to have similar temperaments. Of course, now the females of his world were dying out. All future females would be a hybrid of Zelthranite genes and whatever female the males paired off with. It had been a sad time for his world, but Vordro liked the human females and couldn't wait to claim one as his mate. He'd just never found the right one. They were pretty, but he'd never felt this consuming need to claim one until now.

He hoped it would be Summer.

Summer shifted and rolled off him, giving him the freedom to move. He rolled onto his side to watch her sleep for a few minutes and then got up to shower and get dressed. He closed the bathroom door so the sound of the water wouldn't disturb her sleep, then turned on the shower. Not having a plan for the day, he didn't know what to expect. He hoped Summer would be happy that he'd taken the day off, and thought they could explore the town a little, maybe go see the sights.

After his shower, he pulled on a pair of black leather pants and a black T-shirt. If there was a chill in the air he'd get out his jacket, but his kind didn't get cold as easily as humans did. Vordro brushed out his hair and dried it with a hairdryer. He didn't use one except in the morning, preferring to let his hair dry naturally, but it took forever.

By the time he finished and exited the bathroom, Summer was sitting up in bed rubbing her eyes sleepily. He smiled, thinking she looked too damn adorable for words, and then he walked across the room and sat on the edge of the bed.

"Is it time for you to leave for work?" she asked.

"I took the day off."

Her eyes widened in surprise. "Day off?"

"I thought we could go do something. If you're up for it, we could grab some breakfast out somewhere and then maybe see a museum or the zoo? We can do more than one thing. Whatever you want."

"I haven't been to either the Natural History

Museum or the zoo in a long time. Either would be amazing. Are you sure you won't get in trouble for taking time off?" she asked.

"I'm positive. In fact, I may take off tomorrow too."

Her mouth dropped open, and she seemed surprised, as if no one had ever done something like for her before. Was it really that shocking that he'd want to spend time with her? Or maybe she'd thought last night was a one-night stand. Whatever the case, he was going to prove to her that he could be an attentive mate if she'd give him a chance.

"So, why don't you shower and get ready," he said. "I'll wait for you in the living room."

He could feel her gaze on his back as he went to sit on the couch. He flicked on the TV and watched a movie to pass the time. When Summer stepped into the room, she was wearing jeans and a soft-looking sweater that molded to her curves. It was almost enough to make him ditch his idea of going out and instead spend the day in bed with her. She gave him a tentative smile as he stood and moved closer, leaning down to kiss her cheek.

"You look beautiful," he said.

"Thank you. Are we really going out?"

He nodded and ushered her out the door. Not knowing her preference for breakfast, he chose a restaurant that carried a little bit of everything. They had Southern-style food, traditional breakfast, and even some international choices. It was crowded, but not badly enough that they had to wait for a table. As was true with anywhere he went, there were a few people who stared. His kind had been on Earth for years, and still, they were treated like some exotic species whenever they went out in public.

It didn't seem to bother Summer, though, as she settled into the booth across from him. The waitress left menus with them and took their drink order, then hurried off. Left to peruse the breakfast choices, he found himself watching Summer more than looking at the menu. The sun streamed through the window, making red and gold highlights appear in her brown hair.

"What?" she asked, catching him staring.

"Just thinking about how beautiful you are."

Her cheeks warmed, and she smiled a little before looking back at her menu. When the waitress returned with their drinks, they placed their order. Vordro had ordered everything on the menu at some point, but his favorite was the sampler that came with three eggs, a ham steak, sausage links, three strips of bacon, grits, and hash browns. Summer's order seemed small in comparison, but she assured him it was plenty of food.

"What would you like to do today?" he asked as they waited for their food.

"It's hard to choose. What about the museum? I put my camera in my purse before we left so I can take pictures wherever we go."

"What if I took another day off tomorrow and we have another outing?"

"You're sure you won't get into trouble? You aren't just telling me it's okay but really you'll get written up?" she asked.

Honestly, Vordro would probably be reprimanded for taking off on such short notice, but it wasn't like he would lose his position. He was a revered warrior on his world. He'd seen his share of battles, had even become a prisoner of some nasty space pirates at one point. What was that human term? Hero. Yes, his people considered him a hero. The last thing his council would do was remove him from his position. He just needed to explain why he wanted the time off. If they knew he was courting a female, they would be more lenient.

"I'll call them later and make sure it's arranged. It shouldn't be a problem."

Unless the council member specifically requested his presence. Then it could be an issue, but Vordro didn't think that was likely.

After breakfast, they drove over to the Natural History Museum. Vordro had never been, even though he'd studied human history before moving to Earth. Seeing everything through Summer's eyes would be different, though. He paid for their admission, noting that he could get a membership for them if she decided to become his mate.

Vordro found the exhibit about early humans to be fascinating. There were skeleton copies from the first known humanoid all the way to present-day humans. Summer stopped to read each plaque and took pictures along the way. When they reached the wildlife exhibit, her eyes teared a little as she read the word "eliminated" on many of the exhibits.

"You don't like this part of the museum?" he asked.

"These animals used to live in the wild. Thanks to humans, they no longer have homes. Some have become extinct, and others are only alive thanks to zoos and wildlife sanctuaries. It's sad that we've lost so much beauty because of our greed."

He studied the stuffed creatures. "If you have DNA samples from the animals, why can't you recreate them?"

"Our scientists have made great strides in doing something like that, but there are a lot of animals that are lost to us forever. I've always preferred animals over people, so I guess it bothers me more than it does most people."

He nodded. After dealing with some unsavory humans, he could see where she might prefer the furry beasts. And yet, she didn't have a pet. Would she want one? He'd have to ask her about it later. If Summer wanted something, he intended to get it for her. While he'd never felt the need to own a living being, he understood having pets was a common practice for humans.

They moved on to more exhibits and Summer took more pictures, even a few with him. Then she dragged him over to a large gemstone display and asked a passing couple to take a picture of them together. He curled his arm around her waist and drew her close to his side and waited for the flash on her camera to go off. Was this what being a couple would be like?

Summer thanked the couple and took her camera back before taking him by the hand and tugging him toward yet another exhibit. He found the dinosaurs to be interesting and remembered a movie where someone had brought them back to life. Seeing the lifelike displays made him glad no one had actually pulled that one off. They looked fierce and had more teeth than he was comfortable with.

As they went through the last of the exhibits, Summer looked a little wistful.

"Did you have a nice time?" he asked.

"Yes, I just wish I could come back soon. I love this place. I think I'd come here every week if I could."

He led her over to the membership office, deciding to take a chance on her agreeing to become his mate at a later date. He inquired about the family plan, but since they didn't have children, the woman recommended purchasing two individual plans, which was actually cheaper. Vordro paid for the memberships, and Summer hugged him tight.

"Thank you," she said. "No one has ever done anything like this for me before."

"I want you to be happy, Summer. If coming here every week accomplishes that goal, then I want to make sure you can do it. And on the days I'm off, I'll come with you."

She hugged him again before they went out to the

parking lot. Several hours had passed, and Vordro was more than ready for lunch. He assumed Summer would be hungry as well. Wanting to treat her to a nice meal, he took her to Pesto's for pasta and seafood. Having missed the lunch hour rush, the place was nearly empty. Vordro requested a table near the window.

Summer opened her menu, and her jaw dropped. "We can't eat here."

"Are you allergic to something on the menu?"

"Yes. The prices."

He laughed and set his menu aside. "I wouldn't have brought you here if I couldn't afford it. Order whatever you'd like. If you can't decide, order two things. I want you to enjoy our day out, Summer."

"But everything costs so much," she said.

"Summer, stop looking at the prices and focus on the menu items. I don't care if you order the most expensive thing on the menu. I just want you to enjoy yourself. All right?"

She nodded.

"So, now I know you love museums. What else do you like to do?"

"Well, I've never been to an amusement park before. I've been to the zoo a few times and really liked it. I'd love to go to Washington D.C. sometime and see the Smithsonian. Or maybe go to the beach. I've never seen the ocean before."

She'd never seen the ocean? The beach was roughly two hours away, and there was no reason she shouldn't have gone. Except for money. It bothered him that she'd struggled so much she'd never been able to see the beach or go to the museum whenever she wanted. He decided he was going to make sure all her wishes came true, even if it meant taking a full week off from work. It would be worth it just to see her smile, and it wasn't like he would miss the money. While the humans who worked at the

Terran Station earned vacation time, it wasn't a common practice for the Zelthranites who worked there.

"Summer, I need to step outside for a moment. If the waitress returns, please tell her to give me just a few minutes."

"Everything okay?" she asked.

"Everything is fine. I just need to touch base with work for a moment."

She nodded and went back to looking over the menu. Vordro went outside and called the station. He explained that he was courting a human female and wanted more time with her. After making sure his schedule was clear for at least a week, he went back inside just in time to order lunch. He wasn't sure how he was going to tell Summer about their upcoming trip, but he'd figure things out. There was a large Terran Station in Washington D.C. that had suites for visiting Zelthranites. He just needed to make sure there was a suite available for them, and then he'd set up a trip to the Smithsonian. And after that, Virginia Beach.

Chapter Seven

Summer's nose had been glued to the car window from the moment D.C. had come into view until they pulled into the parking lot at the Terran Station. It was a massive glass structure that was six stories high and wide enough it nearly took up a city block. She'd never seen anything like it before and marveled at everything around her. Vordro carried their bags, and she tried to keep up with him. The receptionist greeted them warmly, perhaps a little too warmly. Summer nearly glared at the woman as she simpered over Vordro. There might have been a bit of teeth baring on Summer's part. She knew she didn't have the right to snatch the woman bald, but it was tempting.

"If there's *anything* you need during your stay," the woman said, "Please let me know. My name is Candy, and I'm here to service all of your needs."

Yeah, Summer just bet she'd like to service all his needs. Wench.

Vordro stared down his nose at her. "You're going to proposition me with my female standing right here beside me?"

Summer perked up a little at hearing him claim her as his woman. It made her heart skip a beat, and she couldn't help but smile.

The woman glanced at Summer and back at Vordro. "I only meant to offer…"

He growled, cutting her off. A guard standing nearby approached.

"Is there a problem, Vordro?" he asked.

"This female propositioned me with my female standing right by my side. You need to better train your workers, or perhaps this one needs to work elsewhere."

Summer could think of a few places she wouldn't mind the woman working. Cleaning toilets would be a good use of her time.

The guard nodded. "I'll see that it's taken care of, and I apologize for any upset your human may have felt over the incident."

Vordro gripped both bags with one hand so he could hold onto Summer. She wondered how the guard had known who he was, or if they had maybe been friends on their world. She figured now wasn't the time for questions, as Vordro still looked fierce. They approached a desk on the far right of the Terran Station and procured a key to a suite. Since he'd convinced her to sleep in his bed last night, she was assuming they would share a room again, but for all she knew the suite held two beds.

Vordro ushered her onto the elevator and pushed the button for the sixth floor. When it dinged and the doors slid open, Summer followed him down the hall to the door marked #602. He unlocked the door and pushed it open, motioning for her to step inside first. Summer's jaw nearly dropped at how gorgeous the suite was. There was a living area and kitchenette and then two open doors. One led to a decently sized bathroom and the other was the bedroom, with a massive bed.

"This place is really nice," she said, as she ran her hand over the back of the couch.

"It's reserved for high-ranking warriors. The council member suites are even nicer."

"You're a high-ranking warrior on your world?" she asked. "You never really talk about home."

"Earth is home now. There isn't much I miss about Zelthrane-3, to be honest. At least here, I'm not going off to fight in wars."

Her brow furrowed. "Your world isn't called Terran?"

"The council decided to call ourselves Terran when approaching Earth's government because they thought it didn't sound as fierce as Zelthranites. We wanted to be welcomed to your world, and so they chose a name they thought would make humans feel at ease."

"I guess I can understand why they would do that. Not all humans embrace change, and Terran makes you sound more human."

He held up his hand. "I don't think I could be mistaken for a human with this skin coloring."

She admired his lavender skin and remembered how sexy it had looked against her paleness. She had to admit that it made him stand out but in the best of ways. Summer thought their differences were amazing, especially since it was all on the surface. Where it counted, they were similar enough to make a relationship work, or so she thought. Convincing Vordro of that was another matter. He'd commented before on her age, and she wondered if it bothered him.

"You like me, don't you, Vordro?" she asked.

"What kind of silly question is that? Of course I like you. Do you think I take off work on go on trips with just anyone?"

"But you like me as more than just a friend."

He moved a little closer and stopped a few feet away. "Is something bothering you, Summer? If there's something you want to ask, don't hold back."

"It's just that we slept together, and you seem to like me, but I'm not sure what this relationship is to you, or if we even have one. Are we just pals hanging out and having a good time with some sex on the side? Or do you see us as a couple?"

Vordro took her hand. "You're more than just a friend, Summer. I care about you, and yes, I see us as a couple. I wasn't sure how you felt about that, though, with me being so much older than you."

"Age is just a number," she said with a smile. "All that matters is you like me, and I like you. I don't care what anyone else thinks, and you shouldn't either."

"There's a group of males we do need to worry about, though. My council would have to approve a mating between us. It's like marriage, but there's no ceremony. We get approval from my council, and they file the proper paperwork."

"So, no dress shopping or worry about where to seat the guests?" she asked.

"Not unless you wanted a human wedding." His hand tightened on hers. "Are you saying you wish to be mated to me?"

Summer nodded slowly. It was crazy, them having just met, but she felt like she'd known Vordro all her life. Being with him was easy and fun, and she wanted many more days with him. Forever, if he'd have her. She didn't care about human weddings. As long as they were together, that was all that mattered to her. She didn't even need an approved mating through his council. Although, she had a feeling that was something he wanted, or maybe even needed. And she wouldn't deny him that.

"You mean that?" he asked softly. "You wish to join your life with mine? Because we don't have divorce like humans do. If you agree to be mine, it's forever."

"I want that," she said. "More than anything."

He pulled her into his arms and kissed her long and deep. Summer's toes curled, and her hands fisted the back of his shirt. All it took was the touch of his lips on hers, and she wanted him. Vordro broke away, smiling down at her.

"Let's go downstairs and use a Vid-comm to speak to the council. We can ask for their approval now."

She smiled and nodded, anxious to get it out of the way.

Downstairs, they found an empty conference room with a Vid-comm, and Vordro placed the call. When the image on the screen came into focus, it showed a table with four Terrans seated around it. They were all dressed in black leather, except for one who wore all white.

"Chief Councilor Borgoz," Vordro said. "I hope this isn't a bad time."

"Not at all, Vordro. We just wrapped up some business and were about to leave, but we can stay a little longer."

"Chief Councilor, this is Summer, my chosen mate," he said, pulling Summer closer to his side. "We'd like to ask the council to bless a mating between us."

"Summer, would you like to tell us a little about yourself?" Borgoz asked. "Do you have family there?"

"Well, not here exactly. We're visiting Washington D.C. right now, but I have parents and an aunt back home," she said.

"And what do they think of your relationship with Vordro?" Borgoz asked.

Summer bit her lip and looked up at Vordro, who didn't seem too pleased with the question. She didn't want to lie, but she hoped her response wouldn't make the councilman deny their mating.

"My family isn't part of my life right now. My dad is very narrow-minded and even cruel at times. He told me never to return. I think I have my aunt's support, but neither she nor my mother will speak to me if my dad is around. They won't want to anger him."

"I see," Borgoz said, pursing his lips. "And if you have a child with Vordro, would it be in danger with your family?"

A sick feeling filled her. She'd never thought of that, but her father was sure to hate any child that wasn't fully human, or fully white for that matter. She didn't think her mother or aunt would care, but again, it was her father's opinion that would rule them all.

"Your silence says a lot," Borgoz said.

"She could already be pregnant," Vordro said.

"We need to discuss the matter further." Borgoz frowned. "Check back with us tomorrow, and we'll let you know our decision."

Summer watched as the screen went black, and she looked up at Vordro to judge his mood. He looked worried and a little tense. But was he concerned that the council might not approve the mating or was he concerned she might be pregnant, and the baby could be in danger? Or maybe it was both. She wrapped her arms around his waist and hugged him tightly.

Vordro held her close and kissed the top of her head. "That didn't go as planned."

"Maybe they'll decide we can stay together," she said. "Just because they wanted some time to think it over doesn't mean they'll say no. Does it?"

Vordro didn't comment and led her back up to the suite. He unpacked their belongings and looked at the clock on the wall. He stared at it a few minutes as if doing a mental calculation of some sort.

"I did some research on the Smithsonian," he said. "There are nineteen museums and each could take as much as five hours to visit. Did you intend to see them all?"

"I didn't realize it was so big. Maybe we could just pick a few?"

He nodded. "We have this suite for as long as we need it, and I've taken a week off from work. But there's one more place I'd like to take you for at least two days before we go home, so let's try to leave in the next three or four days."

"Do you think there's time to see one today?" she asked.

"Since you like the Natural History Museum at home, I thought we'd start with that one here. Although, what I read about it warned that to see everything in that place could take several days, so you may not get to see every single item there."

"Just getting to go is amazing enough. I don't care how much time we spend in the different museums; just seeing them is wonderful." She smiled. "Thank you for bringing me here."

He kissed her softly. "If you need to put on more comfortable shoes, do it now. I think we're about to do a lot of walking."

"I'm good. I can walk for hours in these."

"Then onward to the Smithsonian!" He brandished his cell phone like a sword, making her giggle. He really was like her own personal knight.

She picked up her purse, making sure her camera was still inside, then followed him out of the suite and down to the SUV. Summer knew that today was going to be amazing, no matter what the council decided. Vordro had confessed he wanted a life with her, and now she was getting to see the most incredible family of museums ever.

When they reached the Natural History Museum, Summer was so excited she was practically bouncing. On the first floor, they were greeted with a large elephant and a warning that they were in danger. Summer and Vordro walked all around the base until she convinced the hunky alien to pose. He looked so serious, with his arms folded over his chest, the look on his face clearly stating that he disapproved of the animal's endangered status. She smiled as she clicked the picture.

"I don't understand how humans can hunt animals until they are extinct," he said. "All creatures on my world are valued. We do not hunt them until they no longer exist. We thin overgrown herds, but we would never wipe them out completely."

"I'm afraid humans aren't that smart," she said. "Or maybe we're just too greedy."

He grunted. "Greed is certainly something I've

witnessed while dealing with humans."

Summer tugged on him. "Let's see the ocean exhibit first."

They took their time browsing the area. There were skeletons and a large whale hanging from the ceiling, among other things. Summer thought the skeletons might be some form of aquatic dinosaur, but they hadn't gotten close enough yet to read the display tags. Everything was incredible, and she snapped a bunch of pictures. Vordro took one of her near the eel exhibit and another with the whale hanging over her head. She couldn't remember the last time she'd had so much fun. He was making her dreams come true, and she wished she could do the same for him.

They reached the giant great white shark jaws, and even though they were behind glass, Vordro leaned over like his head was inside the mouth and made a comical face as she took his picture. She had to admit that he was making the museum a lot of fun. She was seeing a side of him that she doubted many people got to witness. He was relaxed and obviously enjoying himself.

When they were finished with the ocean hall, they moved on to human origins, and then the mammal hall. It took hours just to explore the first level of the museum, and while Summer wanted to keep checking things out, her stomach was reminding her it was dinnertime. It rumbled loudly, drawing a chuckle from Vordro.

"There's a café," Vordro said, "but as late as it is, they are probably either closed or have very little left. If you'd like to explore the other levels, we can come back tomorrow."

"I've loved our time here today, but I think I'd prefer to spend tomorrow exploring a different museum. There's so little time to see everything, or as much as I can cram in. Thank you so much for bringing me here, Vordro. I might have gone my entire life without getting to experience this."

Vordro took her hand and led her toward the parking lot. He drove them to a seafood place that wasn't too far from the Terran Station and helped her out of the SUV. With his hand on her back, he led her inside and requested a table. There were two other Terran/human couples inside, and it made Summer wonder just how many of his kind had decided to call Earth home. And was his decision to live on her world permanent? They hadn't discussed the possibility of ever going to his planet, but she'd imagine he would want to eventually.

The hostess seated them at a cozy table and left them with menus.

Vordro reached over and smoothed a finger down her nose. "You're thinking too hard."

"You don't talk about your world much. Don't you ever miss it?"

"Perhaps if I still had family there, I might. I didn't leave anyone or anything behind when I came here, Summer. I no longer own a home on my world, and have no intention of ever going back, unless it's just for a visit."

She nodded. "But what about your friends?"

"I have plenty of friends at the Terran Station back home. I don't need to live on my world to feel content. I'm far happier on your planet than I was on mine." His gaze was penetrating as he looked at her. "What about your friends? You haven't mentioned any."

"You've met my dad. He didn't approve of my friends, so they all eventually drifted away. All I had was my family, and you've seen they're no prize. Until you came along, I was truly isolated."

He frowned. "I don't like the thought of you being so alone. When we get back home, I'll introduce you to my friends and their mates. You should have other females to do things with."

"I'd love to meet your friends and their mates. I only

hope they like me."

He reached out and took her hand. "They will love you."

"Should we check in with the council in the morning before the museum, or in the afternoon when we get back?"

"I have a better idea. Let's stop by the clinic tonight when we get back to the station. There's a quick pregnancy test they can run. I want to be armed with as much information as I can before we face the council again."

Summer's eyebrows shot up. "They could tell I'm pregnant already? Human pregnancy tests can't be used until close to…" Her cheeks flushed.

"Close to what?"

"Nothing. It's a female thing."

He looked curious, but let the matter drop. She was both excited and nervous about the pregnancy test. On the one hand, having a baby with Vordro would be amazing, but on the other, she wasn't sure she was ready to be a mom just yet. She hadn't exactly had the best example growing up.

They ordered their food and Summer tried to think about anything but the visit to the clinic. She asked Vordro more about his world and the things he liked to do. He, in turn, asked her more about what she wanted for her future. She'd always thought she wanted a college degree and a career doing something meaningful, but after spending time with Vordro, she wasn't sure that was what she wanted anymore. Her priorities had changed a bit, now that she wasn't pressed to keep a roof over her head, and no longer had to worry about her family.

Well, that wasn't entirely true. She still worried whether they had a place to live or food to eat, but after the way they'd treated her, she was trying hard to put them from her mind. She knew her father would never accept Vordro, and if they had kids together, he'd hate the babies for their mixed heritage. There were times she wished her father had disowned her long ago.

The meal ended, and Vordro escorted her back to the SUV and drove to the Terran Station. Summer's stomach was tense as he walked her into the clinic. The doctor was walking out with a patient and smiled in greeting.

"What can I do for the two of you today?" the doctor asked.

"Summer needs to take a pregnancy test," Vordro said.

"Of course. I'm Doctor Gerig. Come right his way," he said motioning toward the door he'd just stepped out of.

They followed him down the sterile-looking white hallway to a room on the right. Summer tried to climb onto the table, but couldn't quite manage it on her own. Vordro lifted her and eased her down onto the padded surface. She smiled and reached for his hand, not wanting to let him go just yet. The doctor pulled out a drawer and then rummaged in a cabinet before walking over with some sort of syringe in his hand.

"You might feel a slight prick," the doctor said, and then he slid the needle into her arm.

Summer winced and tried not to tense up. The doctor took more blood than she had thought would be necessary and then watched the screen on the barrel. She'd never seen a syringe like it before, but then she hadn't experienced much of their technology. The doctor stepped across the room to the counter and squirted some of her blood onto a slide, then placed the slide under the microscope.

She wasn't sure if this was normal for a pregnancy test, but it was making her nervous. Was there something wrong with her blood? What if she was sick and didn't know it? The doctor made a humming noise before turning to face them again.

"Is something wrong?" Summer asked.

"You're definitely pregnant," he said, "So, congratulations. I'm a little concerned because you appear to be anemic. From what my tests show, it's from an iron deficiency and it should be easy to treat. I'm going to give you a prescription for iron supplements, and I'm going to give you a vitamin injection today just to give you a little boost."

Summer didn't hear much after the word pregnant.

"This anemia, is it serious?" Vordro asked.

"Well, it needs to be monitored. She may have noticed that she gets tired easily and she may be paler than usual. Not having seen her before today, I can't attest to the latter."

"I just thought it was from stress," she said.

"The prescription I'm going to give you needs to be picked up at the pharmacy here at the station. Wrylok, the pharmacist, can answer any questions you may think of after you leave here, or you may come back to see me or give me a call." The doctor smiled. "The iron supplements have been processed differently from those at a human pharmacy and will not harm the baby."

"Thank you," Summer said.

Vordro ushered her out of the clinic and stood in the corridor a moment, just holding her hand. "Are you all right?"

She nodded. "I think I'm still processing the fact I'm pregnant."

"Why don't you go up to the room?" he suggested. "I'll go wait for your prescription and bring it up to you. After the long day we've had, you should probably take a bath and relax."

She wiggled her toes inside her shoes. Her feet ached from all the walking. "A bath sounds nice."

Vordro kissed her softly and handed her the key to

the room. "I'll be up as soon as I have your pills."

She kissed him once more and then turned toward the elevators. He was right; it had been a very long day. But despite her uncertainty that she would be a good mother, all she could think was that surely the council would approve their mating now.

After they were in their room, while Vordro took care of a few matters, she called her aunt to share the good news. At least, she hoped her aunt would consider it good news. She also swore the woman to secrecy. The last thing Summer needed was her father finding out about the baby.

Chapter Eight

Vordro couldn't contain his excitement over being a father, but he was also concerned about Summer. He didn't know much about this anemia the doctor claimed she had, but he was going to learn everything about it that he could. He wanted to help her in any way possible. If she needed to do less around the house, he'd hire a housekeeper. It wasn't a bad idea with a baby on the way, if she'd agree to it. His Summer was fiercely independent and wanted to… how did that Earth phrase go? Pull her own weight?

He hadn't managed to sleep all night, more than a little worried about the council. Now that he knew Summer was pregnant, there was no way she was leaving his side. He wanted the council's blessing, but if he had to defy them and cut ties with his people, then that was what he would do. They had brought up a good point about her father, but he had a plan for taking care of the man just as soon as they were back in town. Or maybe the council would be willing to help.

Summer slept peacefully beside him, and while he should wake her and take her with him for the call to the council, he didn't want her to worry. He wanted to wake her and give her good news if that was possible. Vordro showered and dressed quickly, slipping out of the room as quietly as possible, and headed downstairs to a meeting room. He accessed the Vid-comm and called the council, waiting for their image to appear on the screen.

"Your chosen mate isn't with you?" Larimar asked.

"No, she's resting. Is Borgoz going to attend this session?"

"The Chief Councilor is otherwise engaged this morning," Larimar said with a hint of a smile, which meant that Borgoz was probably attending to his family. Lucky bastard.

"Before you give me your decision on our mating, you should know that Summer is pregnant. We went to the clinic last night and had her tested. She also has something called anemia and will need to be under a physician's care."

Larimar frowned. "This changes things, then. We were going to deny the mating based on her family, just because we don't need trouble if we can avoid it."

"Her father is the problem, and I think I have a solution. The man is currently out of work. Summer hasn't said what type of job he has, but if I can find out, could the council use their contacts to get him a job outside of Virginia? Maybe move him to a town where there isn't a Terran Station?" Vordro asked.

"You want us to help this man get a job?" Larimar asked.

"I want a way to send him as far from my family as possible, but I know Summer worries about her parents, even if they did turn their backs on her. She'll want to know they're taken care of, at least for the moment. It will be up to her father to keep the job he's given, obviously, but at least they have a fighting chance."

"And the aunt?" Larimar asked.

"She seemed supportive of Summer, and I believe she would be fine remaining in Virginia."

"Very well. Find out what kind of job her father is trained for and I'll see what I can do. Call us back as soon as you have the information. I'd like to have the matter resolved before you return home."

Vordro wanted it resolved before then too. He thanked the council and disconnected the call before going to one of the cafés at the station. He picked up some herbal tea for Summer and some coffee for himself, then returned to his room to wake his sleeping mate-to-be. When he entered the suite, the first thing he noticed was the shower running. It seemed his angel was already awake. He set the tea and coffee on the counter in the kitchenette and went to check on her.

She was humming while she washed her hair and he smiled as he watched through the glass shower door. Vordro cleared his throat to get her attention, but she was oblivious to his presence.

"Summer," he said, hoping he didn't startle her.

She wiped the soap from her face and squinted at him through the shower door. "I wondered where you went."

"I brought you some tea. I thought we could go have breakfast downstairs and meet with the council, or you can browse the station while I speak to them, if you'd prefer."

"Is it safe for me to wander the station?" she asked.

"Hmm. At home, I would say yes. But honestly, I'm not sure about here. Maybe you could just wait in the café for me."

She nodded and rinsed the suds from her hair. "I'll be out in a few minutes."

Vordro left her to finish her shower and turned on the TV in the living area. One of those good-morning-type shows was on, and they had Brexton on their show. It was a little humorous seeing one of his kind on TV in an entertainment capacity. Vordro would have never thought it possible. Obviously, the actor's roles would be limited to aliens with purple skin, so why bother?

Summer made an appearance in a pink sweater and jeans. She'd pulled her hair back in a ponytail, and it was swinging behind her as she stepped into the room. Her eyes lit up when she spotted her tea across the room and she hurried over to fetch it. He hated to kill her good mood, but he needed information about her family. Maybe it could wait until they were eating breakfast.

"What type of breakfast do you feel like?" he asked. "Traditional, something sweeter?"

"I think I'd love a waffle smothered in blueberries and whipped cream," she said. "Maybe with some eggs and bacon on the side."

"So, a little of both." He smiled. "I think we can find something you'll like downstairs."

Summer sipped her tea and set it aside. "You left for more than drinks this morning, didn't you?"

He nodded. "I spoke with the council, but they want more information. I thought we could discuss it over breakfast."

"Just tell me how bad it is. Are they going to deny our mating?"

"I don't believe so. We came up with a solution they approve of, but I'm not certain how you'll feel about it. They are worried your father poses a threat to our child, and I have to admit I'm concerned as well. It's no longer a matter of us not becoming mates in order to ensure nothing bad happens, but now it's paramount that your father is removed from our lives."

She paled and swayed a little. "Are they going to kill him?"

"What? No! Of course not. However, they do feel it would be best if he moved out of the area. He obviously won't go willingly if we ask, so they were going to arrange for a job offer to land in his lap, out of town. But we didn't know what type of work he does."

"He's done a little bit of everything. He's been a bartender, a construction worker, manager of a gas station… he's tried pretty much anything that didn't require a degree or previous experience."

Vordro nodded. "Then I'll see what the council can come up with. I promise that your family will receive enough compensation they will be able to take care of themselves. And your aunt may remain in Virginia, so you won't be completely without family, as long as she understands your father is no longer welcome in the state."

Summer smiled a little, her color coming back. "Trust me, she won't miss Dad."

"Then let's eat, and I'll fill the council in when we're finished."

He took Summer's hand and led her out of the suite and down to the elevator. When they reached the food court and restaurants scattered throughout the second floor, they perused the menus posted on the windows of each until Summer found what she wanted. The hostess seated them and took their drink order before disappearing. When the woman returned, they placed their breakfast order.

Summer fiddled with her silverware and looked around the room.

"Something wrong?" he asked.

"What if my father won't go peacefully? What if he refuses the job and decides to stay in town?"

"We'll figure that part out if it happens. I'm hopeful he'll accept the job offer."

She nodded.

"Which museum do you want to see today?" he asked.

"Could we go to the zoo? Or do you think it's too chilly out for that?"

"You brought your jacket, didn't you?" he asked.

Summer nodded.

"Then I think we'll be fine, but if you get too cold, we can always leave."

They ate their breakfast and then went up to their suite to get their jackets. Vordro didn't get as cold as humans did, but he took his leather jacket in case Summer needed another layer later. At the zoo, Summer dragged him from one animal to the next. She had her camera with her and took tons of pictures, including quite a few of him. An elderly couple walked by as they were looking at the tigers and Summer asked them for help.

She looped her arm through Vordro's and turned him to face the couple, with their backs to the tigers. "Smile," she said. "I want a picture of the two of us."

The couple snapped their picture and handed the camera back.

"Thank you," Summer said.

"You two make such a nice couple," the older woman said. "Enjoy your time at the zoo."

Summer was beaming as she laced her fingers with Vordro's. They stopped at the Panda Overlook Café for some panini sandwiches. They watched the pandas while they ate, but Vordro couldn't help but notice Summer looked a little tired. He wondered what it would take to get her to head back to the Terran Station and get some rest.

They finished their meal, and he slowly started leading her back to the front gates. When they passed a gift shop, Vordro tugged her inside and bought her a souvenir, and a stuffed panda for the baby. It seemed fitting since they'd found out she was pregnant during this trip. They weren't in the car ten minutes before Summer was napping with her head resting against the window. Vordro smiled and drove around for a while, giving her time to sleep before he went back to the Terran Station.

Summer yawned as he parked outside of the station. Vordro went around to her side and lifted her out of the SUV, cradling her close. He shut the door with his foot and then set the locks with the key fob. She snuggled against him and blinked up sleepily.

"Are we back already?" she asked.

"I drove around a little, so you could rest. When we get upstairs, you can finish your nap."

"I don't want to sleep the day away," she protested. "Maybe we could do something stationary?"

"Why don't we pick a movie to watch on TV in our suite and let you get your energy back? I can see if we can get some popcorn or something."

She rubbed her belly. "I'm still full from lunch, but I'd love some chocolate chip cookies."

He smiled. "Then you'll have cookies."

Vordro carried her all the way to their suite and set her on her feet just inside the door; then he went back down to find cookies. There was a small market on the second floor, and he picked up drinks and some snacks for them. When he got back to the room, she was already watching something on TV.

He set some snacks on the coffee table, along with a drink for each them, then stocked the kitchenette with everything else. If they were going to be here another day or two, he wanted to make sure Summer would have everything she could want or need. He sat on the sofa and pulled her against his side. No matter how many times he held her, he would always love the feel of her curves pressed against him.

Her fingers trailed up and down his thigh, making his cock get hard. He looked from the TV down to Summer and found her watching him. Vordro smiled and wondered what the minx was up to. As tired as she'd been, surely she didn't want sex. Did she? Because he was certainly up for it.

"What are you doing?" he asked.

"It's not obvious?"

"Maybe you should tell me what it is you want."

Her hand cupped his hard cock. "I want this. Inside of me."

He chuckled at her bold statement. "Then maybe you should strip out of those clothes."

Summer shot to her feet and started pulling her clothes off. When she stood before him, completely bare, she trembled from head to toe. Vordro stood and divested himself of his clothes and then grabbed Summer around the waist and eased her down onto the couch. He spread her legs and knelt between them. He could see her pulse pounding as he leaned forward and kissed her hungrily. Her lips tasted like the sweetest nectar.

Vordro tugged her ass to the edge of the cushions and lowered his head, his tongue swiping along her slit. Summer hummed and lifted her hips. Vordro licked, sucked, and teased until she was on edge. Her honey coated his tongue as he flicked her clit until she was keening and crying out his name.

"Need you," she whispered. "So much."

"Get on your knees in front of me and face the couch."

She slid onto the floor in front of him and turned to face the cushions. Vordro spread her legs farther and eased inside of her. Her wet walls clamped down on him as he sank into paradise. Being inside of Summer was like coming home. He used short, shallow thrusts until her body adjusted to his size, and then he couldn't hold back another moment.

He pounded into her from behind, every stroke harder and deeper than the one before until he was as deep as he could go. He cupped her breasts and tweaked her nipples as he claimed her thoroughly. Summer screamed out his name as she came all over his cock. As her pussy clamped down tight on him, he came inside of her, his cries muffled against her neck.

He didn't pull away immediately, but as she trembled in his arms, he knew he needed to withdraw and get her cleaned up. He carried her into the bathroom and started the shower. Vordro helped her wash before cleaning himself, and then he shut off the water and dried them both off. Summer gave him a smile that he felt all the way to his toes, and he leaned down to kiss her sweet lips.

"Why don't we spend the rest of the day in our suite relaxing, and then you can decide tomorrow if you want to see another museum, or if you want to move on to your next surprise." Vordro caressed her cheek.

"Can you tell me what it is? It might help me make a decision."

"I'm taking you to see the ocean. I know it's too cold to have a typical beach vacation, but I thought we could always go back in the spring or over the summer."

Summer wrapped her arms around him. "You're pretty wonderful, you know that?"

He grinned. "Feel free to tell me as often as you'd like."

Summer laughed and kissed him before snuggling against him. "Thank you for everything, Vordro. If you hadn't come into my life that day, I don't know what would have happened to me."

His heart ached at the thought of never getting to meet her. "I'm glad we don't ever have to find out."

She nodded and cuddled closer. No matter what it took, he was going to make sure she never regretted choosing him as her mate. He loved her, even if he wasn't certain how to tell her just yet.

Chapter Nine

Summer woke the next morning feeling like she'd eaten something rotten. Nausea welled inside of her, and she rushed to the bathroom before becoming violently ill. Despite her pregnancy, she knew it was way too soon for morning sickness. She curled on the floor near the toilet, afraid to move too far away in case she became ill again. A shadow crept along the floor, and a moment later Vordro filled the doorway.

"Summer? Why are you on the floor?"

"Sick," she croaked.

He leaned down and felt her forehead, letting loose a curse. "I'll be right back."

As she threw up again, she heard him on the phone in the next room. She hoped he was calling for anti-nausea medicine because she couldn't remember ever feeling this miserable before. When she thought she was finished being sick for the moment, she crawled to the sink and pulled herself up. She rinsed out her mouth and stumbled back to the bed, collapsing as she reached it.

Strong arms wrapped around her and settled her back against the pillows. She wanted to cry but didn't think she had the energy for it. Vordro left her for a moment, only to return with a cool, damp cloth. He placed it over her forehead and smoothed her hair back from her face. His gentle touch had her sighing contentedly.

The suite door opened and shut and she wondered who else had access to their room. When the doctor appeared in the bedroom doorway, Summer felt relieved. If anyone could make her feel better, she knew it was Gerig. He checked her over, taking her temperature and a blood sample. He studied his gadgets and made a humming noise.

"Is she going to be okay?" Vordro asked.

"She has a virus. I can treat it, but I don't think I can knock it completely out. It will make her comfortable enough you could take her home, but I would advise that you postpone the rest of your trip."

"No beach?" she asked weakly.

"No beach," Gerig said. "You need rest, and while you could try to get that here, I think you'd rest better at home in your own bed. The trip back to your hometown is only a few hours. I can even give you something to sleep through it."

Summer nodded. She'd been so excited about seeing the beach, but she didn't want to do anything that would jeopardize her health, especially since she was pregnant. If the doctor thought she needed to go home, that was what she would do. Gerig went back to his lab to get the injection she would need, and while he was gone, Vordro began packing their things. After the doctor returned and gave her two injections, one to ease her illness and the other to make her rest, Vordro helped her get dressed, and then he began the task of loading their bags and her into the SUV to return home.

Despite the assurance she would rest during the long car ride, she was awake for most of it. Not coherent enough to carry on a conversation, but she did watch the scenery pass. When Vordro pulled into the driveway at home, Summer was ready to claim her bed. Or maybe the couch. She didn't want to be isolated in the bedroom.

"Living room," she said as Vordro carried her into the house. "I can lie on the couch."

"You don't want the bed?"

She shook her head.

"Very well." Vordro eased her down onto the couch and went to fetch a pillow from the bedroom. Once Summer was comfortable, Vordro brushed a kiss against her brow. "I'm going to get some supplies, and I'll be back soon. Gerig recommended soup and crackers for the next day or two for you."

"I'll be fine."

"Rest."

Summer smiled and nodded.

She heard the door close behind Vordro, and she flicked on the TV, surfing through channels until she found a movie that looked interesting. She already felt a lot better than she had in the morning. Whatever Gerig had given her was working. She still felt a little feverish, but she was no longer burning up.

The doorbell rang a short while later, and Summer frowned. Vordro wouldn't ring the bell, would he? She got up slowly and went to answer the door. As it swung open, her eye went wide, and her heart nearly stopped.

"There's my pregnant slut of a daughter," her father said as he pushed his way into the house.

"Daddy? What are you doing here? How did you find me?"

"All I had to do was tell that ditz who answered the phone at the Terran Station that I was looking for my daughter and she was more than happy to help me track you down. It's bad enough you chose him over us, but now you're carrying his brat too?"

Her father's face was quickly turning purple in his rage.

"Daddy, I'm happy with Vordro. He treats me really well."

He looked around the place, and she could almost see the dollar signs in his eyes. "Looks like you did well for yourself. Is that why you let that filthy alien touch you? So you can keep all these pretty things?"

"It's not like that," she protested.

"Don't tell me you have feelings for that thing."

"He's not a thing! Daddy, I love Vordro. As soon as his council approves it, we're going to be married."

Her father lashed out, his hand cracking across her

cheek. "What you're going to do is pack your shit and come home. We'll sell the baby when it's born."

She cradled her stomach protectively. "No. I'm not going with you, and you can't have my baby."

He slapped her again, her cheek throbbing from the blow.

"You're going to pack your shit, and you're going to come with me. Otherwise, I'm going to put a bullet in that alien of yours."

Summer fought back a sob and tried to back away. Her father reached out and grabbed a handful of her hair, and started dragging her toward the doorway. They'd barely cleared the front porch before a roar made her ears ring.

Her father was ripped away from her and Summer fell to her knees, the world spinning. As she tried to focus, she heard the sounds of flesh hitting flesh. As her vision steadied, she saw Vordro attacking her father, blow after blow. The hateful man tried to fight back, but he was no match for the Terran warrior.

When her father hit the ground and spat blood out at Vordro's feet, her alien sneered down at him.

"I was going to find a way to deal with you peacefully, but it seems you want to do things the hard way. Now, instead of a nice job in a town far from here, you're going to spend your days in a small cell. Since your crime is against my future mate and the mother of my child, it won't be human authorities who hold you."

Her father paled.

"Summer," Vordro said. "Go back in the house. I'll be there as soon as I can."

She nodded slowly and went back inside, but she waited just inside the door, peering through a crack to see what would happen next. Vordro made a call, but she couldn't hear what was said. About fifteen minutes later, two large, black SUVs pulled up, and four Terran warriors got out. They hauled her father to his feet and stuffed him in the back of one of the vehicles. Words were said, but she couldn't read lips and couldn't hear. When Vordro shook their hands and headed up the porch steps, she scurried back away from the door.

He closed and locked it before turning to face her. "The first thing we're going to do is put some ice on your cheek. Then you're going to tell me how your father knew you were pregnant."

She paled a little, knowing he would be furious that she called her aunt. She'd honestly thought the woman wouldn't betray her, though. It stung that her family hadn't thought to protect her or her unborn child. Were they all completely rotten? If she'd hoped she could have a close relationship with her aunt, it was dashed now. There was no way she'd ever trust her with anything ever again. Same for her mother.

Vordro placed the ice pack against her cheek and she winced from the pain. Hopefully, it wouldn't bruise. He pulled out a kitchen chair and motioned for her to sit; then he took the one next to her, turning their chairs to face one another. He looked disappointed in her, and it broke her heart.

"I'm sorry," she said. "I never thought she'd tell my dad."

"Who did you tell, Summer?"

"My aunt. She'd seemed so supportive when I left; I thought she'd be happy for me. I made her swear not to tell my dad, but it seems I can't trust anyone in my family." Tears filled her eyes. "I was just so excited, and I wanted to share the news with someone."

He wiped her tears away and tipped her chin up. "I'm not mad, Summer. Well, that's not entirely true. I'm furious that you were put in harm's way, but I understand why you told your aunt."

"I'm sorry, Vordro. You know I'd never do anything

to hurt this baby. I didn't mean for this to happen." She sniffled. "What's going to happen to my dad?"

"He's going to be held at a facility run by my people and charged with a hate crime. He'll be questioned to determine how he learned of the pregnancy, and then those in charge will decide if the rest of your family needs to be picked up. There's a chance your mother and aunt will be arrested as well."

She nodded, feeling heartbroken.

"I trusted her," she said softly.

"And she betrayed your trust. I'm sorry, Summer. I know that family is important to you, but soon we'll have a family of our own."

She rubbed her belly. "How do I tell our child that their grandparents didn't want them? How do I say that their grandfather wanted to sell them to the highest bidder?"

"You don't." He took her hand. "We tell them that neither of us has a family, and we smother them with as much love as we can. Just because our baby won't have grandparents doesn't mean it will be loved any less."

"Does this mean your council is going to be angry and not let us get married?" she asked. "Now that they know my family is a threat, will they think I'm not good enough for you?"

Vordro kissed her softly. "You are more than good enough for me. And once the matter of your family is settled, they won't have a reason to say no. If they're locked away, they won't be able to harm the baby, or any other children we may have."

She smiled a little. "You want more children?"

"Last I counted, we had at least three bedrooms to fill. If you're up for it."

"I think I'd like that. I hated being an only child. I think our baby should have lots of siblings."

"Lots?" He chuckled. "Sounds like we might need a

bigger house."

"I don't care where we live, as long as we're together."

"I'm sorry I wasn't here when your father came by. And I'm sorry I got mad at you. What happened isn't your fault. You can't help the fact your dad is an asshole."

She snickered.

"Let me unload the car, and I'll fix you something to eat, and then we can snuggle and watch movies until you feel better. I picked up two soups from a local deli, one for now and one for later, and I got a box of crackers at the store."

"Sounds good." She smiled. "I think I'm up to eating at the table. I'll just sit here while you unload, and then we can eat together."

Vordro kissed her again. "I'll be quick."

Summer slumped at the table, feeling drained after the battle with her dad. She'd have never believed he could harm a child, but now she knew differently. What kind of monsters had raised her? How could anyone want to sell or destroy her child just because it was different? Summer loved her baby already and knew that Vordro did as well. As much as she would have loved her family's support, she would just have to learn to live without it. Not that they'd ever supported her much to begin with. Truthfully, she'd usually done all of the supporting.

Vordro returned carrying a bag from the deli and a sack from the grocery store. He put the box of crackers on the table and set some soup in front of her, with a plastic spoon. Her mouth watered when she saw his massive sandwich, but she wasn't about to take any chances on getting sick again because she tried to eat something too heavy too soon.

The soup was tasty, even if she would have preferred a sandwich. By the time she was finished Vordro had not only eaten all of his meal but had tidied the kitchen. Summer threw away the container and spoon, then got a bottle of water from the fridge to carry into the living room. It didn't take her long to select a movie, and she got comfortable while she waited for Vordro. He came in a few minutes later wearing a T-shirt and athletic pants.

"I've noticed you wear your black leather pants everywhere we go," she said.

"It's typical garb for someone of my station."

"But you aren't on your world anymore. Wouldn't you be more comfortable in jeans? You could even wear those pants out in public."

He frowned and studied the pants he was wearing. "There's something wrong with my leather pants?"

"No! I just... I would think they weren't all that comfortable."

"I suppose it depends on what you're used to. I've grown up wearing them, and on my world, you either wear the leather pants or something similar to what the Chief Councilor was wearing, just not in white. That is reserved for his station."

"I wasn't trying to change you," she said. "I just thought you might be more comfortable in something else."

He smiled at her. "I'm fine, Summer. But maybe one day I'll try those jeans you mentioned. Several of my kind wear them, and I admit they have more give to them than my leather. But the leather protects me if I get into a fight at the station."

"I understand."

"Now, what are we watching?" he asked.

"A comedy. I thought after today's events we could both use a laugh."

Vordro curled his arm around her and brought her closer. "A comedy sounds like a fine choice."

Chapter Ten

Over the next week, Vordro received news that all of Summer's family had been arrested and charged. They would be held for a minimum of twenty years, and when they were released, they wouldn't be allowed to live in the same state as his family. The news had been bittersweet for Summer. He knew she'd held out hope that her mother and aunt had been innocent. He didn't understand how people who were so rotten could have raised someone so wonderful.

While he hated that she would lose her family, he was glad that Earth valued his people enough to bend the rules. With so many Terrans settling on the little blue planet, it was guaranteed that his people and their allies would protect Earth if an intergalactic battle ever arose. He didn't see that happening, but he wasn't going to deny that he liked the extra perks.

"Is everything in place?" Vordro asked Krelor.

"The park near the station has been reserved for you, and my mate helped with decorations. We set it up to look like a fancy barbecue so your future mate wouldn't be suspicious. You don't think she knows what's coming?" Krelor asked.

"We haven't discussed our relationship since asking for the council's permission to become mated. She knows they were waiting for news of her family before making a decision, but I lied to her and said I didn't have an answer yet."

Krelor's eyebrows went up. "You lied to her?"

"I didn't want to ruin the surprise. After everything Summer has been through, she deserves to have a special day. You arranged for Larimar to be present?"

Krelor nodded. "He'll be there, along with several guards. Rorval and I asked for the day off so we could celebrate with you as friends and not have to guard the councilman."

"And your mates will be there? I know Summer wants to meet them."

"Rachel and Jenny will both be present."

"Excellent. I'm picking up the ring on the way home, and then I'll shower, and change. I bought a new outfit for the occasion. Summer asked why I always wear leather, so I thought I'd try the jeans I've seen you wear when you aren't working."

Krelor smiled. "You're going to love them."

"If I don't leave now, I'll be late to my own party. Tell Rachel I appreciate all of her help."

Krelor nodded and slapped him on the back. Vordro left the Terran Station and stopped by a jeweler on the way home. He'd already ordered a ring for Summer, but it hadn't been ready before his shift had started. If it wasn't ready now, he didn't know what he'd do. He couldn't very well have a mating ceremony without a ring. Well, he could, but he'd learned that human women liked having a ring to wear when they were married.

The shop owner smiled in greeting as he stepped inside, the bell overhead jingling. "Mr. Vordro, welcome back."

"Is it ready?" he asked.

The man nodded and reached under the counter, producing a small, black velvet box. He snapped the lid open for Vordro to take a look. He had to admit, the ring was rather stunning. He'd chosen an amethyst for the center stone, to match his eyes, and two blue topaz stones on the sides to match hers. The ring was white gold with a scrolling design weaving around the stones.

"It's perfect," Vordro said.

"I hope your intended loves the ring. If she's unhappy with it, bring it back, and I'll see what I can do."

Vordro thanked the man and left the shop. The ring felt like it was burning through his pocket on the way home and when he entered the house, he went straight to the bedroom, calling out to Summer on his way.

"I'm going to shower and then we need to leave for the party."

She appeared in the bedroom doorway as he was stripping out of his clothes. "I don't understand why there's a cookout in the park this late in the day. It will be dark in another hour or two."

"There are lanterns, I'm sure," he said. At least, there had better damn well be lanterns, and some of those outdoor heaters so his mate wouldn't catch a chill. He'd even requested small lights to be strung around the gazebo, where he'd hoped she would join her life with his.

She narrowed her eyes at him. "You've never introduced me to your friends, and suddenly we have to have a barbecue after you've been at work all day. Is this a special barbecue or something?"

"Just a gathering of friends," he said evasively, hoping she'd drop the matter.

She looked down at her jeans and blue sweater. "Am I dressed okay?"

That was a loaded question if ever he'd heard one. To him, she was always stunning, but once she found out they were getting married, he had a feeling she'd be upset she wasn't dressed a little nicer.

"I think you look beautiful."

"But the other women are going to be dressed differently, aren't they?" she asked.

"I think they're dressing up a little more since it's their first time meeting you." That sounded plausible, didn't it?

"To meet me? Why?"

Oh, shit. Why hadn't he thought this out a bit better? He should have known she would ask questions. It would have been better to wait until his day off, but he'd wanted to make her his as soon as possible. Now she was suspicious, and he didn't know how to handle it.

"Because you're special to me. I haven't had anyone serious in my life, and they're curious about you."

That sounded reasonable enough. To him.

"I think you're up to something, but I can't figure out what." She waved a hand. "I'll go change, but I think it's odd I need to dress up for a barbecue."

He breathed a sigh of relief as she opened the closet and started digging through her clothes. He hoped like hell she didn't decide to pick up his leather pants and find the ring. Vordro went into the bathroom and started the shower, taking a moment to brush his teeth before he got in. As the water pelted down on him, he hoped like hell he was doing the right thing. What if Summer was mad and not happy with her surprise? He'd heard that human women liked to make special arrangements for their matings. Would she be the same way?

Washing quickly, he got out and dried off, tying the towel around his waist. Summer had already vacated the bedroom, and he was thankful his pants were where he'd left them. She'd mentioned several times that she'd thought he'd look nice in a pair of jeans, so he pulled out the black pair he'd purchased the other day, along with the blue silk shirt he'd bought to pair with them. He pulled on his clothes, fastened a belt around his waist, and put his boots back on.

Summer was reading a book on the couch when he stepped into the living room to look for her. She flipped a page and held up a finger as she quickly scanned the book. With a sigh, she slid a piece of paper between the pages to mark her place and stood up. With her hands held out, she did a slow turn.

"Do I pass inspection now?" she asked.

The long-sleeved dress she'd put on hugged her curves, and she'd put on a pair of boots with it. He thought she looked enchanting, and he hoped she'd be pleased with her outfit when she found out what was happening tonight. Krelor's mate had insisted on having a camera handy to take their picture as they pledged themselves to one another. She seemed to think it was something Summer would want.

"You look stunning," he said. "Are you ready?"

She nodded and picked up her jacket. He walked her out to the SUV and helped into the passenger's seat. Once they were on their way, nerves plagued him. He knew that he wanted Summer as his mate, but he worried she wouldn't appreciate the way they were tying their lives together. What if she wanted something more? It wasn't common for there to even be a ceremony, but after everything she'd been through, he wanted to make the moment as special for her as possible.

Maybe he should have gotten one of those banquet halls instead.

When they reached their destination, Vordro parked the car and took her hand to lead the way. He heard her slight gasp when she caught sight of where they were going. His friends had outdone themselves. There were lanterns hanging from the trees, twinkling lights wrapped around the posts of the gazebo, and heaters spaced throughout the area. Tables and chairs had been set up with white tablecloths and tea lights in the center of each one. It was romantic, right? He glanced at her to see that her mouth was hanging open.

"This isn't a barbecue," she whispered. "What did you bring me to?"

Councilman Larimar approached a smile on his face and rubbing his hands together. "He brought you to your wedding."

Her eyes went wide. "Wedding?"

"Typically, our males either have a traditional human wedding or Terran mating. Our matings are a simple yes or no from the council, and then we file paperwork. So, Vordro opted to do something in between."

"I don't understand," Summer said. "Vordro, what is all this?"

"I didn't have the patience to wait for a human wedding to take place, and I knew you would want more than just the council's blessing to be mine. So, I asked Councilman Larimar to come here to give his official blessing and have us pledge ourselves to one another."

The councilman nodded. "If the two of you will follow me, we'll begin, and then we can all eat. I've been smelling something incredible by the buffet."

Summer's hand trembled in his as Vordro led her over to the gazebo. Their shoes clicked on the wooden planks as they stopped in front of Larimar. Summer looked around, taking everything in, and there were tears in her eyes when she looked up at Vordro. He reached and smoothed his hand along her cheek.

"Are you displeased?" he asked.

"No," she said softly. "I think everything is beautiful and absolutely perfect."

Larimar cleared his throat. "Let's begin. Vordro, is there something you'd like to say to Summer?"

Vordro turned to face her, holding her hands in his. He took a breath to steady himself as he gazed into her eyes.

"Summer, the moment I saw you, I was taken away by your beauty. The more I got to know you, the more enchanting you became. You love deeply, and selflessly. I am honored that you have chosen me as your mate, and I swear to do all that I can to make your life as comfortable as possible. I won't let another day pass without telling you how beautiful you are, inside and out, and how very much I love you."

Her eyes misted with tears again. "You love me?"

she asked softly.

He nodded.

"Summer, is there anything you wish to say to Vordro?" Larimar asked.

Summer gazed up into his eyes, a slight smile on her lips. "When I first saw you, my heart skipped a beat. I thought you were the most handsome man I'd ever seen. Even when you offered me a place to stay, I knew a guy like you would never want someone like me... but then, something magical happened. You wanted me as much as I wanted you. I fell in love with you long before our first kiss, and that love grows every day. I promise to love you every day for the rest of my life, and to do my best to take care of you, our children, and our home."

"Vordro, I believe you have something for your mate?" Larimar prompted.

Vordro dug in his pocket for the small box, pulling it out and flicking it open. He pulled the ring free, dropping the box as he slid the band onto Summer's left ring finger. He'd studied the human marriage customs and knew that would let other males know she belonged to someone. Tears slipped down her cheeks as she stared at the ring, and then she flung herself into his arms and kissed him until they were both breathless.

"Congratulations, you are officially mated," Larimar said. "Now, I don't know about you, but I'm going to follow my nose to that table of food and figure out what's been teasing me for the last half hour."

With Summer's hand tucked in his, Vordro led her over to his group of friends, all waiting to meet his mate.

"This is Krelor and his mate Rachel," Vordro said as they came to the first couple. "And next are Rorval and Jenny."

"It's nice to meet you," Summer said.

"Do you like pie?" Jenny asked.

Summer blinked, seeming to not know how to

respond at first. "Pie? Um, yes."

"Rachel and I meet every Wednesday afternoon for pie at the local diner. You'll have to join us this week."

Summer's cheeks pinked. "I'd really like that."

"You remember Nyril," Vordro said as he came to the two warriors standing by themselves. "Next to him is Maryk."

"Thank you for coming tonight," Summer said. "It's nice to see you again, Nyril."

He winked at her, drawing a growl from Vordro.

"I should feed you," Vordro said. "Rachel and Jenny organized most of tonight. They had the food catered from a local café."

"I'm sure it will be wonderful," Summer said. "This entire night is magical. Thank you, Vordro. Our wedding was absolutely perfect."

They sampled the fare provided and mingled with their friends. After an hour, Vordro was ready to have some alone time with Summer. They thanked everyone for coming, and Vordro thanked Rachel for overseeing the cleanup, and then they drove home. Silence reigned in the car, but it was the comfortable kind. When they reached the house, they walked inside, hand in hand.

The door had barely closed behind them before he was kissing his sweet mate. Swinging her up into his arms, he carried her down the hall to their bedroom. He wished he'd had time to set a better scene. Maybe some candles and flowers, instead of rumpled sheets and a pile of dirty clothes, but Summer didn't seem to mind. She slowly stripped out of her clothes, as Vordro divested himself of his.

He fell to his knees at her feet and pressed a kiss against her belly. "I also make a promise to you, little one, to be the best dad ever. I will protect you, guide you, and love you with all my heart."

Summer ran her fingers through his hair, and he

looked up to see tears in her eyes.

"I seem to make you cry a lot lately."

"Maybe it's pregnancy hormones. I thought it was too soon for that, but since this baby isn't entirely human, anything is possible."

"Would you prefer that I just hold you tonight?" Vordro asked.

"No. I want you to make love to me. All night long."

"I should have taken you to a hotel tonight, to celebrate our mating."

Summer kissed him. "All I need is you, Vordro. As long as I have you, then I have everything I need."

"You are my everything," he said before kissing her deeply.

Their bodies fell to the bed, a tangle of limbs. With the knowledge that forever stretched before them, a forever they would share together, they made love long into the wee hours of the morning until both were sated. Their hearts beat as one, and Vordro knew that fate had delivered Summer to him that day. No matter what the future brought, he would be forever grateful for having her in his life. She made him complete.

Epilogue

Ten Months Later

A scream tore from Summer's throat, her face flushed and sweaty. She glared at Vordro and bore down on his hand as she gritted her teeth through another contraction. Her hair clung to her face and neck, but it was the least of her worries. Vordro winced as she tightened her grip.

"What do you mean I can't have drugs?" she demanded of the doctor.

"Your contractions are coming too close together. There's not enough time for them to take effect." Prylo smiled as if to soften his words. "You can yell and scream all you want."

"Vordro! I swear if you ever plant another monster-sized baby in me, I'm going to cut your nuts off," she swore at her mate. He paled a little and looked at the doctor.

"She'll change her mind after she's holding the baby," Prylo said.

Summer didn't think it was likely, and as big as this baby felt, she wasn't certain she'd ever be holding it. More like they'd have to cut it out of her. How did women do this? Oh yeah. They had drugs! She wanted drugs! Lots of them.

"I want painkillers," she said, panting between contractions.

"I can give you a little something to take the edge off, but it's not going to numb you completely," Prylo said. He prepped a syringe and then gave her the injection.

A warmth flowed through her and slowly, the pain lessened. As Prylo had said, it didn't go away completely, but it was definitely more manageable. As the next contraction hit, Summer felt the need to start pushing. It took another hour before the blessed sound of a baby crying filled the air.

"Congratulations," Prylo said. "You have a girl. Although, why you didn't want to know before now I don't understand."

Summer reached for the baby. "I wanted it to be a surprise."

"Do you have a name picked out?" Prylo asked.

"We decided to use an Earth name for a girl and a Zelthranite name for a boy," Vordro said. "Her name is Zoe."

Summer stroked her daughter's cheek. "Hello, Zoe. I'm your mommy, and this handsome guy here is your daddy."

The lavender-colored baby blinked her blue eyes up at Summer. Her hair was midnight black just like Vordro's, and Summer thought she was absolutely perfect. The family cuddled together. Summer and Vordro stared at their daughter in fascination, and she stared right back.

"I love you, Zoe," Summer said. "And I promise to be the best mom ever."

"You already are," Vordro said before kissing her. "Thank you for my precious daughter. I'm sorry it caused you so much pain."

"She was worth it."

"Does this mean we can have another one?"

Summer smiled a little. "Don't push it. I need at least a year to forget how much this one hurt. Then we'll talk about it."

Vordro chuckled, and Summer felt a warmth suffuse her as she snuggled with her family. She'd been given the best gift of all, the gift of love, and she was going to cherish it every day for the rest of her life.

Heidi and the Alien Cop (Intergalactic Brides 12)

Jessica Coulter Smith

Heidi's life hasn't been easy since she dropped out of school at sixteen to have a baby. The worst mistake she ever made was moving in with her boyfriend Brent, who turned out to be an abusive bastard, but with no education and no job, there's nowhere for her to go. Her life for the last five years has disillusioned her that happily-ever-after could possibly exist... then *he* comes into her life.

When Raylic rushes to Heidi's aid, the last thing he expects is to end up with house guests, but she and her small son, Shane, are just what he needs. They bring life to his monstrous home and make him want things better left alone. But the more time he spends with the little family, the more he wants to keep them with him forever. Even knowing Heidi is pregnant with another man's child doesn't stop him from wanting to claim her.

Heidi knows that Raylic is one of the good guys, but can she dare trust her heart to someone again? He's everything she's ever wanted, but wanting and having aren't the same thing.

Chapter One

Heidi finished washing the macaroni pot and put it on the drying rack. Her son, Shane, was stretched out on the living room floor making *vroom vroom* noises with his cars. The door opened and her boyfriend, Brent, staggered inside, drunk off his ass as usual. He spent more time at the bar across the street than he did at home, which was fine with Heidi. Brent stumbled over Shane, and his face turned red.

"You little brat! Get the fuck up and get me a beer."

Heidi tensed, ready to jump to her son's defense. Shane looked up at his dad and tried to stand, but Brent shoved him back on the floor.

"Never mind, you useless waste of space. I should have made your mom abort you when I had the chance."

Her stomach churned as Brent made his way to the kitchen. "That's enough, Brent. He's just a little boy."

"He's a pain in the ass is what he is. I should have left your ass back when you claimed you were having my kid. All I've done for the last five years is drag around dead weight."

"I could work," she said. "Maybe find something part-time…"

Brent backhanded her across the face. "Your job is to keep this fucking apartment clean and keep that snot-nosed brat out of my way."

"Don't hit Mama," Shane said as he lunged at his father.

Brent sneered at him and lifted a hand to strike out at the boy, making Shane cower and fall to his knees. Heidi thought she would be sick and yelled for Shane to run. Her son shot up from the floor and raced toward the door. Brent advanced on her, caging her in the kitchen where she had nowhere to run, nowhere to hide. Faced with all his fury, she knew she'd be lucky to make it through the night without any broken bones.

Heidi hoped like hell that Shane had gotten out of the house. She hadn't heard the door open or shut but prayed her little boy had run to safety and not stayed to help her. Despite his young age, he acted like her protector when his dad got mad, which was far too often.

She placed a protective hand over her stomach as she cowered in the corner of the room. Brent towered over her, his face flush from too much alcohol and the rage that was burning in his veins. It wasn't the first time he'd struck her, and she knew it wouldn't be the last, unless she finally managed to escape. But where would she go? Without a job, or friends, or family, only the streets waited for her and their small son.

"Everyone was talking tonight about how you've been whoring around behind my back," Brent said, spit flying from his lips.

"Brent, please. You know how rumors are around here." She swallowed the knot of fear in her throat. She'd learned the hard way that fighting back only made it worse. When she fought back, it pushed him to the point of nearly killing her, and she had to keep living to take care of their son. She couldn't leave him in Brent's hands. Either her boyfriend would kill him, or he'd turn her sweet boy into a monster.

"Stupid, lying bitch. Did you think I wouldn't hear about it? I bet that brat in your belly isn't even mine. Who's to say the other little snot is mine either? You just saw a meal ticket and latched on."

"Of course, it's yours, Brent. They both are. You know I haven't been with anyone else."

He backhanded her across the face again, an explosion of pain ricocheting through her cheek and rattling her brain. Another blow landing in almost the same spot nearly knocked her off her feet. She had just braced herself on the wall when another fist pummeled her stomach. Heidi cried out, her hands clutching her belly, hoping he hadn't harmed their child. She'd tried damn hard not to get pregnant a second time by him, but the condom had broken two months ago.

She saw his hand wind back for another blow and cowered down, but it never came.

"I know humans play by different rules, but where I come from, we don't beat females," a deep voice said with a hint of a growl.

Heidi's eyes went wide as she looked around Brent at the purple alien with the badge clipped to his belt. Was he a real cop or one of those Terran guards? He knocked Brent's legs out from under him, then pressed him face first onto the floor, wrenching Brent's hands behind his back. Her drunken boyfriend was no match for the rather brawny guy manhandling him. The alien slapped cuffs on Brent, then pulled out a cell phone.

"Dispatch, this is Officer Raylic. Can you send a car around to pick up some trash I found beating a female?"

She didn't hear what else was said as the room spun around her. Heidi sank to her knees and tried to process what was happening. Had someone really come to her rescue? How had he known where to find her? A small hand slipped into hers, and she looked into the terrified eyes of her son.

"Shane?"

"I found a police officer, Mama. He'll take care of us, won't he?" Shane asked, looking more troubled than a five-year-old had any right to.

"Are you all right?" the officer asked her.

"I don't know. He hit me in the stomach and the face."

Shane's face scrunched up. "What about the baby?"

"You have a baby?" the officer asked.

"In her tummy," Shane told him.

The officer cursed. Brent took his moment of

distraction to rear up and lunge at Heidi, a murderous glint in his eyes. She jumped to her feet and lashed out at him, kicking him in the shin and hitting him in the eye. The officer made a grab for him and shoved him back down. Brent fell face first onto the floor, getting a mouthful of nasty carpet. Heidi had to admit that it had felt damn good to fight back for once.

Heidi approached her boyfriend. With a well-placed kick between his splayed legs, she had him howling and cursing her all at the same time. She felt a bit of satisfaction, knowing she'd caused him pain, but it wasn't enough. She looked at the officer who regarded her with a bit of mirth for attacking her abuser.

"Want to have another go at him?" the officer asked.

"What I'd like to do is beat him over the head, with a cast-iron skillet, until he can't ever hurt anyone again."

He nodded. "I probably would get into a bit of trouble if I let you do that. But feel free to kick him again. It's just his word against mine."

She looked at her bare feet. "It might contaminate my foot if I kick him there again. I've always heard if someone accuses you of cheating, they're probably the one with the guilty conscience. No telling where he's put that thing."

The officer chuckled a bit. "As soon as backup arrives to take care of him, I'm going to take you somewhere safe. We'll stop by the Terran Station first though. I want our healer to look at you. As small as you are, he could have easily broken bones or caused internal damage."

"Thank you for helping us," she said. "No one's ever helped us before."

He frowned. "Have you called the police before now?"

She nodded. "The officer who answered the call said I was overly emotional and it was just a domestic dispute.

He said if he got another call, he would haul both of us to jail. It was the first and last time I asked for help."

"Asshole," the officer muttered. "Do you remember who it was? I'll make sure he's written up."

"Officer Clarke."

He nodded. "I can see him saying something like that. Don't worry. Your husband is getting locked up this time."

"We're not married," she said.

"Good. Then you can make a clean break when he's taken out of here today. Do you plan to stay in this apartment?" he asked, looking around.

She knew what he'd see. Cracked walls, stained carpets, and the ugliest furniture imaginable. The place reeked of mildew and piss, and unfortunately for her, the rent was past due. It might not have been much, but it had been home for the last year. As often as they'd been late, no way the landlord would renew the lease. Not that she could pay it anyway.

"Where are we gonna go, Mama?" Shane asked.

"I don't know, baby."

The officer tilted his head. "Go pack your things. I was going to take you to a hotel for the night to give you some time to think things through, but it sounds like you need a more permanent solution."

"The rent is past due here," she said. "I don't have a job to pay for a hotel room. Could you take us to a shelter?"

"Don't worry about the cost," he said in a soothing tone. "Just pack your things and be ready to go as soon as possible. Don't leave anything behind that you want to keep."

Heidi took Shane's hand and led him to his room, where she quickly packed his clothes and the few toys and books he owned. Everything fit into one bag. She set his tote in the living room and went to fill one for herself.

Heidi didn't own much, just a few changes of clothes and two pairs of shoes. Since it wasn't flip-flop season, she put on her tennis shoes.

When she was finished packing, she took Shane by the hand and went back to the living room, where a uniformed officer was carting her now *ex*-boyfriend out of the apartment. It gave her a bit of satisfaction to see that he couldn't even stand upright on his own. The hunky alien who had rescued them picked up their bags and motioned for them to follow him. He'd been kind to them, but dread still filled Heidi's stomach. What was going to happen to them now? She couldn't afford rent anywhere, and even if she could find a job, it was Christmas break and she didn't have anyone to watch Shane.

The large SUV parked at the bar across the street looked exactly like the type of car she'd picture the alien driving. It looked every bit as capable as he was. Big, strong, and reliable. Those three things had been missing from her life lately. Actually, they'd been missing from her life since she had Shane at sixteen and dropped out of high school to move in with her loser boyfriend. She never did get her diploma, and Brent had kept her from getting her G.E.D. At first, she'd thought he wanted to take care of them. Later, she'd realized that he just wanted a way to control her. She'd taken some free classes at the library the past few months while Shane was in school and had learned about computer programs, housekeeping tips, and even how to be a better cook, due to taking a cooking class.

The alien put their things into the back of the SUV before helping Shane into the backseat.

"I don't have a booster seat. Do you have one?" the alien asked.

"Couldn't afford one." She licked her lips. "I know it's against the law, but I was always really careful when I drove him anywhere. Brent did most of the driving though. It was his car."

He motioned to the rusted heap outside of her apartment. "That one?"

Her cheeks flushed, and she nodded.

The officer shook his head and finished buckling Shane into the monstrous vehicle. Then he opened the front passenger door for her and helped her up. He reached across her to fasten the seatbelt and then shut the door. When he slid behind the wheel on the driver's side, his scent filled the vehicle. It was spicy with a hint of musk, and Heidi couldn't remember ever smelling anything so good.

He drove straight to the Terran Station, then helped them out of the SUV. Shane slipped his hand into the alien's, then grabbed Heidi's. As they walked inside, she nearly cried when she realized it was the first time her little boy had ever held a man's hand. His father had never wanted anything to do with him. The alien led the way through the hallways and ushered them inside a clinic. Another purple alien in a white coat smiled in greeting.

"Raylic, who have you brought to me?" the doctor asked.

"Xonos, this is Heidi and her son, Shane. Heidi's pregnant and her boyfriend decided to use her as a punching bag. I thought you might be more thorough than a human hospital."

Xonos frowned. "You know I'm only supposed to treat humans who are related to a Terran, either as a mate or as part of the mate's family."

"I'm asking you to bend the rules this once. He hit her in the face and in the stomach. What if the human doctors miss something and she miscarries?"

Xonos tapped his fingers on the counter. "I wasn't allowed to break the rules for my daughter. Why do you think the council would look the other way if I broke them for you?"

"Tell them I'm considering her as a mate. You'd have to check her for overall health then, wouldn't you?"

Xonos seemed surprised. "You'd be willing to claim them?"

"Claim?" Heidi asked. "What are you talking about?"

Xonos studied her a moment. "I'm not permitted to treat humans unless they are either married to a Terran, considering a specific Terran for a mate, or are related to someone who is. And since you are none of those things, Raylic would have to tell the council he's contemplating a mating -- or marriage -- to you."

Her eyes widened. "You can't do that. You don't even know us."

Shane tugged on Raylic's hand. "Would that make you my daddy? You seem nice, and I've always wanted a nice daddy."

Her heart nearly broke at her son's words and her eyes teared again. She blinked the moisture away as she looked up at the handsome cop who had come to their rescue. She didn't know a lot about the Terrans, who had come to their world about nine years ago, but she did know that they mated for life. If he was offering to consider her as his mate, just so she could have medical treatment, it was a huge deal. And something she couldn't allow him to do.

"Just take me to the free clinic," she said.

"Free clinic?" Raylic asked, his brow furrowed.

Xonos was shaking his head. "You need to go to the emergency room."

"I don't have insurance," she said. "I can't afford a trip to the hospital. I'm sure the doctor at the free clinic can check me out just as easily."

"Don't take her to the free clinic," Xonos said. "She'll

get subpar care from a frazzled doctor who's worked too many hours, seen too many patients, and isn't getting paid enough. I've met with the doctor who runs the free clinic here, and the male is an imbecile."

"If you won't treat her, then I guess I'm taking her to the hospital."

Heidi shook her head. "Shane can't sit that long in an ER waiting room. We could be there for hours. This won't be the first time I haven't had medical care after going a round with Brent. I'm sure I'll be fine."

Xonos looked to the ceiling and muttered something under his breath. "All right. Bring her back, but when the council threatens to take my job, I'm sending them after you, Raylic."

The cop grinned and led Heidi and Shane into the back. "Raylic, you should wait out here with the boy," Xonos said. "I need her to strip down and put on a gown for the examination. If I'm going to do this, I may as well be thorough."

Raylic leaned against the opposite hallway wall and held Shane's hand as the door shut, blocking them from her view. Xonos pulled out a cloth hospital gown and set it on the padded table; then he ducked out of the room to give her some privacy. Heidi changed, but she moved slowly, her stomach aching from the hit she'd taken. She wasn't surprised when she noticed a bruise shaped like a fist already forming, and she wondered just how bad her face looked this time.

Once she was dressed, she called out that she was ready, and Xonos re-entered the room. He walked over to the counter and picked up several instruments and a syringe before coming over to her. She eyed the needle with trepidation and wondered if it was necessary.

"I'm going to take a blood sample just to make sure you're in good health, and I'm going to do some scans of your body to make sure nothing is broken. Then we'll take a look at that baby and make sure everything is okay." Xonos smiled. "I promise I'll be quick, and make it as painless as possible."

During the exam, she watched his facial expressions and didn't like all the frowns and the bit of growling that he did. Was there something seriously wrong with her? Was she going to die and leave her son without either of his parents? When Xonos was finished, he tucked his hands into his lab coat pockets.

"I can see the damage your boyfriend did over the time you were with him. Some of the injuries didn't heal quite right. You don't have any freshly broken bones though, and the baby seems to be fine. Watch for spotting and have Raylic bring you back if that should happen."

"So, I'm okay to get dressed and go?" she asked.

"Yes, but I'm going to give you a prescription for prenatal vitamins. I don't know much about your history, but if you're going to the free clinic, I'm going to assume you aren't taking any."

She shook her head.

"You really need to find a doctor you can see on a regular basis for check-ups during your pregnancy."

"I didn't have one when I had Shane. I'll be fine, but thank you for your concern."

Xonos muttered something again as he stepped out of the room. Heidi changed back into her clothes and then opened the door when she was finished. Raylic didn't look pleased as he waited for her and she wondered if she'd taken too long. He held a piece of paper in his hand.

"We're stopping by the pharmacy on the way out to get this filled," he said, holding up the prescription. "And then I'm taking you to the hotel to get you settled in for the night."

"My daddy won't be able to find us there, will he?" Shane asked.

Raylic softened toward her son, and he knelt down.

"No, your daddy won't be able to find you. He went to jail tonight, and he's not going to get out anytime soon."

"I'll have to testify, won't I?" Heidi asked, a sour feeling in her stomach. "Do I need to file an official report about what happened tonight?"

"I'll pick you up in the morning and take you to the station," he said. "For now, I think you need to rest."

"You've been so nice to us. Thank you. I'm Heidi," she said. "And this is Shane."

"It's nice to meet you both. My name is Raylic."

As she followed him out of the clinic, Heidi had to wonder just how much of the officer she would see over the next few days. Would he disappear after she filed her report? Or would he stick around to see how they were doing? There was something about him that made her feel safe, and it wasn't just his badge. His sheer size should have terrified her after what she'd been through, but something told her he'd never raised a hand in anger to a woman before, and never would. From what little she knew of his kind, they revered women.

While he might not have a mate right now, she knew he'd take one someday. And she'd be the luckiest woman on Earth.

Shane tipped his face up to look at her, a smile playing along his lips. "I like him," he said in a mock whisper.

The alien chuckled but didn't say anything.

"I like him too," she whispered back, just as loud.

Raylic looked at her over his shoulder and gave her a wink. Her cheeks flushed as she hurried to keep up with him.

You get the attention of a nice, decent guy and turn into a hussy, she reprimanded herself. Just because he'd offered to consider her as a potential mate for healthcare purposes, didn't mean he'd actually meant it. Guys like Raylic didn't marry women like her.

Chapter Two

Raylic wasn't sure what to make of the female and young boy he'd rescued. Despite the fact he'd found her cowering in front of her male, she didn't seem to have any trouble standing up to him, and had certainly enjoyed kicking her boyfriend when she had the chance. It made him smile to see that spark in her eyes when she'd tried to get her way at the clinic too. It was nice to know the asshole hadn't completely broken her, even if he had left her in dire straits and all bruised up. The few kicks the bastard had received hadn't been nearly enough.

He handed her prescription to the pharmacist and waited as the male scanned it into the system.

"It's going to take about a half hour to get this filled. I'm all out of stock and will have to request some from another local pharmacy." Norco smiled. "I'm glad to see you've found a female."

He couldn't deny the claim on her, or Xonos would be in a world of trouble for treating her. "I'll take them to get something to eat and come back for the pills. If it's going to take longer, just have reception text me."

Norco nodded and turned, presumably to call for the medication.

Raylic reached for the boy's hand and the mother's. Her fingers felt small and delicate in his, and something shifted in his chest. "It's going to take a little while to get it filled, so we're going to go grab a bite to eat. Or if you aren't hungry, we can just get a snack."

The boy's stomach rumbled. "We only had some macaroni for dinner."

Heidi's cheeks flushed. "I was supposed to go shopping today, but Brent drank away our grocery money. And probably the rent too."

He wanted to ask why she'd stayed with such an

undeserving male but refrained in front of Shane. The boy might know his father was scum, but there was no point in making the male seem even more inadequate in his son's eyes. As they neared the food court, he tried to remember what small humans liked to eat. Probably not anything nourishing enough for Heidi, since she was expecting, but he supposed any food was better than none.

"You can pick anything you want," he told them. "It's on me."

"You've already done so much for us," Heidi protested.

He arched a brow. "And did you bring money with you?"

She slowly shook her head.

"I'm not going to let the boy, or you, starve. You can pick anything you want here, and get as much of it as you want. Macaroni isn't enough for a pregnant female, or a small boy, to have for dinner."

"Mama likes Italian food," Shane said.

"That's pasta and pizza, right?" Raylic asked.

Shane nodded. "I like it too."

He guided them over to the Italian eatery and let them look over the choices. Shane eyed a slice of pizza nearly the size of his head while Heidi drooled over the lasagna. He could tell neither was going to ask for what they wanted and it made him want to kick someone's ass. They should have never been made to feel that they didn't deserve the things they wanted most.

Raylic ordered for them, adding a salad and garlic bread for Heidi, then he selected something for himself. He hadn't technically been on the clock tonight when he'd gotten the call about the bust at the bar, but knowing they were shorthanded he'd gone anyway, and missed his dinner. The Chinese takeout sitting on his counter would hold for another day, or he'd toss it. A little ruined food was a small price to pay for being in the right place at the right time though. If he hadn't answered that call, Shane wouldn't have found him.

After their order was ready, he let Shane select a place to sit.

The boy took a huge bite of his pizza and his eyes closed as he savored it.

"Is it good?" Raylic asked.

"The best. The only pizza we get are those frozen ones."

Raylic had tasted some frozen pizza, and it hadn't been half bad, but judging by their current circumstances he guessed the boy meant the ones that were only one dollar and probably didn't have as much flavor, and definitely weren't big enough for a family. He studied Heidi as she ate her food and wondered how old she was. She didn't look old enough to have a son Shane's age, but then he'd met a sixty-year-old woman the other day who didn't look a day over forty.

"Thank you for dinner," Heidi said.

"You're welcome." He smiled. "How does it feel to be free?"

"Terrifying," she said. "I don't know how to take care of myself, much less my son and this baby. I'll need a job and a place to live. How am I supposed to feed us while I try to work everything out?"

She cast a worried glance at Shane, but the boy was happily eating and ignoring them.

For some reason, he didn't like the idea of her choosing a random male, but it would be wrong not to make her aware of all her choices.

"The bride program has recently opened a new section. Previously, all brides were sent to my world to find a potential mate, but with so many of us settling here, they've decided to give the brides the option to be paired with someone on Earth. It would work similar to your matchmaking services. Would you be open to something like that?"

"Who would want a pregnant woman with a son in tow?" she asked. "Aren't most of those women childless?"

"Well, I haven't heard of them pairing a single mother yet, but it doesn't mean it can't happen." He cleared his throat. "And there are those of us who wouldn't mind that you're carrying a child and have another, as long as you were willing to have more."

Her cheeks warmed. "What about you?"

"Me?" His gaze scanned what he could see of her, lingering perhaps a little too long on her rather impressive breasts. "No, it wouldn't bother me that you had kids with another male."

Shane finished his pizza and burped, making him laugh.

"Shane, that's impolite," Heidi said. "Say excuse me."

"Excuse me," the boy said.

Heidi took her last bite and set her fork aside.

"Quite all right." Raylic smiled. "If everyone is finished, do you want to see if your prescription is ready, and then I can show you where you'll be sleeping?"

"Do I have to go to bed when we get there?" Shane asked. "I'm not tired."

He yawned widely, and Raylic hid a smile.

"Bath and bed," Heidi said. "It might be Christmas break, but that doesn't mean you get to stay up all night."

"Will Santa come see me this year? Maybe he won't be afraid of Daddy this time."

Raylic looked at the small boy then his mother. The child had never had a visit from Santa before? Having spent time with his friends' kids, he knew Santa was a big deal. Had they just not had money for such things? Had the boy ever even received a Christmas present?

"I don't know, sweetheart."

Heidi looked miserable, and Raylic knew he would do whatever it took to make sure the family was taken care of this holiday season. While his kind didn't celebrate Christmas, they'd learned to appreciate the human holidays. The mates he knew all celebrated Christmas and made a huge deal about putting a tree up in their homes and wrapping presents. The kids seemed to enjoy it, and it broke his heart that Shane might not have ever experienced the wonder of Christmas.

Raylic threw their trash away and took Shane's hand as he led the little family back to the pharmacy. Norco had the pills ready and said he'd set up an account for Raylic that he could pay off at the end of each month. It was rare for him to need medical treatment, but he appreciated the offer.

He loaded everyone back into the SUV and drove to the hotel that was preferred for Terran use. There was a motel not too far away that also catered to Terrans, but it wasn't as safe because the rooms opened to the outside. He didn't want a single mom and her son staying there, even if the neighborhood wasn't dangerous. At the hotel, he parked and gathered their bags before leading the way inside. The concierge at the desk smiled but looked a little uncomfortable.

"I need a two-bedroom suite for an undetermined amount of time," he told the man.

"I'm afraid I don't have any vacancies right now. There's a large wedding party and a conference in town, so the last of our rooms were taken this morning. I should have something available by Monday night though."

It was Wednesday. Where the hell was he supposed to put them for that long? The motel was out of the question. As a cop, he'd had way too many calls at the other hotels in town to put them up there. Keeping them safe was his number one priority. There was always a suite at the Terran Station, if he could convince someone to let him use one, but then they'd have to share a bed. After everything they'd been through, they deserved to have their own rooms.

The man cleared his throat. "I'm afraid you won't find any hotel rooms in town. Not even the budget motels will have anything."

Heidi pulled on his arm. "Just take us to the shelter. We'll be fine."

He growled a little. "You're not going to the shelter."

"Then where are we supposed to go?" she asked. "At least the shelter is better than being on the street."

"Do you honestly think I'm just going to abandon you?"

Her look clearly said that's exactly what she'd expected. He'd love to get his hands on all the men in her life and pound the shit out of them. Whatever it took to prove to her that not all males were assholes, he'd do it. It was past time that someone took care of Heidi, and he was a little surprised to find that he didn't mind being that someone. From the moment he'd seen her, waiting to be hit again, something inside of him had wanted to protect her.

"Come on," he said, knowing exactly where he'd take them, even if she did balk once she figured out where they were going.

After loading their bags back into the SUV and getting everyone buckled, Raylic headed for his house. His neighborhood was gated, and several of his friends had homes in the community. His home was large, but not as enormous as Syl's. It also felt empty most nights when he came home from work. If he hadn't held out the hope he'd find a mate soon, he never would have purchased something so big, but he'd always wanted a large family.

"Where are we?" Shane asked. "Is that a museum?"

Raylic chuckled. "No, it's not a museum. But we could go see one if you'd like."

"Really?" Shane asked. "I've never been to one before. Or the zoo."

Poor kid. Raylic didn't know how long Heidi would allow him to be part of their lives, but he planned to make the best of it. If Shane wanted to see a museum, or the zoo, then he'd make it happen. Although they might freeze their asses off at the zoo right now. December in Kentucky was still damn cold. At least snow wasn't as common as it was a little further north.

"Come on, let's get the two of you inside and I can show you around."

"Raylic, where are we?" Heidi asked. "We can't stay in this place."

"Why not?" he asked.

"It's too…"

"Rich," Shane said. "Rich people live here."

"I live here," Raylic said. "There's plenty of room for both of you."

Heidi made a sound like she was strangling. "There's plenty of room in there for half the city."

"Now you're just being dramatic," Raylic said. "There are five bedrooms. One is obviously mine, but you can pick from the other four. You can each have your own room."

And maybe, while they were here, Raylic would do something with the empty playroom that had been gathering dust. Well, if his housekeeper ever allowed a speck of dust to enter her domain. There couldn't be many toys or clothes in the tote Heidi had packed for Shane, and he wanted to make sure his guests were comfortable. He just wasn't sure how to get Heidi to *let* him buy things for them.

Raylic got their bags out of the back of the SUV and then unlocked the front door of his home. The alarm went off, and he silenced it. He set their bags down in the front entry and waited for them to step inside. Heidi looked like the house might bite her and Shane stared at everything with wide eyes. He supposed, after the place where he'd found them, they probably hadn't seen anything this grand before. To him, it was just home.

He reached out, tugged Heidi into the house and closed the door behind her, twisting the locks. She stared up at the small chandelier that hung over the tiled entry. The light fixture was a little much in his opinion, but he hadn't had time to change it. He took Heidi's and Shane's hands before leading them through the house, pointing out each room. When they went upstairs, Shane stopped at the first bedroom.

"Can I sleep here?" he asked.

Raylic wasn't surprised he'd chosen the blue room with the full-size bed. The furniture was oak and probably too masculine for a female. Raylic put Shane's bag inside the room and handed him the remote to the TV sitting in the small entertainment center, along with the cable remote.

"Why don't you find something to watch while I show your mom the rest of the rooms?" Raylic suggested. "Do you know how to work those?"

Shane's brow furrowed. "Where's the TV? And why are there two remotes?"

Raylic smiled and opened the cabinet doors. "The skinny remote turns on the TV and changes the volume. The shorter, fatter one is for cable. There are some cartoon channels on there you might like. Push the button that says 'guide' and it will show you what's on right now."

Had the boy never had cable either? The more he learned about the little family, the more he wanted to change their lives. Things that he took for granted, like a home that smelled nice and was safe, or cable, were things the boy had never experienced. It broke his heart, and he vowed to make sure they never went without again.

Heidi balked when Raylic tried to lead her away.

"I can stay in here too," she said.

"Heidi, there are three other rooms to choose from. You don't have to sleep in the same bed as Shane, unless you just really want to." He lowered his voice. "But don't you think he might like having his own space?"

She sighed and followed him down the hall. He showed her each room, watching her expression. When she saw the yellow bedroom with the white eyelet bedspread, he knew it was meant to be hers. He put her bag inside and showed her where the remotes were.

"This particular room has its own bathroom. Shane's room and the other two share a bathroom in the hall. Did you bring any bathroom stuff with you? If not, both bathrooms are stocked with shampoo, soap, razors, and spare toothbrushes. You're welcome to use anything in there."

"Why are you being so nice to us?" she asked.

"Because you're letting me."

She looked like she still couldn't quite believe him, but he'd prove to her, over the next few days, that she could trust him. He left her to settle in and went to his room to shower and change. He unclipped his badge from his belt and placed it on the dresser, along with his wallet, keys, and cell phone. Knowing there was a child in the house, he locked his gun in the safe. Before he undressed, he called the station to request a few days off. Even though prior approval and written notice were policy, he'd not asked for a day off in all the years he'd worked there.

"Sergeant Harper."

"Sarge, I need a favor," Raylic said.

"Does this have anything to do with the woman and child you took off with earlier tonight? Patterson thought it was odd you hadn't brought them to the station after that asshole was hauled in."

"Yes, sir. They're going to stay with me, at least for a few days, and I'd like some time off to make sure they're settled and have everything they need. All of their belongings fit into two tote bags."

His boss sighed. "Are you bringing the woman in tomorrow to give her statement as to what happened?"

"That is the plan. I thought she'd been through enough tonight."

"When you come in, fill out the time off request, and I'll approve it. I'll call Sims and see if he wants some overtime. With that new baby on the way, I'm sure he could use a little extra cash right now."

"Thanks, Sarge. I'll bring Heidi and Shane by tomorrow, after breakfast."

He disconnected the call and stripped out of his clothes. He could hear Heidi and Shane talking down the hall, and heard the water running in the hall bathroom. Bath toys. Did boys his age play with bath toys? If not, he'd find something to make bath time more fun for the boy. Raylic started his shower and stepped under the hot spray. His bathroom had its own water heater, so he wasn't worried about taking up all the hot water if Heidi and Shane needed it.

He lathered his hair then washed his body. His cock was hard and standing at attention, and had been at half-mast ever since those blue eyes had looked up at him back at the apartment. Raylic stroked his cock and braced a hand on the tiled wall. Slow and steady, he let the pleasure build. As he watched his hand slide up and down his shaft, he pictured Heidi on her knees before him. Her plump lips would look damn good wrapped around his cock. He quickened his pace as his balls drew up, preparing to blow.

"Mr. Raylic?" a small voice called through the door.

Fuck! Talk about a fast way to kill an erection. He stared at his rapidly deflating cock and wondered if this was a taste of what it would be like to have kids. "What is it, Shane?"

"Mama is taking a shower, and I wondered if you'd read my bedtime story to me."

"Give me just a minute to dry off, and I'll come read to you."

He heard Shane walk away and he quickly rinsed. As he dried himself, he wondered if it was safe to enter his bedroom naked, or were little eyes still in there? He wrapped the towel around his waist, just to be safe, and opened the bathroom door. His bedroom was wide open, but no one was in sight. He shut the door long enough to pull on a pair of athletic pants before padding down the hall to Shane's room.

The little boy was already propped up in bed with a book in his lap. Raylic entered the room and eased down onto the bed, leaning back against the headboard. He took the book from Shane and looked at the cover.

"The Chicken from Outer Space?" Raylic smiled. "I have to admit, in all my space travels, I've never seen a chicken in a space suit."

Shane's eyes widened. "But you saw chickens out of space suits?"

Raylic laughed. "Not like your Earth chickens. There are similar animals on other worlds. Just like my world has something similar to your elephants."

"That's so cool." He grinned. "Instead of a story, will you tell me about your world?"

"What would you like to know?" he asked, setting the book aside.

"What other animals do you have there?"

"Skerits look like a cross between your skunks and weasels. They are long with bushy tails, and they're black with a pink stripe, and have six legs."

"Cool. Do you have any pictures?"

Raylic shook his head. "We don't really take pictures or videos of things on my world. But, on the next shuttle, I could have a digital camera sent back to a friend of mine, with the request that he take some pictures before sending the camera back. Then we can look through them and maybe print some off for your room. You can decorate this bedroom however you'd like."

"Really?" Shane's eyes lit up.

"I'll get a camera tomorrow and drop it by the station. I think there's a shuttle taking off tomorrow around lunchtime. When I pick up breakfast in the morning, I'll take care of it."

"What other animals do you have there?" Shane asked.

"Hmm. Let's see. We have lilaphants, which are kind of like your elephants. They're a few shades lighter than my skin tone, and the end of their trunks are heart shaped, and they have heart-shaped ears. Their tails look like a zebra's tail, except the stripes are blue." Raylic smiled. "A friend of mine works with them, trying to preserve the species. They have a low birth rate, so Fendrix keeps a few mated pairs in captivity to ensure the species survives."

"Do you have anything like a horse? I've always liked horses, but I've never seen one up close."

"We have loripods, which look like your equines, but they have spikes instead of a mane and their fur is red with black swirls. They look fierce but can be quite sweet."

"What else can you tell me about your world?" Shane asked.

"We have three suns, which keep things warm all year. In preparation for the bride program, we put in an apartment building and a community pool. The pool stays open year-round and is free for anyone to enjoy. We even have a café that has human cuisine. It's run by one of the mates who moved there as part of the bride program. She doesn't like sitting at home all day, so her husband allowed her to open the café."

The little boy looked thoughtful. "I wonder what my mama would do if she was allowed to work."

"She isn't allowed to work?" Raylic asked.

Shane shook his head. "Daddy was really mean to her. He'd hit her a lot."

"Well, your daddy isn't going to hit your mama ever again."

"Promise?" he asked softly.

"I promise. Now, I believe it's time for you to go to bed." Raylic frowned. "I don't have a nightlight."

"I'm not a baby," Shane grumbled.

"No, you aren't. Do you want the door left partially open, or closed all the way?"

Shane stared at the door a moment. "Maybe partially open, with the hall light on."

Raylic smiled and ruffled the boy's hair. He pulled the door most of the way shut and flicked on the hall light. Heidi was leaning against the wall, tears in her eyes. He reached for her, holding out his hand. Her fingers slid along his, and he clasped them, drawing her down the hallway and downstairs.

"You're good with him," she said as they sat on the sofa.

"He's a sweet boy."

"Can I ask you something without you getting offended?"

His eyebrows rose. "I'm an open book. Ask anything you want."

"You're a cop, right?"

He nodded.

"So, how can you afford a place like this? You aren't selling drugs on the side or something, are you?"

He smiled a little. "What do you know of my world or our agreement with Earth?"

"Nothing really. I've never been much for reading the papers, and the news is usually too depressing to watch."

"On my world, I was part of an elite team of warriors. We were paid very well, better than anyone else, except the council members. When I agreed to come to Earth, your government was rather generous with the exchange rate for my credits to your dollars. I paid cash for this house and for my vehicle, and I still have plenty in the bank. I didn't even transfer all my Terran credits. I draw a salary as a police officer as well, so I'm not hurting for money."

"So, you really are rich then." Her lips turned down on the corners. "I always thought rich guys were assholes."

Raylic laughed so hard his sides hurt. "I think your boyfriend was the asshole, but I'm glad you haven't lumped me into the same group."

"You'd tell me if it was inconvenient for us to be here, wouldn't you?" she asked.

"I can assure you that you're not an inconvenience. But speaking of my money, there's something we need to discuss. I know you don't have any cash right now, and judging by the two totes you brought with you, you don't own very much. After we go to the police station tomorrow, I'd like to take Shane and you shopping for some essentials, and maybe some toys for him."

She opened her mouth, and he barreled on before she could protest.

"I have more money than I know what to do with, and I can't stand the thought that he's done without so much. Please, let me do this. You can keep whatever we buy, no strings attached. I'm not doing it to get into your pants, if that's what you're thinking."

Her cheeks warmed, but she shook her head, a bemused expression on her face.

"I wouldn't offer if I didn't have the funds to back it up," he said. "Will you consider it?"

"I'll let you buy us some things, but don't get too crazy. I don't want Shane to think he can have whatever he wants, because eventually we'll have to move on, and I know I can never do that for him. I don't even have a G.E.D., so the best I can hope for is a minimum wage job."

"What's a G.E.D.?"

"I didn't graduate high school because I dropped out when I found out I was pregnant with Shane. G.E.D. stands for General Education Diploma. It would be the equivalent of a high school diploma. I'd need it if I was ever able to apply to college."

Raylic nodded. "And do you want to attend college?"

She smiled wistfully. "Once upon a time, I had planned to attend. Then I found out about Shane, and my dreams changed. Brent is older than me, and he'd already graduated when we were dating. My parents hated him, and when they found out I was pregnant, they disowned me. I was allowed to pack one small bag and had to leave everything else behind. I found out a year later that they were killed when the house caught fire overnight."

"So, you really are all alone," he murmured. "I have a proposition for you."

"What?" she asked skeptically.

"In exchange for entertaining the possibility of becoming my mate, Shane and you can stay here as long as you'd like. Long enough for you to obtain the G.E.D. you want, and to start taking some college classes."

Her eyes widened. "College takes four years!"

"Then at least stay until you get your G.E.D. That should give us enough time to get to know one another, and if you decide by then that you don't want to marry me, then I'll help you get set up somewhere."

Her mouth opened and shut several times, then she tilted her head and studied him. "You really want to marry me? Even knowing I have Shane and there's another baby on the way?"

"I always wanted a big family. Just because Shane and the new baby wouldn't be mine biologically doesn't mean I wouldn't love them as if they were my own. Would you be willing to have more children?"

Her eyes narrowed. "How many more?"

"Well, I'd always thought I'd fill the bedrooms in this place, but if you only wanted one more, I would be fine with that."

She nibbled her lower lip and nodded. "I'll consider it."

Raylic took her hand and leaned a little closer. "Would you allow me to kiss you?"

"I think I'd like that," she said softly.

Raylic leaned closer, and his lips brushed hers. They were soft and supple, and when she parted them, he delved inside for a taste. She tasted of mint, and it was the sweetest kiss he'd ever experienced. When he drew away, her eyes were still closed, and she smiled dreamily.

"Raylic?"

"Yes, Heidi?"

Her eyes opened. "You can kiss me anytime you want."

He smiled. "Then I plan to do it often."

They settled back against the cushions, and she leaned in closer to put her head on his shoulder. He reached for the remote and clicked on the TV, then found a romantic movie for them to watch. It seemed like something a female would like, and he wanted Heidi to be happy... happy enough that she'd decide to never leave.

Chapter Three

The next morning, with a smile on her face, Heidi stretched. She couldn't remember a time that she'd slept so well. Raylic had been so sweet last night, holding her as they'd watched a movie, and then carrying her to bed when she started dozing off. She'd stood in the hall last night, listening to him talk to Shane, and her emotions had gotten the best of her. She couldn't remember a time a man had ever been kind to her little boy. That alone had almost made her agree to be his wife.

While it was true they'd barely spent any time together, sometimes, you could tell someone was a good person right away. When she looked into Raylic's eyes, she could see he had a kind soul. As a police officer, and a warrior on his world, he was a protector, and she and her small son had been lacking one of those the past five years. When she'd agreed to drop out of school and move in with Brent, she'd thought her life was just beginning. Instead, it had turned sour. Rotten. The love she'd felt for Brent had putrefied as the beatings started. And by then, it was too late to escape. She'd been trapped and had stayed that way for far too long.

The more she thought about the sexy alien, the more her body warmed. Her lips still tingled from his kiss last night, and it made her wonder what those lips would feel like on other parts of her body. Her nipples hardened at the thought of the alien's hands on her, caressing her curves and bringing her untold pleasure. Her panties grew damp, and she slid her hand beneath the waistband. She was slick and aching for Raylic, but she didn't dare ask him to satisfy her needs.

Heidi stroked her clit in small circles, spreading her legs a little. Her eyes slid closed as she pictured Raylic lying in bed next to her, imagined it was his hands making her burn for more. Her fingers slid deeper, sliding into her tight channel, pumping in and out. Her breath hitched as she thought about Raylic fucking her with long, deep strokes. Her body flushed, and her lips parted on a silent scream as her orgasm crested and left her breathless.

Pulling her sticky fingers from her panties, she stared up at the ceiling and wondered if she'd ever know what it would be like to have Raylic bend her over the bed and fuck her senseless. The only time she'd ever been able to come was at her own hands, but she'd be willing to bet Raylic had what it took to make her scream his name. Brent had been a sorry excuse for a lover, but she'd stayed with him because she didn't think she had a choice. But if she were to marry Raylic... that would be her choice. And one she was seriously considering. He may not have feelings for her, but he'd treated her kindly and intended to spoil Shane. Being with him intimately wouldn't be a hardship, and she knew feelings could grow over time.

Heidi rolled out of bed. She went into the bathroom to wash her hands and brush her teeth; then she pulled on a pair of jeans and a sweater. Grabbing one of her thin pairs of socks, she put them on and went to check on Shane. His bed was empty, making her frown. Usually, he would come and get her if he woke up first. She hoped he wasn't pestering Raylic. Deciding to see where the guys were, she went downstairs and checked each room. In the kitchen, she saw a note stuck to the fridge.

> *Heidi,*
> *I have Shane with me. We didn't want to wake you. Picking up breakfast and running an errand, then we'll be home. My number is 555-3267 if you want to call and check on Shane.*
> *Raylic*

Well, at least she knew why the house was so quiet.

She wondered how long ago they'd left. Picking up the cordless phone on the counter, she dialed the number Raylic had left and waited for someone to answer.

"Good morning, Heidi," Raylic said when he picked up.

"Morning. Shane didn't bother you this morning, did he?"

"Not at all. I was already up when he woke up. He stepped out of his room just as I was coming down the hall. You aren't upset he's with me, are you? We'll be home in just a few minutes."

"No, it's fine," she said. And it really was. She trusted Raylic to guard Shane with his life. He'd already done as much last night.

"I made a promise to Shane last night, and I needed to see it through. We're just waiting on the diner to finish boxing our breakfast and then we'll come home. I also picked up a booster seat for him this morning, so he'll be safe when we drive around town. He seemed excited about it. Did you want to talk to him?"

"Yes, please."

She heard him hand the phone over.

"Hi, Mama," Shane said. "We went shopping this morning. Raylic bought a camera and got me a booster seat. And then we took the camera to the Terran Station so his friend could take it back to his planet. They're going to take pictures of all the animals up there for me."

Heidi smiled. "That sounds like a lot of fun, Shane. You be sure to thank Raylic for going to so much trouble."

"Yes, Mama. Our food is ready. Love you."

"I love y --"

Shane hung up.

Heidi shook her head, a smile on her face, as she set the phone down. While she waited for them to come home, she explored a little. The tour Raylic had given them last night had been quick, and she hadn't had the opportunity to study each room. His furniture had to be expensive, but it wasn't ostentatious. If anything, his home looked comfortable and lived-in, not like those museum quality homes she'd seen on television.

She eased down onto the sofa and studied the remotes. There were three of them. It took some trial and error, but she figured out how to turn on the TV and cable. She flipped through the stations until she found something interesting to watch. The movie wasn't on long before she heard voices in the kitchen. How had they come home without her hearing anything? Heidi stood and went in search of Raylic and her son, finding them in the kitchen.

"Mama, we got eggs, and bacon, and pancakes, and…" Shane's face scrunched. "What's that other stuff?"

"Grits," Raylic said. "I've heard it's a southern breakfast tradition, and I've become quite fond of them myself."

Heidi smiled and helped set the table. "It sounds great."

They sat down to eat, and Heidi watched as Shane cleaned his plate and finished both a glass of milk and glass of juice. And it wasn't the cheap stuff she'd always had to buy. She'd never known something as simple as orange juice could taste so good. Her breakfast was excellent, and she made sure to eat all of it. She'd been starving herself long enough. Shane had always come first, and if Brent hadn't gotten his fill, there had been hell to pay, which had always left Heidi with the leftovers. It wasn't uncommon for her to have just a spoonful of something to keep the hunger pangs away. She'd learned early on to purchase a cheap box of granola bars and hide them. Sometimes that was all she'd managed to eat during the day, and a box would last for six meals.

"Do you need to do anything before we leave?"

Raylic asked.

"Just put on my shoes," Heidi said. "I'll be quick. I know we need to go to the station so I can give them my statement."

Shane frowned. "Are we going to see Daddy?"

Heidi paused. "Do you want to?"

His little jaw set. "I never want to see him again."

"Then you don't have to," Raylic said. "He's in the jail area, and we're just going to the office part of the department. You'll meet an officer, and your mama and you can tell the nice man or lady what happened."

Shane's eyes went wide. "There are girl officers?"

"Of course." Raylic smiled. "Some of the best officers we have are females. They can be quite fierce when it comes to protecting someone."

Shane nodded thoughtfully. "My mama is like that too."

Raylic's gaze turned her way. "Yes. Yes, she is. Your mama is the fiercest of them all."

Heidi felt her cheeks warm and hurried away before she did something silly, like kissing him again. Not that she was sorry she'd kissed him last night, but it was better not to do that in front Shane, or he might get the wrong idea. It wouldn't take much for her little boy to decide he wanted to keep this life, and she couldn't blame him. Heidi wanted to keep it too, but would it really be fair to Raylic to accept his proposal? Once he got to know her better, he might decide she wasn't the right woman for him. And while she didn't know a lot about the aliens who had moved to her world, she had heard that they mated for life. It didn't stop her from wanting him though.

She quickly put on her tennis shoes, grabbed her purse, and went back downstairs. Raylic and Shane were leaning against the wall, waiting for her in the front entry, both with their ankles crossed and their hands in their pockets. She smiled at the picture they made, and something inside of her broke a little as she realized that her little boy had never known a good man before. Was it any wonder he wanted to mimic Raylic? The sexy alien was all things good, while her ex was all things rotten.

"I hope I didn't take too long," she said as she stepped off the last stair.

"You didn't have to rush," Raylic said. "But if everyone is ready, we'll get the visit to the station out of the way and then we can move on to some fun stuff."

"Like what?" Shane asked.

"Well, your mama and you didn't bring a lot of things from your old home. I thought we could pick up a few things you might need." He hunkered down to get on Shane's level. "And I thought we might go to the toy store."

Shane looked so excited Heidi worried he might burst. The little boy reached for the door, but Raylic steered him back through the kitchen, with Heidi following. They went out through a side door and stepped into the three-car garage. The only vehicle inside was Raylic's SUV, which was already running in front of an open garage door, and they all got inside and buckled.

"I wanted to make sure it was warm enough for you," he said. "Today is warmer than most for this time of year, but I noticed the coats you two are wearing are on the thin side. Didn't want you to catch a chill and get sick."

Heidi was torn between being embarrassed over their poor coats or being happy that someone had thought of their comfort and well-being. Brent would never have started the car early. Of course, their car didn't have heat or air so it wouldn't have mattered.

When they got to the police department, her stomach knotted, and she felt nauseated. They followed Raylic inside, and he inquired about the officer in charge of the case. Once he had a name, he led them back to a room full of desks. They stopped beside a blonde officer, who looked more like Barbie than G.I. Jane. Heidi felt a little frumpy standing next to her.

"Officer Little, this is Heidi. Her boyfriend, Brent, was arrested last night and she's come to fill out a report."

"Raylic." She smiled. "I heard you were taking some time off."

"Yes."

"It was nice of you to bring them in." The officer moved a little closer to him and placed her hand on his arm. "You know, since you won't be getting called in at night, we could go out for drinks."

Heidi took a step back, but what she really wanted to do was rip the woman's hand off Raylic's arm. Just because they'd shared a kiss last night didn't mean she had any right to feel proprietary over him. The alien looked down at the hand on his arm, gently removed it, and stepped back by Heidi's side.

"I'm sorry, Officer Little, but I'm not available for drinks."

Her gaze went from him to Heidi and back again. "I see."

Heidi chewed her lower lip and waited to see what would happen. Was she still filing a report or did they need to leave? She didn't want to cause trouble for him in his place of work. But she really didn't like the gorgeous officer who was undressing him with her eyes either.

"Officer Little, you either take her statement, or I will," Raylic said.

The officer sighed and motioned for Heidi to take a seat. The process didn't take too long, and when they were finished, Raylic took them shopping as promised. She balked at going to the mall because she knew it would cost too much, and instead, asked to go to one of the retail strips in the heart of town.

"We don't have to go to an actual toy store," she said. "The big box stores sell toys."

"I promised Shane a trip to the toy store, so we're going," he said, his tone brooking no argument.

When they reached the store, Raylic insisted on buying her clothes first. He wouldn't settle for her buying less than five outfits, which she thought was too much, and he insisted on a pair of warm boots. He left her in the intimates department to purchase anything else she might need while he took Shane to the kid's clothes. She caught back up with them before too long, but apparently, not soon enough. The shopping cart was overflowing with clothes and shoes.

"Raylic, that's too much!"

He looked at the cart and shook his head. "Looks about right to me. Besides, some of that is your stuff."

She argued all the way to the checkout and finally relented as the cashier began ringing up the items. The toy store was part of the same retail strip but they loaded their packages into the car before walking a few doors down to it. Shane's eyes lit up as they stepped inside and he flitted from one place to another.

When her son saw the trains, he stared at them in awe. There was a table set up in a demo area with tracks and a small train the kids could play with. Shane pushed it around the wooden tracks for nearly a half hour before she was able to pry him away. It didn't escape her notice that Raylic picked up one of the smaller train sets and stuck it into the shopping cart. If he'd picked the big one, she'd have put her foot down, but she didn't see the harm in her son having something he really wanted, as long as it was within reason.

Raylic tried to buy him a bike, but Heidi insisted it was too much and steered them toward the other end of the store. By the time they'd checked out, they had the train set, some Legos, a few puzzles, and a dinosaur playset. It was still too much in her opinion, but Shane seemed so excited that she couldn't really say no. He'd never had so many toys before, especially not nice ones. Most of his old things had come from the dollar store.

Raylic loaded the SUV and drove them back to the house, where he helped Shane set up the train tracks in the playroom. She hadn't even realized there was a playroom until Raylic had carted all of the toys into the closed room at the end of the hall. While the alien and her son set up his toys, she wondered what they were doing for lunch. Her stomach was starting to rumble, and she knew Shane's had to be too.

Raylic looked up from what he was doing and motioned for her to step into the hall. "I know you just had Italian last night, but why don't you order a few pizzas for us? They have pasta dishes too, if you'd prefer that. The menu is in the drawer next to the refrigerator. Tell them I'll pay cash when it gets here. We'll have something healthier for dinner."

She nodded and went downstairs to place the order, glad to have something to do. While she normally helped Shane open his toys, she knew that he needed this time with Raylic. He'd never had one-on-one time with Brent before, and she didn't know when another man might come along who would be nice to her son. Having seen how much food the alien could put away, she ordered a pan of pasta, a large pizza, and two orders of breadsticks. Then she sat on the sofa and flipped through the cable channels while she waited for the food to arrive.

Raylic joined her just before the doorbell rang, looking content and happier than she'd seen him so far. It seemed that playing with her son had been good not only for her boy, but for the sexy alien too. While he paid for their food, she went upstairs to retrieve Shane. She leaned against the playroom doorway for a moment, watching him push the train around the track, making *choo choo* noises. He seemed to be thriving just in the short time that Brent had been out of their lives. How had she stayed so long with such a monster and not seen what it was doing to her child?

Heidi felt like the worst parent, but the important thing was that they were finally safe. Brent wouldn't bother them again, and Shane had a good example to follow, at least for the time being. Heidi didn't know what tomorrow would bring, or the day after, but for now, she was going to enjoy having a caring, attractive man to look at, a roof over their heads, and food in their bellies. Just thinking of Raylic made butterflies flap around her stomach. She'd tried to convince herself her infatuation with the alien was only because he'd saved them, but she wondered if might be something more.

He was her fairy tale prince, the one she'd dreamt of so often over the years. The white knight who would swoop in and rescue her, and they would live happily-ever-after. She'd agreed to consider being his bride, his mate, but she felt selfish for even thinking about it. He deserved someone so much better than her. Someone educated and refined. Someone he could be proud to call his.

Heidi didn't think she met that criteria, but for some reason, he seemed to want her. And he was spoiling her son rotten. Christmas was still nearly a week away, and already Shane had received so much more than he'd ever had. She didn't think she could top it, especially with no money in her wallet. While she'd worried about her son's Christmas for the past few weeks, something told her Raylic wouldn't let the day pass without something special for Shane. She'd seen the look in his eyes when he'd realized that Santa had never visited her son.

"Shane, it's time to eat."

"Do I have to stop playing?" he asked.

"Just for a little while. I'm sure Raylic won't mind if you come back up here after you've finished your lunch. But you need to clean your plate."

He nodded and set the train aside as he stood and walked over to her, hand outstretched. She wrapped her fingers around his and led him downstairs to the kitchen, where Raylic was already setting everything up on the counter. Shane's eyes went wide when he saw the pasta and pizza.

"We get to have pizza *two* days in a row?" he asked in awe.

Heidi laughed. "Yes, Shane. You can have pizza two days in a row. Or you can try the pasta. It looks good too."

"Can I have both?" he asked, then looked upset for asking.

Raylic knelt at his feet. "You can have as much as you want of both, and there are breadsticks too."

Shane sat at the table and waited to be served. Heidi gave him a slice of pizza and a scoop of pasta. As an afterthought, she stuck a breadstick on his plate. She didn't know that he would eat everything, but maybe he'd at least try. She'd tried to feed him as best she could over the years, but she knew he was still on the light side and could stand to gain a little weight. Something told her if they stayed with Raylic much longer, it would happen.

"We bought stuff to occupy Shane," Raylic said, "but you didn't ask for anything for yourself."

"I don't need anything," she assured him. "I can clean, do laundry..."

He shook his head. "I have a maid for that, and I don't want to tell her she's out of work because you're bored. What other things do you like?"

"She likes to read," Shane said. "And she used to paint."

"Paint?" Raylic asked. "What do you paint?"

Her cheeks warmed. "It's nothing. I used to get these little ceramic Christmas ornaments from the store for a dollar, and I'd paint them to put on the tree."

"Before our tree had to be thrown away," Shane said. "We didn't have one this year."

Raylic looked thoughtful. "Since I've been alone all these years, I never thought to put up a tree, but would you like to? I could get one at the store later. I've seen the ones that come with lights already on them."

Shane's eyes went wide. "Really? Ours was just a plain tree with one strand of lights, but the ones in the store have *tons* of lights. Could we really have one?"

Raylic smiled. "Of course. I'll get one today, along with anything else we might need."

Shane yawned before he took another bite of his lunch.

"But I'm thinking your mother and you should stay here for a nap," Raylic said. "It's been a busy day for you both."

Shane looked disappointed but nodded. "Will you get Mama some books too? She likes the ones with kissing on the covers."

Raylic chuckled. "I'll be happy to get her some kissing books."

Heidi's cheeks flamed a brighter red as the alien winked at her, probably remembering their kiss last night. She stared at her plate intently and felt a nudge under the table. She looked up to find Raylic watching her with humor dancing in his eyes.

"Kissing books?"

If she blushed any harder, her entire body would be red. "I like romances. I grew up reading fairy tales, and they're just the grown-up version. There's nothing wrong with reading a romance."

"I was just teasing you, Heidi," he said softly. "I'll

buy you whatever kind of books you want."

Heidi smiled a little as she finished her lunch, then she helped Shane clear the table, and she put him to bed for a nap. Raylic let her know when he was heading out and she settled on the sofa to watch TV. As she flipped through the channels, she realized she couldn't remember a time she'd ever been happier. And it wasn't because of all the things Raylic had bought for them. It was the fact he wanted them to be happy, and he cared that they were taken care of. That was worth more than all the money in the world.

Chapter Four

Raylic stared at the large selection of romance books in Main Street Books. He'd never realized there were so many different kinds, and he hadn't thought to ask Heidi if she had a preference. Not knowing what else to do, he grabbed a variety. Werewolves. Aliens. Cowboys. Lords. He'd like to think she had a preference for aliens, if for no other reason than maybe he had a decent shot at claiming her for his mate.

After he had checked out, he went to the big box store and studied the different Christmas trees. He had a feeling that anything he picked would be well-received, but he wanted the perfect tree. Christmas was important for little boys, from what he'd gathered, and he wanted this to be Shane's best Christmas ever. He selected a seven-foot spruce that was pre-lit with multi-colored lights. When it came to ornaments, he didn't know what they would prefer, so he got a little bit of everything.

Even though he checked the craft area, he didn't see the ornaments you could paint yourself, and he was disappointed. A woman behind the counter near fabrics smiled at him.

"Can I help you with something?" she asked.

"I was looking for the Christmas ornaments you can paint."

She pursed her lips. "We haven't carried those for the last two years, but if you stop at the craft shop over on Elm, you might find some there. They should have a good selection of paints too." She lowered her voice to a whisper. "Better than anything you'd find here."

"Thank you. I'll be sure to check there."

Raylic paid for his purchases then stopped by the craft store, selecting a wide range of ceramic ornaments for the tree, then grabbed a dozen paint colors and some brushes to go with them. By the time he pulled into the garage at home, he was near bursting with excitement over seeing Shane's face when he pulled out the tree and ornaments.

He picked up the sack of books and went inside, looking for his... his what? He'd almost called them his family. Certainly that was what he wanted them to be, but he was giving Heidi all the space she needed. They would take things at her pace, however slow that might be. And if he had a case of blue balls in the meantime, well, that's what his hand was for.

"Heidi?" he called out as he entered the kitchen.

She materialized a moment later, coming from the direction of the living room. "Did you get a tree?"

"I got a tree, ornaments, and some other stuff." He handed her the sack of books. "These are for you."

She set the bag on the kitchen table and pulled out the books, her smile growing with every title she read. "You bought so many. Thank you!"

"I wanted to make sure you had plenty to read. If you get Shane, I'll bring in the tree and other things."

Her gaze narrowed. "You didn't buy more toys, did you?"

He smiled. "No. No more toys. Not until Christmas morning."

Heidi shook her head and left to get Shane. Raylic went back to the SUV and pulled out the tree, and other bags, then took everything to the living room. Raylic didn't think the boy would be able to put the tree together, so he began setting everything up before Shane came downstairs. He was just plugging it in when he heard an excited squeal and turned in time for Shane to launch himself into Raylic's arms.

"It's the best tree ever!" the boy said.

"Why don't you and your mom go through the bags and check out the ornaments I bought. I even got some you can decorate yourselves." Raylic smiled. "Why don't you put the first ornament up?"

Shane and Heidi went through the sacks. He noticed tears in her eyes as she looked through the ceramic ones he'd picked up at the craft store. She set them aside and helped Shane hang the other ornaments on the tree, leaving the top for Raylic. He'd remembered Brielle and Syl had an angel topper on their tree and he'd found one that reminded him of Heidi. He placed it on top and then turned to see Heidi silently crying. While Shane studied the tree from every angle, Raylic wrapped his arms around Heidi and held her close.

"Are you all right?" he asked softly.

"I'm scared that if I blink all of this is going to go away and we'll be back in that apartment, waiting on Brent to come home. It's the most beautiful tree I've ever seen, and you're the kindest man I've ever known. I'm worried I'm dreaming."

He tipped up her chin and placed his lips against hers in a sweet, brief kiss. "You're not dreaming, Heidi. You never have to go back to Brent or that apartment. And all of this," he said with a sweeping gesture, "is yours for as long as you want it."

She sniffled and nodded her head. His thumbs wiped the tears from her cheeks.

"I'm yours for as long as you want me," he said softly. "I did all of this for you, and for Shane, because I want the two of you to have the best of everything. I don't claim to be the best male for you, but I can assure you that I will never go a day without showing the two of you what you mean to me."

She pulled away a little, and he wondered if he'd gone too far. They were still strangers for the most part, but he didn't have to know them for years to decide that he wanted to be part of their lives. He already knew that Shane was an incredible kid, and Heidi was the sweetest woman he'd ever met. She reached up and placed her hand on his cheek before kissing him again.

"Thank you. For everything, but mostly for being you." She smiled. "You make us feel safe, and that's worth more than anything."

Her cheeks warmed, and something like desire burned in her eyes.

"And do I only make you feel safe?" he asked.

The blush deepened. "No. You make me feel other things too. No one has ever made me feel this way before, Raylic, and it scares me a little."

"I will never push you for more than you're willing to give."

Heidi nodded, and she cuddled with Raylic on the couch while Shane studied every angle of the tree, reaching out to touch the ornaments and lights as if he couldn't quite believe the tree was real. Raylic found a Christmas movie for them to watch while Heidi popped some popcorn. The movie couldn't hold Shane's attention, and after he had stuffed himself, he asked if he could bring his toys downstairs to play by the tree.

Raylic smiled. "That's fine. If you'd like, I'll bring your train down tomorrow, and you can leave it in here until Christmas Eve. After that, it will need to go back upstairs to make room for your new toys."

The little boy's eyes lit up. "Toys? You mean Santa is really going to come this year?"

"He really is," Raylic promised. He only hoped Heidi wouldn't get upset when she saw everything he intended to buy for the boy. He already had his eye on a table at the toy store and a larger train set.

Shane scampered off to get his toys while Raylic and Heidi finished watching the movie. When it went off, she made them dinner. Raylic slid his hand around her waist as she stirred something on the stove.

"What did you make?" he asked.

"Pork chops and rice pilaf. I hope you don't mind. I

should have asked if you had something special planned for them." She worried her bottom lip.

"It's fine, Heidi. Make whatever you want. You can use anything in this kitchen, in the entire house, and I won't be angry with you. I told you to make yourself at home, and I meant it. What's mine is yours. You don't need permission to do anything."

She nodded, relief evident in her eyes.

"Heidi," he said softly. "I'm not like your boyfriend. I'm not ever going to strike you, and I don't plan to raise my voice to you. If you ever do something I don't like, we'll discuss it like rational adults. But for the record, I don't see you making me cross. I want you to feel at home here, Heidi, not walking on eggshells hoping you won't make someone angry."

"I know, it's just going to take me a little time. Brent is all I've known for five years."

Raylic brushed a kiss against her lips. "And I'm going to do everything in my power to erase those bad memories and give you good ones."

"You already are." She hugged him. "Now, let me finish dinner, or I'll burn everything. The pork chops should be ready. I hope you like the way I seasoned them. I used your Garlic and Herb mix, and some Worcestershire. They should be good and tender."

"Sounds wonderful. I'll get Shane and then set the table."

He paused in the doorway, watching her another moment, a smile on his face. He'd long wanted a woman in his home, and now that Heidi was here, he didn't want to let her go. She looked right moving about his house as if it were her own. With a little luck, he'd convince her that she belonged here with him, both Shane and her. He'd never seen himself as being a father to a human child, much less two of them, but he would embrace Heidi's children as if they were his own.

Raylic went into the living room where Shane was quietly playing. The little boy looked up, a huge smile on his face. Raylic motioned for him to get up.

"Time to eat dinner," Raylic said. "Your mom fixed a nice meal for us. Go wash your hands and head to the kitchen."

Shane shot up from the floor and raced down the hall to the downstairs bathroom. Raylic smiled and went back to the kitchen, washing his hands at the sink. Then he took down the plates and glasses to set the table. The kitchen smelled amazing, and he couldn't wait to taste Heidi's cooking. When they were seated, and everyone had a full plate, Raylic took the first bite, the seasonings she used exploded on his tongue.

"It's really good," he told her. "Where'd you learn to cook like this?"

"I took a few cooking classes at the library, but I seldom got to use anything I had learned. We didn't really have money for expensive dinners. Hamburger Helper, frozen family meals, and macaroni were staples in our house," she said. "Growing up, I used to watch my mom cook though."

"You haven't talked much about your family."

She shrugged and glanced at Shane, who was too busy shoveling food into his mouth to pay attention to them. "They washed their hands of me when I told them I was pregnant. I told you earlier they died in a fire. They never did forgive me."

"So, you were really young when you had him?" Raylic asked. "I never thought to ask how old you are."

"I'm twenty-one, so don't worry, I'm legal." She smiled. "How old are you?"

"I'm thirty-two. Does our age difference bother you?" he asked.

"No. I mean, Brent was older than me by a few years, but I don't think he ever really matured. You have a stable job, own your own home, and from the way you carry yourself, I'd say you command respect. Brent couldn't claim even one of those things. He was still a child in a lot of ways, and I either ignored it or just resigned myself to my fate."

"You don't have to worry about him ever again," Raylic said.

"He'll eventually get out of jail. What if he blames me for his arrest and comes after me?"

"Then I will protect you, but I don't think he's getting out for a while. Something tells me he doesn't have the means to make bail."

She smiled a little. "No, I don't think so. Not unless he was hiding money from me, which I guess is possible. He seemed to always have plenty for alcohol and never enough for things like food or rent."

They finished their meal and Heidi went upstairs to bathe Shane and get him tucked into bed. Raylic stacked Shane's toys neatly along the wall near the tree. For the first time since he'd bought the place, it actually felt like a home. And he knew it wasn't because of the tree or the toys. It was because of Heidi and Shane. *They* made it feel like a home and made him long for a mate and children. He'd offered to claim her, and she'd promised to think about it, but the more time he spent with them, the more he wanted it to be forever, and not just for right now.

Heidi came back downstairs and stood in front of the tree. Raylic stepped up behind her and wrapped an arm around her waist, pulling her back against his chest. They stood there quietly, marveling at the beauty of the tree, content to stand close to one another. It was probably the closest he'd ever felt to someone before, and he knew that he never wanted to let her go.

"Being here with you, like this, feels more right than anything ever has in my life," he said. "I said I'd give you time to think things over, but just know that if you were my mate, we would have many moments like this. My job can be time-consuming, but I would always put you first."

"Raylic, I haven't agreed to be your mate, not because I don't want to, but because I think you can do better than me. I don't want you to wake up one day and regret settling for me when you could have had someone else."

He tightened his hold on her. "Better than you?"

She nodded slowly.

"Heidi, I've been on Earth for a while now, and I've gone on some dates during that time. Not once has anyone captured my attention the way you have. None of them made me want to hold them all night or wake up beside them the next day. I've never thought of being a daddy to a human child, but I will welcome both of your children into my family and treat them as my own. I already care about Shane and you, and I want you here with me, not just for right now, but forever."

She relaxed against him and placed her hand over his. "I feel selfish accepting your proposal, but if you truly want us, if you're sure, then I'll be your mate. What exactly is involved in that?"

He smiled, kissing the top of her head, happier than he'd ever been before. "I need to speak to the council and ask permission for our mating. There's no reason they would deny me since you've agreed to have at least one child with me. Once we have their blessing, they file some paperwork on their end, and we're officially mates."

"No ceremony or drawn out engagement?" she asked.

"Nothing like that. Although, if you wanted a ceremony, we could have one. I know on Earth you have weddings with rings and everything. Would you like a ring?"

She lifted her left hand and looked at it. "Maybe

something simple. A plain gold band would suffice."

"And if I wore one too, would it tell other human females that I'm no longer available?"

"It would, but some won't care. I think some women like the challenge of trying to get a married man to cheat on his wife. I don't understand it, but that's just how it is. Most will respect the fact you're taken."

He nodded. "Then we'll stop and get rings on the way back from speaking to the council. Would you like to go tomorrow? Or do you need more time to talk to Shane about it? Is he old enough to understand?"

"He'll understand that we get to stay with you forever. He's never experienced a wedding, but he's seen them on TV. If we explain it like that, I think he'll know what it means for me to be mated to you. If we're going to live here, we're going to have to redecorate one of the bedrooms and make it a nursery. I'm only a couple months along right now, but the baby will be here before we know it."

"You can change anything you want in the house."

"Does this…" She tipped her head back to look up at him. "Does this mean I move into your bedroom now?"

"Do you need more time for that aspect of our relationship?"

Her cheeks pinkened again. "No. I want you, Raylic. I keep telling myself that I shouldn't, that it's too soon, but I can't deny that I go all soft and warm with the slightest touch from you."

He smiled and turned her to face him. With his hands cupping her face, he lowered his head and kissed her, softly at first and then more demanding. His tongue dipped into her mouth as she opened to him. Her lips were soft and supple under his. Kissing Heidi would always be one of his favorite pastimes. The way she melted against him, gave herself freely, made him burn even hotter for her.

Without a word, he lifted her into his arms and carried her upstairs, pushing the master bedroom door open with his foot. He eased her down on the bed before shutting and locking the door. Prowling closer, he noticed that her eyes had darkened as she licked her lips and looked him over from head to toe. Raylic removed his black long-sleeve tee and kicked off his boots. Heidi stood and reached for him, her fingers skimming his chest and down his abs. He'd never thought much about how he looked, but she seemed pleased.

"Your body is a work of art," she said as she reached for the button on his jeans. "I only hope you aren't disappointed in mine."

"You're beautiful, Heidi."

She smiled a little. "I have stretch marks from having Shane, and my boobs aren't as perky as they were before breastfeeding him."

He tipped her chin up and kissed her. "You're perfect just the way you are. Do you think I'll look down on you because of those things? They're part of what makes you who you are. You carried your son and nurtured him. That's a miracle, and something to be cherished."

She lifted her sweater over her head and let it fall to the floor. Her bra cupped her breasts, lifting them in an enticing manner. She removed her socks and shoes, then shimmied out of her jeans. He saw the faint white lines on her abdomen where her body had cradled Shane as he grew inside of her. He traced them tenderly, then knelt at her feet to press kisses to them.

"Every part of you is perfect," he said. "Never think otherwise."

Heidi's eyes turned glassy with unshed tears as he tenderly removed the rest of her clothes, before discarding his own. He pulled her closer, wrapping an arm around her waist. She felt amazing pressed against him. His hand skimmed her curves before palming her ass and giving it a squeeze. He'd meant what he said. She was perfect in every way. Raylic toppled her to the bed, smiling as he watched her breasts bounce.

"Before we go any further, you're sure this is what you want?" he asked.

"I'm sure. More certain than I've ever been of anything before. I want you, Raylic. I want you to make me yours."

His fingers skimmed up her leg to the juncture of her thighs, brushing over her damp curls. Even if she hadn't told him she wanted him, the evidence was clear. She flushed a pretty pink as he explored her body. His lips traveled the curve of her hip, across her ribs, and closed over a rosy peak, drawing her nipple into his mouth.

"Feels so good," she murmured.

He lavished the other side with just as much attention before settling over her body. He wanted to spend hours worshiping her body, but he ached to be with her. His cock had never been this hard before, and he worried he'd embarrass himself if he didn't get inside of her soon. Her thighs spread wider as her calves hooked over his legs. Heidi opened herself to him, welcoming him in, and Raylic sank into her one inch at a time.

"You're so tight," he said, straining to hold himself back and not hurt her.

Heidi bit her lip. "I think it's more that you're huge."

He smiled and kissed her. "Tell me if I hurt you."

At her nod of encouragement, he set up a slow and steady pace. Long, deep strokes that had him groaning from the sheer pleasure she gave him. Her nails bit into his shoulders as sweat slicked his skin. Raylic reached between their bodies and brushed her clit with his thumb, making her gasp and jerk beneath him. As he teased the little bud, he felt her body tightening. He knew he wasn't going to last much longer and he wanted her to come with him. As he took her harder, faster, she shattered beneath him, crying out his name and holding on tight.

Raylic spilled himself inside of her and buried his face against her neck as he willed his heart to slow. Heidi wrapped her arms around him, and he rolled them to their sides, drawing her leg over his hip so they could stay joined. She gave him a contented smile as she traced a pattern on his bicep.

"That was incredible," she said.

"Only because it was with you."

"We should get cleaned up so I can check on Shane. We were kind of loud."

He glanced over at the door. "Think we woke him?"

"I hope not. After everything he's been through, a locked door with yelling only means bad things are happening."

That sobered him. "Come on. We'll take a shower and check on Shane; then I want to hold you until you fall asleep."

She kissed him. "I'd like that."

The shower took longer than expected, as they couldn't keep their hands off one another, but once they were clean and she'd pulled on one of his T-shirts, she tiptoed down the hall and opened Shane's door. Raylic peered over her shoulder. The boy slept peacefully, a stuffed bear tucked under his arm and one leg sticking out from the covers. No, not just a boy to him anymore. His son. He smiled at the thought.

"Come on," she whispered. "He'll sleep until at least seven."

Raylic paused at the spare room she'd used. "We should move your things into the bedroom."

"Want to do it before bed tonight or sometime tomorrow?"

"I'm not tired at the moment. You?"

She shook her head.

"Then let's do it now." He smiled. "I think I'm going to like having your things in there with mine. You have your own closet, and I already have two empty drawers in the dresser. If you ever need more space, just let me know."

"It's more than enough room."

"Come on." He swatted her on the ass. "Let's get this done so we can cuddle in bed."

Heidi smiled and shook her head at him before gathering her clothes and shoes. It didn't take long for them to have her things folded or hung up and put away. By the time they were back in bed, her body curled against his, he knew that he'd made the right choice when he'd claimed Heidi. She was everything he'd ever wanted, and so much more. And he would spend the rest of his life making sure she was cherished and taken care of, her and their children.

Chapter Five

Heidi plated the omelet she'd just made, something she'd always wanted to try, and set it on the table. Grocery money had been almost non-existent when she'd been with Brent, and before that, her mother had done all the cooking. It was nice to be able to create filling meals for her family and not worry about the financial aspect. From the size of the house and the way he spent money, she had assumed that when Raylic said he was well-off, it was probably an understatement. Not that his wealth mattered to her. All she'd ever wanted was enough money to pay the bills and put food on the table. She'd never dreamed of being a millionaire or owning a castle.

Raylic kissed her cheek as he pulled glasses out of the cabinet next to the stove. "You're awfully happy this morning."

"We're really getting married today, aren't we?" she asked. "I mean, mated."

"Yes, we are."

There was a squeal from the doorway, and Heidi spun that way, her eyes widening when she saw Shane standing there. He looked confused and excited all at the same time. Her little boy scurried into the kitchen and tugged on her shirt.

"Raylic's going to be my daddy?" he asked.

"Yes, sweetheart. Are you okay with that?"

Shane seemed to think about it a moment. "We get to keep living here? And play with all the toys?"

"Well, yes, but Raylic being your dad means more than just a house and toys."

He nodded sagely. "It means we won't get hit or yelled at anymore. He's nice, Mama."

Raylic knelt at Shane's feet. "So, you're okay with me being your new dad?"

Shane smiled widely and threw his arms around

Raylic. "It's the best thing ever."

"Good." Raylic hugged him tightly. "If you aren't comfortable calling me Dad yet, you can still call me Raylic."

Shane looked at him shyly. "Can I call you Daddy?"

"I'd be honored for you to call me Daddy. Now, did you wash your hands?"

Shane nodded.

"Then have a seat. It looks like your mom is about finished making breakfast. Do you want juice or milk?"

"Juice."

Raylic poured three glasses of orange juice and took out the silverware. Once the table was set and the all the omelets cooked, they sat down to breakfast. Heidi was happier than she'd ever been before, even though she was a little nervous about meeting Raylic's council. What if they didn't like her? He seemed certain their mating would be approved, but if the council denied them, how would she explain that to Shane?

After they had finished eating, Raylic helped her load the dishwasher and then they all went upstairs to get ready. Shane came out his room wearing his nicest sweater and jeans, both gifts from Raylic. Before their shopping spree, Shane's nicest sweater had been faded with little fuzz balls all over it, and his jeans had grass stains on the knees. He'd been in dire need of a new wardrobe, and her sexy alien had seen that it was taken care of.

"Everyone ready?" Raylic asked.

"I guess," Heidi said, trying to calm her nerves. "What if they don't like me?"

"The fact I like you is what matters." He smiled. "Come on. It won't be so bad."

They got into Raylic's SUV and drove to the Terran Station. Heidi still felt like a nervous wreck the entire way there, and entering the building didn't help her anxiety any. He led the way toward the conference rooms and found an empty one, ushering Heidi and Shane inside. Then he shut the doors and began pressing buttons on the large Vid-Comm. A few minutes later, a room that looked similar to the one they were in appeared on the screen, with three Terrans sitting around a table.

"Good morning, Raylic," one of them said. "I see you have company with you."

"Yes, Larimar. I've come to ask the council for their blessing. Heidi and I wish to be mated."

"And the boy?"

"Her son, Shane. My son, as soon as you approve the mating."

"I see. And she's willing to have more children?" Larimar asked.

Heidi gripped his hand tight. "She is, but she's currently expecting, so it will be a little while before we have another child."

Another councilman's eyebrows shot up. "Is it yours?"

"No, Faltz. Heidi was already pregnant when I met her, but I'm willing to embrace both children as my own. I have a large enough home we could have one or two more children if we're blessed with any."

"So, you're welcoming two human children into your home?" Larimar asked.

"Yes, but Reyvor has three human daughters. I don't see that it matters how many human children we have."

The council members talked amongst themselves, too quietly for Heidi to hear what they were saying. She just knew they were going to deny their mating and her grip tightened on Raylic's hand even more. What if they told him he had to toss her out? What if they said Raylic could never see her again? She didn't understand exactly how much power they had over his decisions, but she'd bet it was a lot.

After several more torturous minutes, Larimar faced them again.

"We've decided we will approve your mating. You've done good work for us, Raylic, and you've never really asked for anything. You may claim Heidi as your mate, with our blessing. We'll file the paperwork today. Might I suggest you officially adopt her young son and the baby in her womb? I don't know anything about the birth father, but I'd hate for you to face any nasty surprises later."

Raylic nodded. "I'll meet with someone today about getting the paperwork started."

"Enjoy your new mate, Raylic." Larimar smiled, and then the screen went black.

"That's it?" Heidi asked.

"That's it. We're officially mates now." He smiled. "Would you be all right with me adopting Shane?"

Shane tugged on Heidi's other hand. "Please, Mama? I want him to be my daddy for real."

Heidi leaned down to kiss the top of Shane's head before facing Raylic again. "I'd love for you to adopt him, but I don't know that his father will sign away his rights."

"Leave that to me," Raylic said. "Why don't I walk the two of you to the food court for some ice cream while I go get that paperwork started?"

Shane bounced up and down. "Ice cream!"

Heidi couldn't help but smile at her son. "Isn't it too cold out for ice cream?"

Raylic gave her a mock look of outrage. "It's never too cold for ice cream!"

Heidi just smiled and shook her head as Raylic led them to the food court and bought them each some ice cream. Then he disappeared to go see about the adoption paperwork. As Heidi and Shane sat at a table, she observed everyone around her, watching as Human/Terran couples sat and enjoyed a meal together, or walked by holding hands. She wondered how many were mates and which ones were thinking about becoming mates. A lot of the Terrans sat in groups together, no humans among them. Were those the ones still waiting to find their other half?

She must have looked a little too long at one of the tables because a Terran stood and started heading her way. She braced herself, not knowing what he might ask, or if he would be upset that she'd been watching everyone. He smiled as he stopped beside the table.

"My name is Lovic, and I'm head of security here. It's not common to see a human female alone in our food court. Are you waiting for someone?"

Great. They thought she was a threat? "I'm waiting for Raylic. He said he needed to get some paperwork started so he can adopt my son, Shane."

Lovic looked from her to Shane and back again. "You're recently mated?"

"Just today," Heidi said. "I guess he didn't want to bore us with whatever is involved in adopting Shane. He left us here to enjoy a treat while he took care of everything."

"If you need anything while you're waiting, I'm sitting right over there," he said, pointing to his table of friends. "Any of us would be happy to help you."

"Thank you." She smiled a little. "I'm hoping he won't be much longer."

Lovic nodded. "Enjoy your treat."

With that, he walked off, leaving Heidi and Shane alone again.

"Mama, do you think my other daddy will be mean and not sign the papers?" Shane asked.

"I don't know, sweetheart. I guess it depends on how generous he feels whenever Raylic asks him to sign."

Shane seemed to think about it a moment. "My new daddy isn't going to take no for an answer. I bet he gets my other daddy to sign the papers."

"I bet you're right." Heidi smiled at him. "Finish your ice cream. It's melting."

Just as they were finishing, Raylic slid into the seat next to Heidi. He looked happy, so she hoped that meant things had gone well. He reached over and lifted her hand, placing a kiss against her palm. Her cheeks warmed as she smiled at him.

"I take it that everything went well?" she asked.

"I spoke with Zwyk. He presides over records, and he seems to think I won't have any trouble getting the adoption to go through. Since Shane's dad is currently in jail for abusing the two of you, and I have excellent standing in the community and with the Terran Station, he doesn't think we'll even need his signature."

Shane gave a whoop and launched himself into Raylic's arms.

"Now, what would the two of you like to do today to celebrate our newly formed family?" Raylic asked.

"I've never been to see a movie at the theater before," Shane said. "There's a new one out about a troll king who kidnaps a baby and the princess has to go find the baby. Could we watch that one?"

Raylic smiled. "If it's okay with your mother, it's fine by me."

"I think a movie is a great idea," Heidi said.

"Let me see what times the movie is playing." Raylic pulled out his phone and accessed the internet. After a few moments, he showed a picture of the movie poster to Shane. "Is this it?"

Shane nodded eagerly.

"It looks like there's an eleven o'clock showing. We can get some popcorn while we're there, and maybe hot dogs or something since it will be around lunchtime."

"Theater food for lunch?" Shane asked, his eyes wide. "This is the best day ever!"

Raylic laughed and lifted Shane up, swinging him around to ride piggyback. Then he held out a hand to Heidi. Her fingers slid across his palm, and he helped her from the chair before clasping their hands together. He held Shane in place with his other hand. For the first time in the last five years, Heidi actually felt like she was part of a family again. And this time, it was *her* family. So what if her parents hadn't wanted anything to do with her? She had something much better now. She had Raylic.

When they arrived at the movie theater, Raylic bought their tickets, then ushered them inside and let them choose whatever they wanted from concessions. By the time the movie was starting, Shane was squirming in his seat, had finished his hot dog, and was happily munching on popcorn. Heidi couldn't help but smile at his excitement. He was experiencing a lot of firsts with Raylic, and the alien seemed to want to do even more for them.

The movie started, and Raylic laced his fingers with hers. Her heart raced at his nearness, and it was hard for her to focus on the show. It was cute, and she could see why Shane wanted to watch it. But Heidi was still more than a little aware of Raylic and how close they were, how dark it was, and how damn good he smelled. Nighttime wouldn't come soon enough because she knew one thing was certain, she was getting her sexy new mate naked as soon as possible.

Chapter Six

Raylic leaned against Shane's doorway and listened as Heidi finished reading a story to their son. *My* son. He liked that, and he smiled. It was nice having a family of his own. He'd watched his friends pair off and find their mates, start families, and now it was his turn. Raylic couldn't remember a time when he'd been happier.

Heidi finished tucking Shane in. They both kissed him goodnight and then Raylic led her by the hand to the bedroom, where he pulled out the sack of swimwear he'd ordered online the other night. She looked at him, one eyebrow raised.

"You do know it's winter?" she asked.

"There's a hot tub downstairs. It's in the far corner of the sunroom, so you may not have seen it. I thought we could go relax for a little while."

She smiled and snatched the suit from his hand. "Then why didn't you just say so?"

Raylic chuckled and watched hungrily as she stripped out of her clothes and pulled on the two-piece swimsuit. The aqua color looked fantastic on her. It wasn't until she gave him that look again that he realized he wasn't getting dressed. He pulled off his clothes and stepped into the swim trunks. When they were finished, he tossed her over his shoulder with a smack to her ass and carried her downstairs. Just as he cleared the front entry, someone rang the bell.

Raylic froze and turned to look at the door, wondering who the hell would be stopping by his house so late at night. Trepidation filled him as he set Heidi on her feet and motioned for her to stay behind him. None of his friends would show at this late hour unless something was wrong. He opened the door, and his eyes widened when he saw who was on his front steps.

"Lieutenant Ardis, is something wrong?" Raylic

asked.

"You weren't answering your phone."

"I'm sorry. I must have left it in the bedroom earlier. Did you need me to come in tonight?"

The lieutenant shook his head. "May I come in? I have some news, and I'd rather discuss it inside."

"Of course." Raylic took a step back and let the man enter.

Lieutenant Ardis shoved his hands in his pockets and gave a nod to Heidi. "Ma'am. I'm sorry to disturb you so late."

Heidi's hand curled around Raylic's biceps as they faced the Lt.

"I thought the two of you should know that Brent King was scheduled to see the judge as the last case on the docket. On his way back to jail, he somehow broke free of the officers and tried to make a run for it. They chased him down, but he managed to get his hands on one of their weapons."

Heidi gasped and tensed beside him.

"The other officer tried to wrestle the weapon from him, and it went off. I'm afraid Brent King was fatally shot during the altercation. He died before paramedics could arrive on scene. So, while he won't be getting any jail time, he won't be bothering you ever again. Thought you'd want to know," Lieutenant Ardis said.

"He's dead?" Heidi asked, sounding oddly calm.

"Yes, ma'am. I'm sorry if that news distresses you."

A laugh escaped Heidi, and her hand tightened on Raylic. "Distressed? Are you kidding? After the hell that asshole put me through the last five years? I'm going to throw a party to celebrate his demise!"

The Lt. smiled a little. "Then I'm happy I got to be the bearer of glad tidings for a change."

"Thank you for stopping by to tell us," Raylic said. "We'll think of the best way to tell Shane when he wakes up in the morning."

The Lt. nodded. "I'll let you get back to your swim. I'll see you when you come to back work next week, Raylic."

Raylic shook his hand and then closed the door behind him, twisting the locks. He turned to face Heidi, who looked a little stunned, but happy with the news of her ex's demise. He couldn't really blame her. It also meant adopting Shane would be a lot smoother since the father wouldn't be in the picture at all. He grabbed her hand and led her to the back of the house and out into the sunroom, then walked over to the corner of the room where the hot tub hid in the shadows.

He helped her over the edge of the tub. She sighed and closed her eyes as the hot water lapped around her. Raylic stepped in as well, pulling her close to him. If he'd thought this through a little better, he'd have bought strawberries and champagne for their celebration. Then again, he wasn't certain if a pregnant female could have champagne. Heidi didn't seem to mind not having anything other than his company though.

His hand caressed her stomach and froze. "I didn't think this through. I bet this water is too hot for the baby. I remember a friend's mate complaining that she missed hot baths."

Her eyes went wide. "I didn't think of that either."

Raylic stood, lifting her into his arms, and got out of the hot tub. Instead, he carried her out a side door he was betting she'd never noticed and took her to the indoor pool. It was small, not big enough for laps or anything, but the water would be soothing, and not too hot for their unborn child. He walked down the steps and into the cooler water, keeping a tight grip on her.

"We have an indoor pool?" she asked, as she looked around and then up. "And a ceiling made of glass? What exactly is the purpose of a glass ceiling?"

"It lets in natural light during the day, and you can see the stars at night. As long as a tree doesn't fall on the house, it's pleasant to have. The pool isn't as big as the outdoor one, but this will do in the colder months. We'll bring Shane down here tomorrow if you'd like. It's not large enough to invite too many people over, but some of my friends have kids. If you think Shane would like to meet them, we can have a few people over for a pool party."

"I'm sure he'd love that. He loves to swim, and he doesn't have friends outside of school."

Raylic let her slide down his body until she was standing with him in the shallow end of the pool. He smoothed her hair back from her face, marveling at how beautiful she was. It was no secret he'd wanted a mate for a while, but he was glad he'd waited for Heidi. He'd never met a sweeter woman, and while he knew she liked the things he was able to buy for her, he knew she hadn't agreed to marry him because of his money. There wasn't a greedy bone in her body.

"Why are you looking at me like that?" she asked.

"Like what?"

She shrugged. "I don't know. Like…"

"Like you're the most amazing thing in the world?"

She blushed.

"Because you are," he said. "I was just thinking how lucky I am that you're mine. Having Shane and you here makes me feel complete, and I can't wait to add this little one to our family," he said placing a hand on her belly.

"You're really going to adopt Shane?"

He nodded. "And this one too."

Heidi nibbled her lower lip. "Or I could just put you down as the father on the birth certificate. You'll be the baby's father in every way that counts. Brent never wanted anything to do with the baby, never really believed it was his. Trust me, if he were still alive, he wouldn't have fought you over custody."

"You would do that? Will they let you, since I'm clearly not the father? Any children we have will have my coloring."

"I guess we'll find out when the time comes. Right now, I don't even know if I'm having a girl or a boy."

Raylic rubbed her belly lightly, a smile tilting up the corners of his lips. "It's hard to believe there's a life growing in there. I can't wait for your belly to swell and the baby to start kicking."

Heidi laughed. "Let's not rush the kicking. Shane used to kick pretty hard and then he'd sit on my bladder. Pregnancy is a miracle, and I'm thankful for both of my children, but being the size of a small whale is not exactly fun, especially during the hotter months."

"You'll have whatever you need. I promise."

She kissed him softly. "Just knowing you're here with me is enough."

"I also promised you a ring, and I haven't bought you one yet. We'll go tomorrow and pick out something that will show the world you belong to me and I belong to you. I also need to make sure my affairs are in order before I return to work so that the kids and you will be taken care of if anything happens to me."

Her grip tightened on him. "I have a better idea. Don't get shot."

He chuckled. "I will endeavor to dodge any bullets that head my way."

"Part of me wants to be selfish and tell you to quit, but if you weren't a police officer, then Shane and I would still be in that apartment, or Brent could have killed me that night. It wouldn't be fair of me to ask you to give up something you love, and it's obvious you make a difference in people's lives. I'd never forgive myself if someone died because you were meant to save them and I'd kept you from it."

He buried his hand in her hair. "Heidi, I'm always careful at work. I can't promise never to get hurt, but I will do everything in my power to come home to you every night. I have something to live for, a family."

Heidi kissed him, her fingers sinking into his hair and her leg going around his waist. Raylic wrapped his arms around her, pulling her tight against him. All it took was one touch from her, and he wanted more. Her mouth opened under his and he took advantage, pressing her back against the side of the pool. Heidi was sweet and so very much his. Raylic felt possessiveness well up inside of him as the kiss deepened. His to cherish. His to protect.

His hand slipped into the bottoms of her swimsuit and stroked her pussy, feeling how hot and slick she was. Her clit was already swelling, and he stroked the little nub, making her moan into his mouth. There was nothing like having Heidi in his arms. With her, past lovers blurred, and there was only the present. There had only been a handful of human women since he came to Earth, but with sweet Heidi riding his hand, all memories of them vanished.

Raylic stepped back just long enough to remove her swimsuit and toss it onto the side of the pool with a wet *smack*. He lifted her onto the edge, spreading her thighs. Her pussy glistened and beckoned to him, making his mouth water as he wondered how she'd taste. Parting the lips of her pussy, he leaned forward and teased her with his tongue, stroking her hard little clit until she cried out and thrust her hips upward. He teased and tormented her, making her whimper and writhe as she begged for more. When she came, he thrust his tongue into her tight channel, slowly fucking her until the last ripple of pleasure was wrung from her body.

Heidi lay panting on the concrete beside the pool, and Raylic knew he needed to have her. He levered himself out of the pool, stripped off his swim trunks, and carried her to one of the lounge chairs. With one swift motion, he embedded himself in her sweet warmth, making her cry out in pleasure. His hips rocked against hers as he ravaged her mouth, taking everything she had to give and still wanting more. He thrust into her harder, deeper. As she cried out her release, her pussy gripping him tightly, he drove into her one last time, coming deep inside of her. He tried not to crush her with his weight as he kissed her slowly.

"I will never get enough of you," he murmured against her lips.

"I hope not, because I plan for us to have many more nights like this one."

Chapter Seven

Heidi looked around the jewelry shop and held Raylic's hand a little tighter. She was glad Shane wasn't with them, even if she was a little leery of having a stranger sit with him. Of course, Raylic assured her that Avelyn was great with kids, and she had to admit that while Lily, the little red girl with black curls, had been a bit off-putting at first, she was rather adorable. She'd also been great with Shane, despite the five-year age difference.

Raylic led her over to a case with bridal sets on display. Some of the diamonds were so large that Heidi didn't even want to see the price tags attached to them. Honestly, she'd have been fine with a plain gold band, but something told her Raylic wasn't going to let her get away with that. They perused the cases before coming back to the middle one. An older man came over, dressed in a three-piece suit and a smile that only salesmen seemed to master.

"See anything you like?" he asked them.

"I'd like to see the set with the yellow stone," Raylic said pointing to the rings he liked.

Heidi's jaw dropped a little when the man pulled it out of the case. He didn't really expect her to wear something so flashy, did he? She was a police officer's wife. She didn't need something the fiancé of a movie star would wear. She tugged on his hand and pointed to a more sedate setting and his eyebrows lifted.

"You don't like this one?" he asked.

"It's too much, Raylic. I just need something simple."

"What if I want you to have a ring to complement your beauty? You deserve more than a plain band or a tiny diamond. I want you to have the best."

"Something that large could scratch the children," she reasoned.

He glanced at the ring again and sighed. "Do you have something that will be child-friendly?"

The man put the ring back and drew out a platinum band with diamonds across the top; they were almost seamless, with no rough edges. Raylic picked up the smaller band and slid it on her finger. Heidi had to admit it was gorgeous, and if he insisted on buying her something with diamonds, then this was the ring she would want. The man's ring that complemented hers was a solid band. She picked it up and slid it on his finger, surprised that both rings fit perfectly, almost as if they were made just for them.

"We'll take them," Raylic told the man.

The salesman rattled off a price that had Heidi paling a little. It was more money than she'd ever have seen in a year had she been able to work, but Raylic merely pulled out his wallet and handed the man his bank card. After their purchase was rung up and the slip was signed, Raylic led her back out to the SUV parked outside.

"We have two stops to make today," he told her. "The first is the Terran Station to make sure the proper paperwork has been filed so that all of my assets will transfer to you in the event of my death."

She scowled at him.

"I know. You want me to live forever."

"Is that so wrong?"

He kissed the back of her hand. "Not at all, and I'll strive to live long enough to see our great-grandchildren. Maybe even our great-great-grandchildren."

"You'd better," she muttered.

"Then we're stopping by the mall, and no arguments from you. Both Shane and you need new winter coats. I can feel you trembling whenever we're outside. I'll not have either of you catching a cold when there's something I can do about it."

"Fine. Two coats and nothing else. You don't have to

constantly buy us things. We're with you because we want to be with you. Not because you have a lot of money."

"I know." He smiled a little. "Doesn't mean I can't spoil you though. I promise to lay off the presents until Christmas. It's less than a week away now. We really should get some things for Shane and get them wrapped and under the tree. It looks a little bare."

"You want to go back to the toy store, don't you?"

He shrugged. "We do have a sitter for a while. Might as well take advantage of it. Besides, he's playing with Lily. I'm sure she'll keep him occupied, or convince him to watch a princess movie."

"All right. A quick trip to the toy store."

He smiled and kissed her cheek before pulling out of the parking space and heading for the Terran Station. When they got there, he took her to the food court for a mocha and left her to enjoy the hot brew while he went to the records department. She didn't know how long he was gone, but she'd finished her mocha by the time he returned, and judging by the smile on his face, she'd assumed things went well.

"Zwyk said we should stop by my bank on the way home," Raylic said.

"What for?" she asked.

"He said I should either add you to my bank account, or if you weren't comfortable with that, he said you could open your own account, and I could arrange for a monthly transfer to give you funds for things when I'm not around. I also need to arrange for transportation for you before I return to work next week. I doubt you want to wake Shane early to take me to work in the morning so you can have the SUV."

"You're buying me a car?"

"Well, I was thinking of something a little bigger. You're going to have two kids soon, and with some luck, we'll have a third later. I thought we could get an SUV with third-row seating."

Her eyes widened. "Those things are huge."

"And I'm sure you will handle it beautifully."

Her shoulders drooped. "We just added a car lot to our list today, didn't we?"

"I already called Avelyn, and she's agreed to take Shane to her place and keep him until we're finished. She said she'd feed him lunch and even dinner if it takes that long."

"He needs to be in bed by eight-thirty."

"We'll be done in plenty of time to tuck him in tonight. And maybe we'll get him a small prize for having to go without our company all day."

"The coat will be enough."

He looked like he wanted to argue but merely nodded and held out his hand. She allowed him to help her up from the chair and they walked out to the parking lot together. In the SUV, she looked out the window and realized her life had changed so much, and while his crazy spending was going to make her a little bonkers, she had to admit, it was nice to be taken care of for a change.

At the mall, they went to a children's store first and found a warm coat for Shane, then Raylic took her to an upscale store to purchase a coat for her. Heidi protested the cost, but he shushed her and started grabbing coats off the rack and holding them up to her. Heidi gave in and picked the one she liked best, then dragged Raylic out of the mall before he could decide to buy anything else.

The toy store wasn't far away, and when they arrived, the lot was nearly empty. Raylic grabbed a shopping cart on the way in and went straight to the little boy's department. With her help, they selected some action figures and an Army man set. Then Raylic convinced her that Shane really needed the train table and larger playset. She tried to rein him in, but on the way to the register, he threw in some puzzles before stopping in front of the handheld video games.

"No. We aren't rotting his brain with video games until he's older," Heidi said. "Besides, he'd probably drop it and break it."

"You're no fun," Raylic said with a mock pout.

"You can get him a game system the Christmas after his seventh birthday. Deal?"

"Deal."

"Now let's check out before you buy half the store."

Raylic smiled and went to the first available register. Heidi did her best not to pay attention to the total and then helped him load everything into the back of his SUV. She had no idea how they were getting all of the stuff past Shane. Or what they were going to wrap it with. She hadn't seen a single roll of Christmas paper in the toy store and didn't think Raylic had any at home since he'd never celebrated Christmas before.

He surprised her when he went a few doors down to a discount store and picked up five rolls of Christmas paper and gift tags. With all of their shopping done, they took a break for lunch at a bistro Heidi had always wanted to try. The sandwiches and soup were divine, and she knew she'd come back as soon as she could. While she didn't plan to spend money like Raylic did, it would be nice to have the funds to eat out every once in a while, or to treat herself to a mocha from the trendy coffee shop near the house.

They finished their meal and Raylic took her to the car lot where he said he had purchased his SUV. The same salesman helped them.

"Officer Raylic," the man said, smiling widely. "It's a pleasure to see you again. What can I help you with today?"

"My mate needs a car. I was thinking about one of the SUVs with third-row seating, or something that would handle three kids."

The man nodded. "And would you use this vehicle for out of town trips with the family?"

"Yes," Raylic answered.

"Might I suggest a minivan?" the salesman said. "They're popular with the moms in town and will comfortably seat seven. We have models with built-in DVD players too, which are great for long distance car rides."

Raylic looked at Heidi, and she shrugged. She'd never driven anything other than Brent's rusted heap, but a van couldn't be any harder to drive than one of those monster SUVs. Or so she assumed. The salesman went inside and came back out with three sets of keys, showing them different models. The silver one was her favorite with gray leather interior, the built-in DVD player the salesman had mentioned, and power everything.

They took it for a test drive, and Heidi had to admit she liked the way it handled. She was surprised by how smooth the ride was, and fell a little in love with it. By the time they returned to the dealership, Raylic was already negotiating on a price. It took another hour to sign the papers, and then the salesman handed her the keys and wished them well.

"See," Raylic said. "We finished in plenty of time to pick up Shane and let him swim a little, then figure out dinner for tonight. There's stuff in the fridge, or we could order out. There's that new taxi service for a few local restaurants. I have their menu in the drawer by the fridge."

"Should we go home first and drop off one of the cars?" she asked.

"We can take my SUV home. I bet Shane would love to ride in your new van."

Raylic kissed her cheek and then they drove home. At the house, Raylic parked his SUV in the garage, grabbed Shane's booster seat and new coat, then climbed into the passenger seat of her van, giving her directions to Thrace and Avelyn's home. It was small, compared to Raylic's house, but looked cute. The red brick home had blue shutters, white trim and sat in a quaint neighborhood on a cove.

Heidi parked in the driveway behind a large truck and a sedan. When they rang the bell, a dog started barking from somewhere inside the house. Shane had always wanted a pet, and Heidi knew he'd probably had a blast playing with Avelyn's dog. She could already hear his pleas for a puppy of his own, and she had no doubt that Raylic would get him one.

A large Terran in black leather pulled open the door then smiled when he saw Raylic.

"This must be your new mate," the alien said, motioning for them to enter.

"Thrace, this is Heidi. Heidi, Thrace is mated to Avelyn, and the little girl you met earlier is their adopted daughter. Speaking of adoptions, I hear you may be gaining a new family member soon."

"There's a boy from Helon-9 who lost his parents in a skirmish last month. He doesn't have any remaining family, and no one on their world wants the responsibility of raising yet another male child. Their situation with females isn't as dire as ours, but there is only one Helios girl born for every seven Helios boys." Thrace shook his head. "I can't imagine giving up a child, though, just because he wasn't born a girl. The boy is four and probably doesn't even understand what's going on."

"What's a Helios?" Heidi asked.

"They're an alien race who are green with dark brown hair. Their eyes are usually a golden color, but sometimes there are variations," Thrace answered. "We will gladly welcome the boy into our home, but we're waiting on the paperwork to be processed. My mate and I have been trying to adopt another child since Lily was only two. We've been denied countless times, so we're very happy about this boy."

"I'm sure he'll adjust quickly since he's so young," Heidi said. "And this is a lovely home. He'll be lucky to have parents like Avelyn and you."

"Thank you," Thrace said with a nod of his head. "The children and my mate are in the sunroom at the back of the house. I had it added on this past year, and Avelyn likes to do crafts out there. I believe she pulled out the paints and easels."

Thrace led the way to the sunroom and Heidi smiled when she saw Shane painting a rainbow. The room was warm despite the wall of windows that overlooked a decent sized backyard. Heidi stood in the doorway and just watched her son for a few minutes. He chattered away to Lily and Avelyn, oblivious to the fact his parents had arrived.

Heidi moved further into the room and went to check out Shane's painting.

"That's really pretty," she said.

Shane dropped his paintbrush and flew into Heidi's arms.

"You're here!" he squealed. "You've been gone forever."

"I'm sorry it took us so long," Heidi said. "We have a surprise for you though. Two surprises."

"Really?" His eyes lit up.

Raylic handed him the sack with his new coat. "This is something you need, more than something you necessarily want."

Shane pulled the blue coat out of the bag and hugged Raylic and Heidi. "Thank you. My old coat got a hole in it today."

"How on earth did you get a hole in your coat?" Heidi asked.

Shane shrugged. "It wasn't there when I put it on, but when we got here, there was a hole in the sleeve. I did catch it on the door of Miss Avelyn's car though."

"We were going to offer to replace it," Avelyn said.

Raylic waved away her offer. "Not necessary. I had planned to buy this new coat today anyway. His old one wasn't anywhere near warm enough."

"What do you tell Miss Avelyn and Mr. Thrace?" Heidi asked.

"Thank you for letting me come to your house," Shane said. "I had fun playing with Lily."

Lily smiled, showing off a set of fangs. "I had fun too. It was good practice for when I get my new little brother."

"I'm going to have a new little brother or sister too," Shane said. "The baby is in Mama's tummy."

"Congratulations," Avelyn said. "You must be so excited."

"We are," Raylic said. "We aren't going to take up any more of your time. Shane, the second surprise is waiting in the driveway. Your mom got something new today too."

Shane scrambled to put on his new coat, hugged everyone goodbye, and then raced to the front door. When he saw the van parked in the driveway, he could barely contain his excitement, especially when Heidi told him he could watch movies in it. Raylic buckled their son, and then they headed home.

"We do have one more surprise for you," Heidi said. "Your daddy bought you a swimsuit, and we have an indoor pool."

Shane clapped his hands and bounced in his seat. "We can go swimming?"

Heidi smiled. "Yes, we're going swimming when we

get home. Then you're going to take a bath, put on PJs, and we'll order dinner."

"Pizza?" Shane asked.

Heidi groaned. "No more pizza for at least a week. Daddy said there's a menu at home we can look at, so we'll see what they offer, okay?"

Shane sighed and nodded.

It didn't take long to reach the house, and Heidi pulled into the garage. She hoped Shane wouldn't look in the back window of Raylic's SUV and see the toys stashed there. They managed to get inside without incident and Shane took off upstairs with Heidi and Raylic following at a slower pace. They gave him the swimsuit before leaving to change into theirs. When Shane saw the pool, he went running for the steps that led into the shallow end.

"Don't you dare go deeper than where you can touch the bottom," Heidi warned. "You don't swim well enough for that just yet."

"Maybe we should get him a swim instructor?" Raylic said softly. "I could probably find someone to come a few days a week until he gets good enough that you won't worry."

"It's not a bad idea, but don't mention it to him just yet. I'd hate to get his hopes up and then you not be able to find someone. It is winter, after all. Most swim lessons are during the summer months."

"I'll see what I can arrange."

She kissed him softly and then went into the pool to keep an eye on Shane. They splashed and played together as a family for over two hours, and then Heidi hustled Shane out of the pool and upstairs for his bath. After he was dressed for bed, Heidi rinsed off in the shower and put on her pajamas as well, then went to check out the menu with Shane while Raylic showered and dressed.

"We should probably all order from the same

restaurant," Heidi said. "You pick first, and then your daddy and I will find something at the same place. But no pizza!"

Shane sighed and handed the menu to Heidi. "Can we order from somewhere that has chicken?"

"Like chicken nuggets or a chicken breast?"

"The big pieces with those little lines on them."

"You want a grilled chicken breast?" she asked.

He nodded.

Heidi looked over the menu and read off the choices that matched what he wanted until he picked one. Then she figured out what she wanted and handed the menu to Raylic as he entered the kitchen. After the order was called in, Raylic lifted Shane and carried him to the living room with Heidi trailing behind them.

"We get to eat in here?" Shane asked.

Heidi looked at the pristine floors and furniture. "Raylic, I don't think that's such a great idea. We should eat in the kitchen."

"Heidi, there isn't anything in this room that can't be replaced. I thought we'd watch a movie while we ate. I know it's going to be a little while before it's delivered, but we can go ahead and start the movie now."

She sighed and agreed, even if she did worry that Shane would destroy something by spilling food or drink on it. Shane picked an animated movie on Netflix, and they settled in to watch it while they waited for their food. Heidi yawned as she leaned her head on Raylic's shoulder, with Shane cuddled against her other side. It had been a long day, and she wasn't certain she'd stay awake for very long after they ate. She could only hope that Raylic would find a fun way to wake her up if that happened. After the multiple orgasms last night, she was hoping for an encore.

Chapter Eight

Days passed, and Christmas inched ever closer. Now it was Christmas Eve, and Shane was buzzing around the house with so much energy they were having trouble keeping up. Raylic had to admit that Shane's excitement was starting to rub off on him. The presents had been wrapped the other day and were under the tree, except for the train table and new train set. Those were going under the tree tonight from Santa.

Heidi had been in the kitchen all morning and afternoon cooking one thing after another. The dining room table had a festive tablecloth on it and had been covered with one tray of food after another. Raylic had picked up a ham from a local shop earlier in the day, and it sat sliced and ready to eat in the middle of the table. Heidi had made candied yams, green bean casserole, pigs in a blanket, some sort of pumpkin spread, a spinach artichoke dip, and no less than four desserts.

The first of their guests had already arrived, and Shane had taken Reyvor's girls up to the playroom. Raylic had told his friends to come in when they arrived so he wouldn't have to answer the door every few minutes. They were waiting on Thrace and Avelyn, Syl and Brielle, Xonos and Victoria. Each couple was bringing their children so Shane would have someone to play with. They'd decided against doing a gift swap since the gathering had been last minute.

"I promise no one bites," Raylic whispered in Heidi's ear. "You look ready to bolt."

"What if they don't like me?"

"Everyone is going to love you. Just relax and enjoy yourself. And remember, each of the mates was once a single woman who had fallen on hard times. Victoria lived in an apartment, not much better than yours, and her daughter was dying. Brielle had been engaged, and her ex came back to inform her she had to move out because he was marrying someone else. Avelyn had been divorced after living with an abusive male. Every woman here has been in a difficult situation, so don't feel like they're better than you. They've all struggled, and no one will look down on you."

She nodded and moved away from him to mingle with their guests. As more people arrived, Heidi slowly looked like she was relaxing and having a nice time. Raylic enjoyed having the Christmas Eve gathering at his house and decided he'd do another gathering again soon. Syl usually hosted everyone at his place, but his six-year-old daughter, Emily, had taken ill the night of their party and the celebration had been canceled. Thankfully, she was better this evening and had been able to come with them.

Syl's daughter, Evie, and Reyvor's daughter, Nikki, were the oldest kids at fifteen, and they'd curled up in a corner to talk and play on their phones, too old to play with the other kids and too young to mingle with the adults. Reyvor's daughter Winnie was the next oldest at twelve, and was upstairs keeping an eye on the younger kids, with the help of Dexter, Syl's adopted son, and Lily.

Raylic's home had never been so full of love and laughter before, and he was enjoying every minute of it. The buffet was waiting whenever someone was ready to eat, and Heidi had even placed some snacks on the table upstairs in the playroom for the kids. As the hours passed, Raylic felt the anticipation building. It would be his first time playing Santa, and he couldn't wait.

"You're over here grinning like a crazy person," Syl said. "You'd think you'd never had friends over before."

"It's Christmas Eve," Raylic said.

"I'm aware."

"I get to be Santa tonight," he whispered in case any little ears were nearby.

"I remember the first time I got to do that, when Dexter came to live with us. You didn't go overboard, did you? Brielle made me take back half of what I had bought that year."

Raylic shook his head. "Heidi was with me when I went shopping. What's under the tree is the bulk of what Shane is getting, but Santa has two big gifts he's delivering, and one extra thing that even Heidi doesn't know about."

"Surprising the mate on Christmas morning?" Syl asked. "Are you sure that's wise?"

Raylic shrugged. "I've arranged for Shane to have swimming lessons starting next week. I asked the instructor to give me something I could put under the tree for Christmas morning, so she printed off a certificate for a month of swim lessons."

"You, uh, did think to get your mate something, didn't you?" Syl asked.

"I went shopping yesterday, claiming that there were some things I needed to take care of at the Terran station. I made sure I went to the mall so I could have them gift wrap everything. Her packages are in the back of my SUV. I thought I'd send her up to bed, before I stick them under the tree, so she'll be surprised tomorrow."

Thrace joined them. "What are we discussing?"

"Christmas presents," Syl said. "It's his first Christmas with a family."

Thrace sighed. "That first Christmas was the best ever. Make sure you take lots of pictures, even if it's just with your phone. You'll want to look back on them as your son gets older."

"Thanks," Raylic said. "I'll make sure I charge my phone tonight."

"Did you give your mate the means and time to buy you something?" Thrace asked. "I screwed up the first year with Avelyn, and she never had a chance to shop for me. She was so pissed when she saw all her presents under the tree, and I didn't have any."

Raylic's eyes widened. "Oh shit."

Thrace chuckled. "You are going to be in so much trouble tomorrow."

Syl leaned a little closer. "Unless you convince her that sex tonight is the best Christmas present you've ever received."

"She's going to kill me tomorrow, isn't she?" Raylic sighed. "And here I thought I was doing so well at this mate and father thing. It seems there's still a lot I need to learn."

"Just tell her that she's the best gift you've ever had and nothing could have topped claiming her as your mate," Thrace suggested. "Women love that romantic stuff."

Raylic nodded. "I can do that. It would be the truth anyway."

Thrace slapped him on the back. "Good luck. I think I'm going to gather my mate and Lily and head home. She still believes in Santa, so I need to get her to bed before too long. With some luck, the car ride home will tire her out."

"I think we're going to head out too," Syl said. "It's nearly eight o'clock, and it's bedtime for Emily. I'm sure Dexter will be awake a while longer, but I'm hoping they're both passed out within an hour. I have plans for Brielle tonight that don't include children."

Raylic smiled, having those same types of plans for his mate as well. He bid his friends goodbye, helped everyone get out the door, then leaned against it and breathed a sigh of relief. It had been great having everyone over, but he was more than ready to have his family to himself for the rest of the night. Although he had a feeling Heidi would send Shane to bed.

He started putting away the leftovers, so Heidi

wouldn't have to do everything herself, then went upstairs to find his family. Heidi was just tucking Shane into bed when he stopped in the bedroom doorway. Their son was yawning widely and insisting he wasn't tired. He smiled when he saw the new Christmas-themed pajamas he'd picked up the other day. Since pictures were mentioned, he was glad he'd picked some up for everyone.

"I want to see Santa," Shane whined.

"If you're awake, Santa won't come," Heidi said. "It's part of the magic of Christmas. Only little boys who are asleep get presents from Santa."

Shane's eyes went wide. "Really?"

Heidi nodded. "Now, close your eyes and have sweet dreams. It will be morning before you know it and you'll get to open all your presents."

"Night, Mama. Night, Daddy."

"Goodnight, sweet boy," Heidi said, brushing a kiss on his cheek.

Raylic pushed off the doorframe and went to kiss Shane goodnight. "Sleep tight, and we'll see you in the morning."

Shane yawned again and nodded before turning onto his side and closing his eyes, his bear clutched tight against his chest. Raylic followed Heidi into the hall, flicking off Shane's light and pulling his door shut. Then they tiptoed downstairs to set up the train table and new train set. Raylic, thankfully, had all the right tools, and after an hour, the table was together, and the train was placed on top.

"Why don't you head upstairs?" Raylic suggested. "I want to check all the windows and doors, and then I'll be up. I won't be long."

Heidi kissed him, flicking her tongue against his lips. "You better not be. I have plans for you tonight, Santa."

He smiled and swatted her ass as she walked away.

When he was certain she wasn't coming back down, he went out to his SUV and pulled her presents from the back then placed them under the tree. As he was hiding them amongst Shane's presents, he noticed one package that looked like it had been wrapped by a bear. The tag read *To Daddy, From Shane*. His heart melted at the thought of his son giving him a gift. As he stood, he noticed an envelope tucked into the branches of the tree with his name written across the front. It seemed his family had found a way to give him gifts after all, and he couldn't wait to see them.

Raylic checked the locks on the windows and doors then made his way upstairs. His sexy mate was lounging on the bed, completely bare. After closing and locking the door, he began removing his clothes, eager to get his hands on her. Once the last of his clothing was gone, he crawled across the bed and eased down beside her, turning her to face him. His mouth claimed hers gently, and when her lips parted, his tongue slipped between them. Raylic could taste the sweetness of the eggnog she'd consumed earlier in the evening as he devoured her.

Heidi moaned sweetly and shifted so that her leg was draped over his hip. Sliding his hand between their bodies, he caressed the damp curls between her thighs. It seemed his mate wanted him every bit as much as he wanted her. His finger teased her clit, and she thrust against his hand. Raylic eased two fingers inside of her, feeling her silken walls clasp the digits and pull them in further. He pumped them in and out, his cock jealous that it wasn't inside her yet.

Raylic pressed down on her clit with his thumb, rubbing it in small, tight circles. Her breath came out choppy, and her skin grew damp, as her hips thrust against him. Raylic pumped his fingers faster, pressed on her clit harder, and when she came, he swallowed her screams with another kiss. As tremors wracked her body, he continued to stroke her, drawing out her climax. Before her body could relax, another release claimed her, leaving her shaking against him.

"I love watching you come," he whispered against her lips. "So beautiful."

"Take me," she said. "Make me yours. I want you more than I want my next breath."

With a grin, he rolled onto his back, taking her with him so that she lay sprawled across him. Heidi seemed to take the hint and pushed herself up, her thighs squeezing his hips. His cock was so damn hard it nearly hurt as it brushed against her ass. Raylic lifted her and eased her down until she sheathed him. Heidi groaned and closed her eyes, tilting her head back as her hips thrust forward, taking him even deeper.

As she rode Raylic, he cupped her breasts and teased her nipples, drawing them to hard little points. Watching her rise and fall on his cock over and over was a mesmerizing sight, one he wouldn't forget anytime soon. Heidi came again, her cries filling the bedroom, and Raylic fought for control, not ready for it to come to an end just yet.

Raylic flipped them over, pulling her hips back as he thrust deep, filling her completely. Heidi tilted her hips, and he slid in even deeper. He used hard strokes, driving both of them toward a climax.

"What do you want?" he asked, his voice harsh as he slammed into her again.

"Faster." She panted. "Take me faster."

"Like this?" he asked, taking it up a notch.

She moaned and gripped the sheets tightly as he pounded into her from behind. Their bodies were covered in a sheen of sweat as he plunged into her, over and over. Her back arched as she gave another cry and she felt her pussy tighten. Another orgasm claimed her, leaving her breathless and sated, as Raylic took her fiercely, finding his own release.

Spent, he collapsed onto the bed and pulled her into his arms.

"Best Christmas present ever," he said.

Heidi smiled and kissed him. "I'm the one who had multiple orgasms. I think that's my line."

"We should get cleaned up and get some sleep. I have a feeling we'll have a little boy waking us up early, wanting to see what Santa brought."

"Since it's his first real Christmas, we'll be lucky to sleep a few hours. Better make sure we're wearing our new Christmas-worthy pajamas," Raylic said. "I've been told that pictures are a must in the morning."

Heidi leaned over the bed and pulled Raylic's phone from his discarded pants then plugged in the charger. "Better make sure you have a full battery then."

"I meant to do that, but someone distracted me when I got to the bedroom tonight." He kissed her shoulder. "Come on, Mrs. Claus. I'll wash your back."

She gave him a saucy smile. "In that case, race you!"

She bolted out of bed and took off to the bathroom. Raylic shook his head, smiling, and chased after her. He hadn't lied. Sex with her was definitely one of the best presents ever. No matter how many times they made love, he always wanted her one more time.

Chapter Nine

Raylic slowly opened his eyes the next morning only to find Shane kneeling beside the bed and peering over the mattress at him. He smiled and rubbed the sleep from his eyes. Heidi still slept peacefully next to him.

"How long have you been here?" he asked Shane.

"A while. It's Christmas."

Raylic looked over at the windows and groaned when he saw the sky was barely streaked pink with the rising sun. A glance at the clock on his phone showed it was a little after six in the morning. Heidi had warned they wouldn't get much sleep, but he hadn't expected quite so early a wake-up call.

"Are you ready to see what Santa brought?"

Shane nodded eagerly.

"Go brush your teeth and give me a minute to wake up your mama. Wait for us in your room. No peeking downstairs!"

Shane grinned and took off, leaving the bedroom door open. Raylic watched as he dashed into the bathroom and heard the faucet running a moment later. With a sigh, he rolled over and pulled Heidi into his arms. He gently kissed her cheek, her ear, then her neck. She murmured something he couldn't quite hear and snuggled against him.

"Time to wake up," he said softly. "We have a little boy eager to see his presents."

Heidi groaned and slowly opened her eyes. "We just went to sleep."

"Not quite, but it's definitely early. I'll let you use the bathroom first. I told Shane to wait in his room for us."

Heidi rolled out of bed, and Raylic waited until he heard her brushing her teeth before he went into the bathroom. When they were finished, they went to get Shane, who raced down the stairs and started squealing with excitement before they even reached the bottom step.

"Santa brought me a new train! And a table!" he yelled.

Raylic smiled and snapped a picture of Shane playing with the new train, while Heidi reached under the tree and pulled out a few presents to put in a pile next to Shane. Raylic pulled out a few for Heidi, and she gave him a narrow-eyed glare.

"What are these?" she asked.

"Your presents."

"You bought me a van this past week. I didn't need Christmas presents."

Raylic took a few more pictures of Shane before facing her again. "The van was a necessity. The presents are just things I thought you might like. Now stop complaining and open something."

There was a hint of a smile on her lips as she reached for the first one. While she opened her gifts, Shane dove into his. Raylic spent the next half hour taking pictures of both of them. When he thought he had enough, he sat on the sofa near Heidi and watched as Shane opened his last present. It was a photo album filled with the pictures his friend had taken of the animals from his world. Shane squealed and flipped through the pages, his eyes bright as he looked at all of them. When he was finished the album, he played with his new toys.

Heidi was still unwrapping her presents and she'd just pulled an envelope from a small gift bag. She gave him a look filled with curiosity as she opened the flap and pulled out the paper inside. He saw her eyes sheen with tears and hoped he'd done the right thing.

"You signed me up for a G.E.D. class?" she asked.

"You said it was something you wanted to do. There's a class starting in February, so I put your name on the list and went ahead and paid for it. All you have to do is show up and learn."

Heidi gave him a watery smile and nodded as a tear slipped down her cheek. "Thank you. It's perfect."

Only one gift remained under the tree, and Heidi got up and handed it to him, along with the envelope. He gave her a kiss before opening the present from Shane. It was a green elephant shaped out of clay that had a heart cut into its side. He gently traced the trunk with his finger and smiled.

"Thank you, Shane. I'll put it on my desk in my office, that way I can look at it every time I'm in there."

Shane gave him a wide smile and went back to playing.

Raylic opened the envelope Heidi had given him and pulled out a black and white photo. He frowned, not understanding what it was at first, and then it hit him.

"This is the baby?" he asked, his gaze clashing with hers.

She nodded and gave him a hesitant smile. "I know you probably wanted to be with me the first time, but I couldn't think of anything to give you. So, I drove to the clinic at the Terran Station while you were napping the other day and asked them to do a sonogram. When I explained that I wanted the picture to give you for Christmas, they were happy to help."

Raylic wrapped an arm around her waist and kissed her slowly, softly. "Thank you. I'll get a frame and put it on my desk with the elephant."

"They gave me a second copy in case we wanted to start a baby book. I didn't get to do one for Shane, and I regret it."

"Then we'll do one for this baby. And there's nothing that says we can't start one for Shane. You may not have baby pictures of him, but you could still fill in what you remember, and we could add pictures from this point forward."

"I'd like that," she said.

"If you think we can pry Shane away from his toys, I thought we could go to the diner and get some breakfast. I saw a sign in their window the other day advertising they would be open on Christmas. That way you don't have to cook this morning."

She nodded and went over to Shane. While she tried to coax their son away from his new toys, Raylic went upstairs to get dressed. A few minutes later, he heard Heidi down the hall helping Shane find something to wear. He passed Shane's room on his way downstairs, peeking in to make sure their son wasn't giving her a hard time, and then he went out to the garage to warm up the SUV.

It wasn't long before Heidi and Shane joined him. On the way to the diner, dark clouds rolled in, and it started to snow. Just a flurry, but it was enough to excite Shane and have him rambling about snowball fights and building a snowman. The diner was nearly empty when they arrived, and they claimed a booth near the window so Shane could keep watching the snow fall.

A waitress came over and placed menus on the table. "Can I get you something to drink?"

"Orange juice for Shane and me," Heidi told her.

"Coffee for me," Raylic said. He was going to need the caffeine if he was going to last all day. It was his last day off with his family before returning to work, and he wanted to enjoy every moment of it.

When the waitress returned with their drinks, they placed their order and then sat back to wait. The snow was falling harder, but Raylic still didn't think there would be enough for Shane to play in. Not unless it kept falling all day. He didn't have a problem with a white Christmas, but driving to work in the morning would be fun, especially if the streets iced over. Unfortunately, with his job, it didn't matter if the weather was bad. He still had to go in.

"You seem preoccupied," Heidi said.

"I go back to work in the morning."

She bit her lip, and her gaze fell to the table. He reached across and tipped her chin up, giving her a reassuring smile.

"I'm going to be fine," he said. "Yesterday and today were the crazy days. It should be pretty calm until New Year's, and I think my rotation has me off that day."

"We'll miss you tomorrow," she said. "Do you want anything special for breakfast?"

"I want you to sleep. I'll fix my own breakfast and coffee in the morning, and I plan to leave before seven o'clock. Shane and you should sleep as long as you can. I don't expect you to get up just because I'm awake."

She nodded. "If you'll call me on your way home, I'll start dinner. By the time you shower and change, it should be ready."

"I can do that."

Their food arrived and they dug in, though Shane still focused most of his attention on the snow outside. The meal was good and filling. After Raylic paid and tipped their waitress, they drove back home so Shane could play with his new toys again. At least, that was, until there was enough snow on the ground for him to go out and play.

Raylic pulled through the four-way stop near the house and took his eyes off the road just long enough to glance in the rearview mirror at Shane, but it was one second too long. A horn blared, and lights flashed across the SUV a moment before the crunching sound of metal and Heidi's screams filled the air. Raylic fought for control of the vehicle, but the impact pushed the SUV across the two-lane road, and it tumbled over the side, rolling down the incline until it came to rest at the bottom, thankfully right side up.

His body ached, and everything was spinning. As the pounding in his ears lessened, he noticed the car was silent. Too damn silent. He looked into the back and saw Shane, his eyes wide and tears streaking his chubby cheeks. A whimper escaped the boy as he looked to Raylic for reassurance.

"We're okay," Raylic told him. "Are you hurt?"

Shane shook his head, but he still had a white knuckled grip on the arms of his booster seat. Raylic looked across the SUV to check on Heidi, and his heart nearly stopped. The glass of her window was shattered, and the door was pressed in against her. There was blood running down her face from various cuts, and she was deathly pale. And very still.

Raylic reached across the SUV and took her hand. "Heidi. Can you open your eyes? Heidi?"

She didn't stir.

Raylic's heart pounded as Shane started crying in the backseat. He fumbled for his phone and called in the accident, trying to remain calm and clearheaded as he talked to dispatch, relaying all the pertinent information. He didn't know the status of the other driver, but no one was coming down the hill to assist them. As they waited for help to arrive, Raylic got out of the SUV and checked the vehicle. Other than having the passenger door smashed in, it seemed rather sound and didn't seem to be in danger of catching fire. He didn't dare leave his family to check on the other car, even though he worried they might be injured as well.

He left Shane buckled into his booster seat, knowing the paramedics would want to check him over before moving him. No matter how hard he tried, he couldn't get Heidi's door open. He'd never felt so helpless in his life. Sirens could be heard in the distance, and what felt like hours later, his fellow officers and two EMTs were heading down the hill toward him.

"Jesus, Raylic. Are y'all okay?" Officer Timmons asked.

"I'm fine. Shane is shaken up, but I can't rouse Heidi."

One of the EMTs went to Shane while the other checked Heidi's door. When he called up the hill to the firemen to request the jaws of life, Raylic thought he might pass out. He locked his knees, and tried to be strong for his family, as he fought back tears. If Heidi didn't wake up, he didn't know what he would do. He needed her as much as he needed air in his lungs.

"Raylic, we need to ask you a few questions," Officer Timmons said.

He nodded and did his best to answer everything they threw at him. When they were done, Raylic looked up the hill. "What about the other driver?"

"They abandoned their car and ran, but they left a trail of blood. Simpkins was going after them on foot. Our best guess is that they're drunk. We can't think of another reason they'd run unless they were just too disoriented from the accident to know what they were doing."

"So, I'm not at fault?" Raylic asked.

"There was a witness who claims the other car ran the stop sign. If you're blaming yourself for what happened, you can stop."

Raylic nodded, but it didn't ease his guilt. If he hadn't looked in the rearview mirror, would he have seen the other car in time to avoid the crash? He knew there was no way of knowing for sure. He'd seen the aftermath of enough accidents to know that sometimes bad things just happened and were completely out of your control.

Shane was cleared, having been secured in his seat and not having so much as a bruise, and Raylic pulled him from the SUV, holding him close. The boy cried on his shoulder as they waited to see if Heidi would be okay. Once they'd removed her from the SUV and placed her on the stretcher, a brace around her neck, the EMTs checked her over once more.

"We're taking her to the hospital," one of the EMTs told him. "I know you want to go with her, but it's no place for a small boy."

"I'll take him to a friend's house."

Officer Timmons placed a hand on his shoulder. "I'll drive the two of you home."

Raylic grabbed Shane's booster seat from the mangled SUV and put it in the back of the squad car, then slid in next to him. Shane clutched his hand tight on the way home, and Raylic wished he could reassure him that everything would be fine. The house was covered in snow when they pulled into the driveway, and Raylic lifted Shane out. He reached back into the squad car and grabbed the booster seat before ushering Shane into the house.

"Why don't you play with your toys while I make some calls, okay?"

Shane nodded, but tears still streaked his cheeks. "Is Mama going to be okay?"

"I hope so. She's very sick right now, but the doctors are going to do everything they can for her. We have to be brave while we wait for her to wake up."

Shane nodded and moved over to the Christmas tree, grabbing some of his action figures and settling down on the floor to play. Raylic pulled his phone from his pocket and called Xonos. When he explained the situation, the doctor agreed to head to the hospital to meet with the physicians there.

"Why don't you bring Shane over here?" Xonos said. "Victoria will be happy to watch him, and he can play with the kids."

"Are you sure? It's Christmas, and I'm sure you had plans with your family."

"We're sure," Xonos said. "I'll meet you at the

hospital. Let Shane bring some of his new things with him or a favorite toy. Does he still sleep with a stuffed animal? He might need it for comfort."

"I'll grab his bear and have him pack some things in a tote to bring with him. Thank you."

He disconnected the call and retrieved Shane's bear from the bedroom upstairs then grabbed the tote out of the closet. When he got back downstairs, he told Shane that he was going to go play with Dexter and Emily. The boy packed a few of his new toys into the tote and hugged the bear tight. Raylic put the booster seat into the back of the van and drove across town.

Victoria opened the door as he pulled into the driveway and stepped out onto the porch. Raylic unbuckled Shane and helped him out of the van, grabbing his tote and carrying it up the porch steps.

"Shane, Dexter, and Emily are in the living room playing with their new toys. Why don't you take your things in there and show them what you got today? They opened some new board games from Santa this morning, so maybe the three of you can play one."

Shane nodded, took his tote from Raylic, and went inside.

"Thank you, Victoria. I'll try not to stay at the hospital too long. I know Shane needs me just as much as Heidi does, but I'm hoping to find out more about her condition before I come home. With some luck, she'll be awake when I get there and can come home today or tomorrow."

"Call and let me know how she's doing. I'm sure Shane would like the updates, if it's good news."

Raylic nodded, kissed Victoria on the cheek, and then drove to the hospital. By the time he pulled into the parking lot, his hands were shaking. He went in through the ER entrance and stopped at the triage desk to ask about Heidi. The nurse had him fill out several forms, and then they showed him into the back where they were keeping Heidi. A doctor was filling out something on a tablet when he stepped behind the curtain.

"You must be her husband," the doctor said, holding out his hand to shake. "I'm Doctor Treadwell."

"I'm Raylic, and yes, Heidi is mine. How is she?"

"Her vitals are actually good, but I'm going to order a CT scan and an MRI just to be safe. Once we get the results of those, we'll know more, and hopefully, she'll wake up. We had to stitch two of the cuts on her face but the rest we just cleaned because they were surface abrasions."

"Do you know why she hasn't woken?"

The doctor shook his head. "There are too many possibilities to guess without running those tests first. You can sit here with her, if you'd like. I know the chairs aren't the most comfortable, but if we have to keep her, she'll move upstairs to a nice room with comfortable seating."

Raylic didn't give a damn about the chair. He just wanted Heidi to wake up and be okay. He eased around the side of the bed and picked up Heidi's hand, mindful of the IV. He turned to ask what they were giving her, but the doctor had already left. Raylic pulled the hard chair over and sat down, not letting go of Heidi's hand. After a while, an orderly came to take her away for testing, leaving Raylic alone with his thoughts and worries. By the time she came back, he'd received a few texts from Victoria with pictures of the kids playing, and she had assured him that Shane was fine.

It was another two hours before anyone came to check on Heidi, and he was more than a little relieved to see Xonos. His friend clapped him on the shoulder before checking on Heidi. He scanned her and studied the readout. The frown on his face wasn't encouraging, and Raylic worried even more.

"There are no broken bones, and I don't see any trauma to her neck or spine. Before you ask, the baby is fine. Heidi has cerebral edema, which is likely why she hasn't woken yet. The doctor presiding over her case wanted to operate to try to reduce the swelling, but I told him to hold off. I ran by the clinic and picked up a little something to see if we can give her a boost and get her back on her feet."

Xonos pulled a syringe from his lab coat pocket. He inserted the needle into her arm and pushed the plunger. The blue liquid rushed into her arm and Raylic watched her for any signs of improvement. How long would it take for the stuff to work? He knew some of the drugs from their world worked instantly, while others took a while. Her hand twitched, and her eyes moved back and forth rapidly behind her eyelids. Raylic reached for her as her fingers twitched again. "Is she coming out of it?" he asked Xonos.

"Not just yet, but it looks like the serum is working. I'd give her a few hours and then she might open her eyes. The swelling should be gone by morning. They will probably admit her and keep her overnight. I'm sure they'll want to run more tests in the morning to check on her progress."

"But she's going to be okay?" Raylic asked.

"She's going to be fine. Stay with her until she wakes and then go home and give your son the good news. He's going to need you tonight, but I wouldn't bring him up here. The stuff I gave her should help her cuts heal a little faster too, and she won't look quite so rough tomorrow. You don't want to scare the boy more than he already is."

Raylic nodded. "I can't thank you enough."

"It's my job, Raylic. But I'm glad it seems to be working. I'm going home, but call if you need anything else. And don't worry about Shane. He's fine right now, and we'll keep him as long as you need us to."

"Once she's awake, I'll pick him up."

Xonos patted his shoulder and moved out of the curtained area. Raylic held Heidi's hand, willing her to open her eyes. It was nearly three hours later before his miracle was granted. Her eyes fluttered and then opened. Her disoriented gaze landed on him, and she frowned.

"Where am I?" she asked.

"You're in the hospital. What do you remember?"

"We were driving home."

"A drunk driver hit us, or so they think. They were trying to track down the other driver. He apparently bailed after the accident. You were hurt, but Xonos came and gave you something to make you better."

"Shane?" she asked. "The baby?"

"He's fine. I dropped him off at Xonos' house, and he's playing with the kids, and the baby is fine too. You were the only one injured." Raylic swallowed hard. "I'm so damn sorry, Heidi."

"It's not your fault. It was an accident, Raylic. You can't protect us from everything."

He knew she was right, but it didn't make him feel any less guilty. She was his to protect, and he'd failed her. If he'd been paying more attention or had been a little faster to react... he knew all the what-ifs in the world wouldn't change what happened though. All he could do now was be grateful that she was healing and would be fine by tomorrow. If it weren't for the technological and medical advances of his kind, she could have very well died. "I love you," he said softly. "I didn't understand what I was feeling for you until I damn near lost you. I don't expect you to say it back. I know it's too soon, but I needed to tell you how I felt."

She opened her mouth to say something, but he placed a finger over her lips to shush her. "Rest," he said. "I need to get Shane and tell him you're okay. I'll come back tomorrow morning to see if you're being discharged.

I think it's best if Shane doesn't come with me though. I'll see if Avelyn will sit with him for a little while. Maybe she'll bring Lily, and they can all go swimming or something."

Her hand lifted and stroked his cheek. "I'll miss you."

"I want to stay with you, but I know I need to take care of Shane."

"I'd much rather you be with him than stuck in that hard chair all night. I'll be fine."

Raylic hesitated. "I'll be back in a moment. There's something I need to do before I leave. I promise I won't go without saying goodbye."

She nodded and closed her eyes. Raylic stood, releasing her hand, and left the ER area. He went in search of the hospital gift shop and was happy to see they were open. With it being a holiday, he'd had his doubts. Inside, he selected a few magazines and a romance novel he didn't think she'd read yet. He also picked up a fluffy white bear with a pink bow, paid for his purchases, and carried them back to the ER. Heidi still had her eyes closed when he stepped behind the curtain, and he laid his gifts on the bed next to her.

Leaning down, he pressed a kiss to her brow, watching as her eyes fluttered open. She gave him a drowsy smile and looked at the presents he'd bought her.

"Thank you," she said.

"I hate leaving you alone in the hospital on Christmas Day, but I thought this might help you pass the time, and I thought the bear might make you feel a little less lonely."

"You're so good to me." She yawned widely. "Go take care of our son. I'll be fine on my own."

Raylic kissed Heidi gently and then left to pick up their son and try to salvage what was left of Christmas, if he could. So much for the perfect Christmas Day.

Chapter Ten

Raylic had been pacing her hospital room for the last hour. Heidi honestly felt completely healed and was anxious to get out of the bed, but the doctor had insisted on running more tests to be certain she was well again. Even the Terran doctor had been by and assured the human doctor that Heidi was one hundred percent back to normal. The man wasn't listening, though. So, after another CT scan and MRI, she was finally being released to go home.

"I know you probably want to listen to the human," Xonos said, "but I can assure you that you're perfectly fine and can return to your normal duties."

"Whatever you gave me must have been a miracle drug." Heidi smiled. "Thank you for taking care of me."

Xonos waved away her thanks. "It's my job. As a mate to one of my kind, your treatment falls to me, but since Raylic panicked and called the humans in after the accident, you were brought to the hospital."

Raylic glared at him. "I did what I thought was best for her."

"Yes, well, in future, bring her to me," Xonos said. "I can do much more for her than these humans can."

Raylic sighed and nodded, then went back to staring out the window. From what Heidi could see from where she lay, everything outside was covered in snow. If she knew her little boy, he would want to go out and play in it. Raylic had handed her his cell phone when he'd first arrived today and let her call Shane to talk to him. Her poor, sweet boy was so worried about her, but she could tell he was trying to be brave. Just like his daddy.

"I'm going to sign off on the forms to turn your care over to me," Xonos said, "and then they can process your discharge papers. You should be able to go home in about a half hour if you'd like to go ahead and get dressed."

Xonos moved closer and worked on removing her IV and unhooking her from the machines. He also removed the stitches from the cuts on her face, which were almost completely healed already. When he was finished, Heidi stretched and sat up a little straighter in the bed. Once the doctor left, she stood up and reached for her clothes on the nearby chair. Raylic hovered, as if he worried she'd topple over at any moment. True to his word, Xonos brought her discharge papers a half hour later, and she was free to go home.

"Weren't you due back at work today?" Heidi asked as Raylic helped her into the van.

"Yes, but they gave me another day off for obvious reasons. I told them I'd call today and let them know if I was coming in tomorrow."

Heidi narrowed her eyes at his tone. "You're going. I'm perfectly fine, just like Xonos said. You can stop worrying about me."

"You could have died," he said softly. "I nearly lost you and I... I don't want to go through that again."

Heidi reached over and took his hand. "People die every day, Raylic. From something as simple as choking on a piece of food, to stepping off the curb at the wrong time. Accidents happen all the time, and you can't protect me from them. Just because I got hurt doesn't mean I'm going to live my life afraid of my own shadow. I'm going to live every day to the fullest, and I hope you'll be right there beside me."

He sighed and leaned over to kiss her cheek. "I'll try not to worry so much, but it may take a few days for the fear to subside. I can handle lots of things, Heidi. I've been shot and stabbed, I nearly lost my life in a battle years ago when I was still on my world, but none of that compared to seeing you unresponsive and bloody. I've never been so scared in my life as I was when I realized you wouldn't wake up."

Heidi settled back and tried to relax, but her heart raced when they neared the stop sign where the accident had occurred. It wasn't until they were safely home that she was able to breathe a sigh of relief. She'd barely cleared the door before Shane was hurtling toward her. He threw his arms around her and held on tight.

"Hello, sweet boy. Did you miss me?"

He nodded, and she felt dampness on her clothes from his silent tears. Heidi went down on her knees and wrapped her arms around Shane, stroking his hair and murmuring words of comfort to him. She heard Avelyn and Raylic talking quietly and then heard the front door open and shut.

"Did you have fun playing with Lily today?" Heidi asked.

Shane nodded. "I was worried about you, though. Daddy said you could come home today, but it took forever."

"I'm sorry I couldn't be here with you yesterday, for Christmas."

"Daddy played games with me yesterday, and we went swimming and played in the snow. I just wish you could have been here too."

"Next year we'll all be together, and you'll have a brother or sister too. Won't that be fun?"

He nodded eagerly.

"What do you want to do today? Daddy goes back to work tomorrow, so it's our last day together until he's off work again." Heidi smoothed his hair back from his face. "Anything at all."

"Can we go to Puck's Pizza Palace?" Shane asked.

"I don't know that your mama is up for that just yet," Raylic said, coming back into the kitchen.

"I can sit while we're there," Heidi said. "Shane's never been before, but I've heard it's secure. He should be able to run and play while we sit and talk."

Raylic reached out and stroked her cheek. "Are you sure? I don't want you to overdo it your first day home."

"I'm fine, Raylic. Really. Never felt better."

"All right. Why don't you go shower and change clothes since those are bloodstained from the accident? I'll make a call to the insurance company while you do that. I need to get my SUV replaced. While we're out, I should probably pick up a rental until they can get things sorted. I don't want to take the van to work and leave you without transportation."

Heidi nodded and went upstairs. She showered quickly and dressed in a comfortable sweater and jeans. She put on a pair of boots Raylic had purchased for her and then dried her hair and pulled it back in a messy bun. When she got downstairs, Raylic and Shane were waiting patiently in the living room, flipping through channels on the TV.

"I'm ready if you two are," she said.

Shane sprang up from the couch and went running to the garage. Heidi smiled and shook her head. Reaching for Raylic's hand, she stopped him long enough to press a kiss to his lips. He wrapped his hand around the back of her neck and kissed her harder, deeper, before taking a step back.

At Puck's, Heidi had to wonder if she'd made a bad decision. Kids were running and screaming everywhere, the machines dinged and whistled, and harried looking servers delivered pizza and soda to the tables scattered throughout the place. They found a table in a quieter section and Raylic took Shane to the counter to order their drinks, pizza, and get a wristband for Shane.

Their son was off like a shot running from one place to another as he rode the rides, played the games, and climbed through the tunnels. Raylic returned to the table and sat next to her, putting his arm around her shoulders and holding her close to his side. She tried to keep an eye on Shane, but having Raylic so close was a distraction. She'd missed sleeping in his arms last night and couldn't wait for the day to end.

They let Shane play for a few hours and ate their pizza. When it looked like their little boy was tiring out, Heidi insisted they go home. The rest of the day was spent by the pool, and by the time night fell, Shane was yawning and could barely keep his eyes open. Raylic carried him up to bed, and Heidi helped him put on his pajamas and then tucked him in.

Raylic grabbed her hand after they closed Shane's door and he practically dragged her down the hall to their room, shutting and locking the door. Heidi watched Raylic prowl toward her, every inch the alpha male, and a flutter of excitement made her lick her lips as she reached for him. It had only been one night since they were last intimate, but it felt longer.

Her sexy cop pulled off his clothes and dropped them on the floor, advancing on her until her knees collided with the side of the bed. He reached for her, a hungry expression in his eyes, and began removing her clothes. It seemed whatever reservations he'd had about her health had been resolved as his mouth slammed down on hers in a kiss that curled her toes and heated her from the inside out.

Raylic toppled her to the bed and dragged her ass to the edge of the mattress before falling to his knees. His fingers teased her pussy before parting her folds. His tongue swiped against her, flicking her clit and making her cry out in need. He teased her, as if savoring every moment, his tongue drawing lazy circles around her clit before plunging inside of her. He sucked on her tender flesh until she was crying out his name, her orgasm crashing through her and leaving her breathless, and still, she wanted more.

He leaned back, his hands braced on her thighs, as

his gaze roamed her body. He seemed to be taking in every inch of her, memorizing her curves. Her body hummed from her orgasm, but her pussy still ached and felt empty. She reached for him, curling her hands around his wrists and tugging.

"I want you," she said. "I need to feel you inside of me."

"Never let it be said I don't give my mate what she wants, what she needs."

His body covered hers, his cock brushing against her. He nuzzled her neck as he sank into her, her pussy stretching to accommodate him. It felt like heaven as he thrust into her again and again, each stroke harder and deeper than the last. With every plunge of his cock, she lifted her hips, needing more. Heidi could feel another orgasm cresting, and her nails bit into his shoulders.

Gazing up into his eyes, she felt more complete than she ever had before. She knew, at that moment, that what she'd been feeling for him wasn't just affection. It was an all-consuming love that made her dizzy and a little frightened. Heidi had never felt anything like it before, and tears pricked her eyes.

Raylic slowed, his expression concerned. "I didn't hurt you, did I?"

"I love you," she said softly.

"I love you too."

His mouth covered hers as he drove her into a frenzy that had her urging him on. As his hips slapped against hers, Heidi let herself go, crying out her release and letting wave after wave of pleasure infuse every cell of her body. As Raylic came inside of her, she wrapped her legs around him to hold on tight, never wanting to let him go.

"You're my everything," he murmured against her lips, kissing her again.

"You're my fairy tale," she said. "My Prince

Charming. I never thought I would have a happily-ever-after, but you make me believe that dreams really can come true. You've given me so much, and I will spend the rest of my life loving you, and showing you what you mean to me."

"All I need is your love to feel complete," he said. "As long as I have that, then nothing else matters."

Raylic rolled to his side, pulling her into his arms. She curled against him with a dreamy sigh and a smile on her lips. She had the love of a good man, a son she adored, and another baby on the way. Finally she had a real family, one she would cherish until her last breath. Life couldn't get more perfect.

Jessica Coulter Smith

Award-winning author Jessica Coulter Smith has been in love with the written word since she was a child writing her first stories in crayon. Her first romance was published in 2008, and since that time she's had over one hundred short stories, novellas, and novels published. She's particularly fond of writing paranormal and science fiction romances, but she also writes overly hot contemporary romance as Harley Wylde. Romance is an integral part of her world and Jessica firmly believes that love will find you at the right time, even if Mr. Right is literally out of this world.

Jessica on Changeling: changelingpress.com/jessica-coulter-smith-a-144

Harley on Changeling: changelingpress.com/harley-wylde-a-196

Dulce on Changeling: changelingpress.com/dulce-dennison-a-205

Changeling Press E-Books

More Sci-Fi, Fantasy, Paranormal, and BDSM adventures available in E-Book format for immediate download at ChangelingPress.com -- Werewolves, Vampires, Dragons, Shapeshifters and more -- Erotic Tales from the edge of your imagination.

What are E-Books?

E-Books, or Electronic Books, are books designed to be read in digital format -- on your desktop or laptop computer, notebook, tablet, Smart Phone, or any electronic ebook reader.

Where can I get Changeling Press e-Books?

Changeling Press ebooks are available at ChangelingPress.com, Amazon, Barnes and Nobel, Kobo, and iTunes.

Changeling Press, LLC

ChangelingPress.com